D0752548

"SAMANTHA,
DO YOU KNOW WHAT YOU'RE DOING?"

"Yes . . ." Her fingers touched his arm and moved down to take his hand. "I'm not afraid."

Alex groaned, closing his arms about her as he pulled her into the curve of his hard body. Her hands reached out to touch him, to caress him, and the feel of those hands was his undoing. They swept all reason, all caution from his mind. He bent his face to hers for a searing kiss.

Their bodies touched and Samantha shuddered. Through the thin flannel of her nightshirt, she could feel his every muscle. Trembling with pleasure, she returned his kiss, not even trying to understand. She knew that Alex was the only man who could arouse such an urgent, glowing need. He was the first . . . the only man she could ever love.

SIREN SONG

Kathryn Kramer

A DELL BOOK

Published by
Dell Publishing
a division of
Bantam Doubleday Dell Publishing Group, Inc.
666 Fifth Avenue
New York, New York 10103

ISBN: 0-440-20391-0

Printed in the United States of America

Published simultaneously in Canada

January 1990

10 9 8 7 6 5 4 3 2 1

OPM

To my grandmother, Elsie Margaret Vickery, who came out west from the East, married the man of her dreams (a gold miner, geologist, and mining promoter), and proved her tenacity and strength. She is an inspiration to the entire family and has proven beyond a doubt that East and West are most definitely compatible.

And to my mother, Marcia Vickery Hockett, who gives so unselfishly of her time and knowledge. Having lived so many years in the West, her information was invaluable.

A special thanks to Kathe Robin for her suggestion that I write a story about Central City and Black Hawk.

"For where your treasure is, there will your heart be also."

Luke 12:34

At first the Rocky Mountains were obstacles to be crossed. Later, miners discovered the mountains held riches beyond compare. People from all parts of the United States came pouring into what came to be called "the richest square mile on earth." The gold rush was one of the greatest mass migrations in the world, sending four million people "west" in forty years. Both seasoned miners from the West Coast and novices and greenhorns from the East came to the Colorado Territory hopeful of striking pay dirt.

The West usually brings to mind cowboys, but for every cowboy there were nearly a hundred miners. A gold strike could create a town overnight. Fortunes were often made in a day and unfortunately could be lost just as quickly. The lucky ones were those who first established their claims, built a nearby cabin to live in, and were patient enough to wait it out until their dream of striking gold came true. The discovery of a rich vein of gold or silver was the reward for diligent work, a gamble that paid off as no game of cards could. Many rags-to-riches stories can be told and have become a part of American folklore. Myths, songs, and legends grew up around many of the early miners, their women, gamblers, gunfighters, and the "shady ladies." Although women were fewer by far than men, they were a hardy lot and learned to be independent in order to survive not only the harsh conditions but the often rough, tough lawlessness of the frontier.

Central City was not an average mining town. People of culture came and built opera houses, schools, and hotels as well as other businesses. Lawyers, doctors, bankers, and railroad moguls made this thriving area their home. Unschooled prospectors and cultured aristocrats lived side by side and were instrumental in making Colorado a state one hundred years after our founding fathers secured independence from foreign domain. Colorado is known as the "Centennial state" for that reason. At one time the wealth in gold taken from its rugged peaks secured the wealth of our nation. Central City points proudly to the fact that it is the oldest mining camp in the United States that still actively mines.

It is against the backdrop of Central City and the surrounding area that this story takes place. A lovely young woman, who has been raised by her prospector grandfather, searches for the golden dream of love and finds it in the arms of a handsome man from Boston.

One

THE DUDE
AND THE HOYDEN
Central City
and Surrounding Area
Spring and Summer 1871

"Oh, rank is good, and gold is fair,
And high and low mate ill;
But love has never known a law
Beyond its own sweet will!"

John Greenleaf Whittier,
"Amy Wentworth"

1

The steady rhythm of horses' hooves was decidedly unnerving as the stagecoach lurched and bounced over the bumpy road. Alexander Nicholson stifled an oath as his head touched the hard wooden roof of the coach none too gently. Hopefully he would reach Central City all in one piece, he thought with a grimace of pain. He braced himself against the agonizing jolts. Ah, well, if he had wanted comfort he should have confined his traveling to the routes that were linked to the railroad, he reasoned. He'd wanted to come west and this bone-jarring ride seemed to be his initiation into Colorado Territory.

It had been a relatively easy journey until now. He had been able to travel most of the way by train. The first transcontinental railroad, built during the war, connected Boston to Denver with tracks. In Denver, however, the rails had ended and it was only by stagecoach that Alex could continue his journey. Up before the crack of dawn, he had set out upon this phase of his excursion.

With a snap of the whip and a stream of swearwords, the

driver kept the six brown horses traveling the winding roads at an astonishing speed, stirring up a choking dust that drifted through the open window like a thick dark cloud. By the time he reached the stage depot, his new suit would probably be more brown than gray, Alex thought with a wry smile. He'd be glad when this journey was over.

Five other people were squeezed into the rounded confines of the stage, each struggling to find a comfortable position. The guadily dressed woman at his side looked at him from the corner of her eye, making use of the crowded conditions to move closer to Alex whenever she had the chance.

"You look nearly as uncomfortable as I feel, mister," she said.

"I must admit that I've had smoother rides," Alex answered with a polite smile, trying to ignore the elbow pressed into his ribs, "but then again, I've also had much rougher ones." During the war he'd ridden in an amunition wagon a few times, a far more grueling experience than this. Then the war had ended and he'd grown used to luxury and comfort. A rugged environment would do him a world of good, he mused. Life in the Colorado Territory would be a far cry from the dull routine he'd endured in Boston working with his father and brother. He came from a line of traders and businessmen, men who won victories on the strength of their ledgers, not on their daring. Men who had nothing to fear but figures going into the red. He hoped that coming west would change all that. He wanted to have a hand in shaping the new territory.

Looking at the faces of the other travelers, he smiled. What an assortment. They certainly appeared to embody everything he'd heard about the West. The woman sitting at his side and the woman seated across from him were clearly "fancy women." They had come to work in one of the bawdy houses in Black Hawk, or so the grinning stagecoach driver had told him. Directly across from Alex, taking up more than his share of space, a stern-faced preacher gripped his Bible as he furled his thick black brows. His disapproval of the two women was obvious, for he grumbled beneath his breath about "sin" and chastised them severely with his frowns.

"Damn do-gooder wants to ruin all our fun," the stage driver had mumbled a few stops back. He had told Alex that the preachers spoke of hellfire and damnation as they traveled about the streets. "Oughtta mind their own damned business, that's what they *oughtta* do." It seemed ironic to Alex that this stony-faced parson and the very women he was preaching against should arrive in the same rickety stagecoach.

A lean, bespectacled doctor carrying the black bag of his profession, and a jovial, square-jawed man who proclaimed his intent to open a butcher shop, completed the passenger list. The butcher fidgeted nervously, the doctor tried to sleep, as the stagecoach groaned and creaked over the rutted road.

"You keep looking at that watch of yours as if you think it'll give this stagecoach wings." The woman next to him bent down to lace her shoe, giving him a look at her decolletage. "I for one am not in any hurry. Not with such, uh . . . good-looking company. I have a preference for dark-haired men."

Alex pushed his watch back in his vest pocket. "Just anxious to reach my destination," he said.

"Someone waiting for you?" At Alex's nod she sighed. "Ain't that just the luck. Well, if you ever have a spat, remember me. My name's Honey. Honey Wells. I'm taking over the Silver Garter Saloon as well as another . . . uh, business. I can take a man's mind off of just about anything and turn it in the *right* direction." Her smile left no question as to her meaning. "Just remember me, you hear?"

Alex didn't have time to answer. A violent jolt, then a splintering crash, sent him sprawling to the floor. The driver's furious shout confirmed his suspicion. The stagecoach had struck a large rock. Struggling to his feet, he looked out the window.

"Hellfire and thunderation! I'll be gawddamned!" The gray-mustached driver kicked at the spoked wheels in frustration. "Axle's broke. I warned 'em. They don't make these here carriages near as sturdy as they oughtta. Now we're stuck. Won't be another stage comin' this way until tomorry. Have to hope for a wagon passin' by." Taking off his hat, he threw it on the ground.

"Is there anything I can do to help?" Opening the door, Alex pushed his way outside.

"Help? Nope. Don't have the necessary tools to repair it. Ain't a thing we can do but wait." Circling the stagecoach, the driver swore and blustered.

"No tools?" A search of the stagecoach revealed several bottles of whiskey where the tools should have been.

"Man's gotta have somethin' to quench his thirst on a long, rocky ride," the driver mumbled, his face flushed with guilt.

"If I owned this stageline, I'd make it a point to be prepared for emergencies at all times," Alex remarked. Inconveniencing paying customers just seemed to be bad business. Much stricter discipline was necessary.

"Ain't nobody's concern. Couldn't fix an axle nohow."

"It's my concern." His smile gone, the butcher cast the driver an angry frown. "I have an appointment in just a few hours. Being late could very well ruin me." With purposeful strides he walked toward the horses, fumbling at the reins.

"Hey, what are you doin'?" With a snort of outrage the driver looked angrily at the man who was unhitching the horses. "They hang men for stealing horses in these parts."

"Borrowing, friend. Just borrowing." Somehow managing to hoist his girth onto the horse's back, he rode away, promising over his shoulder that he would send someone back for them in a wagon or a buggy.

"Sure he will. And a horse is a cow. His only concern is for hisself!" The stagecoach driver punctuated his opinion by spitting a stream of tobacco juice on the ground.

The doctor, too, appeared to have his own pressing concerns. Tying his black bag to a horse's harness, he rode off without a word. Half an hour later the preacher deserted them as well, walking down the road with the "intent of getting help" from one of the nearby cabins. Apparently it was going to be every man for himself, Alex thought. He could very well have done the same thing, but he chose to stay. Years of rigid training had made him too much of a gentleman to leave the women. Surely a wagon or buggy would come by eventually. Judging by the wheel ruts carved into the dirt, the road appeared to be well traveled. Surely they would not have to wait much longer.

The thundering sound of horses' hooves and wild yelling proved him right. Three horsemen were approaching at a furious pace. Taking off his hat, he began to flag them down. The trembling driver grabbed his arm.

"Not them! Don't want their help. They're meaner than tigers. That's the Tyburn gang."

Frantically clutching their reticules, the women shrieked at his words. "They won't get my money. It's all I have," Honey gasped. As the horsemen neared, they both picked up their skirts and fled down the hillside, stumbling as they ran. With a strangled oath the driver followed.

"So much for being a *gentleman*," Alex mumbled. Ah, well, he'd been in much graver situations. Facing a battalion of yelling rebel soldiers was far more dangerous than facing these men could ever be, he reasoned. And they'd soon decide he wasn't worth the bother. Luckily his money was coming later on the Wells Fargo stage. He had taken a precaution against just such an occurrence as this. If his father had taught him nothing else, he had always warned Alex to be cautious where money was concerned. It was often the "root of all evil," particularly in lawless areas such as the Colorado Territory.

"Oo-ee! Got us one boy that stayed behind. He's either mighty brave or mighty stupid. Which do you suppose, Slim?" The man who led the riders smiled, showing large white teeth as he waved a long-barreled revolver in a threatening manner.

"Maybe he's just trustin'. By the look of them clothes he must be new around here. La dee da, ain't he the one." The tall, thin man eyed Alex up and down.

"Must be an undertaker."

"A lawyer."

"A real dude, that's for sure."

Alex held his ground, refusing to back down. "If you're after money, I'm afraid I must disappoint you."

The three men snickered loudly. "He thinks we're gonna rob him. Don't know whether to laugh or be insulted, boys. What do you think, Buck?" Like three tomcats spoiling for a fight, they got off their horses and circled Alex.

2

The vivid blue sky shimmered with golden rays of sunlight that cast a shining halo on the world below. Westward as far as the eye could see were mountains, layer upon layer of rock rising majestically. The distant peaks seemed to beckon the sun to melt their snowy caps and send the glacial waters tumbling down to the green valleys below, or so it seemed to the young woman who gazed at the wide expanse of the Rockies. Was there anything in the world half as beautiful? At this moment Samantha didn't think so. Surely this was God's country, as near to heaven as anyone would ever care to be.

Sitting cross-legged, Samantha Marie Claybourne leaned back against the gnarled roots of a huge tree and sighed her contentment. Life couldn't get much better than this. She had everything she needed. Fresh air, sunshine, all the food that she could eat, the sheltering protection of her grandfather's cabin, and, most importantly, Gramps himself. His love always warmed her as surely as the sun warmed her beloved mountains.

Closing her eyes, Samantha smiled as she thought of her grandfather and how close they'd become over the years. He was all she had in this world, her only family since both of her parents had been killed in a train accident twelve years ago. She remembered how frightened she had been of her grandfather's stern visage and scowling brows, but she'd soon learned to love him.

Enoch Claybourne hadn't known what to do with the five-year-old girl at first. How was he going to work a mine with a child to care for? He had no choice but to take her along with him, letting her amuse herself by playing in the ore car, on the dump, sacking dirt or piling up rocks. In time Samantha had become quite inventive and helpful as well. His mountain property had become her playground. The days had passed with a regularity that Sam, as Gramps had nicknamed her, had grown used to. They were up at dawn, hunting, fishing for the day's food, lessons. Then there were chores while he worked the mine and the hours she spent helping him, and finally the hours spent together around the fire when he would tell her stories of the old days or read from the Bible.

Enoch Claybourne had been one of the first to stake out his claim in the Rocky Mountain wilderness. Now people from all parts of the world and all across the United States were streaming in. Not that it would do them any good. Most of the rich land had already been claimed, though there were always those who might try, as Gramps said, "to bamboozle ya." Gramps had warned Samantha to be wary of anyone who asked too many questions. There were ruthless scoundrels who would "do most anything" to get a claim in their own name. Even steal or kill if it suited their purpose. Perhaps that was why he had taught her to shoot. A time might come when she would need to know how to defend herself.

"Too damned lazy to work as I did," Gramps said of the con men he had encountered. "Not only finding gold, but *keeping* it is what it is all about." And Enoch had found gold. He had been one of the lucky ones, making a moderate strike seven years ago. Enough money to keep them fed and clothed while he went on hunting for the main vein.

Samantha glanced down at the gold nugget that dangled

from the chain around her neck. It was a gift from her grandfather in remembrance of that first gold strike. Though it had been but a small pocket, it had given Gramps enough hope to keep him digging. It goaded him to work and work and work, digging so deep that he swore he could hear the devil laughing on the other side of the rock.

"I know the mother lode is farther into the mountain and I'm determined to find it 'fore I die. To secure your well-being and your future," he told her.

"I don't care about the gold, only about you," she had answered, but Gramps was persistent. He said he could smell gold, feel it, nearly taste it. He worked from dawn till dusk and, after locking up the entrance to the tunnel door, came home exhausted but not too tired to teach her to read, to write and do her sums.

"Yep, Gramps is a mighty fine man," she said to herself softly, glancing at the fishing pole she had balanced against a rock. Someday she'd make him proud of her, make up to him for all he had done. That she could hunt, fish, shoot both rifle and revolver as well as any man was a start. And she was proud of her accomplishments. Why, she could ride a horse as well as Clint Landry, the sheriff's deputy. She could guide a wagon with only one hand on the reins. A woman couldn't be any more accomplished than that, she thought with just a hint of vanity.

Samantha stretched her legs, wiggling toes that were unencumbered by boots at the moment. Staring out at the stream, she saw a fish jump out of the water in search of his breakfast, and thought what a fine meal it would be. "No finer victuals in all of this world than Rocky Mountain trout," Gramps was always saying. She picked up the pole with a smile. It wouldn't be long until she'd hook that ole trout. She and her grandfather knew the perfect bait, one the fish couldn't resist. Dragonflies! It was a secret they kept closely guarded. Fly fishing was quite an art.

Squinting against the sun, Samantha tossed the line into the water, flicking her wrist to send the dragonfly skimming across the surface as if in flight. She laughed gaily as the trout lost no time in latching on to the insect. Arching her back while tugging at the line, she pulled the fish into shore. A fish for Gramps; now to get one for herself.

It took much longer to catch the second fish. Samantha grumbled in irritation as she stood on the edge of the bank. It was hot; the breeches and the long-sleeved cotton shirt she wore made her uncomfortable. It was not that she intended to look like a boy; trousers, shirt, and high-topped, front-laced boots were simply appropriate attire for mountain living and working at the mine. A jacket was added during the autumn months when a body had to keep warm in the cool mountain air. Now, however, it was hot and she would have stripped off her shirt if only she'd had something underneath. Up until a few years ago, it hadn't been a problem, but her body had changed, and now her grandfather discouraged such action. Still, there were times when she couldn't resist skinny-dipping in the pond.

Another trout, a bit smaller than the first, tugged at the line and she quickly hauled it in. "Aha, at last a companion for the other," she said in triumph. A third and a fourth followed before Samantha decided she had enough for supper. Putting the fish in a creel, she went in search of her boots and put them on, fumbling with the lacings. The position of the sun, straight overhead in the sky, told her it was time to take the wagon up to the mine. If today was a profitable day, she'd help him sack the ore.

Samantha's hair had come unbound and now she sought to tidy it, rebraiding the waist-length reddish-gold tresses. Burnished sunshine, her grandfather called it, exclaiming on its rarity. Didn't really matter what color it was, she thought. She usually wore it pinned atop her head, hidden under a wide-brimmed hat to keep it from being a nuisance. She would have gladly cropped it short as a boy's, but Gramps was staunch in his refusal to let her part with her crowning glory. Someday, he predicted, she'd give in to feminine vanity and appreciate the thick, beautiful hair God had given her. Sam doubted it. The buns, bangs, and silly curls that women in the towns wore were not for her. So thinking, she plopped the brown felt hat on her head, rehitched the horses that had been grazing nearby, and climbed aboard the old rickety wooden wagon.

The wagon wheels rolled unevenly over the rutted path, and

Samantha muttered an oath beneath her breath as she held on to the reins. "Damn fool stagecoach wheels have played havoc with the road," she muttered. It was what she called a "two-handed ride," yet she maneuvered the horses along the winding pathway as if by second nature.

Though she had driven this way more times than she could count, the beauty of the land never ceased to amaze her. Bright splashes of green dotted the hillsides—pine, spruce, and fur trees swayed slightly to meet the breeze. Wildflowers of blue, yellow, and red covered the sloping meadows. Hell, even the weeds were pretty. Sam was musing on the peace and majesty of the wilderness when the staccato pop of gunfire startled her to attention.

"What in tarnation?" Flicking the reins, she goaded the horses forward, intent on investigating. It was a hunter, no doubt, in search of a hare or a deer and she would have to inform him to seek his prey farther from the road. That was the unwritten rule among the miners ever since one poor unfortunate had been wounded by a huntsman's stray bullet.

The sound of gunfire echoed again, this time accompanied by loud laughter. Sam saw a stagecoach standing in the middle of the road, its axle broken. A few feet away three men were making sport, shooting at their victim's feet and making him dance. It appeared that the other passengers had fled for there was no one to offer the poor man aid.

"*Oo eee!* Just look at that dude move his feet!" The tallest of the men slapped his hand against his thigh, laughing uproariously. "Now just what dance do you 'spect he's doin', Slim? The Virginia reel? Naw, he don't look like no southern dandy. Maybe its some fancy footwork like they do back east."

"Ain't never seen that step before, Cy, but it sure looks fine. Heard tell them easterners think they do *everythin'* better." Walking forward and circling his victim, he eyed him up and down. "Do you s'pose that's true?"

"Naw! Looks like a sissy to me. Why, just look at that purty gray suit. Wouldn't want to get such finery dirty." The man named Cy seemed to tire of his fun for he drew back his gun and just stood staring at the stranger for a while. "But I sure do like that hat he's wearin'." He addressed the stranger. "What do they call that thing?"

"It's called a bowler." Seemingly trying to appease his tormentors, the eastern gentleman held out his hat for their inspection. "Try it on, if you like."

"Try it on?" Taking the proffered chapeau in his hands, Cy put it on his head, prancing around amid gales of laughter. "Ain't I the stylish one?"

"Handsome!" the two others agreed. "Jest like a gentleman."

"Gentleman, hell!" Cocking his long-barreled revolver, taking off the hat, Cy threw back his head and laughed, a thundering sound that caused shivers to crawl up Samantha's spine. She'd hoped that they'd let the stranger go if she didn't interfere, but now she was not so certain. Cy's evil chuckles usually announced trouble with a capital *T*. His next words proved her right. "Wonder just how many bullet holes we can fill this here thing with before it hits the ground."

"Ten!"

"Twelve!" Ominously the men inched forward, surrounding their captive. If they had more than shooting at his hat in mind, Samantha didn't wait to find out. She'd had enough of their tomfoolery. Guiding the wagon to a halt behind the stagecoach, she bounded from the seat, grabbed her rifle, and fired, sending Slim's hat flying from his head as the bullet struck.

"Hold it right there! Take one more step and I'll aim for your head, Slim Walker." She waved the gun in a threatening manner, pointing next at Cy and then at Buck. "You know that I will. I don't cotton much to the odds here. Three against one, and an unarmed man at that. You bullies ought to be ashamed, but I know you don't have the sense for that."

"Aw, get on out of here, Sam. This ain't none of your concern." Taking the chance that she was bluffing, Buck Cameron, the burliest of the three, turned back to the stranger and raised his gun. Sam fired off another well-aimed shot. "God damn!" Holding his suddenly weaponless hand, Buck looked daggers at her. "You'll be sorry for this."

"And you'll all be sorry if you don't ride on out of here." Cocking her rifle, Samantha took aim for another shot. "Go on. Get!"

Hesitating only a moment, Buck Cameron was the first to leave. "All right, I'm goin'." Jumping astride his horse, he rode off without a backward glance.

"If you know what's good for you, you'll git too." Without a word in reply the lanky, red-haired Slim retrieved his hat and with a grumbled oath, followed after Buck. Only Cy hung back, glaring his defiance. "Go on, Cy. What are you waiting for?"

"Seems to me the odds are even now. Why don't you let the dude take care of hisself? Let's see just what he can do when it's man to man. Give him a gun and we'll see how well he can handle it." Folding his arms across his chest he strode to within inches of the tall man in the gray suit. "How 'bout it, dude? Want one of *my* guns?"

Stiffening his shoulders, the Easterner stood straight and tall. Samantha feared he might be pushed into a dangerous game. "He'd have to be a fool, Cy," Sam shouted. "You're the fastest draw around." She turned her gaze to the Easterner, cautioning, "Don't do it, mister."

The hard, chiseled lines of his mouth softened as he smiled at her. "Don't worry. I intend to be peaceable." His piercing blue eyes radiated gratitude and Samantha thought at that moment that she had never seen a more handsome gent. "But thank you for the word of caution."

"It . . . it was the least I could do." Samantha felt suddenly tongue-tied as her eyes appraised him, sweeping from the top of his dark-haired head to the toes of his black shining shoes. He was fascinating. Why, he looked as if he'd walked straight out of the pages of a picture book. It wasn't just his clothes. She'd seen others dressed this way, the men her grandfather dubbed "snobs." No, it was the way he wore those clothes, as if he'd been made for them. He was every inch a gentleman.

The severe cut of the dark gray coat showed off the width of his shoulders, the slimness of his waist and hips. The coat was even lined in silk, Samantha thought. Everything seemed to match, in fact. Even his waistcoat was gray-and-black-striped. He was tall and it appeared that, were he to harness his strength, he might be a fearsome man to reckon with.

Samantha couldn't seem to take her eyes off him. Slowly she took in every detail as if to memorize his face. The dark brown hair had just a hint of curl, his jaw was strong, his nose well-defined above the neatly trimmed mustache. But his eyes were his most startling feature, fringed with dark lashes beneath brows set at just the right angle to complement the rest of his face. A cleft in his chin, far from marring the perfection of his face, lent it character.

"Is something wrong?" He quirked a brow and Samantha suddenly realized that she was staring.

"I . . . I thought you might want your . . . your hat."

"*I'll* give it back to him!" Throwing it up in the air, Cy emptied his six-shooter at the eastern confection, then strode away before he could become the object of Samantha's wrath. The thud of horses' hooves told her he had ridden off, but somehow Sam still couldn't take her eyes off the stranger.

"Looks like everyone deserted you. Can I give you a ride, stranger?" Her heart quickened as he flashed her a grin and she saw that, like everything else about him, his teeth were perfect. Straight and white. "Where are you headed?"

"Central City. Probably miles out of your way." It was, but Samantha found herself shrugging her shoulders, insisting it would be no trouble at all. "Then I have one more reason to thank you. I'm very grateful." Bending down he picked up his hat, examining it with a laugh. "Seems I won't be wearing this again. Might as well throw it away. Besides, it does mark me as a dude."

"Can I have it?" Why she'd asked such an inane thing Sam would never know, yet somehow she wanted to have a memento of this meeting. "It's . . . it's different from any hat I've seen before. I'd like to show it to my grandfather. Said he's seen just about every kind of hat there is, but I bet he's never seen one like this." She took it from his outstretched hands and giggled as she poked her fingers through the bullet holes. "Think I'll tell him it's supposed to be like this."

"Maybe I should keep it. Might set a fashionable new style."

"I suppose it could." Samantha laughed again, striding one pace behind him as he walked back to the stagecoach. Though his carpetbags were very heavy, she gave him a hand, settling his baggage into the back of the wagon. "Ain't gonna be a comfortable ride but I'll take you to where you're going. By the way, what's your name?"

"Alex. Alexander Nicholson, to be exact." He held out his hand, grasping hers in a handshake that caused an odd tingle, a jolt that she felt all the way down to her toes.

"Alexander. Alex. I like that name." As his eyes met hers she blushed a shade and turned her eyes away, busying herself with adjusting the reins. "Well, better get going."

"Shouldn't we look for the others?" He didn't like to desert them even though they'd had no second thoughts about him.

"Don't see no use in it. They're more than likely far, far away by now. Gunshots would have spooked 'em. We could search every inch of this mountain and still not find 'em." Impatiently she climbed up on the wagon. Alex climbed up beside her. "In these parts folks just have to take care of themselves."

"Well, in that case . . ." Alex braced himself as a sharp flick of the reins made the wagon jolt forward. They had ridden only a short distance when he suddenly realized he didn't know his young rescuer's name. "What's your name, lad?" The look of hurt in the wide brown eyes puzzled him.

"My name's Sam. Samantha Marie Claybourne and I'm not a *lad.*"

"Samantha Marie . . . ?" He'd assumed by the breeches, hat, and shirt that she was a boy. "I'm sorry," he said, embarrassed by his mistake. "I meant no offense."

"None taken." Samantha tried to hide her wounded feelings with a smile. Strange that being mistaken for a boy had never bothered her before. Now she was mortified. As the wagon bumped down the road she swore that this Alexander Nicholson would find out just what a fine *female* she was.

3

It was an exhilarating ride down the rutted mountain roadway and Alexander Nicholson braced himself against the wagon, clutching tightly to the side. He held his breath from time to time, certain the wagon would be upended or toppled over the bank. He felt every jolt but had to admit to a grudging admiration for the young driver's skill.

When at last the roadway leveled off, he cast her a sideways glance. How could he have been such a fool as to think she was a boy? he wondered. His eyes were drawn to the gently rounded breasts beneath her shirt. No boy had ever looked like that! And the eyes. Enormous. Wide. Framed by long, thick dark-brown lashes, they looked like big copper pennies. Those eyes were her claim to beauty. Strong, agile, and pertly pretty, she was unaware that she was so pleasing to the eye. Perhaps that was part of her charm, and charm him she did. He'd met a lot of people in his twenty-nine years, but never one like Samantha Claybourne.

"Sorry if the bumps are bruising your backside," she said,

smiling apologetically. Her grin was that of a naughty cherub. "I told you it wasn't gonna be comfortable. A sight rougher than the stagecoach, I'd wager."

Alexander couldn't keep from smiling at her colorful way of expressing herself. "I believe my *backside* will survive. I'm only grateful that I wasn't stranded by the roadside. As you saw, my companions deserted me at the first sign of trouble. Two of the men rode off with the horses, two women, the preacher, and the driver fled."

"Ran away and left you?" Samantha was angrily astounded. "Even the driver?"

"Even the driver." Briefly he told her the story.

"Huh. Well, I'll be damned." She pursed her lips as she thought a moment. "Guess that isn't really so surprising. Cy Tyburn is known to be a hellion when he's whiskeyed up. Not what I'd call a congenial fellow. Not by a long shot."

"You managed to handle him, though. I doubt anyone else could have been as poised."

"Aw, it was nothing." Samantha couldn't help the blush that stained her cheeks as she basked under the warmth of his praise. "Cy and I practically grew up together. I used to wallop him good until he grew taller than me. But I can still outride and outshoot him and he knows it."

"I see." He laughed in spite of himself, imagining her wrestling with the tall blond ruffian. He was certain she must have been as much of a handful then as she undoubtedly was now. He couldn't help but admire her spunk. It must be hard on a woman living in the wilderness. "Tell me all about yourself." He had a sudden curiosity to know everything he could about this interesting young woman before they parted company. As she hesitated he added, "Please."

"There really ain't much to tell. Some things I don't rightly know. Only go by what Gramps tells me." She focused on his blue cravat, afraid of meeting his eyes. Why was it that every time he smiled at her, her fingers trembled? "He says I was born in Kansas City. That my father was a railroad man." She turned her attention back to the road.

"A railroad man?"

"A conductor! He eloped with my mother."

"Sounds romantic."

She shook her head, sending wisps of hair out from under her hat. It was Alexander's first glimpse of the color and he thought how it suited her. Strawberry blond, he'd heard it called. Unusual, just like her. "It wasn't really. My mother's family disowned her. The only person she had in this life was my father. I guess she must have loved him very much." There was a wistful tone to her voice, eliciting his sympathy. "I was their only child."

"Was?" He was confused.

"My parents are *dead*. Killed in a train accident." Samantha gripped the reins so hard that the horses slowed their pace, but with a flick of her wrist she sent them galloping again. "They were on a second honeymoon, Gramps said."

"I'm sorry!"

"It was one of those things that no one could have helped." She sighed. "Gramps took me in, though he didn't have much use for kids, at least not at first." As if to vindicate her grandfather, she rattled on. "But he came to love me. No one could have raised me half as good. He taught me everything I know. Gramps is no fool. He's a well-educated man . . . and . . . a gold miner. Caught gold fever and it became his life's dream. But he doesn't spend his money in the saloons in town like the others do; he comes home every night to teach me and read to me." Fearing she had monopolized the conversation, she asked, "What about you? Where do you come from?"

"Boston. My family owns a shipping yard. Very profitable, but not very stimulating or challenging." He laughed. "That's why I came here. Or at least one of the reasons. To see this 'West' everyone in Boston is talking about. To see if all the tall tales are true."

She echoed his laughter. "Oh, they're true. They're true. Just wait and see." A sudden bump nearly unseated them both and Samantha swore beneath her breath. Cautioning herself to give her full attention to the road, she grew silent. They'd be in Central City in thirty minutes or more and then her handsome gentleman would be gone. She didn't want that. She wanted to see him again. Such things were a puzzlement to her. Surely there must be something she could say that would let him know.

Noticing Samantha's sudden silence, Alex glanced over at her. He liked her laughter, her smiles, the way she averted her eyes when she thought she might have been too bold. She was like a breath of fresh air. A far cry from the stuffy ladies and matrons of Boston. He had the feeling she would never prove dull.

"I'm glad you came along when you did, Samantha. For more reasons than one." He was enjoying himself. He, too, hated to see their journey come to an end. The company was pleasant, the scenery spectacular, the ride in the open wagon a soothing contrast to the stuffy stagecoach. He cast his eyes over the mountains' splendors and was undeniably impressed. The hills and valleys seemed to go on forever, crisscrossed by creeks and rivers that clearly marked it a wilderness paradise. He thought of the elk, bear, and other wildlife he'd heard lived in the forests covering those hills. A man could nearly forget his troubles here, the nightmares of the past.

"I'm glad I came along too, Alex." Samantha clenched her jaw, trying to gather up her courage. If she didn't say something now, she never would. "I've never met a man like you . . . and . . . and I don't think I ever will again." *Ask him! Ask him to call on you,* she thought. *Just say it before you lose your nerve. Alex? Alex!* It was no use. Her mind was willing, but her tongue seemed to get tied in knots at the thought of saying more.

"Where I lived there was house after house. It was not anything like this. Though I did have a view of the ocean. Massachusetts Bay, to be exact." With a faraway look in his eyes he ran his hand through his hair, as if remembering the ocean's breeze. "Have you ever seen an ocean, Samantha?"

"No. But we got lakes aplenty. I fish up there sometimes. . . ." She wanted to tell him that she'd show him her private lake, but another jolt in the road took all her attention.

"Your grandfather sounds like an interesting man."

"He is. Would you like to meet him?" At last she saw her chance to prolong their acquaintance at least for a little while. "I caught four fish today. After you get settled in town I could take you up to the cabin. We could all have supper." She waited expectantly.

"Thank you very much for the invitation but I'm afraid I have other commitments."

"Tomorrow, then."

"I don't think so." Seeing the disappointment in her eyes, he added, "I'll be starting a new job at the bank and I fear it will take up a great deal of my time."

"The bank?" Somehow he didn't look at all like a banker, despite his fine clothes. Bankers were always tight-lipped and unsmiling. At least the few bankers she had seen. Gramps never used money, so they had few reasons to visit banks. Instead they used gold dust for their purchases. They'd had a disagreement with one banker in Central City, though, a man Gramps called a "chiseler." He'd tried to talk her grandfather out of his mine, tried to buy it right out from under his nose.

"Does that sound like a pompous profession? That's what I thought, too, until Caroline convinced me otherwise."

"Caroline?" Jealousy coiled in Samantha's belly at the sound of the feminine name. Somehow in her own mind she had already branded Alex Nicholson as her own.

"It's her father's bank. I promised to give banking a try."

"Oh." She wanted to know who this Caroline was but was afraid to ask. Instead she jerked her hand and pointed out beyond the road. "Better look while you have the chance. Once you get to Central City, its gonna be a different story. Kinda like where you came from, house to house, mine tunnel to mine tunnel. Hell, Gramps always says he hates the city. Can't spit out the window for fear of it going down your neighbor's chimney and putting out his fire. Better look now."

Alex did as she suggested, letting his eyes take in the view. The air was so pure and clear that objects were visible at great distances, a far cry from the smoke and dirt of the city. Birds soared high in the air, fearless in their flight. The dark green of the forests and light green of the meadowlands teemed with life. Alex even spied a herd of elk grazing by the roadway. They seemed undisturbed by the wagon.

"I pass this way all the time," Samantha said by way of explanation.

The scenery changed dramatically, however, the closer they came to their destination. The foliage grew sparser. There were patches of earth where the forest had been cleared. The timber, Samantha told him, was used to build cabins and to shore up the mine tunnels. Those very tunnels soon came into view and looked to Alex like gaping open mouths. Log houses now dotted the hillsides. Shafts and dumps, looking like gigantic anthills, attested to the presence of men foraging in the earth, digging down to search for the gold buried deep within the rock.

"Gramps has a cabin just like that." Samantha pointed to a tiny house made out of logs. "Built it himself with no one but me to help." Samantha's brow puckered in concentration as she recollected.

"You helped your grandfather build a cabin?" Alex was notably impressed. "I can't imagine Caroline being so daring."

Again he'd mentioned Caroline and Samantha could control her curiosity no longer. "Is Caroline your wife?" she asked before she could stop herself.

"No."

"Your cousin?" she asked hopefully.

"Caroline is my fiancée."

"Your *fiancée*?" Her large brown eyes opened wide in question.

"I met her in Boston and it was love at first sight. We're going to be married. She's the other reason I came out here."

Samantha's hopes were dashed. She could only take solace in the fact that she had not made a total fool of herself. He was engaged to be married. Strange how that knowledge caused such intense disappointment. She had thought . . . she had hoped. But it didn't matter. Alex Nicholson would never be hers, no matter how much she wished it. Urging the horses on to a faster pace she was anxious now to reach Central City before the lump in her throat and the expression on her face gave her feelings away.

4

The wagon groaned down Eureka Street, turned right onto Main, and Alexander was afforded a full view of the sprawling metropolis that was most appropriately named Central City, the center of all mining activity in the Colorado Territory.

"Central City, county seat of Gilpin County," she announced, gesturing with her left hand while the right one held the reins. "Well, what do you think? Want to go back to Boston, mister? Damned sight more rugged here, I'll wager."

"A damned sight more," he returned with a grin, scanning the town with a skeptical eye. Wooden buildings with false fronts lined the narrow street. Here and there stood brick or stone buildings in a hodgepodge of styles and sizes, mainly two stories with flat roofs, though he noted several pointed roofs on the houses that dotted the hillside. Looking up, he could see a scattering of crudely designed structures blending into the mountainside. A far cry from Boston's elegant brownstones and artfully crafted brick houses, yet not without a certain charm.

He liked it, although Caroline's letters had most certainly exaggerated. "Little Boston," indeed!

"Hard to believe that gold was first discovered only twelve years ago. All this built in only eleven years. I'd say that's an accomplishment." There was a certain hint of pride in her voice.

"Boston is a great deal older. Ancient in comparison, you might say." He suddenly stiffened as a horse-drawn cart rumbled down the dirt road toward them. "Look out!" His shouted warning came just in time. With an oath Samantha adroitly guided her wagon out of the way.

"I'd better watch where I'm going or we'll end up in Mr. Roworth's Central City Bakery. Horse and all." She smiled mischievously. "Lot of horses and wagons on this road." That statement was true. Vehicles of every kind clogged the wide dirt main road. People in wagons, buckboards, and carriages, as well as those walking, crowded the thoroughfare. It was noisy. The boardwalks on each side of the street were crowded with people of every shape and size. Gamblers, lawmen, and teamsters rubbed elbows as they walked along. Well-dressed matrons stuck up their noses as they spied the women of ill repute whose "charms" were far too freely displayed. Heavy-booted miners covered with grime jostled dapper salesmen and immaculately groomed bankers.

"Over to the right is the blacksmith's, the baker's, the butcher's and a boardinghouse. To the left is the liverer's, the barber's, the gunsmith's and a hotel. You be needing one, Alex?" Or would he be staying with this Caroline? It was, as Gramps would say, "none of her business."

"Hotel? No, I don't believe so. Caroline and her father were kind enough to ask me to be their guest. I'll be staying with them for a while." He wondered if they would be worried about him. Pulling out his pocket watch, he could see that it was two-thirty. His stage had been due to arrive at one. "I do need to find the bank, however. West and Hatcher. My future father-in-law is Mr. West. I believe Caroline said it was located near Spring and Main. Do you know where it could be, Samantha?" He wondered at the frown that had suddenly marred her face. "Samantha?"

"Yes," she snapped, clenching her jaw in indignation. She'd been there twice before and remembered the location very well. Mr. West was the very same banker who had tried to cheat her grandfather. "It's up ahead. The one with the rounded windows." The fanciest building in town, she thought with a snort of derision, and every nook and cranny erected on some poor miner's back. Enoch Claybourne wasn't the only miner Mr. West had tried to dupe. He was a merchant as well as a banker, "dabbling in everybody's pie," as Gramps put it.

"The one with the awnings over the window?" Alex craned his neck for a better view. "Caroline's standing out in front. She must be frantic." Looking at his pocket watch a second time, he shook his head, then slipped it back into his vest pocket. Punctuality had always been one of his strong points, but he supposed there were a great many things about his life that were about to be changed.

"Yes, the one with the *awnings,*" Samantha answered. How she guided the wagon to a halt without having an accident, Samantha didn't know. She was staring so hard at the vision in pink that she most certainly did not see the street. So this was *Caroline.* Dressed most fashionably in various shades of rose muslin, a bustle tapering out in back, she looked like the porcelain doll Gramps had once bought her. Perched upon the artfully coiffed blond hair was a straw hat trimmed with flowers and ribbons of a darker hue than the gown, a bonnet Samantha knew would cost more than two weeks wages. Caroline. She knew the type. Never a hair out of place, delicate leather shoes immaculate despite the dust of the road. Though it pained her to admit it, this woman had to be a perfect match for Alex, as flawlessly perfect as he was.

"Caroline!" Waving frantically to get her attention, Alexander said the name with such poignancy that Samantha's last hopes were shattered. "Over here."

"Ohhhhhhh." A piercing shriek cut through the air. "Alex! Alex, darling!" Picking up her skirts, she trotted gracefully to the wagon. "I'd thought . . . I'd feared . . ."

Bolting from the wagon, Alexander swept Caroline up in his arms as Samantha tried to avert her eyes. How she wished she were the recipient of such a passionate embrace.

"I'm all right, Caroline. The stage broke down. A wheel struck a boulder, the axle broke, and we were stranded."

"Oh, Alex, I was so worried. I was just certain that something dreadful had happened." The woman's wide blue eyes filled with tears. Laying her head on Alex's shoulder, she sobbed. "I had visions . . . of . . . of . . . horrible . . ."

"There, there, Caroline. I'm all right. Really I am. Don't cry, dear heart." In a gesture of comfort he gently stroked her shoulder, then, thrusting her an arm's length away, dried her eyes with his handkerchief. "I wasn't injured. No one was, although we could have been." Taking her hand in his, he feasted his eyes on her beauty. She was just as lovely as he had remembered. How could he ever forget that first time they had met? It had been at one of his aunt's soirees, an evening party with the Colorado territorial governor as the honored guest. They had spied each other from across the room and soon found themselves in each other's company. Caroline had been inconsolable when it was time for her to accompany her father back home, but Alex's promise to join her in Colorado had soothed her distress. Now he was here.

"You weren't harmed?"

"No. Thanks to a very special young woman, I escaped intact." Looking up at Samantha, he smiled. "Caroline, I'd like you to meet—"

"Samantha Claybourne . . ." It took all of Samantha's will but she managed a smile as she introduced herself. A smile that was met with haughty disdain.

"Alexander, what on earth are you doing with that *horrid* creature?" Though the words were whispered, meant only for Alex's ears, Samantha did hear and seethed with anger.

"Caroline!" Alex was aghast. It was not like her to be so rude. She was the epitome of charm and good breeding. Seeking to make amends, he looked apologetically at Samantha, knowing that she had overheard. "Samantha . . . I . . ."

"Save the fancy words." She didn't know why she was angry at him, but she was. She was furious with both of them. Suddenly they were a harsh reminder of all the other snobs who had always looked down their noses at her and Gramps, at all the miners who labored in the mountains.

"I'll tell you what he's doing with me, *lady*. I saved his hide for him, and that's a fact. If I hadn't come along when I did, he'd be wearing holes in his head instead of his hat. Those fancy breeches of his would be marked with more than just the road's dust. They'd have the imprint of Cy Tyburn's boot, right on his backside!"

"Ohhhhhhh." Putting a white-gloved hand to her mouth, Caroline was obviously shocked at Samantha's outburst.

"Course, now I don't expect *your* thanks. You probably don't appreciate the fact that I brought your fella back. But I did. Like it or not, you're beholden to me for bringing your Alexander Nicholson back in one piece. I most sincerely doubt you could have done the same. So call me horrid if you like, but I did *you* a favor."

"Yes . . . yes, so you did . . . and I . . . I thank you, Miss Claybourne." Caroline managed an uncertain smile. "I was just . . . just so overwrought. You must understand . . . I didn't mean . . ."

"Yes, you did, but I'll accept your apology if it's given."

Caroline's smile faltered. "Then I apologize."

"Three ruffians accosted me on the road." Alex hastened to tell the story while there was a small measure of peace between the two women. "They frightened off the other passengers and thought to have a bit of fun with me." He laughed. "I think it was my hat that caused the trouble. It marked me as a greenhorn. When Samantha came along they were shooting at my feet to make me dance. Most embarrassing. An experience I won't forget for a long time, though I suppose I can truthfully say that I have been initiated into this West of yours, Caroline." Though he spoke to his fiancée, he was looking right at Samantha.

"Samantha did, as she put it, 'save my hide' and for that I will always be grateful. If there is ever anything that I can do for you, Samantha, don't hesitate to let me know. I never forget a friend." His sincerity was mirrored in his blue eyes and Samantha couldn't help but be moved by his words. Her anger evaporated just as quickly as it had materialized.

"And I never forget a friend either, Alex." She knew for a certainty she would never forget *him*. Even now a funny little quiver danced up her spine as their eyes met. That he felt affection for her she could tell, and the thought warmed her. It wasn't exactly what she might have wished for, but it would have to do.

"Perhaps you would join us for a drink. I need to inform the Overland Stage Company of what happened, but then—"

"Alex! I'm . . . I'm sure Miss Claybourne has more important things to do." Caroline forced a smile. "We wouldn't want to keep her. And . . . and Daddy's schedule . . ." She looked over her shoulder, watching as her father sauntered up at just the right moment.

"Alexander. Good to see you again. Good to see you." Jeremiah West took Alex's hand in a firm handshake. "Was I correct in assuming there was some kind of trouble? Was it *your* stagecoach that fool doctor was babbling about? Suppose it had to be."

"Alex was in an accident and then he was set upon by Cy Tyburn and his gang, Daddy. Oh, those villains. They should be thrown out of town! Alex. Poor, poor Alex." She reached out possessively to cling to his arm. "You'll have to tell Daddy all about it, darling." She turned her back as if to dismiss Samantha from her presence, but Alex did not follow her. He stood looking at Samantha as he retrieved his baggage. "Do you have time for a sarsaparilla, Samantha? I'd be most honored if you would join us."

Samantha wanted to go. Really did. But at the thought of keeping company with Caroline and her father, she shook her head. "No. Thanks anyhow. Some other time. Gramps will be worried about me if I don't get a goin'."

"She has to help her grandfather. We don't want to keep her, Alex." Caroline had a habit of wrinkling up her nose, a habit Alex had found endearing. Now as she did it in disdain he found it surprisingly irritating. For all her pretense of being polite, he thought Caroline could learn a great deal from this young woman she openly scorned.

"Good-bye, Alex." Samantha held up the gray felt bowler hat. "Thanks for the hat. Take care of yourself and make damned sure some other ruffian doesn't get you cornered.

Could prove to be very expensive and cost you a whole heap of new hats." She grinned. "I might not be around the next time."

"Good-bye, Samantha. Take care."

"I will." She hurried the horses along before she could change her mind. As much as she liked Alex, she didn't belong in the company of those who thought her beneath them. "Self-made aristocrats," her grandfather called them. Samantha guided the horses along the crowded road without once looking back. Still, as the wagon pulled out of Central City her eyes were lightly misted with tears.

5

"Well, Alex, what do you think of our miniature metropolis? Hope you'll be happy here. As for myself, I've always found it better to be a big frog in a small puddle than a . . . well, you get the idea." Jeremiah West scowled as he suddenly realized Alex was ignoring him. He was not used to such treatment and it certainly was not what he expected from a future son-in-law. Clearing his throat loudly, he repeated his statement.

"I beg your pardon, sir." Alex had been so busy watching the retreating wagon that he'd been oblivious to Jeremiah West. With so much on his mind, his thoughts were elsewhere. For the first time since being swept up in his surge of feelings for Caroline, he wondered if perhaps he had been a bit too impulsive. What if Caroline was not the woman he'd imagined? Certainly she'd surprised him with her outburst.

"Daddy asked how you like our mountain city. Of course, I'm certain we'll be happy anywhere as long as we are together." Looking up at him through the thick fringe of her eyelashes, Caroline offered Alex her most seductive smile. "Isn't that right, darling?"

"Happiness is a state of mind," he answered evasively. "I've every expectation of being content." Ignoring Caroline for a moment, he studied Jeremiah West, measuring him man-to-man. He was distinguished-looking with a slightly receding hairline and wire-rim spectacles. A tall, lithe physique belied his fifty-five years, yet the tiny lines at his eyes and the wings of gray in his light brown hair made it clear that youth was long behind him. He liked to boast that he was a self-made man and for this Alex couldn't help but admire him. Now Alex would be working for him, preparing himself to take over the bank when Jeremiah retired. "Keeping it all in the family," as Mr. West had said.

"Content? Is that all?" Caroline pouted prettily. "Why, I remember those moonlit nights when you whispered in my ear, and the times we stood together watching the sunrise when the others were abed. I want to recapture those passionate moments, darling. Remember?" He did, all too well. She had most definitely bewitched him. Just one kiss and he had been like tinder, ready to ignite. "Mmm, I thought you would."

Her laugh was musical as she led him to the family carriage, a one-seated topless vehicle with padded brown leather seats. Putting his valise and carpetbags on the luggage rack, Alex took a seat beside her and put his arm around her shoulders to draw her near. The magic of their first meeting was recaptured as Caroline settled herself into its curve.

"I will never forget that sapphire blue dress, the one with all the buttons. I'd like to see you wear it once again. Will you? For me?"

"I will on one condition." Her manner was coy.

"That being?" He was suddenly wary.

"That you promise to behave yourself." She touched the tip of his nose with her finger.

"Behave?" Alex raised one brow.

"You must give your word that you will have nothing to do with that . . . that creature. Such a scruffy little thing! She's a hoyden if there ever was one. Certainly not a lady. Why, she's the scandal of the town. Wears those hideous clothes, spouts profanity with every other word, and hasn't spent a Sunday in church." She pursed her lips. "Why, I was humiliated when I saw you drive up in that wagon of hers. What on earth will people say?"

"Frankly, I don't give a damn!" Alex's anger exploded. No one, not even Caroline, would tell him who he could associate with. "I've already explained the circumstances."

"Alex, really. Lower your voice." People walking down the boardwalk turned their heads, regarding them with curiosity. Feigning playfulness, she pushed him away. "We mustn't create a scene." As her father took his seat beside her, sandwiching her tightly between himself and Alex, she looked to him for help. "Daddy, please tell Alex how we do things here."

Jeremiah West gave Alex an indolent smile. "We have a . . . a certain social structure here, much the same as in your Boston. I'm sure I don't have to go into it in detail. You know what I mean. Enoch Claybourne is a miner. And a ne'er-do-well at that." He emphasized his words with a crack of his whip, setting the horses in motion. "He keeps to himself and his kind, as do we. It's a most agreeable arrangement."

"There's a feud going on between the merchants and bankers and the miners, Alex," Caroline explained. "You must be loyal to Daddy."

"I see." Clenching his jaw, Alex looked from Caroline to her father. At the moment there was a striking resemblance between them. Both had the same haughty profiles, the same self-righteous expressions.

"A little misunderstanding over who is dependent upon whom in the supply business. The miners complain that they're at the mercy of the merchants and bankers for the goods they need. They claim they're forced to pay usuriously high prices, but they don't understand that such things are really out of our control. The merchants are dependent on an irregular and frightfully expensive transportation system. Of course, the railroad should be coming to Central City soon. The townspeople have just approved a bond issue to finance construction of a line from Denver. But until that train comes, we have to rely on Wells Fargo."

"So I've heard. I read it in the newspaper before I came. I tried to find out everything I could about the West."

"And then there's the matter of barter. The miners refuse to use coins or paper money. They pay their bills with gold dust. A pinch between thumb and forefinger is supposed to be the equivalent of twenty-five cents; larger amounts are determined by using a scale. Makes it easy to have differences of opinion. Of course, the miners always insist they've been cheated."

"And have they?" Alex thought he had a right to know.

Jeremiah West laughed nervously. "Of course not. However, gold dust is very elusive. Sticks to scales, pouches, and the hands. A nuisance, really. But you'll learn all about that when you begin work at the bank." With a sudden wave of his hand he changed the topic. "See that building across the street?" He pointed to a tall, three-story building with oblong windows. "That's our newspaper office. *The Register-Call.* Hasn't missed an issue in ten years, not even when Indian raids on the plains cut off supplies." He chuckled. "Published on anything available, including wallpaper and wrapping paper. Made for some very interesting stories. There's a Masonic temple on the third floor." He eyed Alex over his spectacles. "You a Mason? Never thought to ask."

"No, sir, I'm not."

"I'll make certain that you are. I'm not without influence in such things." His statement made it clear that Alex would have little say in the matter. "But forgive me for letting myself talk too much. You two have been apart for quite a few months. I'm sure you have much to say to each other."

There were several things Alex had been anxious to tell Caroline, a great many questions he'd wanted to ask. Now, however, the silence between them stretched out like a long, lonely road. They had nothing to say to each other at the moment. Perhaps too much had already been said, Alex thought, settling himself back in his seat to view the buildings as the carriage passed them by.

Like many other rural towns Central City had its fair share of stores and shops, each with its name and type of business boldly displayed in large painted letters across the front of the building or on a sign hanging by the door: DRY GOODS. BIL-

LIARD HALL. VARIETY STORE. Pharmacist, barbershop, and dressmaker's shop all sat neatly side by side. But the saloons, hotels and boardinghouses had been built in an odd crazy-quilt fashion. They were jumbled together at the bottom of stark, treeless gulches or perched at crazy angles on the surrounding hills. Some had been built on stilts or were balanced precariously on the rock walls. Alex soon learned that Eureka Street and Lawrence were continuations of the very same street, one taking up where the other ended, seemingly at the intersection of Main. One building, a corner saloon was even shaped like a slice of a pie because of the upslant of the street. This mining "city" seemed to have a personality all its own.

The carriage rocked and swayed, pitching slightly backward as it started an upward climb. "Our house is on West High Street," Caroline said, breaking the long silence. " 'Bankers Row' is what some call it because so many in that profession have built there." She made it clear beyond a doubt that the hill above Main Street was considered the "right side of town," an area where large, elaborate homes gave evidence of prosperity. The district on the other side of the gulch, she explained, was frequented only by gamblers and miners.

The houses they passed now were of a style favored in Boston: Victorian with a hint of Gothic revival. Alex liked them. They had strong character with a hint of a romantic disposition. The houses seemed to rise steeply, their verticality accented by board-and-batten siding, narrow strips that rose to the height of the structure. The steeply pitched cross gables and sharp eaves added to the distinction, as did the tall, slim chimneys.

"This is our little home." With a smug smile Jeremiah slowed the carriage to a halt. "Had it specially built three years ago."

As they alighted from the carriage Alex scanned the structure. What made the West home different from the others was the bay window, the intricately designed bargeboard trim outlining the downward slant to the roof, and a large porch jutting out from the stone foundation. Because it was built on a hill there was no backyard, only a mountain behind them, and he rightly supposed it was on this porch that the family spent a great deal of time in spring and summer.

"Don't worry about your luggage. Chun Lau will see to it." Jeremiah West hastily summoned the diminutive Chinese houseboy, explaining that there were many orientals in the town as well as Cornish and Irish.

"We have a Cornish cook, a 'Cousin Jennie,' as we call them." Caroline was all smiles, touching Alex's arm flirtatiously. "Her culinary magic is divine."

"Cousin Jennie?" Alex was confused, thinking for a minute that the woman was a relative.

She trilled her laughter. "Women are 'Cousin Jennies' and men are 'Cousin Jacks.' Seems everyone who meets a Cornishman wants him to bring all his cousins here to work because they are so knowledgeable about mining. That's the way the name came about. Our cook is named Mrs. Trenoweth. Enid Trenoweth. But I always call her 'Jennie' and she doesn't mind." She gently tugged at his arm. "Follow me, darling and I'll show you to your room. I'm sure you'll want to get all freshened up for dinner. Cousin Jennie has prepared a surprise."

"I most definitely need a bath and a shave. The roads are very dusty." Anxious for such necessary amenities he followed her to the door.

"Not so much different from Boston, is it, darling. Daddy had all the furniture shipped from the East. That's what I meant when I wrote you that you were coming to 'little Boston.' There's really no reason to spend much time anywhere else, except for the bank, of course. Everything you need is right here. I know you'll be very comfortable. I certainly hope so."

She took him on a brief tour, accustoming him to his surroundings. The front door opened into a hall, the hall to the parlor and living room. On the ground floor were the dining room, washroom, kitchen, fuel room, and a storage room with a root cellar beneath. Upstairs was a reading room, gaming room, and several bedrooms, one of which decorated in shades of blue was to be Alex's.

"This will be yours, until we share *our* own bedroom. Oh, Alex, I can hardly wait." Rising up on tiptoe, she wound her arms around his neck. Alex feasted his eyes upon her beauty and for the moment all his doubts were swept away. Were any eyes so blue, any mouth so tempting?

"Caroline!" His mouth claimed hers in a kiss that told of his longing, of his delight in being with her again. "I'll wait until July but not a moment longer," he whispered as he pulled away.

"July. July twentieth? Only seven weeks! It will be the wedding of the year. Daddy has already begun to make the arrangements."

"It will seem like an eternity." Although he had released her, he could still feel the press of her breasts against his chest. The warmth of her body seemed to brand him, made him remember all those passionate nights they had spent together in Boston. "After all, I'm only flesh and blood. Not a saint."

"I don't want a saint. I want a virile, handsome man just like you. I want *you*. I did right from the first moment I saw you, standing so tall and proud. I love you, darling. I know that what we are doing was meant to be. And . . . and I'll try to be a very good wife. You'll see." She sounded so sincere, so breathlessly happy, that he was reassured. He was doing the right thing. Didn't his heart, his body's urgings tell him so?

Alex watched regretfully as she left the room, closing the door behind her. His eyes swept the room, appreciating the artful decor. Hangings decorated the walls and matched the drapes at the large bedroom window. In the center of the room was a large bed with carved oak posts that matched the small oak table and the high-backed chair. That chair now acted as a rack for Alex's coat and vest. He stretched his arms over his head, glad to be free of the restraining garments. Walking to the table, he found soap, razor, brush, comb, and other accessories. Caroline and her father had seen to his every need.

Yawning, Alex suddenly realized how tired he was. It had been an interesting, confusing, exciting, tiring day. Perhaps he would lie down for a few moments before he took his bath. So thinking, he stretched out on the bed. Caroline. Soon she would be his wife, would be sharing his life and his bed. Closing his eyes he thought to conjure her image but another visage, one with large brown eyes, an impish smile, and a nose lightly dusted with freckles appeared instead. Samantha Claybourne. She'd made more of an impression on him than he'd realized. He wondered what she was doing now, if she was with her "Gramps" and if they would ever meet again.

6

The steady rhythm of pumps, the whir of steam hoists and the pounding of sledges resounded from hillside mines as Samantha guided her wagon up the steep winding road. The noise sounded like the mountain's heartbeat, thundering nearly as loudly as her own.

"Jeremiah West is nothing but a lamebrained jackass," she mumbled beneath her breath, "and that highfalutin daughter of his holds her nose so uppity one would think she was a princess."

Gramps works hard, she thought. What did that ole Jeremiah West know about working? He might know banking, might know how to invest and deposit somebody else's money, but he sure as hell wouldn't have a bank if not for men like her grandfather. How dare he judge them, try so obviously to cheat them. Gramps had made the mine all that it was. He had known long ago that gold in a placer could indicate proximity to another type of gold deposit, a lode.

Enoch Claybourne hadn't spent his time in panning, oh, no.

While others were searching the streams, he had chosen the more difficult but profitable hard-rock mining. Far more complex but more lucrative in the long run. He was inventive, with a genius few fully appreciated. Now there were others doing hard-rock mining, using methods her grandfather had devised. Even Jeremiah West had imitated her grandfather's techniques in his own mines. If he was as smart as he thought he was, why didn't that wily banker do something original for a change? Let him try to build a headframe, that wooden tower capped by a wheel over which her grandfather had run cable from a hoisting engine. Gramps had figured that out so that he and Sam could lift the ore more easily.

As she neared the mine and cabin, the road narrowed severely, becoming more trail than roadway. Though Samantha had traveled this way more times than she could count, she still cringed as the outer wheel of the wagon crossed an open notch in the edge of the trail. Here the hill dropped off sharply to the boulders below. With grit and courage she tugged at the reins, avoiding a near accident. She continued on her way, glad to be back up in the high mountains where the air was fresh, unpolluted by the smoke of city fireplaces. Although she wished him well, she was determined to put Alexander Nicholson far from her mind. Though she could not abide Caroline West, she hoped he would be happy. She wished him luck. He would need it!

Reaching the mine entrance, a small cabinlike structure built right into the side of the mountain, Samantha pulled off the roadway and secured her wagon to one of the few remaining trees. Wood was precious. Gramps said the mountainside reminded him of a balding man losing his hair, but lumber was needed for building and for shoring up the mine shafts. Many a miner had been killed by a collapsing tunnel. Sturdy timbers were a matter of life and death.

The door to the mine entrance stood slightly ajar. Samantha hoped her grandfather would not be too worried or annoyed with her for being so late. Well, she would manage to soothe him. Gramps had the roar of a tiger but was in truth a pussycat. Perhaps it was better if others thought him gruff and easily angered. It helped keep any would-be claim jumpers away.

"Gramps! Gramps." The sound echoed as she entered the

main tunnel. Walking carefully as the way grew dark, she paused to light a kerosene lamp. Once inside, branch tunnels spread out like spiderwebs from the main tunnel and the shaft. Although she knew the mine like the palm of her hand, she still had to be careful. Many a skilled miner had fallen to his death because of a misstep. A forgotten ledge, a misjudgment could be fatal. Samantha remembered being with her grandfather when most of the tunnels and shafts had been dug. The mine had grown bigger over the twelve years, just as she had, yet she was always wary of where she placed her feet.

"Gramps . . ." Her voice echoed eerily down the tunnels and back again, answered by his deep grumbling voice. She followed the sound and found him at last down in the winze, a sloping passageway connecting two tunnels that were at different levels.

"Where have you been, Sam?" Her lantern reflected the worried crease of his forehead, the thick gray beetling brows. "You're late!"

"I was fishing. Caught four fish for supper, in fact. I had just started back for the mine when I heard a ruckus. Seems the stagecoach had a breakdown. The driver and most of the passengers had run off but Slim Walker, Buck Cameron, and Cy Tyburn had arrived on the scene. They were shooting at an easterner making big pests of themselves as usual. I had to help, Gramps. I couldn't just stand by, so I frightened them off. Then I gave the man a lift into Central City."

"Humph! Easterner, you say?" He took off his wide-brimmed felt hat and wiped his brow. "I told you to be careful. Don't like you taking up with strangers. Could be dangerous." His piercing hazel eyes peered out at her from under his heavy brows. "He didn't get too familiar, did he?"

"Oh, no, Gramps. He was such a gentleman. Handsome and dressed so fine." She sighed dreamily, remembering. "I've never seen a man like that in these parts before. They're either old, ugly, or snooty." She wrinkled her nose distastefully. "Only ones with any appeal at all are ruffians. Cy. Buck. But he was a man any gal would be right proud to claim."

"Oh, he was, was he?" Enoch snorted his disapproval. "Even

more reason to stay away." He pulled at his beard, a thick gray thatch that hung to midchest. "And did he sweet-talk ya?"

"No. But I wish he had." She kicked at a rock in frustration. "He had himself a fiancée. One of those dainty beauties who live up on the hill. He wouldn't give too winks for the likes of me." That thought somehow hurt.

"Like stays with like. That's the way it should be. Besides, you're too young to be thinking about courting. You're just seventeen. Won't be eighteen for three whole months."

Samantha pouted at the reminder. Her grandfather thought she was still a child. "My mother was married and had me by my age," she protested.

"That she was and did. But she was city bred and knew much more about life than you do. I don't want you to get hurt. I love you too much, Sam."

"Yes, I know," she sighed. She didn't want to argue. There was really no point. It would be a long time before she'd even contemplate getting married. "I don't want you to worry. Most likely I'll never see him again. Leastwise not for more than a minute." Would Alex even want to associate with her when Jeremiah and Caroline had finished gossiping?

She could imagine just what they would say. There were some who considered Gramps a rough, tough, uncouth old coot who should do better by the young girl in his care. At least take her to church, it was whispered. But Samantha knew Gramps had given her a fine upbringing. He was as kind and gentle as a man could be, showing her how much he cared by every word and deed.

Looking at her grandfather now, Samantha remembered how she'd once been certain that he was Santa Claus. He greatly resembled that Christmas elf with his thick gray hair, mustache, and beard. Of medium height and stocky build, with a strong weatherbeaten countenance, Enoch bristled with defiance when anyone angered or tried to take advantage of him. Yet she remembered one Christmas Eve when she had stayed up spying to see if he would harness his two mules for a secret night's journey to visit the town's children.

"You don't think you'll see him again? Good." His mood softened. "Course now, I expect you did the right thing. Cy

Tyburn needs his comeuppance once in a while." He chuckled. "And as I remember you've always been the one to give it to him. Even when you were just a child."

"I whopped him good. I would have done the same today if he'd given me reason."

Enoch Claybourne's eyes took on the glow she knew so well. His mind was on the gold again, she could tell by the look in his eyes. "You should see what I found today, Sam. I know the mother lode is nearby. I just know it! You and I are gonna be rich and then you can have any man your heart desires. When you're old enough, that is."

"Hope we're rich enough to hire a cook," she giggled. It was a joke between them that Samantha's skills in the kitchen left much to be desired. There had been no women around to give her instruction. What little Sam knew she had learned on her own. Needless to say, she had invented some "interesting" recipes. But the bulge of Gramps's stomach proved that he had not only survived but was in fact well fed.

"A cook it will be, but come along."

Together they made their way through the maze of tunnels and Samantha felt a rush of pride. Each and every passage reflected her grandfather's genius. He had extended his tunnels underground. Most gold was far below ground level. To begin with he had sunk two shafts along the supposed vein, one for working, the other for ventilation and pumping water. Water collected at the bottom of the shafts, but her grandfather had solved that problem by deepening the holes and digging connecting horizontal tunnels to drain off the water. Later as the mine extended deeper underground, he had found it more efficient to blast his tunnels in from the hillside so that they could push the ore out of the mine rather than having to haul it up.

At first they had used a wheelbarrow, but as they went deeper into the mountain Enoch had added rails for an ore car to travel down the main tunnel to the outside. When the ore was collected, it had to be sorted and the waste rock discarded. This was part of Samantha's job. The valuable ore was then carried to nearby bins, huge wooden receptacles with chutes that could easily discharge the ore into the wagon. Then they would take it to the mill in nearby Black Hawk for processing.

All the years her grandfather had been working and searching were just a prelude to finding the real treasure. Oh, how she hoped he would find it soon. So far the pockets had contained more rock than gold.

"See here. Look at the shine in that quartz. Isn't a prettier sight this side of the Rockies. Gold. And the deeper I dig, the more there is." Picking up a loose rock that had fallen to the ground, he held it up for her inspection.

"Lord, what a beautiful sight. More gold dust for our coffee tin, Gramps. Soon it will be full again. All the way up to the top by the looks of this!" She caressed the hard piece of ore in her hand, thinking of how many men would willingly die to possess it. Hell, just to touch it.

"There's gold in there. But I have a sneakin' notion that the main lode is still some distance into the earth. I'm gonna have to dig another tunnel to follow the vein. Pick and shovel won't do the trick. Got to open it up. I'm gonna have to use powder."

"Powder? You're not as fleet of foot as you used to be, Gramps. . . ." She tugged at the sleeve of his shirt to get his full attention and shook her head. "Don't."

"I'll be careful, Sam. Been mining since forty-nine. Been to California and back. If there's anything I know, it's how to find gold and get it out!" His surly look silenced any further protestations. "I can do it."

His confidence soothed her. "Of course you can."

"Gonna find it, Sam. Gonna find that mother lode. It's something I gotta do. Gotta strike it rich. Guess you just might say it's my end of the rainbow right here." He held the ore up to the lantern's light, muttering beneath his breath.

"Just wait until the town hears this!" Samantha said, caught up in her grandfather's excitement. "They'll think twice before calling you a 'crazy old miner' again." She wanted to shout the news to the mountaintops. Her grandfather was going to find it. He most surely was.

"*No.* Gotta keep quiet about this." Enoch's voice sank to almost a whisper. "Can't let *anybody* know. From now on we'll sack ore and load at dusk when it's too dark for nosey strangers to see we've finally struck somethin'." She had a good idea of just who that "nosey stranger" was.

"But . . ."

Despite his long beard his smile looked strangely boyish. "Gonna make it up to you, Sam, for all those lean years. You've brought light into my life, given me a reason to keep on going." His eyes shone with tears and he quickly turned his back. "But we can't stand here jawin' all day," he said, his voice suddenly gruff. "Gotta get busy. Come along." Without looking back he made a broad gesture and Samantha followed him.

7

The shadowy outline of the mountains was a deep purple against the dark pink haze of the sky as Samantha and her grandfather returned to the cabin, a wooden structure with a sod roof. They were tired but happy. It had been a profitable day that would replenish their dwindling supply of gold.

"Are you hungry, Gramps?"

"So hungry I could eat my shovel."

"I'll hurry and cook the fish." With a twinge of guilt Samantha realized that she had been so busy with Alexander Nicholson that she had forgotten the matter of her grandfather's lunch.

A large wood-burning cookstove stood in the center of the cabin. It was used for heat as well as cooking and now Samantha hurried to light it, striking a match on the sole of her boot. She fed the fire with wood from the pile just outside the front door then stood watching the intricate mica window in the stove door until she could see the flickering flames dancing about behind it. Taking off her hat, she tugged at her braids, letting them fall to her shoulders.

"Do you really think I have nice hair, Gramps?" She toyed with a braid absentmindedly.

"Uh-huh. Never seen a color like that, except on your mother. She was nearly as pretty as you." Taking her hat he hung it on a peg beside his own. To save room they hung nearly everything on pegs on the wall: brooms, hats, kettles, pots, pans, tools, and guns. Even the chairs were hung on the wall when they were not in use.

"I'm *not* pretty." She really didn't think that she was, certainly not in the same sense that Alex's blond fiancée was. For just a moment she wondered what it would feel like to be soft and fragile and feminine with hands that never had scratches or calluses. Hastily she put the thought from her mind. She was what she was. And yet maybe she'd wear her hair free of its restraining braids and pins, at least the next time she went into town.

"Gonna fry that fish or are you gonna stand looking into the fire all night?" Gramps sounded peeved as he sat on the sofa and pulled off his boots. "What's got into you, Sam?" He frowned. "Not thinking about that stranger again, are you?"

"Oh, no!" She answered all too quickly, turning her head to avoid his searching gaze. Taking a large iron skillet down from the wall, she greased it with lard from a tin can near the stove. "Wish we had some cornmeal. Guess flour will have to do." Without really thinking, she set the pan on the stove while she went to the cellar to get the flour. There was only a two-pound sack left and most of that was gone. The cellar was in fact nearly empty, depleted from the long, hard winter.

Meat and wood were the only commodities that miners provided for themselves. There was no place for a garden on the sloped, rocky land. Samantha and Enoch went into town for just about everything else, usually to Black Hawk, where the prices were cheaper and the merchants friendlier. Of course, Sam thought, she *could* go into Central City just this once to compare prices. And while she was there she could drive past the bank. Wouldn't hurt to be neighborly, even if Caroline West wasn't. Alex had made an overture of friendship that Sam couldn't ignore.

A sharp crackling sound brought her back to the present and sent her scurrying up the cellar ladder to take the pan off the stove before it caught fire. It wasn't like her to be so addled. For the twentieth time she resolved to wipe all thoughts of Alexander Nicholson from her mind.

"Supplies are dwindling, Gramps. We have a sack of potatoes, a half sack of turnips, two bunches of carrots, four or five onions, and one or two apples."

"How's the coffee?"

"About enough for another week." Enoch Claybourne savored his coffee. He said it was the only thing that would keep him full of steam to keep digging. He'd invested in his own coffee grinder, a smaller version of the one they had at the general store. It had a wheel that needed cranking to crush the coffee beans. The grinder was Enoch's only concession to "frivolity."

"Enough for a week? Better be going into town, then. Do it this Saturday."

Samantha darted a glance at her grandfather and saw that he was writing in his journal again. He kept a careful record and never failed to scrawl an entry at the end of each day. "Want some fried potatoes with the fish?"

"Potatoes will be just fine." Returning to his scribbling, he balanced the journal on his lap. Samantha wished that he had a desk but knew that such an expensive piece of furniture was a luxury they could ill afford. They had very little in the way of furnishings—two beds, a table, three chairs, one with a broken leg, a washstand, and the sofa her grandfather was sitting on—all handmade by Enoch. If it wasn't fashionable, it certainly was sturdy.

Enoch Claybourne was very independent, a quality Samantha valued and thought to emulate. "When all is said and done," he'd always told her, "the only person you can really rely on is yourself. Remember that, Sam." If that made him a "grizzly old hermit," as some people called him, then so be it. A man had to do what was best for himself. It did present a problem in the mine, however, one that could have been easily rectified by hiring a man or two to help with the digging. But her grandfather refused to trust anyone. Until she'd seen the quartz he'd chipped off today, Samantha had wondered if he'd ever find the vein. Now she was certain that he would. It was only a matter of time until all her grandfather's dreams became a reality.

Samantha busied herself preparing the trout, scooping a handful of flour onto a discarded page of a newspaper. Rolling the fish over and over, she covered each one completely with a powdery white coating, then put it in the pan. Cutting two potatoes as thin as possible, she squeezed the slices in between each fish and peppered the concoction lightly. It wasn't fancy cookery but it would fill their stomachs. Perhaps tomorrow night they'd have a chicken. There was a coop right next to the cabin that sheltered a small flock of layers. Once in a while one of the birds would end up in the stew pot.

"Supper's ready, Gramps," Sam said, poking at the potatoes with a fork to make sure they were done.

Enoch washed his face and hands in the chipped china basin that stood on the washstand. There was a well with a pump outside the door, but Samantha always kept a large bucket of water filled to the top to save them the trouble of going in and out. Tonight her grandfather didn't bother heating his wash water but used it right from the bucket, then took a seat at the small round table.

"Smells good, Sam." He eyed his dinner appreciatively, then attacked it with zest, using his fork as sturdily as his pick. There was little suppertime conversation. Enoch ate quickly and avidly. Though his body was at the table, his thoughts were still at the mine and Samantha had little doubt that tomorrow he would be up at the crack of dawn.

"Think the vein's just a few yards off to the left of the spot I showed ya, Sam." The air was filled with a pungent fragrance as Enoch lit his pipe. The odor of burning tobacco was a fragrance Samantha had grown used to. He had smoked a pipe for as long as she could remember. "Been making some calculations. If what I think is true, we just might have a real bonanza on our hands. Yep, a real bonanza. Then I can buy you all the things I been longing to get you, honey."

"Don't really want anything. I'm well contented."

"I know you are. You've never asked for much. You're a fine young'un, Sam. It's just that I want you to have all the things I've never had. I want you to reach out and be able to touch a star. Want you to be able to walk down the street and thumb your nose at all those so-called ladies who look down on us. Wouldn't you like that?" His bushy brows danced up and down as he asked the question.

Thinking of Caroline West, she smiled. Oh, how she *would* like to put that haughty miss in her place. "Well . . . yes!"

"I know the townspeople say I ain't done right by you. That you should be more feminine, more mannerly . . ."

Samantha sniffled in disgust. "You've taught me all the things I need to know, Gramps. Hell, I wouldn't want to be as helpless and dainty as some of those women I see. Why, they look as if they'd faint if they got mud on their shoes. All they know is gossip and stitchery, sitting around on their backsides, twittering behind their fans. I thank the good Lord that I'm not like them. I'll bet there's not a one of them that can shoot a gun or knows the difference between a tunnel and a shaft, or can tell when a rock is nothing but fool's gold. She held her chin up with pride. "But I can."

"Yes, you can." For just a moment his eyes looked sad. "But there's more to life than shooting, hunting, and scratching about with a shovel all day helping your old grandfather. I taught you how to do all those things but I didn't teach you female things. Guess I just didn't know anything about such matters. Hope I haven't done you a great wrong, child."

"Wrong? You've made me strong like you. Hell, I don't need anybody else. Why would I when I've got you?"

"But what if you didn't?"

"But I do!" She didn't like the turn their conversation had taken. Though she knew her grandfather wouldn't live forever, she couldn't bear the thought of being without him.

"I'm an old man, honey. You've got years and years ahead of you but I'm well into the autumn of my days. I want security for you, enough money so that you can tell the governor himself to go to the devil if you want to. I want rainbows and roses for you, Sam." Rising from his chair, he stretched his arms. "And

I'm gonna get 'em, too. Yep, I'm gonna find that rich vein of ore just for you." His voice was stern with determination.

Once again he busied himself with his journal while Samantha did the dishes, then swept the planked floor. It was a small one-room cabin. A partition between Samantha's bed and her grandfather's gave them their only privacy. There were those who scoffed at the Claybourne cabin, calling it a shack, but it was the only home Samantha had ever known, or at least the only one she remembered. Home, "the next best place to heaven," or so she'd heard it said. The mine and the cabin were all she and Gramps had, all they wanted. She clenched her jaw with determination, as eager to protect her grandfather as he was to watch over her. She'd never let anyone take their property away, never let the mine go, no matter what happened. It was a vow she promised herself she would keep, gold or no gold.

8

The blare of the noon whistle pierced the air, shattering Alex Nicholson's reverie as he stood gazing out at the wagons, horses, and people that thronged the wide dirt street. The whistle signaled a change of shifts in the mines, that much he had learned. It was hard, grueling work the miners did, and yet at the moment he nearly envied them. At least they had something to do to while away their time, something to make them feel productive. As for himself, he'd arrived on a Monday, started his job on Tuesday, and so far, though it was Thursday, he still hadn't done a thing. A man could only sit idle so long.

"Well, what do you think of your office?" At nine o'clock on Tuesday morning that was the first question Jeremiah West had asked.

Alex had wanted to give Jeremiah an honest answer. It was a big room dominated by a large mahogany desk. Against the back wall, between two windows, a bookshelf displayed an assortment of leather-bound books. A large settee and several upholstered leather chairs completed the furnishings. "Impressive is the word, though I really don't need anything quite this grand."

"Nonsense. You are going to be my son-in-law. I want you to be comfortable. I want you to have the very best." He had pointed proudly to the name painted in gold lettering on the door: *Alexander C. Nicholson, vice-president.*

"I really haven't done anything to warrant such a title yet, sir." Alex had expected to work his way up, not start at the top. Even at his father's company he had earned his way by diligence and skill. "I don't expect to be handed such a responsibility on a silver platter, son-in-law or not."

"Nonsense." Jeremiah West had rewarded his sincerity with an indulgent smile, one he might have given an errant child, then left the room without another word. He had not visited Alex's office again. Back at the house, he shrugged Alex off, sternly stating that he never discussed business at home. Thus Alex had spent the last three days in a perpetual state of boredom. It seemed an uneasy beginning to his new career and his vision of helping to build the new territory.

Well, I can't spend my time smoking expensive cigars, drinking whiskey, and drawing a salary for staring out the window, he thought in irritation. He hadn't come all the way from Boston just to "sit on his backside," as Samantha would have said. He had expected something quite different. He had expected the world west of the Mississippi to be free of the restraints that bound the eastern half of the continent. There were said to be many who had acquired riches and status with little else but their grit, daring, and good business sense. He had thought this a place to make his own way, his own fortune. He had wanted a challenge he could master. Why, so far he'd been about as useful as the cigar store Indian that decorated the boardwalk!

Alex was determined *not* to become a mere puppet in Jeremiah West's hands. He was his own man, determined to make his own way. Had it not been so, he would have stayed right where he was in Boston and insisted that Caroline come to *him.* He had wanted to have the same chances and challenges that had spurred his great-grandfather to success. Edward Nicholson had come to the American colonies with nothing but the clothes on his back, had worked and toiled and built one ship

into a shipping empire. With tenacious courage he had insti-
gated the Boston Tea Party and stood firm against the king of
England himself. Edward Nicholson had made the money that
future generations of Nicholsons had spent. Alex, however,
wanted the chance to prove his own worth. He wanted to get
away from his father's domineering presence. Alexander Cur-
ran Nicholson would be no man's shadow.

"You are a fool!" his father had shouted at him, "leaving a
veritable empire that will one day be yours to go traipsing off
into the wilderness. A fine place for a war hero to be, amidst a
bunch of unlawful scoundrels no better than those rebels that
you fought in the war."

The war. The war. Alex was tired of hearing about it. It had
been the most devastating four years of his life and yet his
father would never let anyone forget about it. "My son, the war
hero," he would always say when introducing Alex. As if win-
ning a medal for obliterating other human beings was an act of
heroism. The South *had* fallen to its knees, the North had won
the war, but at a terrible price. Alex had spent the last six years
trying desperately to forget. It had been just one more reason to
leave Boston for Colorado.

And now I am the vice-president of West and Hatcher, he
thought glumly. Vice-president, a meaningless title if he never
made any decisions. Indeed, he would be better off working as a
teller. At least then he'd have something to keep him busy and
people to talk with. He'd be earning his salary instead of twid-
dling his thumbs in isolated grandeur. Another week like this
and he would go mad, he thought, pacing up and down, listening to the wood beneath the the scroll-patterned carpet creak as
he walked.

"Careful or you'll wear a pathway in Mr. West's expensive
rug. I don't think he'd be pleased about that." A tall, thin
auburn-haired man with an infectious smile peered in through
the doorway. Anxious for some company, Alex invited him in.
"Robert Cunningham is my name. I'm a lawyer."

"Alexander Nicholson. I'm—"

"Jeremiah's soon to be son-in-law. He's told me all about
you. I'd be lying if I said I wasn't envious. Caroline is just about
the most eligible young lady around here. I know I've been

giving her the eye for quite a while. But all's fair in love and war, or so I've heard said." His easygoing manner showed he held no hard feelings. "Congratulations on your triumphant wooing."

"Do I take that to mean you've called a truce?" Alex raised his brows in question as the young man took a seat behind the desk, in Alex's chair. One thing that could be said for the young lawyer, he wasn't at all shy. He seemed brazenly sure of himself.

"Of course. I know when a woman is out of my reach." He grinned again, reminding Alex of a mischievous elf. "Besides, I think I'm going to like you. Just a feeling I have." Reaching into his coat pocket, he pulled out a cigar and offered it to Alex. "Have one? A gesture of welcome to our fair city."

"No, thank you. I don't smoke."

"Better start. Jeremiah will tell you that it looks *distinguished.*" Removing the band from the cigar he had chosen, Robert tossed the paper band over his shoulder with a devil-may-care shrug. "Jeremiah always gets his way."

"Not with me, he won't." Alex folded his arms across his chest, bristling his defiance. "I am my own man."

"Are you now?" The lawyer seemed surprised. "That's good to hear." He lounged in the leather chair, propping his feet on the desk, looking all the while at Alex. "Have you told J.W. that?"

"Not yet, but I'm planning to." Drawing up another chair, Alex sat down across from his visitor. "Just how do you know so much about Jeremiah?" he asked, intrigued and a bit amused at the lawyer's boldness.

"My office shares the building with the bank. That's usually the case in a building such as this. Numerous businesses use the building. Mine's on the second floor. I pay Jeremiah rent. There's an assayor's office up there too. Make's it handy for all of Jeremiah's ventures." Lighting the cigar with a strike of a match he took a puff, relishing it slowly before he spoke. "J.W. deals in many areas. That's how he made all his money."

"Such as?" Alex was anxious to know.

"Oh, he owns a few stores, holds shares in some gold mines. The usual. Hear tell he's going to invest in that railroad, the one that's going to connect Black Hawk and Central City to Denver. Then, too, he's begun making plans to build a fine hotel here. The one spearheaded by a fellow lawyer, Henry Moore Teller." He took another puff. "Some might say he's a bit over-ambitious, but that's what has made Jeremiah what he is. He's what they call a self-made man." He lowered his voice conspiratorially. "Hear he's even going to buy out his partner. Old Thaddeus Hatcher had better look out. I'd say J.W. is preparing to make this bank read West and *Nicholson.*"

"I sincerely doubt that." Alex thought a moment. When he had argued with Caroline about the wisdom of working for her father, she had given him a mysterious smile. He would not regret it, she'd promised: now he began to understand what she meant.

"And just what do you know about my future father-in-law?" Alex asked.

"He was educated in a country school near Omaha, Nebraska. That's where I'm from. He was a friend of my father's before he came here. Used to be called Jeremiah Westbrook but he shortened it to "West." While he was still a lad, he left home to make his own way in the world and went to New York City. Became a bank messenger. It was there he learned his trade, rising to the position of assistant teller. By the time he was twenty he was sent to Kansas City to become a cashier for the Bank of Missouri. The rest sounds like a fairy tale." Robert grinned, flicking the ashes of his cigar into his boot. Taking the hint, Alex searched for and found an ashtray. "Met a wealthy woman, a widow. Caroline's mother in fact. She had some connections, enough to set him up in business. A branch store in Denver. Formed a partnership with another merchant, Mr. Hatcher. Few years later they heard about the gold strike and came here. They invested in mines, hiring others to do their digging for them."

"Jeremiah is involved in mining?" Alex was a bit surprised. He'd never mentioned that fact. "Does he know a man named Claybourne?"

"Enoch Claybourne? Yes, indeed he does." Robert leaned forward, a smile tugging the corners of his mouth upward. "Do *you* know him?"

Alex shook his head. "I don't know Enoch Claybourne but I did meet his granddaughter, Samantha. She saved me from certain embarrassment." Alex saw no need to elaborate. "A most interesting young woman. Do you know them?"

"Haven't met them, but I've heard enough to fill a book. Seems J.W. tried to buy out the old man's claim a while back and was told in no uncertain terms to take his money and—"

"I see." No wonder there was so much tension between Samantha and the Wests, Alex thought. Unwittingly he had put Samantha in an awkward situation. Now he knew why she had scowled at the mention of Jeremiah West's name. And hadn't Jeremiah himself said something about trouble between the miners and the bankers?

"Caroline says the Claybournes are *quite* . . . uh . . . unusual. Suffice it to say I refrain from mentioning their name whenever she is near." Once again his voice lowered to a near whisper. "Personally I believe it was all just a misunderstanding. J.W. wants to have a firm hand in the future of the territory, that's all. All the talk about the questionable source of his fortune is merely rumor. I can't believe he would cheat anyone. I believe J.W. when he says he has the miners' interests at heart, that left to their own devices, they'd fritter away all their hard-earned profits on gambling, whiskey, and women. I surely do."

Alex scowled. Something in Robert Cunningham's manner suggested that he was hiding something. "What do you mean when you say there's talk of impropriety?" The answer was not forthcoming. Just as Robert was about to answer, the door swung open and Caroline swept into the room with practiced grace.

"Sorry, darling. I didn't know you had a visitor." She smiled, wrinkling up her nose. "Hello, Robbie."

Robert Cunningham sprang to his feet in much the same manner Alex had seen Union soldiers do when confronting an officer. "Hello, Caroline. Just thought I'd extend a welcome to old Alex here. Thought he might need a friend, or a lawyer in the future. Whichever it is, I'll be right here."

"How kind of you. Alex doesn't know many people in town yet. Course, now we're having a little gathering next Friday evening at our house. You are most certainly invited. Seven o'clock, Robbie."

"Seven?" For all his talk of love, war, and truces, he seemed completely captivated by her. "I'll be there."

"We're turning the parlor into a dance floor. I'll save *you* the second dance." Fluttering her eyelashes, Caroline seemed to be making the very most of the situation, using Robert to spark Alex's jealousy.

"Thank you, Caroline." Robert was obviously flattered.

"The first dance is already promised to Alex." She took Alex's arm coyly. "Isn't that so, Alex darling?" Without waiting for him to answer she hurried on. "All the important people will be there. Even Mr. Teller. Daddy has some splendid ideas about the hotel. He's anxious to talk with him about it. I'm sure you've heard all the details."

"Robert's just been telling me about it. Sounds like a most ambitious project." Robert slowly made his way to the door. "We've already got hotels." Then, noting her scowl, he added, "But perhaps another one won't hurt. Your father told me that they plan to begin soon, the excavation, that is. Seems a site has already been selected."

"The corner of Eureka and Pine. Across from the newspaper office." Reaching up to adjust her hat she turned her back on the lawyer as if suddenly tiring of the chatter. "We'll talk about it some other time. Right now I have a surprise for Alex."

Realizing that he had been dismissed, Robert Cunningham took his leave, offering Alex a friendly farewell wave.

The moment the door shut, Caroline wound her arms around Alex's neck, bestowing her most dazzling smile on him. "I thought you might be hungry, darling. A man's work awakens a healthy appetite."

"Work? I've done little enough of that lately. I'm beginning to wonder just what I'm doing here." He softened his tone as he realized it was not her fault. "I want to talk to your father about the situation but he refuses to talk business after hours and God knows he's never here. But we have to get a few things settled. I won't sit around and be part of the furniture. You can tell him *that* for me."

Caroline stuck out her lower lip in a pout. "Don't be bothersome, Alex. I didn't come here to have you rant and rave at me."

He was more than a little annoyed and realized that it showed. Throwing his hands up in frustration, he shook his head. He wanted to talk, to vent his anger, to seek her advice and understanding, but the expression on her face told him she didn't want to listen.

"All right, I'll drop the subject, but do let your father know that I want to be involved in what's going on. I want to make some decisions."

She sought to placate him with a smile. "You will be involved, darling. You will. Give Daddy time. You've only been here a few days. He's had a great deal on his mind." She pirouetted gracefully before him. "Do you like my new dress? My hat? I had them made up specially for you because I know how much you like blue."

"You look lovely." He knew that was what she wanted to hear.

Playfully she pushed him toward the door. "We won't talk unpleasantries any longer. I'm starved. Cousin Jennie made some sandwiches for us. They're in a basket in the buggy. I need to have some dresses fitted this afternoon and I thought we could have lunch together first. Remember when you took me out in your boat and we ate sandwiches while we sailed Boston Harbor?" She laughed. "Food was really the last thing on our minds."

How could he forget? It was the first time he had kissed her. "The very last thing, as I recall." He opened the door for her. He was still frustrated but kept his emotions bottled up inside. She couldn't help what her father did or didn't do. He wanted to be fair. Everything would work out if he gave it time. Still, as they approached the carriage, Alex wondered once again if he had been too hasty in letting his heart rule his head.

9

Samantha awoke just as the first rays of the sun crept through the cabin's lone window. It was not the light that disturbed her sleep, however, but the quiet. She'd grown so used to her grandfather's snoring that whenever the gentle rumbling ceased it usually did not take long before even her soundest slumber was disturbed.

"Gramps?" There was no answer. Rising from her bed and hurrying to dress, she looked about, not really surprised to find him gone.

The cabin was empty but the smell of brewing coffee gave proof that Enoch had already eaten his breakfast and embarked on his labors. Pouring a cup of coffee for herself, Samantha grabbed a handful of crackers from a small barrel, popped them into her mouth, and hastily washed them down. It would have to do for breakfast. She had to get going.

Without stopping to redo her braids, she grabbed her hat down from its peg on the wall, plopped it on her head, opened the front door and headed for the mine. There were four outbuildings near the cabin: a crudely constructed outhouse, a shed to house the animals—four horses, two mules, a goat for milk and cheese,—a chicken coop, and another building for the wagons and tools, Beyond this, less than sixty feet away, was the entrance to the mine. Lighting the kerosene lamp that her grandfather had left behind for her, Samantha entered the darkened labyrinth.

She found her grandfather in the stope just as she had expected, his clothes already dusty and stained, his boots muddy, the front brim of his brown felt hat turned back from his eyes as he delved into the cavern walls with his pick. He turned abruptly when he heard her call his name, his eyes lighting up at the sight of her.

" 'Fraid you was gonna sleep all day," he teased.

"You should have wakened me, Gramps." She crept closer to see what he was doing.

"Gotta get what ore I can. Take it to Black Hawk first thing tomorrow morning. Don't even need to get it assayed, Sam. I can tell right away just how fine a grade this is. Didn't I tell ya?" His voice lowered conspiratorially, as if fearful someone might overhear. "We'll keep a secret. Won't tell nobody."

"Someone will find out eventually." News of a gold strike traveled like lightning.

"S'pose so." He grunted. "But we'll keep it from 'em as long as we can. Striking out with his pick, he sent a cascade of loose rocks showering down. "But I'm gonna need some money for equipment and the likes, so's I can go down deeper. Can't keep picking away like I'm doing."

Samantha took a deep breath, knowing what her grandfather's reaction would be but speaking her mind nonetheless. "You need help, Gramps. You can't do it all alone."

"No! Don't need no one else." His tone of voice softened. "Except you, Sam."

She understood his determination. Until two years ago Stephen Tyburn, Cy Tyburn's father, had been Enoch's partner. They had nearly lost the mine by his foolishness. Since then, her grandfather had refused to trust anyone. Once the cabin had rung with the laughter and chatter of other miners, but now her grandfather chose to frighten them away.

"But if you hired some men . . ."

Enoch Claybourne shook his head. *"I* can do it. You and I been working together for the last two years. Been doing just fine." The stern set of his jaw informed Samantha that nothing more would be said about the matter.

They worked all day, pausing only for lunch. At dusk they packed the ore into gunnysacks and loaded them aboard the wagon. First thing in the morning they would take the ore to be smelted. In the meantime the wagon would be secured behind the walls of the storage shed, away from prying eyes.

It was a hard day. A grueling day. Only when the wagon was filled did they take the time to rest, and by then it was supper time. Samantha had killed a chicken the day before and now she prepared a stew while her grandfather wrote in his journal. Totally exhausted, she found the words a blur as she sat down by the fire to read over his shoulder. She must have fallen asleep right then and there and been carried off to bed, for when she opened her eyes she was still dressed in her clothes with a blanket thrown over her.

"Breakfast, Sam." Greeting her with a loving smile, Enoch Claybourne surprised her by already having the morning meal prepared. A "gift" from the layers. "A little token of my appreciation for your hard work yesterday, Sam. Man couldn't ask for a better partner." He smiled sheepishly. "Eggs again. Thank God for the chickens."

It was a long, steep, rough ride into Black Hawk, one that nearly made Samantha regret taking a second helping at breakfast. Nor was it easy guiding the four horses necessary to pull the heavy load of ore. At last the smoke rising into the blue sky from many smokestacks announced their arrival.

Known as the "mill city of the Rockies," Black Hawk was a town much like its neighbor, Central City. Buildings, mills, churches, stores, and residences were sandwiched in between gulches, ravines, mines, rocks, and projecting mountain crags in a most irregular manner, the whole city seeming to cling to the hillsides. The difference, however, was the thunderous noise and the dark cloud of smoke that hovered in the air. Black Hawk shuddered from the din of blasting, the crash of mill stamps, the shriek of whistles.

The streets were built one above another, terraces cut into the hillside. At one point the streets crossed above the level of the housetops below and Samantha could nearly look down into the fiery chimneys of the smelters, into the seemingly bottomless shafts and excavations. A little beyond the lower end of town was the site of Professor Nathaniel P. Hill's smelter, The Boston and Colorado Smelting Company, their destination. The denuded hillsides would have announced the place even if the noxious smell and the blackness of the smoke had not.

"You stay in the wagon, Sam. I need to talk to Professor Hill." The owner was a scientist turned mine owner, a man from Boston just like Alexander Nicholson.

"All right, Gramps, I will." Fighting the urge to cough, wiping the sting of the smoke from her eyes, Samantha watched him walk to the main building. Her grandfather had more than one reason to be thankful for the Professor, she thought. Before he had built his establishment, all ore had to be shipped across the ocean to Wales, where the gold was separated from the other minerals. Stamp mills had been useful at first and still operated in freeing the precious metal from the worthless rock, but smelters were a vast improvement. Wealthy investors had contacted Professor Hill and after testing ores in the area, he had been persuaded to build his furnaces in Black Hawk. His smelting works had revitalized the mining industry and given her grandfather new hope.

Enoch was back very soon with one of the foremen, a man with a flat nose and weaselly eyes. Something about the man made Samantha wary, though her grandfather didn't seem to have any qualms. She kept her eyes riveted to him as he helped her grandfather unload the sacks, just in case he had any ideas of keeping some ore for himself.

"Gonna take six weeks to process. They're gonna set the ore ablaze and let it burn in the open air. We'll have better than gold dust. We'll have solid gold. Enough to buy anything I need to get to the womb of the ore."

"Six weeks?" Usually her grandfather was so guarded that she wondered at his sudden trust now. "We're gonna leave it?"

"I've got a receipt that says just how much quartz I brought in. Got an advance in gold dust for half of what it's worth. That will tide us over for a while. Has to be done, Sam, if I mean to get to the main vein." He helped her down from the wagon. "Come on. The Professor said he'd show us around."

"All right." Samantha paused, watching the foreman drag the last of the ore sacks away. An eerie feeling tickled the back of her spine. He'd done nothing unseemly, yet as he looked back at her, she couldn't shake an uneasy feeling.

"What on earth is this, Sam? Hadn't noticed it before." Her grandfather's laughter stirred the air. "Silliest-looking hat I've ever seen. But clearly well ventilated." He held the hat aloft for a better view.

Forgetting her apprehension, Samantha joined in her grandfather's laughter. "That's the Easterner's hat. The man I told you about. He gave it to me as a sort of souvenir." She had tried to put Alexander Nicholson out of her thoughts, but at the sight of the hat it all came flooding back. She could nearly see him perched atop the wagon, clinging to the sides as they shared the bumpy ride. Once again she thought of going into Central City to see him. Should she? Gramps seemed to frown on her furthering the relationship, but she did so want to see him one more time.

10

The midmorning sun cast a shadow of the wagon across the dirt-packed road as Samantha guided the horses down Eureka Street. It was Saturday, the day she and her grandfather had chosen to get their much-needed supplies, but her mind was on an entirely different errand. She intended to pay Alexander Nicholson a friendly call. With that thought uppermost in her mind, she was relieved that Gramps had found himself too busy to accompany her.

He belongs to someone else, she reminded herself more than once along the road. It would not do to have foolish fantasies. Still, she couldn't control the erratic beating of her heart whenever she thought of seeing him. "Like stays with like." Gramps had said it again and again but Lord, she sure liked looking at him and wanted very much to be in his company if only for a short while.

The main street was crowded. It was the end of the week and the last day to get everything a body needed before the seventh day of rest and churchgoing. Samantha saw a few old miners leading mules burdened with their purchases. Others were to be seen on the boardwalk, chewing tobacco, chatting or whittling as they talked of the week's gains or losses. All of the saloons were open and some of the men from the larger mines idled in and out enjoying their liquor and the bright Colorado sunshine. There were women going to market, carpetbags and carryalls slung on their arms. Though their husbands might be lounging, a woman's work was never done, or so it appeared. Samantha guided the horses to a spot in front of the Hazard Powder Company and brought them to a stop. Bounding from the wagon, tying the horses to the hitching post, she joined the throng on the boardwalk.

Samantha had tried hard to look her best. Instead of leaving her dark green shirttails outside her pants, she'd tucked them securely inside her breeches, notching her belt a couple of holes looser to make up for the bulk of the flannel. She'd nearly outgrown the tan canvas pants and she hoped they didn't look too snug on her hips. She wore her old brown hat, but she'd left her hair unrestrained, free to cascade down her back to just above her waistline. Did she look presentable? Strange, but she'd never had such concerns before. Well, it was too late to worry now, she scolded herself.

Clutching the leather pouch of gold dust tight, she made a mental list of her errands. There were four places in all she had to visit: the powder company, to get the blasting supplies her grandfather wanted; the city bakery; the grocery store; and the bank. Since she was already just outside the brick powder house, it would do well for a start.

"I need a keg of powder, thirty paper cartridges, and a spool of fuses, please," she informed the man at the counter.

"You want powder and fuses?" He eyed her warily, obviously reluctant to give such items to a woman. "Seems you'd be better off purchasing a length of cloth. Then you might be able to sew yourself a *dress,* miss. Explosives are dangerous. I'd hate to see such a pretty young thing blow herself to kingdom come."

"I know enough to be careful. Besides, they aren't for me. They're for my grandfather."

"For your grandfather? He's a miner?" He seemed a bit too inquisitive for Samantha's liking. Remembering her grandfather's words of caution, she answered his questions about hard-rock mining with a glib reply.

"He's going to use it to get rid of termites." It was her way of telling him to mind his own business. "Now are you going to get me what I need or aren't you?" Putting her hands on her hips, she stared the man down.

"I suppose." Mumbling under his breath, he went off to return a few minutes later with the items Samantha had requested as well as a wooden hammer and a pointed copper chisel. "Got to use these when you're working, to avoid the danger of a spark. Iron can set off the powder. Please, be careful, miss." He looked so concerned that for a moment she regretted having been so snide.

"Thank you, I will," she replied, giving him an extra pinch of gold dust. Returning to the wagon, she carefully hid her newly purchased items under a canvas tarpaulin then walked in the direction of the bank. If she didn't see Alexander Nicholson soon, she might very well lose her nerve. Besides, maybe he would renew his offer to buy her a sarsaparilla and accompany her to the general store. The thought warmed and encouraged her. She paused to appraise her appearance in one of the bank's larger glass windowpanes, then opened the door.

Inside, the bank was a flurry of activity. Cashiers from the mines were taking in gold dust, nuggets, and retorts to be weighed. Tellers gave out and took in bank notes and made exchanges of coins. Would Alex be too busy to see her? Samantha suddenly wondered just what was his job at the bank. If he had told her, she couldn't remember and as she looked around anxiously she didn't see his face in the crowd. Had she been foolish to come? Nevertheless she craned her neck in search of the offices beyond the main banking floor. Could he be there? She would never know if she did not investigate.

Samantha walked down the hallway reading the names lettered in gold on the doors. *Thadius Hatcher, Oliver Greenway, Jeremiah West.* On the last door was the name she sought: *Alexander C. Nicholson.* Raising her hand, she started to knock when a voice from behind startled her.

"Can I be of some help?" Turning, she found herself scrutinzed by Jeremiah West, whose piercing blue eyes peered at her from above his spectacles.

"No . . . I . . . I . . ." She felt at a sudden loss for words, wondering how she was going to explain herself. "I was just paying a call," she managed at last. "Alex . . . uh . . . Mr. Nicholson forgot his hat and I . . . I had hopes of perhaps returning it." It was a blatant lie but she hoped it sounded convincing.

"His hat?" He gave her a sudden smile. "How thoughtful, Miss Claybourne, and how opportune that we should meet instead." Before she could even think to reply, he had taken her by the arm and led her into one of the other offices. "Sit down. Sit down, my dear. I've been meaning to pay a visit, but this will save me a trip up that long, steep winding road of yours." He pulled up a red velveteen upholstered chair.

Samantha eyed him suspiciously and remained standing. "Just what you got in mind, Mr. West?"

He laughed a bit nervously. "Why to apologize, of course. My offer to buy your grandfather's claim must have sounded a bit presumptuous, a bit overbearing. If so, then I'm sorry. I realized, in thinking the matter over, that there must be a great deal of sentimentality attached to that mine."

"Most certainly there is. Gramps has spent his sweat, his time, his very blood in working it over the years. He'd never let it go. It means too much to him." She clasped her hands together tightly and swallowed hard. "And to me . . ."

He clucked his tongue sympathetically. "Of course. Of course. I do understand. The amount of money I offered must have seemed a paltry sum, an insult, as it were. But now I'm prepared to offer a great deal more." He paused just an instant before he blurted, "Two thousand dollars."

"Two thousand dollars?" Samantha could hardly believe her ears. It seemed like a great deal of money, a fortune, yet she knew what her grandfather would say and answered accordingly. "The claim is not for sale. There is not enough money in this world to make my Gramps part with that mine."

His smile faltered perceptibly. "I see. But then, of course, that is your choice." Since she had decided not to take a seat he also remained standing, but he did prop one foot upon the footrest of the chair he had offered Samantha. His jaw tensed as he thought a moment then amended, "Two thousand five hundred."

"No!" Samantha turned to leave, but he detained her.

"Miss Claybourne, just listen to me." He answered her frown with a benevolent smile. "I like you. I like your grandfather. I hate to contemplate all the hardships you've both been subjected to. That mine is a losing proposition for one man to work. Enoch can never realize its full potential. He needs capital behind him, men to work the mine for him, machinery that will do the same amount of work in one day that takes him a week or a month."

There was a stubborn tilt to Samantha's chin as she stared back at him. "You think my grandfather should make money off the backs of other men like you do, Mr. West, paying them less than a hill of beans for busting their tails down in some dark, damp tunnel? If you think Gramps would ever agree to that, then you are plumb crazy. He *won't* sell you that mine."

"Not sell." He took out a cigar, rolling it between two fingers as he looked at her. "What I had in mind was a partnership. He keeps the mine. I provide the money he needs to get to the—as he might call it—'bonanza.' Enoch can manage the mine as he sees fit, as long as *I* maintain a certain profit margin." With a self-assured smirk on his face he went to the large mahogany desk in the middle of the room and opened the drawer. "I've drawn up an agreement right here. Sixty–forty. Of course, I would hold controlling interest, which would only be equitable under the circumstances. I'm certain you'll agree it's more than fair." He came to her side and held the document in front of her nose as one might hold a carrot before a donkey, grinning in a way that incensed Samantha. Had it been any other man, perhaps she might have given the matter thought. As it was, she shook her head furiously.

Sixty–forty? More than fair? Oh, yes, Jeremiah West had the money to finance the digging, but it was her grandfather who knew where the gold was. "In my way of thinking, Mr. West, you need my grandfather a whole heap more than he needs you."

"Absurd! Enoch Claybourne will never be able to realize that mine's potential without my money to back him." Shocked at at her response, he had forgotten his fine manners and was shouting. "Why am I even talking to a *woman* about the matter anyway? Tell your grandfather I insist on speaking to *him*."

Samantha's eyes flashed and her mouth tightened. "His answer will be the same. *No!* My grandfather and I always see eye to eye. He doesn't think of me as *just* a woman. He will give you the same answer he did before. Take your money and . . . and you know what you can do with it! You'll never get your hands on that mine." She left the office, slamming the door behind her. She did not hear his parting words.

"You will be sorry for this. Before I'm through with you, Samantha Claybourne, you will be begging me to buy that mine."

11

The barbershop was alive with sounds—the slapping of the barber sharpening his straight razor on the leather strop, the snip, snap of scissors, the clink of hair tonic bottles. These noises blended with the murmurous din of men's voices exchanging the latest news as they waited their turn in the chair. Alex breathed in the odor of cologne, hair balm, and soap, and thought it a bit too sweet for his taste. In Boston his barber had concocted a special fragrance for him that smelled a bit more like spice.

"You have to agree, there is nothing half as relaxing as being so pampered," Robert was saying as the two men sat side by side in the barbers' chairs. "Aren't you glad I stole you away from your weary routine?"

"It was a good suggestion, my friend. Besides, I was badly in need of a haircut as Caroline reminded me."

"Mmm." Robert sighed his pleasure as he leaned back and let the barber lather his face. It was the first time since meeting the brash young lawyer that Alex had seen him so quiet. Undoubtedly Robert had no desire to find his face nicked and cut. He sat as still as a statue as the white-coated barber cut away the lather.

Alex watched in the mirror as the barber at his side snipped at his hair. "I like it long on top, just above my collar in back, with just a hint of sideburns. My fiancée tells me it makes me look distinguished."

"Yes, sir."

Alex clenched his jaw slightly as he thought about his fiancée. Last night they had quarreled about the most foolish thing. Such an unimportant matter that he could not even remember what it was. Unless they were talking about what dress Caroline was going to wear or who was doing what in town, it seemed they had very little to discuss. Caroline did not seem to want to be "bothered" with serious matters. She was confounding. What had become of the laughing blond beauty who had so captivated him in Boston? How could she have changed so drastically right before his eyes? It was a puzzlement. How could a relationship he'd thought so perfect suddenly disintegrate before his eyes. Could he really have been so blind, so ensnared by a woman's beauty?

"Be careful with that thing!" Robert's exclamation sent Alex's eyes in his new friend's direction. "My nose might not be perfect, but I like it just the way it is."

"Sorry, sir." The barber was contrite, hurriedly applying alum to the small cut between Robert's mouth and nose.

"J.W. is always telling me that if I'm not careful I'll cut my nose off to spite my face. But I don't need your help, my good man." He laughed in spite of himself. "Guess my nose is a fairly good target, Alex." Prodding the tip of his uptilted nose, he assured himself that no real damage had been done, then breathed a sigh of relief. "By the way, how are things in paradise?"

"In paradise?" It was hardly that lately, Alex thought. Jeremiah West was a domineering man used to issuing orders and having them obeyed. That Alex was meant to become part of his "empire" was obvious. Things were to be done in a certain way, according to Jeremiah's wishes. Caroline in turn always sided with her father. Was it any wonder that there had been an atmosphere of tension at the house for the past few days? Unlike the others Jeremiah came in contact with, Alex refused to back down when he had a different opinion. It had brought them to loggerheads on more than one occasion, much to Caroline's dismay.

"I don't need to tell you again that you are a very lucky man. Caroline's lovely, elegant, graceful, and . . . so why the frown?" Robert cocked a brow. "Trouble in paradise?"

"You might say that."

"Mmm. I'd guess J.W. might be partly to blame, am I right?" At Alex's nod, Robert whispered, "My advice to you is to marry her and take her far away from her father."

Alex shook his head, saying no to the barber as he moistened his hands with hair tonic. "I believe I know exactly what you mean. Caroline seems to be more than just a trifle spoiled."

"You might as well be prepared for the fact that Caroline dotes on everything her father says and does. And he in turn does spoil the devil out of her. It's always been that way. Caroline's mother died when she was born and J.W. has made his only child his sun and moon. Can't blame him for that. But it does present a problem or two for you, Alex. Jeremiah West's shoes seem a bit too big to fill, at least in Caroline's mind." Pressing himself against the back of the chair, Robert awaited the hot, steaming towel that would finish his shave. "Oooooh. Ouch! Ahhh . . ."

"Well, she will have to let me fill them, *if* we are going to be married. There will only be *one* head of my household and that will be *me.*" Alex awaited his own shave, watching as the barber took a china mug from the wall. He noticed the rack of shaving mugs. The entire wall was filled with them, each emblazoned with the name and occupational symbol of the barbers' most valued patrons. He had heard that the most reliable gauge of a barber's stature was the number of such mugs on his racks. If that was correct, this barbershop must be one of the best.

"Your mustache, sir?"

"I guard *that* with my life. Just the stubble. Shave only the whiskers." The hot lather was soft and soothing. Alex closed his eyes as the razor glided over his face. Unlike Robert's barber, this one had a more certain touch and managed the task without a single nick.

"What about you and J.W.? How are you getting on with him?" Removing the towel, Robert donned his jacket, paying the barber ten cents for his shave. "Ten cents! Highway robbery. Everything in this fool place keeps going up, except the fees for my services. But then that's a lawyer's fate, I guess, to be poor." Taking a seat near the window, he interested himself in watching the people walking by as he waited for Alex. "How are things at the bank?"

"I would be much happier if I were kept better informed about fiscal and investment matters. Is Jeremiah usually so secretive about what's going on?" Alex was distracted from his questioning as a gray-haired man with a drooping mustache took the seat next to him.

"Shave, haircut, and somethin' to make me smell less like an old goat," the raspy voice said. Alex recognized the man at once. It was the driver of the stagecoach. "Tobias F. Catwaller has plans for tonight. Gonna spend my time with a pretty piece of fluff named Honey. And if she don't give pleasure to the eye—"

"Tobias. I'm Alexander Nicholson. I was on the stage the day the axle broke. I'm glad to see that you made it back into town safely. I did worry, you know."

"The Boston fella." The old leathery-faced man looked a bit sheepish. "Sorry I took off like I did. S'pose you think I'm as yeller a coward as ever lived, leavin' you there to face Cy Tyburn and his gang. But . . . but I just felt I had to take care of the *ladies*. Hope you won't hold it agin me."

"If I'd had any sense I would have been right behind you. Guess I have a lot to learn about the West, even though I read all about it before I made my journey. Some men around here appear to think they don't have to obey the law. They'd find themselves sitting in a jail cell back east."

"Yep." The old man leaned back in his chair as the barber cut his shoulder-length hair. "Some men just lets out their feelings here. 'Bout as cross as a bear with two cubs and a sore tail, that's ole Cy Tyburn at times. Takes after his pa more than likely." He squinted as he looked at Alex. "Don't look like they hurt you none."

"Just made nuisances of themselves. Showing off for each other. Harmless if you don't give in to fear. I've seen that type before. They'd be the first to run at any real sign of danger. For all their bravado a woman ran them off with a rifle." Alex smiled as he remembered Samantha Claybourne's timely intervention. "A most interesting woman."

"Is that so?" Tobias Catwaller slapped his thigh with his hand and laughed. "Wish I'd a seen that. Bet ole Cy was hoppin' mad. Hee-hee yep." He watched as Alex's barber brushed him clean of hair. "Me and the girls ran off quite a ways. Got an ole miner to take us back to town. I came back the next day with a crew of fellas to fix the stagecoach. Good as new now. Yep, good as new."

Alex paid the barber his fee then scanned the room for Robert. Seeing him staring transfixedly out the front window, he tried to get his attention. "Robert have you met Mr. Catwaller? Robert? Robert, what is it?"

"The most fascinating woman I've ever seen. Dressed in breeches. Tight ones, no less. Shows off her—"

"Derriere? Backside?" Since meeting Samantha it was his favorite new term.

"Yeh, her *backside*. Seldom see curves like that, but oh, how I wish I did. Well-shaped fanny, long legs, small waist. The rest of her is nice too. Beautiful hair. Haven't seen that color before. Red-gold."

"Let me see!" Alex had a feeling he knew who it was, and he was not disappointed. Striding down the street, passing by the barbershop with a defiant scowl on her face, was Samantha. "It *is* Samantha!"

"Samantha? Samantha Claybourne?" Robert was astounded. "Enoch Claybourne's granddaughter."

"That's Samantha Claybourne?" A smile curved Robert's lips. "Why didn't you tell me she was so pretty? A fine friend you are. Here I thought, from Caroline's description, that she was . . . was . . . Will you introduce me?"

Alex didn't answer, he was too anxious to catch up with her. Bounding through the barbershop door, he ran headlong into another man, not taking much notice of the denim-and-leather-clad drifter who stared after his retreating form.

"Seems he was in a bit of a hurry," the man snarled at one of the barbers. "Someone ought to teach him a lesson." Taking off his wide-brimmed hat, he slapped it on his leg, releasing a cloud of dust. Without his hat he was even more ominous-looking, the barber thought, hurrying forward to placate him. It wouldn't do to anger such a man. The set of the jaw, the expression in the wide-set eyes, the way he kept touching his gun, suggested that he might be a gunfighter. Hopefully he would not be staying in town long. As if reading the barber's thoughts, the man curled his lip. "I was just passing through, but now I have second thoughts. Who was he? What's his name?"

"I . . . I don't know. Never saw him before today. Didn't tell me his name."

"Could be I'll be staying for a while if he's who I think he is. An old, old army *buddy* of mine. Yes, siree." Throwing back his head, he laughed chillingly. "It's a small world."

From his place by the window Robert studied the newcomer, deciding at last that Alex couldn't possibly know such a man. No, it had to be a case of mistaken identity. He certainly hoped so, for Alex's sake.

12

Alex pushed through the thick knot of men on the boardwalk and followed Samantha as she hurried down the street. Samantha. He'd been afraid he'd never see her again. Now here she was, like a ray of light on a cloudy day. "Samantha! Samantha!" She didn't seem to hear him, but he watched as she got into her wagon, manuevered it down the road, and tied up in front of the bakery. Dodging horses, wagons, and carriages, Alex crossed the road. He saw her go into Roworth's grocery store, and headed in that direction.

Stepping inside, he quickly scanned the large room. A variety of provisions was heaped in bundles, occupying every inch of available space. From foodstuffs to tobacco, cracker barrels to canned-food tins, not an inch of space was wasted. The store smelled of fresh ground coffee, kerosene, dried meat, and pickled fish. Hams, sausages, and slabs of other smoked meats hung from the rafters along with cooking pots and pans. Kegs and barrels brimmed with sugar, flour, molasses, and vinegar. On a large counter stood glass jars filled with striped peppermint sticks, horehound drops, and licorice. He spied Samantha leaning over the counter. It was just as Robert had said: She did have a very nicely curved derriere. He must have been blind to mistake her for a boy.

"You sneaky varmint," she was saying to the clerk. "I saw you put your thumb on that scale. I ought to climb right over this counter and pull out every hair on your head."

"I wasn't doing any *such thing.*" The man was indignant.

"I saw! Don't give me any of your lip, mister. I know when someone is trying to cheat me. Now you just weigh that slab of bacon again and keep your hands far away from that scale." The grocer did and Samantha laughed triumphantly. "Aha, I knew it. I knew it. You're just lucky I don't anger easily, mister."

"Samantha. Samantha!"

She recognized that voice and turned around, a flush staining her cheeks. "Alex?" She brushed at her shirt and tugged at her hair, hoping she looked presentable and that he hadn't overheard.

"Hello, Alex." Her brown eyes shown with undisguised joy at seeing him again. All she could do was stare. She'd so wanted to see him, but now she couldn't think of a thing to say. How could she have forgotten just how handsome he was with his dark hair and blue eyes? Standing there dressed in a brown suit with a green cravat he made a striking picture. The picture of elegance. Once again his coat showed the perfection of his form, the width of his shoulders, his slim, well-proportioned frame.

"I was hoping to see you again," Alex said, amazed by her glorious hair—hair that he longed to reach out and touch. Would it really be as soft and as silky as it appeared?

"I wanted to see you again, too, Alex." She could see the straight, hard line of his jaw as she looked up. The barber had missed a spot in the cleft of his chin. Without even thinking, Samantha reached up and flicked the dab of lather away.

"What?"

"You must have just had a shave. There was a bit of lather on your chin and I . . ." She liked touching him.

"Yes, I was at the barbershop. I saw you walking by and followed you here." His eyes traveled leisurely from her face downward and back. "It's good to see you, Samantha." There was no use denying it, he was disturbingly drawn to her. After Caroline's haughty snubs and slights, Samantha was like a breath of fresh air. "What a lucky coincidence."

"Oh, it's not really a coincidence. I came into town today especially to see you." There was no use hiding the truth. "We usually get our supplies in Black Hawk or Nevadaville, but I came to Central City so's I could stop by and say hello. I went by the bank but you weren't there, or so your . . . your fiancée's father informed me. Now I know where you were." Something in his intense gaze forced her to meet his eyes. "I'm glad I came to town."

"So am I." He looked deep into her eyes, intrigued by the tender passion so innocently revealed whenever their eyes met. She had such unforgettable eyes. Expressive. Wide. She was an alluring mixture of child and woman, alternating like quicksilver between the two. And yet the longer he stood there, the more aware he was of her womanly side. It was all too evident in the way her green flannel shirt clung to her firm young breasts. He noticed the rise and fall of those breasts as she breathed.

"I was thinking that maybe I'd get a second chance to share a sarsaparilla with you. After I get the supplies, that is. Got some things to load onto the wagon and then—"

"I'll help you. We can get it done much faster that way." He put his hand on her back with an air of familiarity as they moved down the cluttered aisles of the general store. Samantha felt a sudden weakness in the pit of her stomach at his touch, a coiling sensation that was foreign to her. Suddenly, the barrels, kegs, the people—everything seemed forgotten. For just a moment it seemed that they were the only two people in the world. She wished she could think of something to say, but how could she when all her senses were swimming.

"How do you like the Colorado Territory so far?" she somehow managed to ask. "Do you miss all those fancy Boston drawing rooms?"

"No. I think I like it here in the mountains. Makes me see things quite differently." He knew his idea of women most certainly had changed. He'd thought until now that all a woman wanted was satins and laces to wear to a whirl of parties, soirees, and teas. Now he'd begun to realize that there was much more to a woman than that. Alex had begun to realize that there was an inner beauty that was much more important than a woman's appearance. Caroline was perfection to gaze at, but she was shallow and self-centered. Samantha was as different from Caroline as night was from the day. She made him want to see the world through her eyes. Perhaps then he might be able to forget some of his disillusionment, the pain and frustration of the past. "I most definitely like it here."

"I'm so glad to hear that, Alex." She found herself hoping that he would stay for a *very* long time.

It took half an hour to complete her purchases. There were the usual staples—flour, beans, sugar, potatoes, bacon, and coffee as well as soap, kerosene, and a pouch of Gramps's favorite tobacco. The cellar would be well stocked. She even bought a dozen rolls and two loaves of bread at the bakery, since she hadn't the time or inclination to bake them herself.

Samantha watched in fascination as Alex took off his coat, rolled up his shirt sleeves, and helped her load the wagon. She had supposed he would be muscular but was surprised to find out just how lean, hard, and appealing he was. As he worked, the front of his shirt gaped open, exposing a view of his chest and the dark hair covering it. It was a tantalizing sight that kept drawing Samantha's eye.

If she was aware of Alex, he was equally aware of her. Standing beside Samantha, he noticed that her red-gold hair glinted like fire in the sunlight. The wind swirled about her slim form lifting the long strands of her strawberry blond hair, making it float about her like a shimmering cape. She was lovely without artifice. She didn't flutter her lashes, had no practiced smile. Even so, Alex thought, she was a born enchantress. Her sparkling brown eyes glowed with so many emotions. She was open, honest, and steadfast in her loyalty to her grandfather. She was a free spirit full of fun and enthusiasm. Watching her from the corner of his eye, he noticed the way the corners of her mouth turned up when she was telling him something she found amusing, the way she would stretch her body like a supple young colt. With an innocent abandon she seduced him slowly and surely without even meaning to.

"Whew, I'm all tuckered out," she said, smiling shyly. "How 'bout that sarsaparilla now, Alex?"

Wiping his brow he returned her smile. "It seems a most appropriate time."

He bought her the sweetened carbonated beverage flavored with sassafras. They sipped their drinks as he related a few amusing travel anecdotes. "It was on a riverboat down in New Orleans that I learned my lesson about gambling." A seemingly respectable woman had taken a seat beside him, inducing him to play a hand of cards just to while away the time. Alex had thoroughly beaten the woman for four straight games and, being a gentleman, had promised her a chance to win the money back. "She bested me with four kings but, fool that I was, I played another game. I thought to call her bluff by raising the stakes to fifty. I didn't think I could lose with a straight flush."

"But did you?" Her eyes were steady as they met his in question.

"She had a *royal* flush, aided by her stack of marked cards." He shook his head, remembering. "When I dropped my money pouch and bent to pick it up, I noticed a pearl-handled bowie knife in her garter. The initials *Q.H.* were carved on it in flowing letters. She was a professional gambler, the "Queen of Hearts." I was only eighteen at the time, but I haven't touched a deck of cards since."

"Why, hell, I wouldn't either. Gramps says gambling is a sickness. He never gambles!" Gambling nearly lost the mine, she thought. She clutched her glass tightly as she remembered, bending her head forward as she listened to Alex intently. He was even more worldly-wise than she had supposed; indeed, he had traveled to nearly every state in the Union, but now it seemed that he planned to settle down and make the Colorado Territory his home. With a wife. She must not forget that he had come to Central City to marry Caroline West. Still, just being with him was a delight. For just this moment in time she could pretend that Alex Nicholson belonged to her.

"But enough talk about me. I want to hear about you." Alex took her hand, little realizing how deeply such a gesture would touch her. No one but her grandfather had ever held her hand before.

"Aw, not much to tell. Been mining with Gramps since I was old enough to hold a shovel. This territory was a sight to see then. Yessiree." She chuckled, remembering. "Weren't many women around the territory in those days, so whenever the miners got together for a square dance they had to dance with each other. The men who took the women's parts wore bandannas around one arm." Her voice lowered to a whisper. "There were even some miners who made certain they'd be the belle of the ball by wearing crinolines. It was one strange-looking wingding."

"I'll bet it was." Alex liked to hear her laugh. It was a soft, bubbling sound like a running brook. Time passed all too quickly. He hated to take his leave of her, but she told him it was time to return to the hills. As they walked to the door of the general store, Alex took her arm in gentlemanly fashion. Her arm where he touched her tingled with a warm glow, though it was her face that was flushed. She couldn't help but wonder what it would be like to be kissed. She'd never been kissed, never even thought about it really. Looking at the softened curves of Alex's mouth made her wonder now. Would his mustache tickle? She felt certain that it would and scolded herself most severely for even wondering. Even contemplating kissing Alex made her stomach dance with butterflies, sent a tingle squiggling up her spine, and brought the blood rushing frantically to her cheeks. Oh, if only she'd met Alexander Nicholson first, she thought, before that haughty Caroline West had tethered him.

"A penny for your thoughts, Samantha." Alex paused in front of the wagon, looking down at her with a smile.

She cast her eyes somewhere in the direction of her boots, fearing he might be able to read her thoughts in her eyes. "I was hoping . . . thinking that it would be nice if you would . . . would have dinner with Gramps and me sometime. I'd like for you to meet him. Course now, I know that Caroline wouldn't like it and . . . and you probably won't have the time . . . but . . ."

"I'd like to come, Samantha." He needed a change of pace

from the boring evenings he'd spent so far. Caroline always talked about her day at the dressmaker's, the tea or party she was planning or her endless list of social calls. Jeremiah's somber sermons on all the ways a "wise man" could invest his money were equally irritating. The Wests didn't own him. Nor did their aversion to Samantha and her grandfather prejudice him. And he found himself looking forward to meeting Enoch.

"You'd like to come?" She lifted her chin to smile at him. There was a soft, glowing quality about that smile. It lit her face with a gentle radiance and made her at that moment nearly beautiful. "Oh, Alex, I'm so glad. Gramps has a ton of stories. He'll keep you entertained. Course, I'm not much of a cook but I'll whip up something special just for you."

"Anything will be just fine. I don't want you to go to any trouble." Her exuberance touched him. He had the sudden feeling that Samantha needed friends, that she and her grandfather had been isolated for far too long.

"Maybe next week?"

"Next week would be just fine." He helped her onto the wagon with a gentle push at her waist. *I will determine my own friendships,* he thought. Besides, it was becoming clear that there was much in his relationship with Caroline that needed testing *before* she wore his ring. If he'd made a mistake, he had better find it out before the wedding.

"I'll come down to the bank to see you again, Alex, and then we'll make our plans." With a flick of the reins Samantha set the horses into a trot. Perhaps when her grandfather got to know Alex, he would change his mind about "strangers." After her argument with Jeremiah West, Samantha suspected she and her grandfather needed all the friends they could find.

13

The aromatic scent of freshly ground coffee beans filled the air as Samantha turned the crank of the grinder. The wheel seemed to spin as she took out all her frustrations in the task. For the last two days she'd been trying to convince her grandfather that it would be wise to cultivate the eastern gentleman's friendship, but to no avail. Enoch Claybourne held stubbornly to his opinion of strangers.

"But you'd like Alex, Gramps. He isn't a snob." Her brown eyes took on a special glow. "He's patient, strong but gentle, and very polite."

"Humph!" he snorted in annoyance as he positioned a small gunnysack to collect the coffee that fell in a trickle from the grinder. "What has you all agitated is that he gives pleasure to the eye. Now don't try to fool me, Samantha Marie." The use of her first and middle name contained a warning to drop the subject.

"Yes, he is handsome, Gramps, but that's not why I invited him. I want you to get to know him. Old Mr. West has given us more proof that he intends to be our enemy and I thought we might have need of friends."

"Don't need no one poking around here. Haven't I been clear? Tarnation, gal, here we are on the verge of discovering enough gold to make us rich forever and all you can harp on is some fool man. I'm surprised at you." Putting down the coffee sack, he folded his arms across his chest and studied his granddaughter with concern. "You tell me this Alex is going to get himself hitched to Jeremiah West's daughter yet he's hanging around you. If you ask me, you're treadin' on dangerous ground."

"I don't think . . . I . . . I don't know that . . ."

"That's just the point. You don't *know.*" The old man fought against the lump in his throat. Had he made a mistake in not teaching his granddaughter the ways of the world? At the first smile from a handsome young dandy she seemed to have lost her head. He'd sheltered her as best he could, taught her all about digging for gold, but he hadn't taught her about the ways of men. "He's a man just like any other," Enoch chided gruffly. "Puts his pants on one leg at a time. He ain't no prince. Now I don't want to hear no more."

"I'm sorry, Gramps. I won't mention Alex again." Sam hung her head contritely. She'd been so swept up in the magic she'd felt with Alex. Now, as she thought about it, she realized her grandfather was right. Alex had his future and she had hers. It wasn't likely they had anything in common. Hadn't she realized that the moment she'd seen him standing next to Caroline?

"You're actin' like a twitterpated squirrel in spring." Enoch threw up his hands in the air. "Oh, Sam! Sam!" He knew he shouldn't be angry at her but with himself. He'd ignored all the signs. Instead he'd kept in his mind the image of Sam as a little girl. But Sam was a *woman,* full grown. Why hadn't he realized it? Soon it would be time to find her a suitable husband, to give the one person he loved in the world up to the keeping of another man. It was a truth that saddened him. Selfishly, he wanted to cherish the pigtailed child who followed in his tracks, and warmed him with her smiles.

"I'm sorry." Samantha said again. She didn't want to upset her grandfather, had in fact only wanted to see Alex one more time. It was just that the moment they'd spent together had given her hope—a hope that defied common sense. Alex would marry Caroline West. She had to accept reality.

Enoch Claybourne pulled at his beard. "Don't be sorry. It's me that's been blind. But not again. No sir." Now more than ever he had to find that mother lode. He had to make her future secure. He wanted her to be so rich, she could have any man that warmed her heart. Even if it was this Alex Nicholson. Besides, it would give him pleasure to put one over on Jeremiah West. That cagey banker thought himself as clever a critter as ever lived, but Enoch would have the last laugh. Why the nerve of the man, hinting that he, Enoch Claybourne, couldn't find gold without some fool banker's financing. "We'll show Jeremiah just what can be done when a man gets his dander up."

"What, Gramps?" Scooping out a few spoonfuls of the freshly ground coffee, Samantha measured it into the coffeepot and set the pot on the stove. How had Jeremiah West's name gotten into the conversation?

"I said I'm gonna prove that you and I can work miracles, gal. We'll make that gol' darn banker eat crow. Calling the Siren's Song a losing proposition! Ha! I'll show the whole damn territory a thing or two." He chuckled, reaching for his journal. "You'll be the most sought-after young heiress in the West, Sam. Ole Jeremiah's daughter will be pea green with envy. Why, you'll be rich enough to marry a crown prince if you so choose."

"A prince?" Samantha laughed, envisioning the gossip *that* would create. It was so much fun to dream. That her grandfather had put aside his pique, eased her mind. She never should have mentioned Alex in the first place. And yet if she had her choice of any man in the world to marry, she knew it would be *him.*

"A king! Only man who'd be good enough for you, Sam." He took his usual seat upon the sofa and motioned for her to sit beside him. "Want you to see what I've been writing. It's important that you know." He explained all that he intended to do in the days to come, scribbling pages as he spoke. He was in a lighthearted mood. Happy. Seemingly content. Only once did a shadow crossed his brow. "The Siren Song's been a friend to me and to you as well. I'll never let her go. Not to Jeremiah West. Not to the governor. Hell, not even to the devil himself. Promise me you'll hold on to her, Sam, no matter what."

"I promise." She leaned her head on his shoulder in the gesture of affection she'd shown since she was a child. "I'll never give up the mine. Not if I live to be a hundred."

She gave little thought to the promise at the moment, but she fully intended to keep it one day, a long, long time from now.

14

The air was heavy with smoke from the day's blasting. Samantha coughed, trying to clear her lungs of the suffocating, sooty vapor. Her efforts did little good, only sending her into choking spasms. Her eyes burned and trying to wipe them clear only added to her discomfort. As bad as it was for her, however, she knew that it was even worse for her grandfather. In his position deep in the tunnel he had no respite at all from the smothering mists.

"Gramps, are you all right?" Leaning over the hole, she waited for his answer. The man at the powder company had been right. The black powder was dangerous, though often used in the larger mines. Despite all her grandfather's protestations that he knew exactly what he was doing, she knew she would be glad when the blasting was over. "Gramps?

"I'm all right except that I just hit my gol' darned thumb," came the reply. Samantha paused at the shaft's opening, listening to the sound of his swearing. His cusswords were soon replaced by the sound of hammering.

It was a tiring process. If ever Enoch needed help, it was now. In order to blast, holes had to be cut in the rock by either double or single jacking. Double jacking required two men, one to hold a hand drill while the other hit it with a sledge. Gramps was stubbornly single jacking, work that took a toll on his muscles and his temper as well. Still, he had been adamant that Samantha stay above ground where he knew she would be safe. This acknowledgment that something could go wrong gave Samantha more reason to worry.

"Sam, I need the change drill." Her grandfather's voice echoed eerily in the tunnel. "And send down my spoon."

Samantha hurried to comply, placing the chisel-tipped rod and copper miner's spoon in the bucket of the small hoist. Turning the crank, she lowered the bucket down the shaft. The change drill was six inches longer and a fraction of an inch narrower than the other drill so that it would follow easily into the hole and increase the depth. The copper spoon would be used to scrape out the rock dust so that the aperture would be clean. Though most miners used a pattern of seven holes and charges, her grandfather preferred to use three in a rough triangle angled to meet at the apex of the overhanging rock. Her grandfather was repeating a process he had done several hours before, one that had taken at least an hour or so.

"Are you sure you don't need help, Gramps?" She couldn't help thinking how much sooner the whole thing would be finished if only he'd let her give him a hand.

"No. You stay right where you are, Sam. I'm nearly done. Gonna measure out the powder into the paper cartridges and then insert the fuses. One more blast ought to do it. Just one more." There was a brief silence before he amended, "But you can help me if you'd like by cutting the fuses. Better make them a foot and a half long."

Samantha busied herself cutting the jute and twine cord into three equal pieces. Figuring the length of her boots to be just about eight inches, she measured accordingly. Her grandfather had told her that the fuses burned at a reliably uniform rate and seldom failed, so she tried her very best to be accurate. Gramps would need enough time to get out of the tunnel before the explosion.

Like the drill and the spoon, the fuses were carefully lowered into the hole and she laughed as her grandfather referred to them as "rattails." She supposed that was what they would resemble, hanging from the ends of the caps.

"As soon as you are finished, Gramps, let's go home. I shot a squirrel just this morning to put into a stew. I know for a certainty it's your favorite dish. If you're not too tired, maybe we can play a game of chess after supper. I know also for a certainty I can beat you *this* time." A loud rumble was her answer, not from her grandfather but from the earth. Samantha gasped in surprise as she was hurled backward. "Gramps . . . !"

The sound of splintering timbers, then another grinding rumble reverberated through the silence. A violent rush of air extinguished her lantern. "Gramps!" Her voice was a shriek of fright in the darkness. She thought she heard a groan, then a scream of pain, then silence again. "Gramps, answer me! What happened?" Before she had any hope of hearing an answer, a falling rock struck her head and she slipped into unconsciousness.

Samantha awoke to utter blackness. She did not need a lantern to know what had happened. A cave-in. Her worst fears had come to pass. She fought to remain calm. Panic would only add to the danger.

"Gramps! Gramps, can you hear me?" Dear God, he did not answer. "Gramps!" She had to find him. She had to get him out of the lower tunnel.

Her head hurt violently, but despite the pain, the dizziness she felt when she moved about, Samantha inched her way across the floor of the tunnel. She was extremely careful. If she fell down the shaft, she would be no use to her grandfather. Above all she must not give in to terror.

"Gramps? Gramps!" There was still no answer. Had she expected that there would be? Yes. It was a foolish hope. The falling rocks and debris would block off any sound. She was as isolated from her grandfather as he was from her. Taking a deep breath, she tried to relieve the tension and stop the feeling of panic that swept over her. She could reach him. It was not an impossible task. She could. She must. "Dear God, let him still be alive," she said aloud. Finding the gold wasn't important.

She'd make him understand that when she reached him. Oh, why had she ever let him use powder in the first place?

Cautiously, Samantha edged her way. Fumbling about in the dark, she found the fallen lantern at the edge of the shaft and lit it with one of the matches she always carried in her pocket. She knew a slight sense of relief as light once again flooded the tunnel. At least now she could see. Holding the lantern aloft, she investigated the extent of the damage, scrutinizing each nook and cranny. A sloping tunnel led to the next level below ground where her grandfather was, but it was blocked off by fallen timbers and large, heavy rocks. Samantha judged that it would be useless to try to move the debris. It would take too much time, even if she had the strength to do it. Time might well be her enemy. If her grandfather was injured in any way, she had to get him out of the lower tunnel and quickly.

"The shaft!" It was the only way, though it was the most dangerous. The shaft went straight down through the earth at three levels. One false step could be fatal, and yet she had to take the chance.

Moving to the edge of the vertical passage, she examined it carefully. The bucket was down with her grandfather, but even if it hadn't been, she could not possibly lower herself without someone to hoist the rope. Most miner's shafts had wooden ladders but Enoch had carefully imbedded long steel pegs in the shaft's side. Set at intervals of a foot and a half, they would make a convenient ladder *if* she was careful and did not slip. As a precaution Samantha tied a length of hoisting rope around her waist. Securing one end to a firmly entrenched timber to act as a lifeline if she fell, she carefully eased herself through the small opening.

Samantha could not take the lantern, she needed both hands for her descent, so it was dark once again. Her hands and knees were scraped raw, her head ached, her heart pounded so violently, she swore it sounded like thunder. Carefully placing her feet on one steel peg at a time, she clutched at the peg above with her hands. It seemed to be taking forever and she fought against both her frustration and her fear. Her grandfather had always told her that patience was a virtue and now she found that saying being tested.

"Gramps, I'm coming. If you can hear me, I want you to know you're going to be all right. Gramps . . . *ahhhhhhhh!*" She screamed as she lost her footing, hanging like a spider from its web. Her feet dangled in the air. She felt helpless. Cold, stark terror at last took hold of her. "No! No!" Frantically she kicked, trying to regain her footing. Her movements only added to the precarious sway of the rope. For what seemed like eternity she hung there, until at last she managed to reach out and catch a metal peg. Carefully she maneuvered herself back into position to continue her descent.

A sigh of relief escaped her throat when at last her feet touched the floor of the lower tunnel. Inching herself cautiously along, she felt in her pocket for another match and lit the candle she had carried in her pocket. She was devastated by what she saw. It was much worse than she had imagined. The cave-in had nearly obliterated the area. Rock upon rock and timber upon timber separated Samantha from her grandfather.

Dread clutched at her heart as the candle went out, leaving her again in darkness. "Gramps . . . !" Her voice was a mournful cry. She would not listen to the voice inside her head that whispered that he was dead, that she was too late. There was nothing that could have been done to save him, her reasoning told her, yet she would not allow herself to hear. Her grandfather couldn't be dead. Not Gramps! She rushed forward in the darkness, tearing at the rocks and boulders in a frenzy. Like one possessed she had only one thought—to clear the rubble away so that her grandfather would be free.

Samantha labored until her fingers and hands were bruised and bleeding, until she was so exhausted that she could barely stand up. At last she lit the candle again, placed it on a dry ledge, and continued working in the light. The water dripping from the ceiling and coming in steady trickles out of the rock walls added to her worry. She had to get to her grandfather soon in case the tunnel flooded.

"Gramps! Gramps, please answer me." It was so silent. Tears stung her eyes. There was no answer. "Gramps . . ." This time his name was a wail of grief.

Sinking to her knees, Samantha gave vent to an uncontrollable flood of tears. "Oh, Gramps. Gramps." At last her emotions were spent and she stubbornly resumed her labor. No matter what his fate, she would not leave until she found him.

Digging about in the rubble, Samantha located her grandfather's sledgehammer. Angrily she dashed at her eyes with grimy hands. Now was no time to cry. She had to keep on. Somehow she sensed what she would find next, yet even so she was not prepared for the sight of her grandfather's body. "Gramps . . ."

Pushing and shoving at the rocks, she at last had him free, but it was too late. Putting her ear to his chest, she listened for any sign of life, but the proud and noble heart had ceased beating. His face was pale, his breath stilled, his hazel eyes stared sightlessly back at her.

"Gramps!" The pain of her grief wrenched through Samantha like a knife. It was an anguish she was certain she could not bear. Sobbing, she sought comfort in the only manner she knew, by throwing her arms around her grandfather. Always his encircling arms had been haven from sorrow, just as his nearness was now. "Oh, Gramps, I love you so!"

A thousand memories assailed her, dancing before her eyes like a vivid dream. Happy times all of them. She remembered tagging along behind him on his forays to the mine, the times they'd sat together on a large rock waiting for the fish to bite. He'd been her only companion, her only family, and most importantly of all, he'd been her friend—the only person who loved her. Now he was gone and the desolation was shattering. From this moment on Samantha Marie Claybourne knew she would be all alone.

15

It was silent in the cabin, so distressingly quiet that Samantha could hear every breath she took. Burying her face in her pillow, she cried until her eyes were dry of tears. Even an ocean of tears, however, could not wash away the pain. Her grandfather was gone. She would never see him again, never hear his voice, join in his laughter, feel the touch of his large, callused hand ruffling her hair.

She had stayed with him until the candle burned low and then somehow had managed to find the strength to bury him. It was a very fitting place that she chose. Samantha had dug a grave deep in the floor of the main tunnel. The mine had been the place where he had spent so many days, now it would entomb him forever.

There had been no mourners at her grandfather's funeral. No preacher to whisper sacred words. Samantha knew instinctively he would not have wanted that. He was a solitary man, who trusted almost no one. Instead she had quoted her grandfather's favorite Scriptures by memory. "The Lord is my shepherd; I shall not want. He maketh me to lie down in green pastures: he leadeth me beside the still waters. He restoreth my soul. . . ." Why did she have the feeling that she would one day see him again? Though her grandfather was not a churchgoer, his deep sense of wrong and right had brought him very close to God. She had no doubt that he was in heaven now. It was the one thought that brought her comfort.

Samantha rolled over on her back to stare up at the blackness of the ceiling. Darkness enveloped her and she was suddenly afraid. Would she ever be able to forget what had happened today? The helplessness she'd felt in that cold, unlighted cavern? No. As long as she lived she would remember. Now she was all alone with no one to take care of her. She had no one to rely on but herself. What was she going to do?

At first she had been filled with anger, as if it had been the fault of the mine itself. She had sworn and she had raged, vowing never to set foot inside again. Gold. Such a fanciful quest. The obsession to possess it had led her grandfather to his death. And yet her reasoning told her his quest for treasure had also given him a great deal of joy. It had been his life. He had put his blood, his sweat, and even his tears into that mine. Most importantly, he had done it for *her*.

"I want you to always keep a hold on the Siren Song," he had said. "She's been a friend to me and to you as well. I'll never let her go. Promise me you'll hold on to her, Sam, no matter what happens."

She had given her word last night without even knowing she would be tested so quickly. "I'll never give up the mine. Not if I live to be a hundred." Childish words. A foolish, impulsive promise, perhaps, that Samantha now realized she must keep. The mine was her grandfather's legacy, his tomb. She could never let it go.

Closing her eyes Samantha tried to push away the thoughts that clamored in her head. She wanted and needed sleep, but the stark silence was as unnerving as any loud noise might have been. She missed her grandfather's snoring. It had been much like a lullaby that calmed her into sleep. His presence had been her security. Somehow she had thought he would always be there, but now there was no such word as *always*. Like a candle in the wind, life could be snuffed out just as her grandfather's had been today.

Another flood of tears welled up behind her eyes, but Samantha refused to cry again. Gramps would not have wanted her to act this way. She had to regain some control. If there was any chance at all that her grandfather could look down from high in the sky, she had to make certain he would feel proud of her.

"I *can* work the mine. I *will* work the mine. Somehow. Some way," she whispered, more to her grandfather than to herself. Her resolution gave her a strange sense of peace.

Samantha waited impatiently for the dawn, when the first pink glow of the sun peered over the horizon, she was up and dressed. She ran out of the door without once looking back, hurrying toward the mine before she could give it another thought. She had to finish the work her grandfather had begun. First and foremost she had to flush the water out of the tunnel by way of the shaft. She couldn't let the water stake its claim.

For just a moment her hands trembled as she touched the latch. Once inside the mine tunnel it all came rushing back into her mind: the rumbling, her fear of the darkness. The smell of water-soaked timber nearly sickened her. Water was even now trickling onto the tunnel floor.

"I can't do it, Gramps! I just can't." A feeling of hoplessness washed over her. She knew the taste of defeat. It was far too great a task. *Give up,* a voice seemed to say. *Leave this place and never come back.*

A Claybourne never gives up, Sam. Remember that. Another voice inside her head insisted. "Hold on to the Siren Song! Hold on! Hold on! Hold on!" it echoed, reverberating in her mind.

Taking a deep breath, Samantha stilled her fears. She lighted the lantern then went to the toolshed and got her grandfather's favorite pick and shovel. It was an awesome task, but by the love she bore her grandfather she would do it. She would muck out the water and renew the search for gold.

16

The planks of the boardwalk creaked in rhythm to Alex's stride as he hurried along Main Street. It was late. Most respectable people were at home for the evening meal or on their way. Except for several horses tied to the hitching posts and a wagon or two, the business area looked deserted, but Mr. Reich, the tailor, had promised to stay open as a special favor to Alex. A look at his gold pocket watch told him that he was tardy for his appointment and he quickened his pace. Punctuality was something he took seriously, but Jeremiah West had detained him on a trivial matter just as he was leaving the bank. At least, however, he was becoming involved in the bank's dealings. It was a start.

Time, he thought in exasperation. It was something he usually had in excess. But today an endless stream of wealthy matrons and entrepreneurs had vied for his time, each of them selfishly demanding his full attention in quests that seemed to have no other purpose than to bolster their inflated self-esteem. Which was not to say that he was totally dissatisfied with the work that he was doing. He enjoyed dealing with those enthusiastic merchants and miners who had newly acquired their riches. One young rancher's wife had even reminded him a great deal of Samantha with her eager smile, her spunk, her determination.

Samantha. Therein lay the real reason for his ill humor. Nearly a week and a half had come and gone and she hadn't returned. Alex could only suppose that she had changed her mind or been too busy to come to town. Her grandfather was said to be very taciturn. Perhaps Enoch Claybourne had no wish to meet him. Whatever the reason, it seemed to take away the promise of sunshine from his days. Samantha had briefly brightened his usually dull routine and he had looked forward to seeing her again.

Alex had even toyed with the idea of paying the Claybournes a surprise visit, but had cast the idea aside. He didn't want to cause a rift between Samantha and her grandfather. Besides, he didn't really know just where to find her. And no one was willing to give him the information. It seemed that the townsmen feared Enoch Claybourne enough to grant him his gruffly requested privacy. Thus they kept their distance from the "grizzeled old miner," as they referred to him. He would have to be patient, Alex decided. And yet, how he missed the sound of Samantha's voice, her smile. They came from worlds so completely opposite, it was startling, and yet he was drawn to her. The air of loneliness about her touched his heart. He had known that kind of loneliness in his own life.

I wish her well, he thought. He hoped she and her grandfather would discover the gold they were looking for. He couldn't help but compare Caroline and Samantha, wondering what Samantha would have been like if she had grown up with Caroline's advantages. Maybe the day would come when she would know such comfort. Security, he thought. He had taken a hand in guaranteeing his own future, carefully investing his money in stocks the last few weeks. The railroad, a grainery, a stamp mill, and a telegraph company were his initial investments with more to come as soon as he familiarized himself with the opportunities. Even in Boston he had realized that Wall Street looked toward the West with interest. Alex had never really had to worry about money before. It had been a plaything to him. Now he was as addicted to investing as gamblers were to gambling.

Other buildings had long since extinguished their lights but, since the miners worked in shifts the brothels and saloons never closed. Alex heard loud laughter and raucous singing as he approached the area. Now and then a staggering townsman toppled out a doorway into the street below the boardwalk to sleep off his "refreshment" before morning. There were, Alex reflected, two Central Cities: Central City by day, populated by merchants, workers, and customers, the peaceful side; and Central City by night, frequented by gamblers, shady ladies, and men who took what they wanted at gunpoint. Once or twice he had seen such a man rush through the throng shooting his pistols, creating havoc. And Robert had told him of a bank robbery a few weeks before his arrival, but so far things had been relatively tranquil.

The sound of broken glass, splintering wood, and swearing suddenly put an end to that. Piano music stopped and shouts broke out. With a resounding crash a man came hurtling through the swinging doors with such force that he nearly toppled Alex over backward. Only by his presence of mind was Alex able to keep his balance.

"Well, lookee here. If I didn't run into the *dude* again," said a voice he remembered only too well. It was one of the three ruffians who had accosted him on the road to Central City a few weeks ago. Alex tried to discern which one it was. Not Cy, he quickly recalled. Cy had been the one who had challenged him to a gunfight. "Evenin', dude."

"Good evening." Alex kept his eyes level. He hadn't been afraid before and he wasn't afraid now. This man had far more brawn than brains, that much was obvious.

"Got me a little fight in there. Might need some help. You good with your fists? Think you can handle a little fight, Mr. Easterner?" He took a swig from the bottle he held in his hand.

Alex answered with an amused smile. Didn't this ruffian have any better way to spend his time? He reminded Alex of a mischievous boy. "Some other time, perhaps. Right now I'm late for an appointment." To emphasize his answer he pulled his watch from his vest pocket, clicked open the lid to check the time.

The man's mouth fell open. He stared at Alex in astonishment, then took a threatening step forward. "Appointment, my ass! If you ask me, you're just afraid to get your hands dirty. Or maybe you're a coward. Which is it, dude?" He spat a mixture of saliva and whiskey at the toe of Alex's shoe. "Now, you can either fight with me or agin me. Which is it to be?"

Alex maintained his calm. "I don't choose either." He had seen enough danger and brutality during his army days to know that fighting created more problems than it solved. If he fought this man, there would be another and another. Once he might have taken the challenge, when he was younger and unschooled in the ways of the world. Over the years, however, he had learned to be a reasonable man.

"Don't choose either?" Alex's composure seemed to unnerve him, though he seemed intent on intimidating Alex. "You're a gawddamned coward, then."

"I'm no coward." Alex knew this type of man, a bully. The West didn't have an exclusive claim on them. Men like this fed on fear, but Alex was not afraid. "Now, as I said, my good man, I have an appointment and I intend to keep it." Squaring his sholders, Alex walked right on by the scowling gunslinger, who mumbled swearwords under his breath but didn't attempt to stop him. Instead he shouted to his friend inside the saloon, obviously feeling the need for reinforcement.

"Slim! Slim! Hightail it on out here. Our fancy Easterner is right outside this door and I wouldn't want you to miss greetin' him. Hurry or he'll get away."

There was the sound of stumbling feet, then the door opened again, this time with such violence that it slammed against the wall and stayed open. A tall, skinny man with hair the color of fire stood in the doorway, a bottle of whiskey in his hand.

"Well, I'll be damned if you ain't right, Buck." Standing with his hand poised at the handle of his gun, he asked, "You alone, dude? No Sam around to save yer ass this time."

"We can start right where we left off." Succumbing to his partner's example, Buck Cameron pulled out his pistol and aimed it playfully at Alex. "Shall we make him dance again?"

"Naw, we done that before. I wanna do something that takes real inspiration. Wonder if I could shoot an apple off his head? Heard tell of a man who done that with an arrow once. William A. Tell was his name, or somethin' like that." Coming up behind, he put the barrel of his revolver to Alex's temple. " 'Spose if he could do it, I could too. Don't think I'd miss from this distance, do you, dude?" He laughed deep in his throat as he cocked the trigger.

Beads of sweat broke out on Alex's forehead, but still he maintained his composure. "No, I don't think so," he said. The street was not as deserted as it seemed. There were enough witnesses, he thought, to deter any real act of violence.

"I need a little target practice too." Buck took several faltering steps. "I'll go find an apple." He started to leave then shook his head with a long-drawn-out "naw . . ."

Both men were drunk, drunk enough to be dangerous. And yet the two inebriated miscreants held no real terror. They wouldn't shoot him. They merely wanted to see him cower. That thought gave him courage. "If I were you, I'd put that pistol down. Shooting an unarmed man is a hanging offense in this town, or so I've been told. Put it *down,*" Alex said with authority. "I'm not going to beg you for my life."

The tone of command was successful, perhaps because both men were used to taking orders from their absent blond leader. Alex breathed a sigh of relief as he felt the cold, hard gunbarrel pulled away, saw Slim sheath the weapon.

"Well, I'll be damned if he ain't as cool as a cucumber. Don't think we're gonna have much fun with him."

"He's just a coward like I say. If we weren't in town, I'd shoot him just like I said. But I won't. Not this time." Buck Cameron waved his gun right under Alex's nose. "But if I ever find you off somewheres alone, you'd better watch out. I owe Sam one and I owe you one as well." He rubbed at his hand. "That little hellcat drew blood when she shot that gun out of my hand."

At the mention of Samantha, Alex stiffened. Though she was spirited, courageous, and strong, she was still a woman. He knew he would protect her if this bully pushed the matter.

"I wouldn't advise harming Miss Claybourne," Alex said gruffly.

"You ordering me, dude?" Buck Cameron's nostrils flared.

"Merely suggesting."

"Suggesting?" Buck Cameron bristled. "Talk like that just might get you a gunfight. Care to join me in a shooting contest?"

Alex's jaw tensed, but he managed to maintain his composure. Only a total fool would contemplate a contest of firearms with a man like Cameron. Not that Alex was without ability. During the war he had been an expert with weapons, distinguishing himself time and time again in battle. But he firmly believed that nothing was ever solved by a daring show of prowess. Violence begot violence in a never-ending circle of destruction. It took far more fortitude to avoid a fight.

"I'm much more interested in maintaining peace than in spilling blood, Mr. Cameron. I don't think there is any matter in this world that can not be settled peaceably." He stared his adversary down. They were a study in contrasts, one outwardly calm, standing with his shoulders thrust back, chin up; the other clenching and unclenching his fists. "I do, however suggest once again that you leave Miss Claybourne alone."

Surprisingly, Slim agreed, adding his voice to Alex's. "Sam and me have had our differences, but I wouldn't go starting anything with Sam, Buck. For all that she goes around in them pants, she's really quite a looker. You gotta admire her spunk. Ain't many women like that. Hear tell she's actually begun work on that mine. Digging, shoveling, and the like, just like that old grandfather of hers. Working from dawn to dusk without even taking a rest. Don't even think *I* could do that. But Cy's seen her."

So, Alex thought, that was why Samantha hadn't come to town. For just a moment he found himself growing angry with Enoch Claybourne. What kind of man would let his own granddaughter do such grueling labor? Though it was none of his business, he determined to at least voice his opinions to the man. *If* he ever met him. He couldn't help feeling sympathy for Samantha. She really hadn't had much of a chance in life. Caroline had always been pampered and spoiled. Jeremiah West had never expected Caroline to lift a hand while Samantha was working her life away when she should be enjoying herself. She was young and pretty, yet he was almost certain she'd never had a suitor. Caroline had had dozens of beaux and had learned the art of coquetry. Even her avowals of love were practiced and sounded hollow. He couldn't help but wonder what Samantha would be like when she really fell in love.

"Cy been spying on her?" Buck sounded interested.

"Naw, just saw her puttering about with a pick slung over her back once or twice. He lives not too far from her, you know. His pa was partners with Enoch Claybourne until they quarreled and parted ways." Bored with the banter, Slim nodded his head toward the saloon. "Ain't gonna get no kick outta *him*," he said. "Let's go back and finish our whiskey." "So long, *dude.*" Somehow the way he said the name didn't sound quite as much like an insult as it had before. "See ya around some time."

Alex continued down the boardwalk toward his destination. A light in the window showed that Mr. Reich was still there. Alex needed something suitable for Caroline's "little gathering." Most of his suits were in grays and browns. The tailor had come to his rescue, skillfully making a fashionable black suit. It needed one more fitting, however, before he could wear it to the party.

It was to be a gathering of Central City's "finest" citizens. He found himself wishing that Samantha could be there. Had Samantha ever been to a party? Would Enoch Claybourne let her rest from her toil long enough to enjoy herself? He doubted it. A man who would let his own granddaughter slave away in a mine must certainly have a piece of quartz for a heart.

"Alex! Alex!" The West buggy lumbered down the road, narrowly missing Alex as he stepped off the curb but hurling dust and dirt in his face. "Climb in. Quickly." Caroline seemed in a bit of a dither.

"I don't want to go home yet, Caroline. I was detained. I'm on my way to the tailor shop. You go home without me. I'll walk back when I'm done." Alex started to turn away, but she guided the carriage to block his path.

"I was on my way home when I saw you, Alex. Those two

terrible men. Buck Cameron and Slim Walker are nuisances, as you must have discovered."

"We were just getting *acquainted*. A man needs to get acquainted with his neighbors, Caroline. There was no real harm done." He sought to placate her, not wishing another argument.

"No harm done?" Her voice was shrill. "I saw them pointing a gun at your head, Alex. You should have called for the sheriff. What were you thinking? *Daddy* would have had them arrested. He's consigned them to more than a few days in jail before." She flicked the reins impatiently.

"A man has to handle some things on his own." Leaning against the carriage, he did his best to reassure her. "They did *not* harm me."

"They wouldn't have *dared*. Undoubtedly they know you're under *Daddy's* protection." Her jaw tensed with determination. "But from now on you must carry a gun, Alex. Daddy does. You don't want everybody in town to think you're a coward, do you? Daddy will get you a revolver."

"So that I can be just like Cameron, Tyburn, and Walker? No. I don't believe in guns, Caroline." His eyes were on hers, his gaze just as intent. "At least not for me. Violence is never the answer. I've seen for myself the all too sad truth of where it can lead." He'd seen enough blood and killing to last a lifetime, enough to make a promise to himself to lay down his arms. He was not a coward, merely a man who thought it was time to use other means. He had sworn he would never shed blood again.

Caroline tossed her head back with a haughty air. "We'll see what Daddy says about that. I don't intend to find myself a widow before I'm even a wife."

"That would be inconvenient."

"You know what I mean, Alex." Her expression softened and she pouted. "I don't want anything to happen to you. I love you."

"You love me, Caroline?" She hadn't done anything to prove it. She seemed far more concerned for herself.

"Of course I do. How can you doubt it? Haven't I told you I would marry you?" Her blue eyes were wide with confusion. "We're very suitable for each other, darling."

"Suitable?" The word left a bitter taste in his mouth. So

that's what he was. Suitable. The most promising petitioner for her hand. It was hardly what he had envisioned on those moonlit nights. Suitable. He wanted a woman to love him, to feel bereft when he was not near her. He wanted a woman who understood him, shared his thoughts and his dreams, a woman who accepted him and loved him for what he was, a woman who wouldn't try to change him. Was that too much to ask? To expect? Somehow he knew it was not.

"Every other woman in town is jealous, darling. Everyone is talking about how handsome you are. It's whispered that we make such a good-looking pair." Her words left Alex cold. Was Caroline only interested in having a presentable man on her arm? Was he only that to her?

"I'm afraid I won't be so very handsome if I don't get to the tailor's for my fitting. I'd hate to see you attend your gathering all alone, Caroline." He spoke the words with biting sarcasm, folding his arms across his chest as he backed away from the carriage.

Comprehension flooded slowly over her. Her eyes were wide, her mouth formed a perfect *o*. All concern for his safety was put aside as she said, "Then by all means you should hurry, Alex. You can't even think of missing the party! What on earth would people say if you did?"

"Indeed, what on earth *would* they say, Caroline?" She had made her feelings all too plain to see. Alex stood watching as the carriage pulled away, feeling as if he were wrapped in an icy shell. Any last, lingering hopes he might have held for a future with Caroline seemed to die at that moment. Even so, he felt strangely serene. Confusion, disbelief, and a bit of anger washed over him, yet he felt no remorse. How could he mourn the end of something that had never existed? The love he had thought he felt for Caroline, the affection he had thought she felt for him, had been nothing more than an illusion after all. But having realized that fact, what was he going to do now?

17

Squinting, angry gray eyes followed Alex as he continued down the boardwalk. Pulling his hat down over his eyes, the man followed at a safe distance. It was *him,* all right. Despite the moustache, he knew it to be Alexander Nicholson. Major Alexander C. Nicholson, to be precise. Rich man's son. Overbearing, self-righteous taskmaster who had pushed his troups unmercifully, punished deserters ruthlessly, and earned a Medal of Honor in the bargain. Alexander C. Nicholson. Major Nicholson. The man who had ruined Ben Cody's life.

"Pious son of a bitch!" Cody hissed beneath his breath as he watched Alex go into the tailor's shop. He'd watched his encounter with those two bullies with interest, hoping one would pull the trigger. Instead they'd backed down, succumbed to that authoritative tone of voice he knew so well.

A muscle in Ben Cody's cheek ticked nervously, a tick he'd acquired since the war had sent myriad memories flashing through his brain. They'd been the same age when they'd joined the army, but because he was just a poor watchmaker's son he'd had to watch from afar as the "miracle boy," as he'd dubbed the Major, had slowly but surely risen in the ranks. It had been said that the wealthy shipper's son had earned his way by daring and bravery, but Ben Cody had never been fool enough to believe that. Ah, no. Having a rich old man for a father had been Alex's claim to fame. It had bought him a major's uniform. Was it any wonder that he, Ben Cody, had seethed with resentment? It was a rough, stinking life of trudging through mud up to your knees, getting shot at, listening to the groans of men bleeding to death, fearing you'd meet the same fate, all the while taking orders from stiff-necked disciplinarians like Major Nicholson.

A shimmering haze of whiskey had been Ben's only consolation. It had sustained him, succored him, given him courage. He wasn't the only one who drank himself senseless, and yet he was the one who had been punished for being "drunk and disorderly." One night while they were encamped, he'd taken a swing or two at the high-and-mighty Major Nicholson and for that been sent to the brig. He'd been unarmed and unable to flee when the enemy had invaded the camp. Taken prisoner, he'd been condemned to the hellhole of Libby Prison in Virginia.

But I survived, he thought. He'd longed for death each day, but it had passed him by. Now he'd learned to conquer fear, to use it as his ally. Brushing his fingers over the pearl handle of his gun, he curled his lip in a twisted grin. He'd come to the point where he relished seeing that look of fear in a man's eyes, hearing that pleading tone in his voice when he begged for his life. It gave him power. Made him feel like a god.

Oh, no, Alex had not been frightened by those two blustering ninnies. He'd played his hand like a skillful gambler, bluffing his way to a win. With Ben Cody he would not be so lucky. Not by a long shot. He'd let Alexander Nicholson feel secure for the time being. One of these days when Alex thought he had everything he'd ever hoped for, Ben Cody would strike.

18

The party was anything but a "little gathering." It was an elbow-to-elbow crush of Central City's wealthiest and most influential citizens. Men in frock coats talked politics and smoked cigars, women dressed in a variety of fashionable colors and rich fabrics buzzed gossip, all the while putting on airs. Nouveaux riches, Alex thought, hoping to hide their own humble roots by scorning others.

It soon became obvious that he was on display. Alex from Boston. Still, he was determined to enjoy himself. Let the guests stare and gawk, he really didn't care. Jeremiah West had intended to procure the perfect consort for his little princess. For the moment, Alex would play the part. But the time of reckoning was just around the corner.

The air was warm, the stars glittered like candle flames, and a soft breeze wafted the faint scent of wildflowers and pine. It was a perfect evening. Alex was determined not to let anything spoil it. Standing on the front porch, he watched as the carriages took turns depositing their passengers. He smiled as he saw Robert Cunningham arrive. It was good to see a familiar face.

"Guess you could say J.W. throws a very fine party." Robert greeted Alex with a wide grin, gesturing at the lanterns strung across the patio. "Even a quartet of Central City's finest musicians to serenade. Quite a show. Yes, sir, J.W. knows his stuff."

"An imitation of the soirees of Boston. Jeremiah is a keen observer," Alex answered dryly. "Mrs. Trenoweth has been in the kitchen all day preparing food." Slaving away, he thought, with not one word of appreciation from either Jeremiah or his daughter.

"Food! Did you say food?" Robert massaged his stomach. "I'm starved!"

"Come with me and we'll sample a dish or two." Alex led the way. The living room furniture had been pushed against the walls. Long planked tables were laden with artful displays of culinary fare: bowls of steaming vegetables, glazed hams, an assortment of cakes and pies. Before either Alex or Robert could take a plate, however, Jeremiah appeared. Taking Alex by the elbow, he led him across the room. Nudging his way through the throng, he approached the bearded man who stood at the center of the group.

"Alex, I want you to meet Henry M. Teller. Henry, this is my future son-in-law. Like you he is from the East." He said the word like a benediction. "Boston."

Henry Teller held out his hand. "I grew up in New York State. That makes us neighbors."

Alex returned the handshake. "Yes, I suppose it does." So this was the man who wanted to build the lavish hotel, Alex thought, the lawyer who seemed to have so much influence in the territory. He looked pleasant enough.

"We easterners know the importance of good investments. I understand you have some personal capital to be used for our fine hotel. We're going to start excavating any day now. Jeremiah has the papers drawn up." Henry Teller glanced at Jeremiah with a grateful nod. "He said I can count on you for a percent of capital."

Every muscle in Alex's body tensed. He was infuriated that Jeremiah West would make such a pledge without even consulting him. "I'm sorry, there's been some mistake. I wish you every success with your hotel, but I was unaware of any agreement."

"A mistake?" Henry Teller looked from Alex to Jeremiah, then back to Alex again with a puzzled frown.

"Alex. Don't be hasty. Think the matter over before saying no." Forcing a smile, Jeremiah moved closer, whispering in Alex's ear, "It's a very sound investment. Central City is growing faster every day. We need a grand hotel. The return on what you put into it would more than double your investment."

"I'm never impulsive, Jeremiah," Alex said firmly. "I always investigate a matter before I act." Any decision to put money into a hotel would be his own.

"Then perhaps your father or some of your friends might be interested." Jeremiah looked thoroughly displeased, but Alex didn't care. He would not be a pawn in any game.

"My father and my friends would have to speak for themselves." Now he knew why Jeremiah was so anxious to have him at the bank. So much for noble gestures. Future son-in-law indeed.

"You're being pigheaded. Ungrateful. I open up an opportunity for you and you throw it in my face. Embarrass me before my colleague!" Brows furled, face red, Jeremiah West did not even try to hide his anger.

"Henry, good to see you!" Having heard the tirade, Robert hurried forward to alleviate the tension with an outstretched hand. "I hear tell that you plan to make Central City more important than Denver. Hear they're calling you one of the "golden gang," and that you're doing your damnedest to have Colorado made a state. Tell me all about it." He winked at Alex on the sly, giving him a cue to leave. With an appreciative nod, Alex hurried away.

Wandering through the crowd, Alex was greeted warmly and enthusiastically by all the people he met. Soon his own anger began to abate. The gentlemen seemed to like his witty conversation and easygoing manner, the women seemed enamored of his handsome dark looks. He tried to put the incident with Henry Teller from his mind, but he couldn't. Obviously, Jeremiah thought he'd found a pliable puppet, one who could be manipulated at every turn. As he had told Robert, however, he was his own man, willing to take risks and just as willing to accept the consequences—of his *own* decisions. From some of the talk he'd heard, Jeremiah was beginning to sound more like an unscrupulous taskmaster who ruled his domain with an iron hand than a hardworking self-made man. Incurring his wrath, he heard said, was like tangling with the devil. Hardly a man Alex wanted to work for.

"You're wearing a scowl as wide as Main Street." Extricating himself from Henry Teller and the small group of would-be investors, Robert joined Alex again. Together they moved to the parlor.

"I've a great deal on my mind just now, my friend." Alex was oblivious to the ingratiating nods and smiles he was receiving from the other guests.

"J.W. didn't mean to shout at you, Alex. That's just his way. He thinks Teller's hotel is going to be the greatest thing next to heaven and wants you to be part of it." Alex didn't seem to be listening. "Alex? Alex." Trying to regain his attention, Robert poked him in the ribs. "What's wrong?"

"Is it true, Robert, that Jim Andrews shot himself in the head when Jeremiah called in his loan? That Jeremiah ruined him?" Alex had heard two of the younger men talking about the matter.

"Well . . ." Robert hesitated. "The man did owe a great deal of money. Borrowed for some gambling debts, then couldn't pay it back. J.W. only did what any other banker . . ." Robert was fidgety and nervous, anxious to change the subject. "Where is the beauteous Caroline? Heard she has a new dress for this affair." He patted Alex on the back. "One look at your blushing bride's face will dispell all your misgivings." Robert's hazel eyes flitted about as he scanned the assemblage for sight of her.

"She's not here yet. Undoubtedly she's still getting dressed."

"Ah, yes. That's how women are. I love them, but unfortunately all the sweet young things ever think about is what dress to wear, whether the hat they've chosen is a proper match . . . things like that. Bless their hearts, they can be quite boring at times." He shrugged his shoulders.

"Not all women." Samantha's smiling face popped into

Alex's head. "Samantha Claybourne is not like that. She's pleasing to the eye as well as interesting. She's straightforward and honest. She doesn't flutter her lashes or pretend to the vapors if I don't compliment her."

Robert clucked his tongue. "Samantha Claybourne, is it? Sounds to me like Caroline's fallen from grace."

Alex felt the need to talk to someone, to confide his doubts. "I think I have made a most grievous mistake in this matter, Robert. I fear I let moonlit nights and passion blind me. I fear Caroline is not the kind of woman I want to marry."

"Whew!" Robert slapped his thigh. "You don't mince words. It takes a lot of fortitude for a man to admit he's made an error in judgment, Alex. But I don't envy you. Coming up against old J.W. and his daughter is not going to be easy. It's not so easy to break an engagement." He put his hand on Alex's shoulder. "Whatever you do, Alex, be careful. They say there's no fury like a woman scorned. I might add that the same is true of an angry protective father as well. Just watch yourself. Move slowly on this. Do nothing hasty." He chuckled softly. "Do what I'd do in such a situation. Give Caroline reason to break off with *you*!"

Robert's voice faded to a hush as he noticed all conversation in the room had suddenly stopped. The musicians had struck up a majestic air. Under the glittering prisms of the chandeliers all heads turned toward the stairs, where a dazzling vision in periwinkle blue floated gracefully downward. Caroline West was making her grand entrance amids oohs and ahs. Clothed in a low-necked silk dress that swirled about her ankles as she walked, with her golden hair arranged in ringlets that cascaded down her shoulders, she was breathtaking. Robert Cunningham's open mouth attested to the fact.

"Alex. Darling . . ." She reached out a beringed hand, smiling as Alex grasped it. As the music started up again he led her into a dance.

"You look lovely." She was beautiful, he thought, but a bit like the fool's gold he'd heard the miners talk about. He wanted the real thing.

"That was the idea, darling. And, of course, you make every other man look dull and uninteresting. I'm so proud to be seen with you." Alex felt the pressure of her hand on his shoulder as she moved closer, brushing against him as tightly as decorum allowed. Time seemed to stop as they whirled round and round. Her steps were graceful as they moved about the room. "Why, even now every feminine eye is turned your way, Alex. But you are mine and I will never let you go."

"Not even when you give Robert his promised dance?" Once he might have been jealous, but not now. Her preoccupation with being the center of attention amused him instead.

"Then and only then." She reached up and touched his cheek. "But I want you back in my arms as soon as my obligation to Robert is fulfilled. Is that a promise, darling?"

"If I said no, you'd never forgive me would you, Caroline?"

Wrinkling up her nose, she giggled, throwing her head back to give him a pleasurable view of her long neck and what lay below. "No, I would not. I don't want to be with anyone but you. Though while I'm gone you should mingle with the guests."

"I have. I've introduced myself to quite a few of them. Joseph Thatcher, the other banker here, Peter McFarlane, Hans Jacob Kruse. An interesting gathering."

"I suppose. But there is one man in particular Daddy wanted you to meet. Has he introduced you to our distinguished guest Henry Teller? If not, I'll do so."

Alex stiffened. "I've already been introduced. Your father saw to that." He hadn't wanted to mention the matter, but since she had brought it up he couldn't keep silent. "I'm afraid we got off to rather a bad start. Your father was—"

"A bad start?" She cocked her head. "What do you mean, Alex?"

"He introduced me to Mr. Teller and intimated that I had promised to invest some money in the man's hotel. I tried to straighten out the misunderstanding."

"Misunderstanding? It was hardly that. Daddy knows what he is doing, Alex. If he thinks it is a good investment, then it most certainly is." She bobbed her head to punctuate her sentence.

"I make my own decisions, Caroline."

"Your decisions? You should have done as Daddy said." She pulled away from him as violently as if he had pinched her, pursing her lips into a pout. "Daddy asked him here tonight just so he would be made aware of you. He's one of the most influential men in the Colorado Territory. If we become a state, he'll undoubtedly be the first senator. He's been here for ten years. Certainly, knowing a man like that could benefit you a great deal. Perhaps even help you if you became interested in politics." She was mimicking her father's manner of speaking so well that for just a moment it seemed as if Jeremiah had suddenly taken her place.

"Are you saying I should buy his friendship?"

"If that's necessary, then *yes*. Heaven knows there are hundreds of other young men who would welcome the chance even to meet Henry Teller." Her voice was sharp with annoyance, as if she were talking to a dim-witted child. "What must he have thought?"

"I was honest with him. I have no interest in investing right now and I told him so. Your father didn't even discuss it with me. If he had . . ."

"And that is your last word on the matter?" Her nostrils flared in anger. "Then there's no need to talk any further. You've ruined everything." Like a spoiled child she turned her back on him, flouncing away in a swirl of perfume and petticoats. She had only taken a few steps before she had Robert Cunningham in tow.

Alex's jaw tightened in exasperation. She had snubbed him publicly, blatantly. She wouldn't even listen. Had he not known it by now, her behavior made it all too apparent that she was not the woman for him. Certainly she didn't value his opinion. Only "Daddy" seemed to impress her.

Seeking to cool his rising temper, Alex pushed his way through the tide of dancing guests and left the house. He needed some air, needed time to reflect. And he didn't want to say things he might regret later. Robert had been right in cautioning him not to do anything hasty. Above all, he didn't want to lose his temper.

Alex walked down the roadway, kicking at the clods of dirt

in frustration until his anger had cooled. Still, he considered returning to the house, packing his bags, and moving to a hotel. The night air held a hint of a breeze that ruffled through his hair as he stood looking up at the sky. Seeing a shooting star, an omen of good fortune, gave him hope. No one had promised him that life would be easy. Hadn't he had sufficient proof of that during the war? He'd been to purgatory and back and still survived. Certainly this matter would not best him. Before the war his world had been as narrow as Caroline's. War had taught him what was really important in life.

Turning on his heel, Alex made his way back to the house, pausing as he neared the white picket fence that defined the boundary of Jeremiah's West's property. Seeing the figure of Caroline's father standing in the shadows, he decided to have a few things out with him before the night was through. It was time for a man-to-man talk. But a deep rumbling voice called out to Jeremiah before Alex had the chance. "Mr. West! Mr. West! I have to talk to you."

"What is it, Lawton? I've got a lot on my mind." Jeremiah West sounded annoyed.

"You told me to report to you if anything happened. Well, it did. There's been an accident at the Claybourne mine."

An accident? Immediately, Alex thought of Samantha. Was she all right? He took a few steps forward, intending to break in on the conversation and ask, but the question was answered for him.

"Enoch Claybourne was killed in a cave-in. I heard the news just this evening in Black Hawk. Samantha Claybourne came into town to record the death certificate."

"Enoch Claybourne dead? Well, this certainly changes things." Jeremiah West cast a furtive glance over his shoulder, then pushed the man named Lawton around the corner of the house, to make certain their conversation wouldn't be overheard.

"A cave-in!" Alex gasped. Poor Samantha. She adored her grandfather. How terrible for her to have to bear such grief alone. Alex longed to comfort her. He imagined a pair of wide brown eyes clouded by tears. "Samantha . . ." He had to see her, had to give her what comfort he could. It was dark and he didn't know the way. Tomorrow he would get directions and ride out on horseback. The urgent desire to see her pushed every other thought from his mind.

19

It was dark and damp and so eerily quiet in the mine. The only sound was the staccato clank of Samantha's pick as she struck at the rock. Day after day she had worked until she succumbed to exhaustion, chipping away at the rock with her pick, shoveling away at the pile of stones and rubble. Dear God, would it never end? All the dirt, rock, and debris that had been pushed back into the tunnel by the cave-in had to be dug out before she could even hope to turn her attention to looking for gold. It was as if all the years of her grandfather's labor had been for naught.

Hour after hour Samantha had toiled until her back ached, her hands were red and blistered, her leg and arm muscles so sore that she was certain she could not find the strength of will to move them. Her body seemed to cry out "no more, no more," and yet somehow she managed to continue. Only the hard work had kept her from giving in to her loneliness, to the realization that she was completely alone. Night after night she came home so exhausted that she could do little but fling herself down on the bed. Sleep was a luxury; rest, something all too rare to her now. Perhaps she was afraid to be idle for too long. Afraid of remembering that terrible cave-in and thinking about her grandfather's death.

The air was warm and smelled musty. Taking off her brown felt hat, Samantha wiped her forehead with the sleeve of her shirt just as she had seen her grandfather do time and time again. Though she had been raised in the mine, had seen her grandfather do just as she was doing now, she had never realized how truly difficult it was. The actual digging was so much more exhausting than helping her grandfather had ever been.

Samantha had used her wits. She had improvised ways of removing some of the dirt and rock by loading it into the ore car, but it still looked as if a lifetime of labor stood before her. Staring up at the shaft, which was sunk to a depth of five hundred feet, she knew a moment of panic. She was enclosed within these walls. They had become nearly like a prison. Now she never even paused long enough to look at the mountains and the land she so loved. She'd been down in this tunnel so long that she hardly remembered what the sunshine felt like.

"Oh, Gramps. Gramps! What am I to do? I've tried. Truly I have," she cried aloud. "I promised not to give up the mine." Keeping the mine meant working it. Samantha knew this only too well. The laws were firm on that point. No one under sixteen years of age could hold a claim, and all claims had to be improved or worked on. If a claim was not improved, it was declared vacant and could then be reclaimed by someone else. If she failed, she could very well lose everything, even the cabin that was the only home she'd ever known.

The walls of the tunnel seemed to close in on her. Samantha felt a scream welling up. Covering her mouth with her hand, she fought her desperation, afraid that if she opened her mouth, she'd never stop shrieking. Sitting down on a huge boulder, she tried to calm her tense nerves as she reevaluated her situation.

She had hardly made a dent in the pile of rocks which still loomed ahead of her. Even her grandfather would have been hampered by such a monumental task. Rocks, loose dirt and fallen timbers formed a mountain of debris. She had stubbornly hacked away at it. If she went on, she might cause another cave-in. A shower of small rocks plopped to the ground emphasizing her thoughts. She needed to shore up the mine again, reinforce it with timbers. She had to admit her limitations. She could not do this all alone.

"Look here, Samantha Claybourne. You have done your damnedest. Hell, even a man couldn't do it alone," she mumbled aloud. "Oh, sure, you take pride that you can ride, shoot, fish, and take care of yourself, but you have to stop being so gol' darn stubborn." She couldn't timber up the mine alone. She was too short, for one thing. As much as she hated to admit it, she was limited in what she could accomplish. Wanting to do it was not enough.

For days now she had groped along the winding tunnel down into this damp hole. The thought depressed her. She thought she was so independent, had been so cocky on occasion, but the truth was, she needed help. Her hands were small, her body strong but not as muscular as a man's. She was only five feet four, too short to reach the top of the cavern. Her grandfather had insisted on working the mine alone, but she could not. She had to hire at least two men to do the heavy work. But who? Whom could she trust?

The flame in the lantern flickered and went out, leaving Samantha in darkness, and once again she fought to remain calm. "It's all right. I just need to light it again, that's all," she breathed. She laughed nervously as she struck a match on a rock and held it to the wick. She fought the feeling of utter loneliness that overcame her as her heart thumped within her chest. The past few days she had even been talking to herself. Much more of this and she would go mad. Oh, how she needed the sound of a human voice. Her grandfather had given her love and understanding. Now she had no one. She put her face in her hands and sighed wearily.

"Samantha . . ." The voice echoed hauntingly down the shaft. "Samantha . . ." She jumped to her feet, her eyes hastily scanning the tunnel for the source of the voice. Her heart seemed to stop as she imagined that she saw her grandfather standing by the loaded mine car. Rubbing her eyes, she was certain that she had finally taken leave of her senses. Her grandfather was dead. It couldn't be. She must be seeing things. Even so, she crept cautiously forward. It was only the shadow of a long plank, resting against a large rock about the size of a man's head. The apparition vanished as she moved her position to the left.

"A rock and a timber." She felt foolish and most definitely angry with herself for succumbing to such silly fear. Nevertheless, her legs still quivered. Closing her eyes, she could see her grandfather in her mind's eye swinging his pick, drilling holes, shoveling, or pushing the ore car. She had to get away from the mine, at least for a while. She needed a breath of fresh air.

"Samantha . . ." The voice calling her name echoed again. She shook her head to chase away the sound, but it reverberated again through the tunnel. "Samantha . . . where are you? Samantha!"

"Dear God, I *am* losing my mind." Picking up the lantern, she hurried up the sloping tunnel, crawled through the winze, and made her way to the entranceway. There, standing in the open doorway, illuminated by the light of the sun, was the figure of a man. No shadow, no illusion, but reality. "Whoever you are, go away. Leave me alone! You'll be sorry if you tangle with me." Her words belied her sudden panic. She was without her rifle, helpless if this was an enemy. Squinting against the excruciating glare of the sun, she tried to appear brave and menacing. If it was Cy Tyburn, he'd soon find himself involved in a tussle.

"Samantha, it's me. Alex. I've had the devil's own time finding you, but I have. Samantha . . ."

"Alex?" She felt such an overwhelming sense of joy and relief that she shouted aloud. "Alex, oh, Alex!" As if it were the most natural thing in the world, she came to him, finding comfort in the haven of his encircling arms. "Dear God, I'm so glad to see you. Alex. Alex."

"I heard about your grandfather, Samantha. I'm sorry. So sorry. I know how very much you loved him." He was achingly moved by the sight of her and reached out to stroke her hair. "Samantha . . ." His voice was a soft, deep rumble, sending a shiver through her.

"Gramps was working in the mine. There was a . . . a . . ." Her words suddenly stuck in her throat as she remembered. Her face was etched in pain, her eyes were closed as she relived the moment once again.

"He was killed in a mine cave-in."

"Yes . . ." There was little else she could say. She still hadn't fully come to terms with his death. It had struck so swiftly, had bereaved her so deeply that she somehow couldn't get the words out. Her fingers tightened on his shoulder as he held her closer. Just having him near seemed to ease some of the pain.

"I wish there was something, anything, I could do to soothe you, Sam. To make it easier for you to get through your grief." He touched the soft curve of her cheek with one finger, tracing the line of her tears. Samantha responded to the gentle caress by looking up at him. She had a sudden flash of intuition that Alex shared her sorrow, that he had experienced a similar loss once, knew exactly how she felt. "Death is always difficult to understand. I don't think anyone ever gets used to it." He hadn't. Not even after all the deaths he had seen during the war. Nor had he ever gotten over the guilt.

"It makes a person feel so helpless. There was nothing I could have done to save him, though I tried. I tried so hard to reach him before . . . before . . ." She buried her face in the warmth of his chest, amazed at how right it felt to be in his arms. She could feel the heat of his body, the hardness of his chest, could hear the loud thud of his heart. It was pounding nearly as fiercely as hers.

"Samantha . . ." Involuntarily his hand came up to rest on her hip then slid slowly up her back as he pulled her closer. Gently he brushed his lips against her hair. He was conscious of the way her full soft breasts were flattened beneath the pressure of his chest, but hastily pushed all amorous thoughts from his mind. Still, he could not deny the desire that coursed through his body, racing up his spine like wildfire. Passion tempered with a great tenderness rose up in him. She'd been through so much. She looked pretty but tired and pale. So much so that it alarmed him. He wanted to keep her in his arms, cradle her like a child.

"I never knew I could feel so lonely, Alex. Gramps has always been there. Now I have no one who really cares."

"I care, Samantha."

She raised her eyes to the potency of his gaze. His voice evoked a hungry longing deep within her. "Alex . . ." Nothing could mask the desolation that brimmed in the dark copper spheres of her eyes, the need to be comforted and loved. For just a moment Alex regarded her, then with a strangled exclamation bent his head to claim her mouth in a startlingly gentle kiss. It was a chaste kiss they shared, yet it made Samantha aware of her body as she'd never been before. She was giddily conscious of the warmth that spread over her, a pleasurable tingle that tightened in the pit of her stomach. It was her first kiss and she knew the feeling of happiness that Alex had been the one to initiate her into such a tender display of affection. In a burst of emotion she flung her arms around his neck and kissed him back with all the longing she'd held deep inside since that first moment she'd seen him.

Alex was stunned and shaken by his reaction to such a simple kiss. He wanted to deepen the embrace, to part her lips and explore the inner sweetness there, but instead he pulled back. Now was not the time.

Feeling him draw away, Samantha stepped back, her hand going to her mouth as she stared at him wide-eyed. She'd never felt anything at all that could compare with that kiss, even in her imaginings. Nevertheless she did not want to mistake the reason for Alex's gesture. It was sympathy and concern he had shown her, not passion. She should not make too much of his kiss, she told herself, and yet she smiled at him with all the love that brimmed in her heart.

Alex made such a strikingly romantic figure standing there that suddenly Samantha could hardly think of anything to say. *Twitterpated* was the word her grandfather had used and at the moment the word was entirely appropriate. A lock of his thick dark hair had fallen across his forehead and she fought against the impulse to reach out and push it out of his eyes. Her wandering gaze appraised him from the top of his head to the hem of the odd trousers he wore, breeches that were flared from the hips to the knee, where they vanished into the tops of highly polished black boots.

"Riding pants, Samantha." Alex saw the quizzical look in

her eye and answered her question before it was asked. "For want of something more appropriate I put them on. I wore them back east whenever I went horseback riding."

"They're right fine, Alex. Just a little odd, that's all." She smiled again. "But you sure are a sight for sore eyes. I can't remember when I've been so glad to see a man." She gasped suddenly as she imagined what a sight she must be. Her clothes were covered with dust and grime, her hair a tangled mess. Hastily she brushed at her pants. "But I must look as mangy as a coyote. If I'd a known you were coming I would have cleaned up a bit."

"You look lovely, Samantha, but you do have a streak of dirt on your nose." He wiped it away with his fingers. "There."

That touch somehow seemed to interfere with her breathing. The rhythm of her lungs was thrown off as she stared up at him, licking her lips. Good Lord, how she wished he would kiss her again, but she supposed that he would not. The kiss had just been something that had happened, that was all. "How did you find me?" It was the only thing she could think to ask.

"It wasn't easy." He put his hand on his aching hip. Not since the war had he ridden so far. "I went to the land office, found out where your grandfather's mine was located, got a map and a compass. The man at the livery stable gave me directions. As you can see I did *not* get lost, though I did hear two gentlemen in the stable making a substantial bet that I would." He drew up his shoulders and stood tall. "They didn't know I used to be a soldier nor of the times I had to lead my company through unfamiliar territory."

"You fought in the war?" She was noticeably impressed. "Gramps used to talk about it all the time."

"It was a time I would prefer to forget. So many people killed, so much heartbreak. Brother against brother and friend against friend. Tragic. Man is the only animal who kills his own kind. And we like to call ourselves civilized." There was a certain sadness etched on the hard planes of his face that struck Samantha. Had Alex been one of those who had fought against a friend or a relative? Had he killed someone he'd been close to in one of those battles? "I haven't carried a gun in six years, though it's not because I'm a coward," he said, breaking through her thoughts.

"Takes a whole heap more courage not to, I'd be thinking. Why, hell, even I can be brave when I'm aiming with my rifle. Skunks like Cy Tyburn, Slim Walker, and Buck Cameron think carrying a gun makes them men but I know different. They ain't men at all, but you are, Alex." Indeed he was, she thought, so much so that he had completely captivated her. "I feel very proud that I can call you my . . . my friend." Oh, how she wished that it was more, that he felt even a tenth as much affection for her as she felt for him, but she held back her words.

"You must be tired after riding so far," she said. "Come on back to the cabin with me and we'll sit down and talk." She needed to talk to someone so desperately. Her feelings had been pent up for so long, she feared she'd explode. Taking Alex's hand, she led him up the path to the cabin.

20

Alex found the cabin to be little more than a hovel, but Samantha's obvious pride in the log house that she and her grandfather had built made him hold his tongue. He forced a smile as she gestured for him to sit down on one of the chairs she had plucked from a peg on the wall. Nor did he even blink an eye when that chair nearly collapsed under him.

"Are you hungry, Alex? I could whip up some grub, though I must admit I'm not too handy in the kitchen. But I can put on a pot of coffee and fry up some eggs before you have time to whistle." Assuming that his answer would be yes, she rose from her seat, threw wood into the stove and started a fire. "I could add some fried potatoes too."

How could he say no? He smiled at the sight of her bustling about the kitchen. She was definitely out of place before a stove, and yet her anxiety to please touched him. She was most certainly tired and yet all her concern was for him.

"Let me help you," Alex offered. While she cooked the food, he fixed the coffee. As he did so his eyes scanned the cabin.

There was a table and three chairs. A large settee made out of boards and padding sat in the middle of the room. Two small beds stood at the far end of the room, divided by a flimsy partition. It was meagerly furnished. He had to get Samantha out of here. The cabin was no fit place for a young woman, not to mention that she was living all alone.

Samantha noticed him looking about and stuck her chin up proudly. "Gramps made the furniture. Every single bed, table, and chair. Guess we were just about as comfy as two squirrels in their nest." She jerked her thumb in the direction of a brass ring that appeared to be firmly imbedded in the planked floor. "Cellar's heaped full of goods from my last trip to town. Should last me at least two months or so." She missed the anxious look he gave her as she turned her attention back to the stove.

"Samantha . . ." Alex began. What could he say to convince her? "The cabin looks very comfortable and I know you've lived here a long, long time, but don't you think perhaps you should come back into town with me?"

"Into town?" She raised a brow in question.

"You could live at the hotel or at one of the boardinghouses until you got a place of your own. A young woman just can't . . . can't live out in the wilderness by herself. There are dangers. . . ."

"I can't leave!" she retorted stubbornly. "Gramps and I built this place. How would I get back here every day to work the mine. Hell, I hardly get what I need to do done as it is. I can take care of myself. I got work to do."

"Which brings me to another point. You're a woman, Samantha, and although I know how very capable you are, you must think sensibly. You can't work the mine alone."

A few days ago, she would have protested. Now, however, she sighed her exasperation. "I know. I was just telling myself that a little while ago. Mining is damned hard work, Alex."

"You could sell the mine. I understand you've had an offer already. . . ." He watched as her face became transformed by anger.

"Offer, you call it? Your fancy pants soon-to-be father-in-law offered two thousand dollars. Two thousand dollars for all the years my grandfather gave to this mine." She looked him square in the eye, all trace of contentment replaced by resolve. "You can tell that skinflint Jeremiah West for me: I'll never sell this mine. I may be a woman but I'll do it somehow. I will! I will!" All the days of agony and heartache at last took its toll and she succumbed to a full flood of tears, covering her face with her hands.

"Samantha! Samantha, I didn't mean . . . Surely there is someone who would give you a fair price." He put his arm around her, unnerved by her sobs, though he knew she had reason to cry. "I'll help in any way I can. If the mine is so important to you, then by God I'll do everything possible to help you keep it."

She looked at him through her tears. "I don't want to sell it, Alex. Gramps found gold. A new vein of rich ore. Just before he died, we took some of that ore to Black Hawk to be smelted. They still owe me some money for that ore."

"But gold or no gold, you can't work the mine alone, Samantha." Red-gold hair fell into her eyes and he gently brushed it away. "Even your grandfather had *you* to help him."

"Yes, he did. He had me." That thought cheered her. She looked up, all too acutely aware of the firmly muscled body so close to hers. His mouth was just inches from hers as he spoke. Hopefully she closed her eyes, only to open them again as she smelled the odor of burned potatoes. "Oh, no!" Picking up the spatula, she tried to undo the damage, turning the potatoes over in the pan. "I ruined our lunch."

Alex grimaced as he eyed the seared mess. "Nonsense. I like my eggs and my potatoes very well done." Taking the spatula from her fingers, removing the pan from the stovetop, he gestured with his head toward the table. "Get the plates ready, Samantha. Luncheon is about to be served." Somehow Alex managed to make good on his word. They both ate what Samantha had prepared, if not with great relish, then with appetite and good humor.

"Now, as to the mine," Alex said over the coffee. "If you insist on keeping it, you're going to need at least a couple of men to help you. It will mean paying them wages."

"Gramps and I have plenty of gold dust. Keep it in an old

coffee tin under a board in the floor. I'll give any man that works for me a more than decent wage." She wanted to add that she was not as penny-pinching as Jeremiah West but thought she had maligned that man enough.

Alex knew just the two men to suggest. The Cornish cook, Mrs. Trenoweth, had a son who had just found himself out of work when one of the mines closed and the Chinese houseboy's cousin was in similar circumstances. He was pleased when Samantha agreed. "I'll talk with them and send them up here tomorrow," he said.

"Thank you, Alex. You really have proved to be a friend. I'm beholden to you." Reaching across the table, she took his hand, giving it a gentle squeeze. Just touching him was enough to set her heart pounding. Ah, yes, she was twitterpated all right. "A damned sight so," she said beneath her breath.

After clearing the dishes away Samantha motioned to the sofa and tried as best she could to amuse Alex with stories and "yarn spinning," as her grandfather had called it. Her manner charmed Alex. He liked her laughter, her smiles, and the exuberance with which she spoke. If at times she was a bit blunt, still it was an endearing quality. He doubted there was another woman quite like her. Alex thought again about their kiss, surprised at his own reaction. He had wanted to deepen the embrace, had relished the soft yielding of her mouth. She evoked in him a yearning to *give,* a far different emotion than he felt for Caroline. With Caroline he was always tense and guarded, with Samantha he felt as relaxed as if he had known her forever. He found Caroline cold, despite her pretended passion; Samantha was as warm as a summer day.

"I like this West of yours, Samantha. I hope it will be my home for a long time to come." Putting his hands behind his head, he leaned back and made himself comfortable, something he never could quite manage to do at the Wests' house. "I know it's foolish, Samantha but here in Colorado the moon looks larger, the stars closer, and the air seems much fresher than in Boston. The altitude took some getting used to, but I've adjusted. I guess a man could say that the mountains do bring us closer to the sky. It's true, Samantha, just as you said." He glanced over at her only to see that he would get no answer. She was fast asleep, her head resting on one outflung arm, her red-gold hair tumbling across the back of the sofa. She looked like a seductive angel, so lovely that he was mesmerized and would have been content to watch her for hours.

"Ah, Samantha, why do you tug at my heartstrings so?" he whispered. "We really are quite a mismatched pair." Or were they? Just what were his feelings for her? He needed time to sort things out. Picking her up in his arms, he carried her to the bed and watched as she nestled her body into the softness and warmth of the mattress.

For a long time he stood gazing down at her, watching the gentle rise and fall of her chest. Long shadows cast on her cheeks by her lashes gave her a delicate, vulnerable look, but he knew just how strong-willed she really was. Taking her hand gently, he looked at the blisters and shook his head. If only he could convince her to leave here, to sell the mine and live an easier way of life, but she was adamant. He hoped for her sake that she really did find that gold. Of one thing he was certain: Samantha deserved happiness.

Doing his best to make her comfortable, Alex pulled up a blanket from the foot of the bed and covered the peacefully sleeping form. He knew her pride would stop her from taking any money from him. He remembered the upward tilt to her chin when she'd talked about the gold dust. Still, he would keep an eye on her. It would be a most pleasant task. Yet he couldn't help but worry about her. There were a lot of "skunks," as she called Cy Tyburn and his bunch, living nearby. He could only hope that she would be able to take care of herself.

Alex trudged back to the mine where his horse was tethered. With a glance back at the cabin, he drew himself up into the saddle. He'd talk to Mrs. Trenoweth the moment he got back to town. He'd ask her son to come to the mine as soon as possible. Alex knew he'd feel a lot better when Samantha had someone reliable around. She was skilled at handling a rifle, but even the most proficient woman was no match for a bully. Enoch Claybourne's death was not yet general knowledge. Certainly Jeremiah West's informer had acted as if it were a secret. By the time the news was about, Alex reasoned, Samantha would have Mrs. Trenoweth's son and the houseboy's cousin to watch over her. Even so, as he made his way down the mountainside Alex felt a deep sense of regret to be leaving.

21

A pink glow on the horizon touched the mountains and seemed to make them shimmer with rays of light. A glorious sunrise awaited Samantha. How could she help but smile? Over and over again in her mind she heard Alex's words. *I care, Samantha.* There was someone who cared about her after all, she thought, flinging open the cabin's lone window for a breath of the fresh early morning air. Alex cared. Somehow that seemed to heighten her senses to the world around her. The song of the birds seemed more vibrant, the colors of the wildflowers looked more vivid, their heady perfume smelled much sweeter. Her every instinct had been abruptly awakened.

He kissed me, she thought, touching her lips. Though several days had gone by, she still remembered. Could she ever forget? His warm lips on hers had awakened a host of sensations that were complicated to define and certainly confusing. A kiss. Just a kiss and yet it had somehow changed her, made her view the world in a different way. Made her aware that there were other things in life besides finding gold. Happiness. She wanted to reach out for it but cautioned herself. Falling in love with Alex would be treading on dangerous ground. He was engaged to marry another woman. Though his kiss had set her entire world wheeling and spinning, it had not meant the same to him. It had been merely a gesture of affection. She had to keep that in mind. He had offered her friendship and nothing more. Even so, she was ecstatically happy, looking forward to that time when she would see him again.

She lit the stove, put a pot of coffee on to brew, then padded across the cold wooden floor and tried to put her thoughts into perspective. There was work to be done. She couldn't spend her time dreaming, as pleasant as it was. Lifting the creaky floorboard, she took out the rusting black-and-red coffee tin and pried up the lid to take careful stock of the gold dust within. There was more than enough to pay the two miners Alex had sent. Enough for tools and supplies. She also had the document from the Boston and Colorado Smelting Company tucked inside with its promise of gold from the ore she and her grandfather had taken in. Security for the long weeks ahead. Closing the lid, Samantha was pricked with temptation and opened it again. She wanted to look pretty for Alex, wanted him to think of her as a woman, not a waif.

A dress, she thought. Frivolous. Foolish. Bothersome. Yet men seemed to put high stock in women who wore them. Samantha had never even contemplated wearing a dress before, but suddenly found herself inspired to buy one. It would be a surprise. God knew she'd looked like a windstorm had struck her the day he'd visited. Though she knew she could never even hope to compete with Caroline, still she thought it might please him. A plain blue-and-white-checked calico would do, one without that silly contraption called a "bustle." Samantha knew she could never go quite so far as to wear one of those. "Makes a woman look like she's all backside," she laughed to herself, taking out a scoop of gold dust before putting the coffee tin back in its nest. Samantha hurried to dress and had just finished lacing up her boots when a loud, melodious song announced that the Cornishman had arrived for his day's labor.

"Good morning, me beautay." Patrick Trenoweth met Samantha at the door with a polite bow then looked into her eyes with a crooked smile that sent the freckles dancing on his face. "Here be I for another day."

He was a congenial fellow, Samantha thought, and seemed to take particular pleasure in watching over her. She had liked him from the very first. He was short, somewhat stocky with thick black hair framing a face that looked as if it had been in one fight too many. That Patrick Trenoweth was able to do the work of two men was not surprising when one viewed his strength. His arms bulged with muscles built up from years wielding an eight-pound double-jack sledgehammer. Though he showed by every look he gave her that he disapproved of a woman working in a mine, he never said a word.

"I put some coffee on. Come in and sit for a moment." Samantha took a chipped earthenware cup from the shelf and filled it to the brim. "I'm pleased as punch with the job you have done, Patrick. A few more days and we should be able to start working the mine again."

"Ah, it weren't all me oo 'as done it. The little Chinaman has been a 'elp as 'ave you. Together we 'ave moved all the rubble." As if he had been summoned, Wan Lau poked his head through the door.

"We must hully, missy. Plenty work. Plenty work." A small, lithe man, he was hardly bigger than Samantha. She had doubted he could do the work, only to find she had to eat her words. Wan Lau was small, but he was as effective as blasting powder in getting a job done. Unlike Patrick the solemn, pig-tailed man never left the mine site. He lived in a tent right on the grounds and Samantha suspected he had been instructed to do just that by Alex. Despite her fierce pride in being able to take care of herself, that thought pleased her and seemed to be further proof of Alex's affection.

Which was not to say that Samantha could now shirk her own work. Their presence seemed to spur her on. She worked just as hard and as long as they did. They needed her there. No one could ever know the mine as well as she did. Just as it had been her grandfather's blood, sweat, and tears, so was it now her own.

Accompanying Wan Lau and Patrick Trenoweth, Samantha put in another exhausting day, staying at the mine until they were all ready to leave. It was not that she did not trust them. If Alex had sent them, then that was proof enough of their honesty. The reason she stayed was in part pride: the need to show them that although she was a woman, she could work just as long and just as hard as they could. Pride. If anything at all could be said to be her Achilles heel, perhaps it was that. It was her strength as well as her weakness, as her grandfather had reminded her on more than one occasion.

Walking back to the cabin, Samantha thought once again of Alex, wondering when he would come to see her again. When he did, she just might take him down in the tunnel, show him all that had been accomplished. It was important for him to understand why she couldn't let the mine go, why she worked so very hard to keep it. Perhaps tomorrow she might even go into town for the dress.

Looking up to see a carriage parked in the middle of the narrow road, Samantha hastily brushed at her shirt and trousers. Thinking it to be Alex, she paused by the pump, washed her face and hands, then ran her fingers through her hair to chase away the tangles. With a wide smile she approached the door only to give a gasp of outrage. Jeremiah West sat on a large stump, his legs crossed at the knee, casually puffing a cigar. That he dared be so bold filled Samantha with fury.

"What are you doing here? No one invited you." Her eyes sparked with anger, her face was flushed, her breath came quickly between parted lips. It seemed a sacrilege to have this man on her property.

Jeremiah raised the hand that held the cigar. "Now hold on, my dear. My visit is a friendly one. It's a mission of charity that brings me here." He followed her to the door, despite her efforts to dismiss him. Standing in the open doorway, he eyed the interior of the cabin with disgust. "I came here to tell you how very sorry I am about your grandfather," he said.

"How did you know?" Samantha wasn't at all sure that she liked the idea of Jeremiah West being privy to such information and for a moment suspected Alex might have told him.

"Some business associates of mine know the records clerk in Black Hawk." He looked at her over the rim of his spectacles.

"I have an entire network of men who keep me informed, my dear. I am a very powerful man."

"So you know. Thanks a heap for your condolences. You paid your call, now you can go." She had made it very clear that she wanted him to leave, but instead he stepped farther into the room.

"It must be very hard on a *woman* living in a place like this. An attractive young thing like you should be going to dances and socializing, Miss Claybourne, not huddling all alone in a shack."

"It's not a shack. It's my home and I'm damned proud of it. Gramps built it and I helped him. I wouldn't trade it for the queen of England's palace." She was so angry, she wanted to throw something at him.

"But the truth is you will leave it in time. You'll have to." He smiled smugly. "Just to show you what a generous man I am, I am fully prepared to offer you money for something you will soon lose anyway." Reaching into his coat pocket, he pulled out an impressive wad of bills. "Two thousand dollars for the cabin and the mine. With the understanding that you will vacate the premises immediately."

"When it comes to gall you certainly have your share. I'll never sell this mine to you." Taking off her hat, she flung it angrily in his direction. Unruffled by her display, Jeremiah merely smiled. "You look like the cat that swallowed the canary. Well, you can just stop grinnin'. I mean every word I say."

"Come, come, come. I admire spunk and fire but there comes a time for common sense. You're a female, Miss Claybourne, for all your . . . uh . . . pretense. A woman. There is no possible way that you can work this mine. You cannot do it alone nor do I think you really want to. The law is very clear on the matter. I can wait until time defeats you or I can take this losing proposition off your hands. Which is it to be?"

"Neither." Putting her hands on her hips, she glared her defiance. "You can take your money and . . . and stick it in your ear." Anger made her less cautious. "The truth is, you're wrong. I am going to work the mine. Hell, I was raised here, began crawling in and out of those shafts and tunnels as soon as

I could walk and talk. I watched my grandfather and worked by his side. I'm not some foolish female whose head is full of fluff."

He snorted disdainfully. "Work it? Nonsense. I hear there was a cave-in. It would take you the rest of your life to dig it out. You'll go broke. You'll starve to death. When winter comes you'll come begging me to make you the same offer I'm giving you now."

"Never. Gramps left me a slew of gold dust and I'm using it to hire some of the work done. If you can pay someone to do the bull work, then so can I. Got myself a Cousin Jack and a Chinaman. Two men who'd pay no nevermind to you after you just up and let them go. They needed a job and I hired 'em."

"You hired men?" The idea seemed to astonish him. The thought had never even crossed his mind. A wave of emotions played across his face, none of them pleasant.

"I'll make this the richest producing mine in the territory."

Jeremiah West fought to control his anger. The little chit had ruined all his carefully made plans. He had thought that if he bided his time, she would be forced to sell. Now he could see that she was determined to hold out. Stubborn, irritating woman that she was, she might even succeed, unless he took a hand. Rising to his feet, he marched out of the cabin and climbed into his carriage, his mind seething with ways to get his hands on the mine he had learned might yield the richest ore in Colorado.

22

Jeremiah West whipped his horses into a frenzy, taking out his anger on the hapless animals as he drove them farther up the mountain toward a cabin a mile up the road. Stephen Tyburn's name had suddenly popped into his head and he had been granted the welcome recollection that the old man had once been a partner in the Siren Song. Though he had never learned what had caused the rift in a once strong partnership, he intended to find out in hopes that the knowledge could in some way prove useful.

Though he had left Samantha's with a scowl, the sight of the tiny cabin brought forth a smile. The Tyburns were in even worse straits than he'd suspected, the dwelling little more than a shed. A man in dire poverty was an easy target for what he had in mind.

Reining in the horses, setting the brake to the buggy, Jeremiah walked the path to the door, weaving his way amid the rocks, tree stumps, tools, and wagon wheels. He knocked at the splintered door and let his eyes scan the outlying grounds as he waited for it to be answered. An old rusty ax imbedded in a log, an overturned bucket, and a litter of junk indicated the lack of interest Stephen Tyburn had in his place.

"Who are you and what do you want?" The questions were barked out by a cadaverously thin man who peeked out through the suddenly opened door. "Cy ain't here."

"I'm not looking for Cy but for you. I presume you are Stephen Tyburn. I have a business proposition that just might interest you." As the door opened wide he took a step inside the cabin, trying to hide his disdain for the chaotic jumble that greeted him. The interior was filthy. Empty whisky bottles were scattered over the dirt-caked floor, yellowed newspapers were crumpled up in corners or pushed into cracks in the wall in an apparent effort to insulate the cabin from drafts. Piles of dirty clothing covered chairs and a broken-down settee. Nevertheless, Jeremiah West took the seat that was offered him.

"State your business." The words were slurred, the man's hands trembled as he looked at his unwelcome guest with squinting eyes.

"I'll come right to the point. I want to buy the Siren Song and I've been denied that wish. I thought that perhaps you could help me."

Throwing back his head, Stephen Tyburn cackled. "Me? Me help? I haven't been inside the mine for little over two years. Not since Enoch Claybourne kicked me out."

"But you once held half ownership of the mine, did you not?" He waited expectantly, hardly daring to hope.

"Yeh, he did." The voice came from an unlighted area of the cabin as Cy Tyburn took a step forward. "It's all right Pa. He ain't here with the sheriff." Brushing his fingers against the gun he wore in his holster, he grinned a warning. "Hope you ain't here to give me no scolding. What passed between me and that sissy pants soon-to-be son-in-law of yours was just a bit of fun."

"Indeed?" Brushing off his jacket, Jeremiah West curled his lip. "What happened is no concern of mine. What I *am* interested in, however, is finding out more about the mine you once worked. When the claim was staked, by whom, and if there was a grubstake. How is it that the ownership has passed into the hands of a woman? A most stubborn and unfriendly one at that."

"Enoch Claybourne cheated my father. It's as plain as that." Reaching for a half-full bottle of whiskey on a corner table, Cy Tyburn took a long swig.

"He cheated you?" Jeremiah couldn't help the grin that spread across his face. "Perhaps I can be of some help in the matter."

Stephen Tyburn shook his head. "No. No, he bought me out fair and square. Put my half of the claim in his granddaughter's name. Isn't a court in the territory that would argue with that. Enoch Claybourne was careful, knowing it's hard for a woman in these parts. Staked out that claim in sixty-one. We staked out an area fifty feet wide by a hundred feet long, wrote the name of the claim, the date, the direction of the vein, dimensions, and our names. He filed the location with the recorder of the district and duly recorded it. Two years ago he stirred up a hornet's nest when I nearly gambled my share away. Bought me out. Said I was more interested in drinking and gambling than in working. I suspect he was right."

"He took advantage of your good nature, Pa. And now they both swagger around that mine of theirs as if they owned the world. I hate to think just how highfalutin Enoch Claybourne is going to be if he does strike a vein." Taking off his large-brimmed hat, Cy Tyburn slapped it against his thigh, then sprawled his long-legged body in a chair.

"Enoch Claybourne won't be able to act in any manner." Jeremiah West took off his spectacles and cleaned them with the end of his cravat. "Didn't you know? Hadn't you heard? Enoch Claybourne was killed in a mine cave-in."

"Killed?" Cy Tyburn picked up his ears in interest. "Sammie dear is living all *alone*? What a gawddamned shame."

"Enoch dead?" Stephen Tyburn was the only one who seemed to have any remorse. "I always told him that mine would be the death of him." Taking the bottle that his son held out to him, Stephen Tyburn drank it dry, then wiped his sleeve across his mouth. "I'm sorry. I really, really am."

"I'm not, Pa. With that old goat out of the way, maybe we can get our hands on that mine. Sammie's gonna need a man now. Guess I can pass myself off as a pretty likely candidate. Always known I had a way with women." Running his fingers through his tightly curled blond hair, he grinned.

"And if you succeed, I'll pay two thousand dollars for your share of the mine. If you don't, perhaps we can work out an arrangement. I could use a man with your knowledge and skill, Cy." With a conspiratorial wink, Jeremiah West held out his hand for a handshake. "One way or another I think our association could be very profitable."

"You won't hold it against me for anythin' I do? You'll give me full rein?"

"I'll let you handle things as you see fit, just as long as you make certain I'm not connected in any way to your doings. Is it a deal?"

Cy Tyburn grimaced a smile. "It's a deal. And I think it'll be the best gawddamned partnership you ever seen." Rising to his feet, Jeremiah had the same feeling.

23

Samantha was so enraged that despite her fatigue she couldn't sleep. How dare he! How dare Jeremiah West barge into her cabin and make such an insulting proposal. Calling her home a shack! She trembled with anger to think of it. He wanted her to fail. He wanted her to lose the mine. As if he didn't own half the mines and properties of Central City already. The greedy fox! Well, there was one mine he would never get his hands on.

Taking a deep breath, Samantha turned over on her stomach and buried her head in a pillow. She had to get some sleep if she was going to be worth a nickel tomorrow. Poor Alex, she pitied him, having such a man as a father-in-law. Alex deserved much better, she thought, closing her eyes and trying to calm her ire.

She had just begun to relax when a noise startled her. Her eyes flew open and she stared into the darkness. Was she imagining it or was something rattling the door? Could be a raccoon, she reasoned. The mischievous varmints could be a nuisance and sometimes turned to cabin theft for food. Wouldn't be the first time they'd tried to get inside. Covering her head with the pillow, she once again closed her eyes.

Samantha willed her body to relax, her mind to concentrate on the sheep she was counting. Thirty-three, thirty-four. It had always worked for her grandfather but not for her. She kept seeing one wearing spectacles. "Drat and damnation!" Sitting up in bed, she kicked the covers aside. Was she going to let that money-grubbing banker keep her awake?

Was she imagining it or did she hear footsteps? Fully awake now, Samantha sat up and listened. There was no mistaking the *clump, clump* that pounded right outside her door. Could it be Wan Lau? After that set-to with Jeremiah West, she couldn't be too cautious. Wouldn't it just be like him to send one of his cronies to poke around the mine? Dressed in a long nightshirt, feet bare, she grabbed her rifle, stealthily crept to the door, unlocked the latch, and kicked it open.

"Who's there?"

Moonlight shimmered over the rocks and crevices beyond the doorway. A chill of apprehension raced up her spine as she heard an all too familiar chuckle. Stepping back, she cocked her gun.

"Evening, Samantha." Cy Tyburn stepped into the light, leaning against the doorway. "Thought I'd pay you a call."

"If you aren't lower than a skunk, crawling around here. What the hell do you want?" One sniff told her he'd been drinking. Aiming the rifle, she pointed it warningly. "Get on away from here. It's late and I'm in no mood for callers. Especially you."

He pretended surprise. "Now, Sam, is that any way to treat your future beau?" Preening like a rooster ready to mate, he combed his fingers through the thick blond curls of his hair. "Why, I just come on by to ask you to the dance. Ol' Horace Vickery is gonna play his fiddle down at the church and I wanted you to be my gal."

"I'd just as soon go with a polecat." Sam had heard that Cy Tyburn was considered devilishly appealing to the ladies, but his cruel streak, bullying ways, and constant tomfoolery had always made him unattractive to her eyes. Let other women vie to run their fingers through his curly blond hair, Samantha wanted no part of him. "Besides I don't have time. I gotta work." Thinking the matter closed, she motioned him outside and tried to shut the door but his strategically placed boot kept it from closing.

"Now I was gonna be nice to ya, Sammie. I wasn't even gonna hold it agin you, making a spectacle of me and Buck and Slim in front of that sissy-pants stranger. I was gonna let bygones be bygones. But a man can take just so much sass from a woman." His eyes roamed over her in a searching appraisal that seemed to strip her naked. The moonlight clearly outlined the curves of her body through the cotton of her nightshirt. Whistling beneath his breath, Cy Tyburn made it obvious that he liked what he saw. "Oo ee and you are some woman. When did you get all growed up like that, Sammie?"

"You leave this minute, Cy. I'm tired of your foolish gibe." His stare chilled her more than if he had challenged her to a gunfight. Though she might have been secretly pleased to have Alex look at her that way, Cy's gawking sent a flash of fear reeling through her. "I mean it. You turn around and walk on out of here or I'll shoot."

His smile was a flash of white. "Okay. Okay, I'll go. Don't get riled, Sammie. But first I want to tell you how sorry I am about ol' Enoch. I knew him just as long as I knew my own pa. Tanned my breeches for me often enough he did when I was just a boy. I liked that ol' man even if my pa said he cheated him."

"Gramps never cheated your father. He was a lazy no-account and wasn't pulling his fair share. All he did was get all whiskeyed up and gamble. Gramps was doing all the work. He paid your pa a fair price for his share in the mine and you know it!" His accusation reopened old wounds that were better off forgotten. It was true that Enoch Claybourne and Stephen Tyburn had been partners. Equally true that her grandfather had done all the work. It was Stephen Tyburn who, in his spite and rage, had convinced the townspeople that he'd been swindled. Each and every man had shunned her grandfather, and Enoch, in turn, had grown embittered, retreating and creating a cocoon around himself and Samantha.

"Pa is lazy, I'll agree." He threw his hands in the air. "See, we got no quarrel." Sticking his thumbs in his gun belt, he shrugged his shoulders. "Why, as a matter of fact, I been thinking about you lately. Woman needs a man to take good care of her. You pretend you don't like me none, Sam, but I'm not so certain that's true. Woman's blood runs just as hot as a man's, or so I'm told. I could be persuaded to hitch up with you if you gave me half a chance."

Samantha gave a shriek of outrage. "You *must* be drunk to even think such a thing." Holding the rifle up as if to take aim, she laughed as he jumped for the door and pulled it closed behind him. He'd always been easy to best, she thought. The smile died on her lips as he flung the door open and took her by surprise, lunging for her before she could aim her rifle again. The gun went off, blowing a hole in the cabin roof right above Samantha's bed. Cy knocked the rifle away.

"You little bitch. I'll teach you to laugh at me. I owe you for all the times you've pointed that fool rifle at me. You won't be so brave now, Sammie." He carried her struggling, kicking form to the bed, chuckling that evil laugh all the while. "You and that gawddamned dude think you're so smart. Well, I'll get him and I'll show you, too."

"Leave Alex out of this, Cy. He hasn't done anything to you."

"Not to me, but he sure has Buck all riled. Called his bluff in town." Despite the discomfort she felt from his grasping arms, she felt relieved. Alex really could take care of himself. The question was, could she? Cy was becoming a worrisome pest. She pushed against his shoulders, trying to break free, but his hold on her only tightened. Gone were the days when they had been children and she could hold her own. She twisted and squirmed but couldn't budge him.

"Go ahead and fight, Sam. I like it. You got me wound up so tight I'm just ready to burst. I think I want much more than a kiss." With a low growl he brought her up hard against him. At the first touch of his mouth, however, Samantha bit down, drawing blood. With a yelp of pain he loosened his hold just enough for her to wrench free, dash across the room, and pick up a chair.

"I'll knock your head so hard it will meet your shoulder-blades if you don't get on outta here and leave me be, Cy. I will. You know it!" There was something so fierce, so savage, in her eyes that he believed her. Wiping his mouth with his sleeve he backed away, bumping into Wan Lau, who stood in the doorway holding a rifle.

"I'm going. I'm going. You're too much of a hellcat for me. Man doesn't want a woman who wears pants anyway. A woman should be soft and smell like flowers. You smell like that ol' mine of yours. And you're about as feminine as your granddad. No man is going to want you, Samantha Claybourne. No man. If you don't change your ways you'll go to your grave an old maid." Stomping across the threshold, he paused for a moment, glaring at her. "Think on that. And just remember, Cy Tyburn gets even. Somehow. Someday. I'll make you regret what happened tonight. You'll wish you'd been a little nicer to me." He slammed the door with a resounding bang, leaving a shaken Samantha behind.

24

The pop of firecrackers set off by some mischievous boys startled Alex from his thoughts as he stood looking out his bedroom window. He'd been thinking once again about Samantha. He worried about her. Though he'd asked Wan Lau to keep an eye on her, it didn't relieve his anxiety. Sam certainly gave the impression that she could take care of herself, but he knew that beneath her flannel shirt and fiercely independent ways was a sensitive and vulnerable woman. A very lovely woman. Could he ever forget the expression on her face when she'd seen him standing in the doorway of the mine entrance. She had looked so lost and forlorn despite her air of grit and bravado. She had needed him, had run to him as if he were a permanent haven of protection.

"I care, Samantha," he had said, little realizing at the time how very much he meant those words. He did care, far more than he should. Until he was disentangled from his engagement, he was not free.

He didn't want to hurt Caroline. In truth, she had not really done anything particularly odious or appalling to cool his ardor. She was simply not the young woman he had first thought her to be. She was not a lovely young goddess but a very spoiled and self-centered young woman. A perfect companion for moonlit nights, but not the kind of woman Alex wanted to spend the rest of his life with.

Alex had watched the shimmering beauty with an appraising eye these past few days. He had noted the disdain with which she treated the houseboy, Chun Lau, her lack of consideration for Mrs. Trenoweth. Caroline kept late hours and slept until noon. No one who was "anyone" ever went to bed before dawn, she laughingly said. She seemed helpless in the face of the simplest household tasks. Like a gloriously beautiful mantelpiece she was pleasing to the eye but totally useless. Looking fashionable seemed to be the only thing important to her. She spent hours getting dressed, then baited Alex for compliments.

But most disturbing of all, Caroline always talked in terms of what her father would say or do. Alex wanted to be head of his own household. He had come to realize he would not be if he married Caroline West. He would be marrying Jeremiah as well.

The air rang with shouts and laughter, the pounding of drums, and the blare of trumpets as the Fourth of July parade wound its way through the town, but Alex was barely aware of the tumult. His mind was on his predicament. The matter had to be settled quickly. Each day that passed was unfair both to Caroline and to himself. There was no turning back to what might have been. What had flashed between them had fizzled out. But what of Samantha? Just where did she fit into all of this? Just what were his feelings for her?

Slowly he tried to sort his thoughts out. He liked Samantha, genuinely liked her, of this he had no doubt. But was it more than that? He'd never really thought of her in an amorous way before. Or had he? Certainly he hadn't been blind to her pert prettiness, her womanly curves, but up to now he had pushed any lusty thoughts out of his head. He had meant to befriend her. He hadn't expected their kiss to be such a stirring experience. Surprisingly so. And why had he kissed her?

Careful, Nicholson, he cautioned himself. If he wasn't careful, he'd be falling from the cooking pot into the fire. He had thought himself in love with Caroline and that relationship had gone up in smoke before his eyes. Samantha was untried and naive in matters of love. Were he to court her and find that he had made another mistake, it could very well shatter her. She didn't need any more heartache right now. It was one thing to offer friendship, another to entertain thoughts of a more passionate nature. That was why he had kept his distance, though he had been sorely tempted to go back up to see her. He wanted to protect her, even if that meant protecting her from himself.

Closing his eyes he could envision her smile. She haunted his thoughts in the daytime and his dreams at night. Though it had been a very chaste kiss, he couldn't put it out of his mind. There were moments when he found himself aching to hold her. She was young and vulnerable. All her life she'd had her grandfather to protect her. It was only natural that she'd seek another hand to guide her. She was lonely at the cabin. How easy it would be to take advantage of that loneliness right now. But that was a thing that Alex swore he would not do, no matter how very lovely she was.

"Samantha!" Her name sang on his lips. He could still feel the softness of her young, firm breasts against his chest, taste the sweetness of her lips. She'd lived on that mountain most of her life, was inexperienced with men, of that he was certain. Why, she didn't even own a dress and yet she was twice the woman Caroline was. An enticing, innocent creature. Soft and smiling one moment, full of fire and grit the next. Alex didn't want to take the chance of hurting her. Like it or not, he'd involved himself with Caroline West and until that problem was solved he had no right to look at another woman. He was, at this moment, engaged. Strange, he thought, how the word that at one time had made him feel such euphoria now made him feel like a condemned man.

"Alex! Alex!" He heard Caroline's voice through the door, her tone shrill. "Are you ready? Please hurry. Cousin Jennie has fixed some fried chicken for our Fourth of July celebration. Daddy's anxious for us to be on our way." Another pop of fireworks punctuated her sentence.

Slipping on his coat, Alex opened the door. "I'm ready, Caroline."

In spite of his quick response, she looked peevish, and gave him the silent treatment as they walked down the stairs. Not until they were in the carriage did she let him know the reason for her ill will. "How could you, Alex?" she asked between clenched teeth. "How could you humiliate me so?"

"What are you talking about?" He quickly reviewed all that he had done since breakfast. He'd been deep in his own thoughts, had perhaps been sullen and silent, but he'd done nothing to merit her anger.

"Maria at the dressmaker's shop told me that her husband at the bakery said you had asked the man at the assayer's office for directions to the Claybourne cabin. You actually intended to visit that wretched girl! Mr. Howard at the livery said you took a horse up the mountain roadway. You *did* go up there, didn't you? After all my pleading."

"Yes, I went up to see Samantha." His stomach churned with anger. "For God's sake, her grandfather was killed in a cave-in. I went up to offer my condolences."

"Without even a thought of how I would feel when the news was bandied about town." She turned her back with a petulant frown.

"Your feelings were the very last thing on my mind, Caroline. I told you once before that I will not be dictated to. You do not have a ring in my nose yet." His eyes narrowed dangerously. "Nor is my ring on your finger." To marry a woman as obviously selfish as Caroline was tantamount to insanity. If he had never known it before, he knew it now. There would be no wedding. Let the entire town call him a blackguard, he would not tie himself to such a woman.

"Alex . . ." His tone of voice shocked her out of her surliness. "I didn't mean—"

"Yes, you did. If you had a heart beneath the ruffles of that dress, you would feel some sympathy. If you were any kind of woman, you would have gone to see Samantha yourself and offered your sympathy."

"Go to see her?" Her mouth formed an *o* of indignity. "Why, after the way she treated my father, turning down the fair price he offered her for that silly mine, I wouldn't walk the same side of the street with her. Why . . ."

Jeremiah West had been silent, concentrating on guiding the carriage through the crowded streets, but now he spoke sternly. "Caroline is right. That young woman was hardly cordial. I offered to help her out and she practically drove me out her door with a shotgun. She's undisciplined, unruly, and needs to learn her place."

"And that is?" Alex trembled with anger.

"She needs a firm hand. A husband. With ten little children tugging at her skirt she'd hardly have time to think about man's work, I daresay." The din of drums and horns drowned out the rest of his words as the carriage came to a stop on Main Street. Alex jumped out and mingled with the crowd. He needed to put some distance between himself and the two smugly smiling people he had arrived with, before he completely lost his temper. Seeing Patrick Trenoweth in the crowd, he pushed his way toward him.

"Patrick, it's good to see you. How is it going at the mine?"

"Splendid, me 'andsome. Splendid. That little Sam is quite a girl, that I be sayin'." His pugilist's face broke out in a smile.

"Is she working too hard? Is she well? Is she here with you?" He looked anxiously for her.

"To answer yer questions, me boy, she's well, working very 'ard, and no she did not come." He grinned. "But it's pleased I be that you should be making such inquiry. The little beautay thinks the sun rises and sets in you, she does. I know it. Were I not a married man meself, I might give ye some competition for her 'eart."

The thud of drums and blare of horns drowned out Alex's reply. The whole town had turned out—miners, saloon girls, gamblers, merchants. Several soldiers in uniforms they had worn during the war marched down the street, a painful reminder to Alex of a time he preferred to forget. Pulling a two-wheeled wagon with barrels and buckets, the Central City Fire Department joined the throng. Wagons decorated with flowers added a colorful touch. Atop one of these wagons Caroline perched like a reigning goddess. Being queen of the parade was no doubt the special surprise she had been jabbering about all week.

"She isn't the one for ye." The Cornishman's eyes looked in

the same direction Alex was looking. "Samantha *is* gold, that one is nothing but fool's gold. I think ye know it."

"I do, Patrick. But it's not as simple as you might suppose. What a man wants to do and what he does are not always the same."

"If 'e is wise it will be. A woman like Samantha comes along only once in a lifetime, me boy. Remember that." Shouldering his sledge, he took his leave of Alex to position himself for the drilling contest, a main event of the celebration. Soon the sound of hammers striking steel drills created a clamor. A large stone was used to show off the miners' prowess. One by one the men took their turn as a timekeeper looked at his watch. Soon the rock was as full of holes as a Swiss cheese. Alex heard it whispered that Cornishmen usually won such contests because they were experienced with the drill and sledgehammer.

"I'll bet on the dark-haired Cornishman. A dollar says he comes out the winner," cried out an old man. "He and the little Chinaman holding his drill look like winners to me. Heard it telled he's the best one for double-jacking around."

"The Irishman. He's the one for my money. He'll win it this time. He'll drill the deepest in the shortest amount of time."

"Saw a man's hand crushed once in one of these competitions." A man standing next to Alex grimaced at each blow of the sledge. "Ain't as easy as it appears, hitting that drill."

"No, I don't imagine it is," Alex replied. His eyes were drawn to a group of onlookers across from him. One of the men, a tall man with a cruel scar that ran from temple to chin was staring at him. It was a glaring appraisal that conveyed anger and resentment, though Alex was at a loss as to how he had inspired such a glower. He didn't even know the man, or did he? Some dim memory tugged at his brain, but before he could get a better look, the man had disappeared.

25

High aloft a tall wooden flagpole the Stars and Stripes fluttered in the breeze and the sight of it filled Alex with a sudden surge of fierce patriotism. So many had died to keep the Union together. Too many. Would the scars ever heal? The boom of fireworks sounded like exploding shells, and for a moment Alex was drawn back in time, hearing the sounds of battle again. . . .

"Column of Rebs headed right for us. We'll show the bastards!"

"Fire."

"Dear God, I'm hit. My arm. My arm."

"I'm gonna die. I'm gonna die."

"We're outnumbered, sir, what are we going to do?"

"Quite a few casualties, Major. Simpson. Walker. Marshall. Jones and God knows how many more. A bloodbath, sir." . . .

"Alex! Alex!" From behind him, Jeremiah West's hand on his shoulder brought Alex back to the present. "I assume you are enjoying yourself."

"Yes, I am."

"And I think you'll have to agree that our celebration more than rivals any of your eastern observances." His expression dared Alex to say differently.

"I don't think I've ever seen a more enthusiastic crowd, nor a longer parade."

"Nor a more beautiful queen of that parade, eh, Alex." He smiled triumphantly. "I want you to like your new home here."

"I like Central City very much." Alex wondered just how cordial Jeremiah was going to be when he learned of Alex's decision. Now was as good a time as any. Alex had already decided to move to a hotel the first thing tomorrow morning. Patrick Trenoweth was right. A man had to do what his good sense told him to do. To do otherwise made a man worse than a coward, it made him a fool.

"Why, after you and Caroline are married you can—"

"We need to discuss that matter, sir." It was noisy; the shouting, laughter and the pop of firecrackers made conversation impossible. "Let's find a quiet spot. There's something I must say." Without giving Jeremiah a chance for argument, Alex led the way to the livery stable and stepped inside. Ordinarily he would have told Caroline first, but knowing the influence her father held over her, he thought this might be the best way.

"I don't know what on earth we need to talk about. The arrangements are all made. Wedding's just two weeks away." Deep frown lines darkened Jeremiah's expression, as if he sensed what Alex intended to tell him. "Guests have been invited, Caroline's wedding dress is awaiting a fitting, even the territorial governor is planning to attend."

Alex knew exactly what he had to say. Still, it did not make the saying any easier. "I should have insisted on this talk much sooner. For that I ask your forgiveness, sir."

"Forgiveness?"

"Marriage is a most serious commitment. Your daughter and I rushed into this engagement without really knowing each other very well. We were swept away on a tide of physical attraction, an attraction that both of us were eager to consummate. Caroline being a lady and I, a gentleman, we of course kept our respectful distance from one another. We had so little time together before you were called back to the Colorado Territory." Alex groped for the proper words. "What I'm trying to say is that Caroline and I entered upon our engagement far too impetuously."

"Impetuously!" Jeremiah spat the word out with an annoyed grunt. "And now you think to leave her in the lurch, embarrass her before the entire populace of Central City. Is that it?"

"I don't want to see her hurt. You must believe me. But marrying the wrong man will eventually cause far more heartache than—" The crash of a falling lantern startled Alex. Someone else was in the stable. Whirling around, he saw a shadowy figure coming from behind a stall. The shadow held a gun. Instinctively he pulled Jeremiah to the hay-covered ground with him just as a shot rang out. The blow of the lead bullet slammed into the wall just where Jeremiah had been standing.

"Get up. Get up and face me like a man you devious money-grubbing bastard." A lantern overhead took the blast of the next bullet. Shattered glass fell on Alex and the banker like a shower of hail. "I said get up!"

"Who . . . who are you?" Jeremiah's question was a croaked whisper.

It was dark in the stable, with only one lantern left to shed any light, and Alex felt Jeremiah stiffen as the man stepped forward. "James Andrews. George Andrews's son. You remember *him,* don't you? Until you squeezed every dime he ever made out of him, he was pretty successful around here. Owned the dry goods store. Remember? Now he's dead."

"I didn't kill him. I didn't!" Jeremiah fumbled around in his vest pocket for the small derringer he always carried and took aim, but the shot he fired fell short of his target.

"One more move like that and I'll shoot you and your protector there without another thought. I will, you know it," Andrews barked. Despite the warning the voice sounded nervous. Squinting his eyes, Alex studied the man in the dim light. He was hardly more than a boy. "My father shot himself because you ruined him."

"I . . . I didn't ruin him." Knowing he'd fired his only bullet, Jeremiah clutched at Alex, using him as a shield. "I . . . I loaned him money. I . . . I was his friend. But a . . . a man's got to take care of himself. I only asked for what was rightfully mine."

"You tricked him. You know it and *I* know it. And now it's gonna get you killed." He motioned with his gun. "Get out of the way, mister. I have no quarrel with you. I'm warning you. Move."

"No!" Alex had to keep this boy from making the worst mistake of his life. "Killing isn't going to bring your father back. All it can do is ruin your own future. Think, son. Think!"

"I don't care. He cheated my father. He's a skunk that doesn't deserve to live! Now my mother and brothers have lost everything while he's gotten his grimy paws on all my pa worked so hard for."

"You can have it back. I don't want it. I don't need it. It's not worth my life. Please!" Getting to his knees, Jeremiah groveled.

"I can have it back? Your word isn't worth a nickel. As soon as you're safe, you'll change your mind. You don't care if my family starves to death. You deserve to be shot."

Standing up, Alex faced the boy. "If your father was cheated, son, there is a much better way to handle the matter than going to jail for murder. Your mother has had to deal with one tragedy, don't make her face another. She needs you. If what you say is true, if you can get witnesses, then it should be handled in a court of law not here in a stable." As a major, Alex had dealt with many young men in moments of crisis, talking them out of killing, suicide, desertion, or fear. He used that experience now to calm the angry boy. "I promise to do everything I can to help you."

"Promise? What's to say your word's any better than his?" He pointed the gun barrel at Jeremiah's trembling form.

"I'm asking you to trust me." Meeting the young man eye to eye, Alex made a silent promise. The moments passed slowly, agonizingly, but at last the matter was settled. Putting his pistol back in his holster, the young man looked at Alex once more, then left the stable.

"I should have aimed more carefully!" Rising from his position on the ground, Jeremiah brushed the straw and dirt from his coat angrily. "Give him back his property. That will be the day." He turned on Alex. "This is all *your* fault, you know.

Bringing me here to talk nonsense. Not marry my daughter indeed! You will, sir. You will or risk the consequences."

"I'll have to take that risk. I'll leave it up to you how you want the matter handled."

"Humph!" Jeremiah eyed Alex up and down, deciding that on this matter his bluff had been called. "We'll settle the matter at once. Let's go and find Caroline." There was not one word of thanks, not a single acknowledgment that Alex might very well have saved his life. Alex watched the man stalk away, then followed him, determined to keep his word to the young man who had trusted him. He'd have Robert look into the matter and be of what help he could.

They found Caroline surrounded by a ring of admirers: old men, married men, bachelors, and boys. Taking her by the hand, Alex drew her toward the carriage. "Caroline, we need to talk." His voice sounded so intense and serious that she looked at him in surprise.

"Are you jealous, darling? You shouldn't be. My heart belongs to you and you alone. But didn't I look wonderful up on that wagon? I took such special care to make certain I wore just the right dress. I was supposed to be Molly Pitcher. . . . Daddy, what on earth is wrong? You look as if you'd just seen a ghost. You're so pale."

Jeremiah exchanged a look with Alex that told him to keep silent. "Nothing to worry you, Caroline. Nothing that couldn't have been handled better if Alex was smart enough to carry a gun." He glared at Alex as if the matter in the stable had been his doing.

Wrinkling up her nose, Caroline looked from Alex to her father and back again. "Well, what ever happened, I must say you smell strangely of . . . of . . . manure." Taking out her handkerchief, she stifled a giggle.

Alex ignored her teasing remark and got right to the point. If he waited much longer, Caroline would be so filled with chatter that he would never get the words said. "Your father and I were talking at the stables. I'm going to take a room in the hotel tomorrow, Caroline. You and your father have been very gracious, but—"

"The hotel?" She looked completely bewildered. "But why?

Daddy and I enjoy having you at the house. Besides, it will be your home, too, once we are married."

"Caroline, we need some time away from each other. I know if we each think deeply on this matter of our marriage, we will see that we are making a serious mistake." He had said it as gracefully as he could.

"A mistake?" Her eyes nearly popped from her head. "How can you even suggest such a thing? A mistake!" She tugged at her father's arm. "Daddy, do something. Alex . . . Alex is trying to break our engagement but I won't have it! I won't. I won't. I'll . . . I'll look like an idiot. Like some plain-faced spinster who can't hold a man. Daddy!" Her voice was a wail.

"Just a bachelor's jitters, Caroline. I experienced them myself right before I married your mother. Merely a case of cold feet. Don't worry, sugar." Taking her by the arm, he pushed her up in the carriage. "I'll have it out with ol' Alex here." His voice was sinister. "Move to the hotel if you must. We'll discuss this matter again in a few days. I know you will come to realize the consequences and come to your senses. Bachelors always fear an end to their freedom, but you have more to lose than most. Think on that, Mr. Nicholson. And remember that I warned you."

26

Samantha sent a stone skimming over the pond, venting her frustration. Cy Tyburn's words had hurt. Why not admit it? All the more so because they were true. She wasn't soft and feminine, hadn't wanted to be, but the thought of how she must appear to Alex stung her. Did he pity her? Find her outrageously amusing? Think of her as a hellion? Was it because he felt sorry for her that he offered friendship? Like showing concern for a stray kitten?

Suddenly, Samantha saw herself through another's eyes. She supposed she was a bit of a "hoyden" as she knew she was called. Was that so very wrong? A woman living up in the mountains had to take care of herself and be self-sufficient. Was it wrong to be feisty? And yet if she was all bristle and vinegar, perhaps she'd never know what it was like to be loved.

No man is going to want you, Samantha Claybourne. No man, Cy had said. Sighing in dejection, she flung another pebble, counting the number of times it bounced on the water before it sank. She didn't care about any of the others, but she had to admit that she cared about Alex. Was that why he hadn't been to see her?

He's most likely getting ready for his wedding. Hadn't she heard in town that it was to be the middle of July? His wedding! With each day that passed, the date grew nearer. Though she'd mentally prepared herself, the thought still sent a wrench of pain tearing through her. Oh, Alex!

Hunkering down, resting her arms on her knees, she fought her feelings. Right from the first she'd known that Alex was spoken for. She didn't have any call to feel put out. Even so, the knowing didn't make the hurting any easier. She should have known better than to let him into her heart. Hadn't she had the sense of a chicken? Alex had offered friendship and nothing more.

"Ah, there you are, me beautay." Patrick Trenoweth's greeting made Samantha feel guilty. She should have been down in the mine working beside him, not feeling sorry for herself. "I wanted to know, since it be payday and all, if I could 'ave the rest of the day off to go into town."

Samantha bounded to her feet. "Of course you can, Patrick. Hell, you been doing the work of two men around here. It's the least I can do by way of thanks." Brushing off her breeches, she tried to smile. "I got an errand or two myself. I'll give you a lift into Black Hawk if you'd like. You can tie your horse on the back of my wagon. Beats sitting in the saddle. Besides, I'd like some company." Perhaps with Patrick along she could push all thoughts of Alex away.

It was a pleasant journey to Black Hawk. The sun was shining, the birds singing, and Patrick Trenoweth was interesting company. He had brought his wife and seven children to America for a better life, but as he talked, Samantha knew that the gold he'd expected to find at the end of the rainbow still eluded him. Times were hard for him and for his family. His wife took in washing, six of his seven children found what small jobs they could to help, and all of them lived in two small rooms at a boardinghouse. He had brought his widowed mother to Colorado when they'd moved west, but from what Patrick implied, her job as Jeremiah West's cook was far from lucrative. Still, Patrick was full of song and smiles. As the wagon plodded down the pathway he entertained Samantha with strains of "The Wreck of the Arethusa" and "Trafalgar's Boy." If he could sing with all his troubles, then so could she, she thought, putting all trepidation far from her mind. Though she sang a bit off-key, she added a song her grandfather had taught her to the melodious repertoire. By the time they had reached the town, Samantha was laughing.

"Thankee for the ride and the song. This cousin Jack, 'e is going to wet 'is whistle before going on 'is way." He pointed to the saloon they were approaching. "Care to join me?"

"Oh, no!" Samantha's grandfather had been firm in conveying to her the evils of whiskey. "Got some errands to do." Feeling a sudden spurt of affection for the Cornishman, she cautioned, "Be careful, now. Don't get into any fights."

Laughter was her answer, deep and booming, as he pointed to his face. "Got nothing much to lose, me beautay." He stuck out his chest proudly. "Sides, I be a boxer. I'm good with me fists." Playfully jabbing the air, he laughed again, then waved as she rode on down the road. "See ye tomorrow. And smile, everything will be fine."

Though her errand was at the smelters a sudden prick of vanity made Samantha waver as she passed the general store. Jumping from the wagon and tying it to a hitching post, she gave in to the temptation and walked inside. For once she would try to look like a woman, just to see what it felt like. Alex Nicholson wasn't the only man in the world. Why, she might even let one of the young miners court her. Just to see what it was like.

"Can I help you?" A small, plump woman wearing a plain white cotton apron over her calico dress greeted Samantha.

"Well . . ." Samantha suddenly felt like a fool. She knew nothing at all about women's fashions, not even where to begin. "I . . . I wanted to get myself a . . . a dress," she stammered.

"If you're lookin' for cloth, I got just the fabrics." With a chuckle she brought forth a bolt of cloth for Samantha's inspection, red-and-white-checked gingham. When Samantha shook her head, she brought forth another bolt, a green-and-white plaid. "Look real pretty with that hair of yours." At Samantha's frown she shrugged her shoulders. "Got some patterns in the back and some more bolts of cloth. I'll fix you up right pretty. Needles are on sale. Twelve for a penny."

"No! No, don't go." Samantha shook her head emphatically. "I don't know how to sew. Won't do you no good. I don't know one end of a needle from the other. I . . . I thought I could get it done for me."

"Ready-made? That will take a bit of time."

"Oh, but I wanted to get it today. I don't get down to town much and I—"

"You need a dressmaker, miss." A woman Samantha had not noticed before now swept up to the counter. She was elegantly dressed in a yellow gown with white pearl buttons. The two feather birds on her straw hat seemed about to take flight. The makeup she wore gave her a worldly look, but Samantha suspected she was not much older than herself.

"A dressmaker?"

"A dressmaker." Her amused smile was strangely comforting. It was a different kind of look than most of the other women in the town gave Samantha. "Come with me. Let me take you under my wing."

Samantha started to follow her, but the bespectacled woman tugged at her shirt. "Don't you know who she is?" she whispered behind her hand. "That's Honey Wells. She owns a . . . a *house*. If you don't watch your step, she'll make you one of her girls."

"I have no such intention. I just want to help her, that's all." Putting her hands on her hips, Honey Wells looked indignant. "Just want to help you find a dress," she said, turning to Samantha. "I've been looked down on myself. I know how it feels."

"A proper woman wouldn't be seen with the likes of her." Turning her nose toward the ceiling, the woman behind the counter patted her tightly combed brown hair haughtily but Samantha had already made up her mind.

"Well, then, guess I'm just not a 'proper' woman 'cause I'm sure as hell gonna be seen with her. Leastwise long enough to get me a dress." She smiled mischievously at the feather-bedecked woman. "Guess we better get started."

Before Samantha could say another word, Honey Wells was leading her gently down the boardwalk to a tiny shop that proclaimed dressmaking its specialty.

"Give her my dress, Annie. The one I had made for church going."

"Oh, I couldn't . . ." Ignoring her protestations, the women swept Samantha into a back room. Stripped to her long johns, Samantha was embarrassed to be fussed over. A long, flat piece of ribbon marked with numbers was put around her bosom, then her waist, and finally her hips. It was downright humiliating, Samantha thought. If she'd realized what she was in for, she might have put up more of a squabble.

"I knew it, Annie. I knew it. She's nearly my size," Honey exclaimed. As Annie went off to get the dress, the woman turned to Sam. "I'm Honey Wells," she said.

"Yes, I know. I'm Samantha Claybourne and I don't feel right about this." It was an argument Samantha lost. The blue dress with white polka dots was soon adorning her body. She examined herself warily in the mirror, and had to admit she was pleased with what she saw. The dress was full-skirted with tiny white buttons down the front, surprisingly circumspect considering who had ordered it. Perfect for Sam.

"A good color for her," the two women chorused.

"It will do just fine, if you don't need it. Are you sure?" Annie looked hesitantly at Honey Wells.

"It looks much better on Samantha. Too high-necked for me anyways." She winked. "You'll outshine any of those other women now. Do my heart good to know I helped you. Please take it."

Samantha withdrew her pouch, wondering if she was spending her gold dust foolishly. Still, the material was soft to her hands, so much nicer than flannel or denim. And she felt nearly pretty. She wondered what Alex would think.

"The dress is my gift. Put away the gold dust," Honey insisted. Leaving for just a moment, she came back with a ribbon of the same blue to tie in Samantha's hair. Circling Samantha three times, she gave her approval.

The transformation startled Samantha as she took one last look in the mirror. Taking a tentative step outside the door, she was amazed at the stares she inspired. She was the object of men's smiles and a tipped hat or two. What a difference a few yards of material made! Walking toward the wagon, she began to feel more sure of herself, greeting the doffed hats with a wave of her hand.

"Hello there, dolly. Want a ride?" Two young miners stopped their wagon, blocking her path and openly flirting with her. "You're much too pretty to be all alone."

"I'm . . . I'm not alone. I'm waiting for somebody." The way they were appraising her unnerved her. She was used to being snubbed or ignored on her infrequent trips to town. Now they were staring at her as if they had never seen a woman before.

"Waiting for someone? He must be a very lucky man." Slapping his horse with the reins, the driver followed along beside her on the boardwalk as she made her way to her wagon. "A husband? A father? Just who is this somebody?"

"Oh, leave her alone, Fred. She looks like a nice girl. Not the type for you. Come on, I need to get down to the post office." The men took their leave in a cloud of dust, but not before she'd been treated to their smiles. She hoped the second part of her journey would be as rewarding.

Samantha mumbled several swearwords beneath her breath. It was all well and good to wear a dress until it came time to take the reins. Her full petticoats and skirts wound around her legs as she pulled herself up on the wagon seat, displaying a shocking amount of shapely limb. Enough to elicit several wolf whistles from passersby. With a blush, she started up the wagon, determined to keep her mind on the business at hand.

Arriving at the smelters, Samantha clutched the receipt her grandfather had been given and sought out the owner, only to be given the disappointing news that he had gone back to Boston to visit his relatives for a while. Once again Samantha found herself dealing with the foreman. She hadn't liked him before and she didn't like him now. She liked him a lot less when he told her a blatant lie, that after burning the ore it had been found to have a lot less gold than they had first supposed.

"You've already been paid in full for the poor grade of ore you brought in here," he said, daring her to argue.

"There must be some mistake. I know a high content of gold in ore when I see it." A flash of intuition told her exactly what he was trying to do. Now that her grandfather was gone, knowing that few people would believe a woman was experienced in judging the gold content of quartz, he thought she'd be an easy target. "No, there is no mistake, is there? You dishonest badger. You're lying and trying to cheat me. Well, I won't have it! There are laws against doing what you're trying to do!"

"Then go get yourself a lawyer." The man grinned evilly, as if certain she never would. "With Professor Hill back in Boston, it's gonna be your word against mine."

"You lying, cheating skunk!" Samantha clutched her rifle but knew it would do her little good. She was the loser, at least for the moment. "When Professor Hill returns, I'll have him kick your backside right on out of here for this. You haven't seen the last of Samantha Claybourne. No, sir, not by a long shot." Clutching the reins she gave the man a hostile glare, then, cursing and fuming, sent the horses galloping along the road that would take her back to the mine. She most definitely did not enjoy being cheated. Such scoundrels gave the entire industry a bad name. She was glad when the cabin came in view, at least until she took a step inside.

"Drat and damnation! What on earth has happened here?" The lock was broken, the interior in shambles. Chairs were overturned, the sofa was on end, the beds were completely devastated of their coverings. The cellar door was open and Samantha knew without even looking what she would find. All her supplies were gone. It was empty. "I've been robbed!" Dazed, she shook her head, trying to think who would do such a thing. Some thief out on the prowl? Cy? He had threatened her. Her eyes hurriedly scanned the floorboards. She gasped to see the pried-up board. Dashing across the room, she threw herself down on her knees and peered into the darkness below. The coffee tin was gone. The gold dust, her only hope for the future, had been stolen.

27

Samantha sat watching the cookstove fire, listening to the crackling sound as the dry wood burned. She was licked, why not admit it? Whoever took the gold dust had taken all her dreams as well. Someone had carefully planned her defeat and had been disgustingly successful. She doubted the thief had been some poor miner down on his luck. Oh, no. Nor did she really think Cy Tyburn was the culprit. He was ornery, yes, but he had nothing to gain by stealing from her. Jeremiah West, then? She remembered the way his eyes had examined the room in cunning detail. She'd thought he was being condescending, but perhaps he had been planning. Jeremiah West. So he had won after all.

Burying her face in her hands, Samantha felt defeated for the very first time in her life. Even after her grandfather had died, a ray of hope had still nestled within her grief. It had carried her through the worst of her devastation and pain. Now all hope was gone. It would be a long time before the mine would produce any gold. There was still a great deal of digging to be done to get to the stope where her grandfather had proclaimed the mother lode to be. It would take time. She couldn't ask Wan Lau and Patrick Trenoweth to work and sweat for promises. Both men had large families to feed, they needed money perhaps even more than she. No, she would have to let them go. The only good thing about all this was that she had paid them their wages today. At least she wasn't letting them go with money owing.

And so I'm right back where I started, she thought. Alone. If there was any hard work to be done, she would have to do it. She would have to hunt for her food and live by her courage and wits. That would be possible during the summer, but what about the winter months to come? If she hadn't found gold by then, she'd be in serious trouble. Nor did she really think she could get the foreman at the smelting company to renege on his villainy and give her the gold that was due her. Jeremiah's fingers were probably in that scheme as well. A plot to force her to sell the mine or give it up and let someone else claim it.

"Never!" Jeremiah West was dead wrong if he thought she would break. "Damn him! Damn his highfalutin, greedy ways," she cried aloud. At least there were a few coffee grounds left. Adding water to the pot, she watched the coffee as it brewed.

"So all the gold I got is right here around my neck and way down deep in that mine." Reaching up, she touched the nugget sadly. Could she part with it? It was her most cherished possession, and yet what choice did she have? She had to survive.

I ought to confront that bespectacled old scoundrel, she thought in anger. *I ought to march right into that bank and tell him what I'm suspecting.* She wondered how smug he would be if she called the law in on him. There were strict penalties for stealing, and yet who would believe her? Who would go up against Jeremiah West? Who would take the word of a miner's granddaughter over the testimony of a respected banker? No one. In all probability no one would even care. She had thought Alex did, but Jeremiah West was soon going to be his father-in-law. Would he want to cross him?

And yet Alex had said he wanted to be her friend. He had dried her tears and told her that he cared. Would he really give half a damn if it came to a showdown with the West family?

Would he risk losing that pink cloud of fluff to take up for Samantha? She couldn't really ask that of him. She couldn't ask him to jeopardize his relationship with the woman he loved. It just wouldn't be fair. He had his job at the bank to keep him occupied and Caroline to warm him with her embraces. Samantha wouldn't spoil that for him.

Pouring herself a cup of coffee, she grimaced at the bitterness but drank deep, her gaze fastening on the blue-and-white polka-dot dress. Her only reward for a misspent day. A dress. A silly, foolish dress. If she'd stayed at the cabin, she wouldn't be in this fix. Or would Jeremiah West have accomplished his goals at another time? She would never know.

Tugging at the nugget around her neck, she fidgeted as she tried to think what she could do. There was nothing much that could be sold. She needed the horses and the mules to do the work. There were just enough chickens for eggs and an occasional stew. She needed the goat for milk. With no supplies she couldn't even think of selling the chickens or the goat. Or the wagon. Oh, if only she had something of value to sell. But she did not. Her fierce pride would not allow her to ask for a handout.

"When all is said and done, Sam," her grandfather had told her, "the only one you can count on is yourself. A body should be strong so as not to have to ask from others."

But could she make it without help? Sloshing the coffee round and round in the cup, she watched a bit of coffee grounds bob up and down. It reminded her of the way she felt, trying to escape being drowned. "Oh, Alex!" Even he had told her she should sell the mine, and yet when he'd realized how important it was to her he'd said something else as well.

"I'll help in any way I can. If the mine is so important to you then, by God, I'll do everything possible to see that you keep it," he had promised. She had the impression that he'd meant every word he'd said.

"I won't ask him for money that I can't repay," she swore. She couldn't ask for charity. But she could ask him for a loan, one she was certain she could repay when the mine yielded its plenty. A loan. Alex was a banker, he might be able to arrange it. Wouldn't that serve Jeremiah West right? The last laugh would be on him.

She would do it. She would get all gussied up in her new blue dress and go to town. The bitter taste of gall and the sweet taste of success mingled on her tongue as she vowed to do just that. She had her gold nugget to use for collateral and her hardscrabble determination to insure she'd succeed.

28

The walls buzzed with whispered rumors. The voices filtered through the thin walls of Alex's office as he sat at his desk. It was his last day at the bank. The strained relationship between Jeremiah West and himself made it imperative that he leave. He would not be blackmailed into marrying Caroline. Though he'd tried to be as considerate and courteous in breaking the engagement as he possibly could, he would not let anyone change his mind. A skilled puppet master, Jeremiah West ran everyone around him, but no one was going to make a marionette out of Alex.

"Psst! Can I come in?" Robert Cunningham poked his head through the door. His usually smiling face was grim.

"Of course. You're always welcome, Robert. You know that."

"Is the old man around?" Closing the door behind him, Robert looked uneasy.

"He's in one of his meetings. Why? What's on your mind?" It wasn't like Robert to be so wary.

"I came to warn you. J.W. has been maligning you to everyone, Alex. You won't be able to get another job anywhere in the town, not in Black Hawk or Nevadaville either, for that matter. I wanted you to know so that it wouldn't surprise you."

"What?" Alex rose angrily to his feet. "If he thinks I'm going to stand for such a thing, he's damned wrong." In truth Alex did not really need a job, he had a small invested fortune of his own, but it was the principle that infuriated him.

"There's nothing you can do. When J.W. goes into action, he's merciless. I was merely thinking that you might want to get out of town. Go back to Boston, Alex. In truth you *are* out of place here. Not that I think ill of you. I don't. You're a very pleasant fellow. . . ."

"But? Come on, Robert tell me what's really going on." Reaching in the drawer of his desk Alex drew forth a cigar. He'd bought them specially for Robert's visits. To his surprise Robert declined. "Tell me . . ."

"It's being said that you're a coward. That you won't even carry a gun." Shrugging his shoulders, Robert flashed a sheepish grin. "Course, now *I* know that you broke up with Caroline, but it's being said that she left you. She's telling everyone that her father asked you to leave the house. She says you refused to defend yourself even when some members of Cy Tyburn's gang tried to rough you up. That her father won't let her think of aligning herself with such a 'milksop.' "

"I won't carry a gun. But I'm not a coward."

"Then prove it. Make J.W. out to be the liar that he is. If you don't, you'll be the target for every miscreant and bully in town." Reaching into a hidden flap of his jacket he pulled forth a small, short-barreled pocket pistol, the kind gamblers often used. "Here, take this. I've got another. I'll even show you how to shoot it if you don't already know."

Alex looking disparagingly at the pistol. "Thank you, Robert, but I hardly think that carrying this . . . toy . . . will prove that I am brave. Nor do I really care what's being whispered about. I'm not responsible for what others think." So, he thought, that was to be the story. He'd saved the man's life, but Jeremiah hadn't bothered to mention that.

"You can be as peaceful as you like, but just prove to the town that—"

"By carrying a pistol? By getting myself into a gunfight?" Alex shook his head, remembering the vow he had taken long ago, when he had looked into a pair of eyes glazed with terror and then seen them cloud over with death. "Robert, some things a man has to prove to himself and no one else. I thank you for your concern and I hope that I can count on you as my friend, but I won't be prodded into doing something I feel is wrong."

The two men stood looking at each other, tense emotions playing over their faces. At last Robert held out his hand. "No matter what happens you can count on me. I'll even face the old miser himself if need be. If you don't want to be armed, it's your decision. You must have your reasons. I'll not question them." He playfully jabbed Alex in the ribs. "I'm sorry you were kicked out of paradise, but I have a feeling you'll survive."

It was this congenial scene Samantha encountered as she pushed her way through the door. For just a moment she was tempted to turn and walk away, but having seen the bright blue of her skirt from the corner of his eye, Robert moved in a flash to greet her, blocking her escape.

"Well, well, well, what do we have here? A pretty flower to be sure." His approving eyes moved from the top of her head to the hem of her gown. She was hardly fashionable but appealing enough to make him smile. "By my word, I do believe it is Samantha Claybourne." Without waiting for her reply, he introduced himself. "My name is Robert Cunningham. I'm a lawyer. Alex and I are old friends."

Astonishment held Alex speechless as his gaze took in the slim, pertly curved young woman who stared back at him. Her strawberry blond hair was combed back from her face and held in a thick cascade of waves by a ribbon. She was dressed in a full-skirted blue dress dancing with white polka dots, a sash tied around her small waist. One lone petticoat gave the skirt just a hint of fullness, emphasizing Samantha's natural allure. She was a most entrancing sight and for a moment he wondered if this was indeed Samantha. The toes of her boots, peeking from beneath the hem of her skirt gave him no further reason to doubt.

"Samantha?" He smiled.

She felt suddenly foolish, ill at ease in her new attire. The way the two men gaped at her made her fear she had done something wrong. Why, one would nearly think she'd put the dress on backward the way they were gawking. "You're busy. I'll come back some other time." She wanted to flee, seek the haven of her wagon, but Alex stood in her way.

"I'm never too busy to see you. Don't leave." Seeing her brush at the skirt of her dress nervously, Alex said, "Don't be shy, Samantha. You look lovely."

"Do I? Do I really, Alex?" Her coppery brown eyes were wide, gazing up at him searchingly beneath her perfectly arched brows. Samantha lifted her chin with a proud air, suddenly uncomfortable at his prolonged appraisal.

"You are as breathtakingly beautiful as a newly blossoming rose." Before Alex could answer, Robert had reached for her hand and was kissing the palm with a familiarity that made Alex bristle. She was no match for an avowed "ladies' man." Anxious to draw her away, he pulled out a chair, motioning her to sit down.

"I've been meaning to visit you, Samantha, but so much has been happening that—"

"I understand. With your wedding and all." She licked her lips, determined not to show how much the thought upset her. "I wish you every happiness, Alex."

"There's not going to be any wedding."

Samantha's brows shot up in surprise. "There's not?" She tried to hide the cheerfulness from her voice, but it was all too obvious. "I'm sorry," she added hastily. "I wanted you to be happy, Alex." Myriad emotions coursed through her. Alex was not going to tie himself to that haughty, icy beauty. Alex would be free! Her heart pounded so crazily that she put her hand to her breast in an attempt to quiet it. Her head whirled with happiness, her fingers trembled as she clenched her hands together.

"I intend to be happy, Samantha." Though his voice was low, the anger he felt at the thought of Caroline and her father made his tone harsh. He wanted to tell Samantha the circumstances leading up to his decision, but decided against it. First, he would put his engagement to Caroline West far behind him.

Samantha felt very uncomfortable with Robert, a stranger, in the room. She wished he would leave, but when he made no move to go, she came right to the point. "Someone broke into my cabin, Alex. Stole my supplies. Stole the tin where I hid the gold dust. I don't want to let Patrick or Wan Lau go, but now I have no choice. I can do the work myself if I have to. You know I can."

"Someone broke into the cabin? Do you know who?" Alex thought immediately of Cy Tyburn and Buck Cameron.

"It's not important." She wouldn't make accusations now. "But . . . well . . ." It was harder to get the words out than she had realized.

"You need some money. Of course." Without even blinking an eye Alex reached in his pocket and drew forth a roll of bills. "How much do you need, Samantha?"

Her face flushed with embarrassment. Pride made her tilt her nose haughtily in the air. "I won't take charity, Alex. Didn't come here for that." Unclasping the chain that held the nugget, she removed it from her neck and held it forward. "I'll give you this for . . . for collateral. There isn't anything on this earth I treasure more. Gramps gave it to me."

"You're asking for a loan?"

She nodded. "You're a banker. You can arrange it. Hell, I'll be able to pay you back in a month." Her voice lowered to a whisper so that Robert could not overhear. "I told you there is gold."

Alex shook his head. "I can't give you a loan, Samantha. I'm no longer working at the bank. I've quit, you see."

"Quit?" The sudden fear that he would leave and go back to Boston now that his engagement had been broken nearly strangled her. Life just wouldn't be the same without knowing Alex was nearby.

"I can't give you bank funds, but I would be very happy to give you some of my own money." He thrust several bills into her hands. "Please, take it."

"No!" She was fiercely stubborn. "I won't be beholden, not even to you. But I thank you just the same, Alex." She couldn't take his money. Why, he'd just told her plain as day that he was out of a job. He might need it himself before the month was out, she reasoned.

He was touched by her fierce determination. Her courage and perseverance were qualities he thought should be rewarded. "*I'll* give you a loan. My money is just as good as this bank's." He pushed the nugget back into her hand. "I don't need collateral. I have the utmost faith that you are a woman true to her word."

Samantha stared up into his blue eyes and sought a quick solution. How could she keep him here and at the same time save the mine? An idea suddenly occurred to her. If Alex held a share of the mine, if he were a partner, it would give him a reason to stay in Central City. It would give them a reason to be together. It would also be a way of rewarding his kindness and faith in her. She would never forget that he'd been willing to hand her a wad of money. What better test of friendship could there be? Now she would return the favor. Whether he knew it or not, Alex Nicholson would be a rich man one of these days. Then he wouldn't have to worry about a job.

"Perhaps I don't need a loan, Alex." She fumbled with the nugget as she clasped the chain around her neck. "But I do need a partner." She nodded in Robert's direction. "You said you were a lawyer. I want you to draw up the agreement, then."

"Samantha, I couldn't . . ." He didn't want to claim a share of the mine that she and her grandfather had worked so hard to make prosper. It wouldn't be right. And yet he wondered if it wasn't the best way to help her after all. Prideful woman that she was, it might very well be the only way he could help her keep the mine. When it began bringing in money, he would gracefully pull out and leave the entire mine in her keeping.

"I insist, Alex. You understand how important it is to me. I can't think of any other man I'd rather take as a partner. I'll give you a third share, so's I'll still have controlling interest."

"A fourth. I want to be fair."

"A fourth?" She cocked a brow, then smiled. "It's a deal." Shaking his hand in a vigorous fashion, she did little to control her enthusiasm. "Now we'll be partners, Alex. And you can start right now by coming on up with me to take a look at what you just acquired. My wagon is parked right out in front." It was an invitation Alex knew he could not refuse. Besides, he needed to get away from the claustrophobic atmosphere of the city, needed a ride in the fresh mountain air. But more than that, he wanted to be with Samantha.

29

It was a pleasant ride up the mountain road, climbing the long, curving hill out of Central City. Samantha kept Alex entertained talking about a hundred things. The road, the mountains, the mine, how beautiful it was in spring. Her exuberance charmed him. Made him forget his turbulent emotions. She had a passionate soul, a zeal for living, as if she wanted to experience all the wonder of God's beautiful world.

"Gramps always used to say that the song the wind whistled, the colors of the rainbow, the birds, the sun, the sky, were the real treasures of the heart. More important than gold. No matter how hard he worked he tried to take time to appreciate them." Samantha sat proud and tall on the high wagon seat, her face framed by wisps of hair that the wind had whipped free. Alex's eyes caressed her, realizing what a rare, sweet, unspoiled young woman she was. There was only one Samantha, he thought with a smile. And if he didn't watch himself, he could fall deeply in love with her. Perhaps he already had without even knowing it. Surely her innocent beauty seduced him, attracted him as no other woman's practiced wiles had. The wind swirled about her as they rode the bumpy roadway, molding her dress against the gentle curve of her breasts, the slender length of her thighs. She was appreciating nature, but as the wagon bumped along the pathway he was taking special delight in looking at her.

"Black Hawk and Central City were rivals from the start," she was saying. "Black Hawk laid out the first cemetery in the state on Dory Hill. My grandmother's buried there. She died long before I came to live with Gramps. She was from Kentucky. Smoked a corncob pipe. I wish I'd known her. From what Gramps said she was a mighty unusual woman." Samantha suddenly realized how little she knew about Alex, aside from his being from Boston. "But you've never told me about your family, Alex."

"I have a younger brother named Michael who is as fair-haired as I am dark. He's a bit of a bookworm. Studious to a fault. Though he wanted to be a doctor, my father insisted he run the family business. I think he was a bit envious that I had the fortitude to leave my father's ships behind."

"Your father and mother, what are they like? I can't even remember my own. I was so young when they died."

"My mother is warm and loving. Her hair is peppered now, but there was a time when she was said to be the most beautiful woman in Boston. Tall and graceful and very, very gentle. My father is balding, scowling, and determinedly set in his ways. We argued very frequently, but in a way I miss his well-intentioned bickering."

"Are you homesick, Alex?" Samantha's gaze drifted to him, watching as he squinted his eyes against the bright afternoon sun. She hoped that he wasn't, wishing that somehow she could keep him near her for as long as possible.

"No. I'm very content being here. You know, Samantha, you're very good company for a cynical old man like me." Though he laughed, there was a certain tone in his voice that revealed some painful memory.

"You're not old, Alex. I'd say you weren't more than five years older than me." His dark hair was tousled by the breeze and she watched as he pushed it back from his lean, handsome face.

"I'm twenty-nine. Not old in years, perhaps, but in the things I have done and seen. The war aged me, Samantha. I was nineteen when it began and like all brash young men I wanted to be a hero. I thought I would make a man of myself killing Johnny Rebs. I didn't know how wrong I was. It's a time in my life I both want to remember and forget. I—" As they reached a curve in the road Alex saw to his horror that a roadblock of jagged rocks and stones loomed in their path. "Samantha, look out!" Realizing that the sun was in her eyes, he jerked the reins from her hands and frantically pulled the horses to a stop. "A rockslide!" His hands trembled as he peered over the steep incline of the mountain. They were just inches from a collision that in all probability would have sent them hurtling over the edge.

They were a tangle of arms and legs from the jolt. Alex was suddenly all too aware of Samantha's firm young breasts crushed up against his chest, her hip pressed intimately into his groin. He was achingly aware of the warmth emanating from the soft female body so close to his own. So much so that he hurriedly pulled away before he was carried away by the moment. Still, as he watched her climb down from the wagon he found himself regretting his self-control.

Samantha's heart pounded wildly. She had been giddily aware of Alex's nearness, aware of the pleasurable tingle in the pit of her stomach at once more being in his arms. Danger seemed to enhance the senses. Were passion and peril similarly stimulating? It was all she could do to maneuver her legs toward the rock pile. When she did, she was furious at what she found.

"That was no rockslide, Alex."

"No accident?" Alex eyed her quizzically.

She pointed to the upslope of the mountain. "The rocks up above are gray. These are red. They were hauled in here and dumped in the middle of the road."

"Samantha, are you certain?" It was a startling accusation.

"As positive as I can be. Just as I'm sure that my cabin was robbed, that when I went into Black Hawk the payment that

was owing me was wrongly withheld, and that someone is trying to make it so difficult for me that I will sell them the mine."
She put her hands on her hips as she stood looking upward. "If
you need further proof, just look up there. If there had been a
slide, the shrubbery would be disturbed. As you can see, it
ain't."

"But who would do this?" He slid from the wagon and came
to her side, following the line of her gaze.

"Someone who wants to make it difficult, nigh onto impossible for me. Someone who thinks all women are creampuffs who
run at the first sign of a squabble. Some dad-blamed jackass
who thinks he can frighten and discourage me." She wondered
if she dare tell him. "Someone who had better watch his step."

"Who, Samantha? Cy Tyburn? If this is because you came to
my aid, then I'm sorry."

"It wasn't Cy. He's ornery, sneaky, and a cad at times but he
wouldn't have much reason to sabotage this road. He and I
have had our quarrels but I don't reckon he would do this.
Besides, he'd only be hurting himself since he uses this road
nearly as much as me."

"Then who?"

"Doesn't matter, Alex. What's been done is done. We'll just
have to clear it away."

That was not such an easy matter. Some of the rocks were
huge boulders that could not be lifted. Whoever had put the
rocks across the roadway intended that they stay. Samantha
pushed and pulled at two smaller stones, letting them roll down
the hill, but knew the sting of frustration as she labored at the
larger ones. She couldn't budge them.

"Let me help, Samantha." He moved forward, but she shook
her head.

"And ruin your suit?" He thought he saw just a hint of a
smile. "You'll split the seat of your pants, Alex and all for
nothing. Ain't a man alive that can move that hill of rocks."
She knew it must have taken several men to bring them here.
Men and machinery.

"Not a man, perhaps, but the horses can." Without waiting
for her reply he began to unhitch the horses. "During the war

we often had to remove debris from the railroad tracks. Horses were very effective."

"Were you in the cavalry or infantry?"

"I was a major in the Union infantry. As I said, it was a time I've chosen to forget." Taking off his coat, he handed it to her. "Hold this for me. And this." His brown-and-white-striped vest followed. "We'll have those rocks out of the road in no time." He winked at her as he rolled up his shirt sleeves. Without his jacket and vest there was a bold, tenacious strength about him. It was as if, for a moment, she had glimpsed a man of ages past. A pirate, some noble knight, or perhaps a pagan warrior.

Samantha would have been happy just to stand and watch him, but her conscience demanded that she pitch in and help. Working elbow to elbow, they carefully tied the thick leather reins around each boulder and led the horses as they dragged their burdens to the edge of the road. There they loosed the reins and gave the huge rocks the one last push that would send them careening harmlessly down the mountainside.

Samantha felt his eyes on her, his gaze intent as they labored. She judged that a subtle change had taken place in their relationship. She knew it even if Alex did not. For the first time she felt that he was not as far out of reach as she had first supposed, that there was a chance for her dreams to come true.

30

Once again the wagon rolled along the road and though both Alex and Samantha were tired, they were for the moment relaxed and contented. Alex breathed deeply and paused to listen to the chirp of the birds, the whir of the mountain wind, which gusted with an increasing fury as they climbed the hill.

"Samantha, you said that you had a suspicion as to who was responsible for that roadblock. Who was it? Now that we are partners I have to know who is trying to thwart your work at the mine. Your enemies are my enemies too."

She sighed, hating to mention the name, not wanting to raise the question of his broken engagement to Caroline. But Alex had a right to know. "Jeremiah West," she said. "He offered me money for the mine again, made quite a point of telling me that I'd never succeed without Gramps. My refusal made him about as mad as a wounded cougar. He left my cabin stomping and glowering."

"But are you certain he'd actually be a party to theft and sabatoge? I know he's stubborn and overbearing, but is he devious and cruel?" In spite of his own feelings about the man, Alex was reluctant to believe the very worst of him without proof.

"He is the meanest and most spiteful man I've ever known." Samantha spouted for-instances, a lengthy list of victims of Jeremiah West's quest for power. Most of the property that West now owned had once belonged to someone else. West had maneuvered until he managed to wrest the land grants away.

"Zebadiah Grover's mine was stolen right out from under his nose. Roadblocks, stolen ore, one catastrophe after another—the very same tactics he's using with me. But that's not the half of it. He hires others to do his dirty work for him. He sends men down into mines that are downright perilous. He pays wages that couldn't keep a flea alive. Ask Patrick Trenoweth, he'll tell you. Jeremiah West is so tight that he squeaks! He might wear fancy suits, smoke expensive cigars, and go about with a highfalutin air, but he's a crook all the same."

"I see." Alex was resolved to do some investigating into the matter. It was more than possible that Jeremiah's reluctance to involve Alex in certain bank matters might have been a move to keep his misdeeds from being found out. If so, was Robert part of his schemes? Alex was determined to find out.

Looking up at the sky, he watched the gathering clouds and urged Samantha to speed up the horses. "Looks like there's going to be a storm." During the war he'd become an expert at predicting weather. A raging tempest could seriously alter battle plans. One battle had been fought knee-deep in mud; even after all these years, the memory still stirred bleak flashes and grim nightmares.

"A storm? Hell, it's been as dry as a desert well all spring, dry enough to cause alarm hereabouts." Samantha appraised the sky. Dark thunder clouds were mixing with the white, fluffy mists. A flock of birds skimmed wildly across the sky. "You're right, Alex. We better get this rig to the mine in a hurry before we find ourselves in an unpleasant fix." Flicking the reins, she urged the horses into a brisk gallop. The wagon swayed precariously as it turned each bend in the road and Alex clutched at the seat to keep from being hurled out. Though the horses moved at a furious pace, it was soon obvious they were not going to outrun the storm. Thunder rang out with a resounding boom, followed by flashes of lightning.

"It's gonna pour some water on us for sure," Samantha shouted, her voice almost drowned out by another clap of thunder. She gave Alex a tense smile. "Course, now, I don't suppose we can blame Jeremiah for this, leastwise unless it's because we had to take so long pushing those rocks from the road."

Within seconds the clouds burst; rain pelted them mercilessly as the skies raged. Within minutes they were both soaking wet, drenched from head to toe. It was almost impossible to see and once again Alex had the opportunity to admire Samantha as she managed the muddy road with astounding expertise. No Union soldier could have done it better.

"Only a few more turns and we'll be there," she promised.

How lovely she looked with her strawberry hair in wild disarray, Alex thought. Her bodice tightened across her firm young breasts as she raised a hand to push back a stray wave, revealing the peaks beneath the wet material. It was difficult for him to draw his gaze away from the tantalizing view. She looked like a mermaid sitting there, a beautiful untamed mythical creature, and at that moment even the drenching rain could not put out the spark that kindled his desire.

"Samantha . . ." Until that moment he hadn't fully realized the feelings she inspired. Friendship, yes, but also something far more passionate. And yet he felt responsible for her. He had set out to be her protector. How ironic it would be if the one he needed to guard her from was himself. Gentleman though he prided himself in being, he was also a man.

The cabin was a welcome sight, promising shelter and warmth, yet Alex eyed it with anxiety as well. It presented him with a temptation that he was going to have to ignore. As soon as the rain let up he was determined to return to town.

"Come on, Alex," Hugging her arms around her shivering body, Samantha dashed for the cabin. "I'll start a fire." Fumbling in her pocket for the key, she soon had the door open and headed for the tiny alcove she called a kitchen. Alex's eyes followed the gentle sway of her hips as she moved. It seemed impossible to turn his eyes away. She moved with a surprisingly sensuous grace for one who'd been raised as a tomboy.

Alex's stride was long yet hesitant as he followed her. Strange how he had always felt so comfortable with Samantha before. Now he felt as nervous and tongue-tied as some fledgling schoolboy who had never been with a woman. Scoffing at himself, he entered the cabin and closed the door. The scent of fresh-cut wood assailed him.

"Good thing I cut half a cord of wood this morning before I came to town. Now we'll be comfortable and cozy." Throwing a couple of logs into the stove, she soon had a fire blazing. Searching about for a long length of rope, she strung it from wall to wall in front of the stove. "Best take off those wet clothes, Alex. You'll catch your death of chill."

She was right, of course, but the idea of stripping in her presence made him hesitate. "I can step outside while you change, to give you privacy if you'd like."

"Out in the rain?" Her wide brown eyes widened in amazement. "Why on earth would you want to do that? You just turn your back and I'll turn mine. Guess if I can't trust you not to look, I can't trust anybody." She walked across the small room and dug through a box underneath one of the beds. "Here, put these on. They belonged to Gramps and I know they won't fit you, but they will keep you covered while your own clothes dry." Samantha pushed a green flannel shirt and a pair of tan canvas pants into his hands, then picked up a shirt and pair of trousers for herself.

"Whew! That was a Colorado rainstorm all right. Still wailing around outside. Just listen, Alex. Came up so fast, it stunned me. Course, it's like that around here. Weather's always changing. Why, we've been known to have snow as late as May or sunshine in the dead of winter. Always a big surprise." It was such a joy to have Alex with her in the cabin. This was the way it should always be, she thought. She'd never be lonely if only he belonged to her. As much as she hated cooking, she'd even do that gladly if Alex sat across the table. She wanted to please him, wanted him to feel as comfortable as she did right now, as snug and happy as a caterpillar in its cocoon.

"The storm won't last long. Just a heavy cloudburst is what it appeared to be." Turning his back, Alex stripped off his sodden coat and vest and unbuttoned his shirt trying to keep himself from thinking of Samantha unbuttoning each one of those little white buttons at the front of her dress. He wondered if the skin on her shoulders was as flawless and golden as he imagined it. Would her breasts be as soft to his stroking fingers as he supposed? Though he closed his eyes, he couldn't help being aware of how very close she was. Not more than two feet away. The sensation of her nearness taunted him, teased him.

Samantha breathed quietly and listened, heard each piece of Alex's wet clothing fall to the wooden floor. She felt an unfamiliar tremor flood through her, experienced a yearning she had never felt before, but for what, she did not know. She wanted to feel his arms around her, wanted to taste his lips again. It was a longing that made her tremble as she pushed the sopping-wet dress over her hips and watched it fall to a heap at her feet. She wanted him to want her but didn't know the words to say to let him know what was in her heart.

"Alex . . ." The petticoat followed the dress.

"Yes, Samantha." His voice was low and husky, sending more shivers up her spine.

"I . . . I . . ." It was no use. She was suddenly tongue-tied and shy. Hurrying into her shirt, pulling off her wet boots and socks, she stood barefoot on the cold wooden floor, afraid to move. Then she slowly pulled on her trousers.

"I'm fully dressed if that's what you're wondering. Though your grandfather's breeches are a bit too large and too short, they'll keep me dry and warm for the moment."

Samantha whirled around, appraising him with a smile. The pants came well above his ankles and bagged about his narrow waist and hips. The shirt, however, was a closer fit. Her grandfather had had wide shoulders and muscular arms and so did Alex, though the sleeves gave proof that Alex's arms were much longer. "You look like a miner now." With a burst of exuberance she grasped his hand. "I'm so glad you're my partner, Alex."

"I'm glad, too, Samantha." He slowly turned around and was as enchanted by her boyish attire as he had been by the blue-and-white polka-dot dress. Her womanly form was sharply outlined, reminding him of how she had looked in earlier that day —lovely, soft, and glowing. She beckoned his arms with a sweet and smiling allure. She was just ripe for love were he a scoundrel. He wanted Samantha Claybourne and he was only too aware of that fact. He knew also that he could win her all too easily. The look on her face clearly said so. He could so easily seduce her, claim her at this very moment. One look at her trusting brown eyes told him that he would not. The gentleman in him would not let him take advantage of her innocence no matter how deeply he was drawn to her. Samantha deserved far better than that. Wisdom dictated that he leave as soon as he could. Alex was certain that the rain would stop very soon.

Another crack of thunder put the lie to that thought. Rain drummed madly against the roof as the storm unleashed its full fury. Hours passed, but the rain showed no signs of letting up. Nor was leaving possible. Water and mud had made a quagmire of the road. It was impassable. Whether he liked it or not, Alex realized, he would have to spend the night in Samantha's cabin.

31

The fire in the large black stove flickered and sparked. It radiated warmth to the cramped interior of the cabin and shed heat on the garments hung haphazardly across the rope in front of the firebox. Samantha and Alex had enjoyed a hastily prepared supper of roast chicken garnished with wild onions, boiled dandelion greens, and sweet wild raspberries floating in goat's-milk cream.

"I have to hand it to you, Samantha. You never cease to amaze me. Even though your supplies were taken you still managed to feed us a delicious meal." Sitting in front of the fire, his bare feet propped up on the three-legged chair, Alex had to admit he was enjoying himself. Aside from being pretty, Samantha was delightful company. It soothed him to talk of something besides banking, teas, or who was doing what to whom.

"I hated to have to kill old Henny but there was nothing else I could do. With the rain and all I didn't have much time to go hunting. She really wasn't laying anyway, but still . . ." Finishing up the last of the dishes, she wiped her hands.

"Old Henny tasted very good."

"Gramps taught me a long time ago which roots, plants and berries are safe to eat. When I saw that the cellar was stripped completely bare I went out and collected a few things. Just in case I couldn't get a loan. Why, the hills are full of delicacies, Alex, if you only know where to look. Wild carrots, parsnips, and berries of every color and size. Wild asparagus grows along the creek beds. Course, you have to know just which ones are good for eatin'."

"Very few people know that, Samantha. It seems we've gotten away from nature in our quest to be civilized." Putting his hands behind his head, he leaned back in his chair. He'd heard it bandied about town that Enoch Claybourne had not done right by his granddaughter, that he had sadly neglected her education, but it was clear to Alex that the old man had taught her the important things. Samantha was a survivor. She had taught him that tonight. It was a quality he deeply admired in her. "If more soldiers had known what you know, Samantha, more of them might be alive right now."

"Gramps told me he'd heard how the Rebs went barefoot and hungry in the last years of the war. It must have been a sorry sight. Was it, Alex?"

"It was a sight I'll never forget. Dear God, the poor desperate fools fighting on until the end, plodding through the snow with rags wrapped around their feet for want of boots. Thin, pathetic scarecrows fighting for a cause that was already lost. Yet they were brave and valiant right until the end." Closing his eyes, he shuddered at the memory. "Don't ever let anyone tell you war is glorious, Samantha. It is far from that. It's pain and blood and gut-wrenching guilt no matter how much a hero they tell you you'll be." Rising from his chair, he paced the floor in agitation. "I would give everything I possess to undo what was done. Everything, Samantha."

His face wore such an agonized expression that her heart went out to him. Something terrible had happened to Alex during those years, she sensed it. Her grandfather had often told her that it helped a wound to cleanse it, wasn't that also true of the soul? Alex seemed to want to forget, to suffer his anguish alone. Wouldn't it be better for him to talk about it, to share his sorrow with somebody else? To purge the poisoned memories that ate away at him.

"Tell me what happened, Alex. Please." As he passed by she reached for his arm and touched it. "You told me you cared when I was just about ready to give up. You helped me when I needed a friend so desperately. Please let me help you now."

"It's something I've never talked about before, not even to my family." He gave a sad, derisive laugh. "How could I, when they were so busy welcoming me home as a hero? As the man who had led his men to victory? How could I tell them about how it felt to hold a thirteen-year-old boy in my arms while he died? Hearing the cries of his tortured agony as he sobbed with fright. A boy, Samantha. Hardly out of knee pants. A child and *I* killed him." He was consumed by the memory as if it were happening all over again. He could nearly smell the stench of battle on that cold winter's night.

"It was war, Alex. You didn't do it on purpose."

"But I did kill him." Closing his eyes, he told of hearing the rebel yell, of finding himself face-to-face with the enemy. The air had rippled with gunfire and shuddered with the roar of cannons. His men were fatigued by the march through land little better than a swamp. "They were angry, defiant, as dangerous as wounded animals. When the Confederates swooped down with that hair-raising, soul-shattering yell of theirs . . . I shot two men to protect my comrades, wounded them, then I turned and faced a third who came at me with his rifle raised. He was saying something to me but I couldn't hear him. The yelling was too loud. A gun behind me discharged, wounding me in the side, and it was then I fired. I thought the soldier in front of me had shot and so I pulled the trigger." He grimaced as he passed his hand in front of his eyes. "But he could not have fired that shot. He didn't even have ammunition. Did you hear me, Samantha? His gun wasn't even loaded."

"But you couldn't have known that, Alex. You were only protecting yourself. Hell, anyone would do that."

"He told me as he lay dying that he was trying to surrender. That's what he had been saying all the while. He was a farmboy, just a scared child. What did he know about fighting and war? He should have been home with his tin soldiers!"

Tensing every muscle in his face, Alex fought for control. "I took a vow at that moment. One I have kept."

"Not to carry a gun. Oh, Alex!" She wanted to comfort him, wrap her arms around him and never let him go. "If only I could say something . . . could . . ." Her eyes spoke more of the depth of her concern and affection than any words could convey. Looking into her eyes was like a soothing balm, a healing potion. Though Alex could not forget, some of the hurt of that memory was gone.

Slowly his hands closed around her shoulders, pulling her to him. His heart pounded violently as he stood stone-still, looking at her.

"Sweet Samantha. Proud, beautiful angel." Never had he wanted anything quite so much as he wanted to reach out to that love now. To stroke and caress her. He wanted to touch her hair, to let it slide ever so slowly through his fingers. He remembered how soft her hair was. Like silken threads. Everything about her was softness, tempered with the strength of her determination.

"Alex . . . ?"

He studied her face, the wide eyes that so fascinated him. It was said that the measure of a man was the look he held in his eyes, and Alex knew for a certainty that it was the same for a woman. The eyes were the mirror of Samantha's soul, a window through which he could read deep into her heart. And now she inspired a maelstrom of emotions within him. Passion and tenderness. Not only was a storm raging in the heavens, it was in his heart as well.

Alex's eyes were hooded and unreadable and Samantha wondered what he was thinking as he looked at her. Was there any hope that he wanted to hold her in his arms as much as she wanted him to? Perhaps there were times when a woman had to act on her intuition. Lifting her arms, Samantha made the first move, encircling his neck as she raised up on tiptoe. With a silent gasp she melted against him, burying her face in the strong warmth of his shoulder, then raising her head to meet his kiss. The burning possession of his mouth said all she needed to know. She gave herself up to the fierce sweetness of that kiss, her lips opening under his as she tangled her fingers in his dark hair.

His arms were so warm, made her feel safe and secure, yet sparked another feeling too. She felt his breath ruffle her hair and experienced the sensation down the whole length of her spine. She felt as if she were flying, as if her feet didn't even touch the ground. Was that her heart beating so loudly that it shook her body? Her voice whispering his name as he bent down to kiss her again? The world seemed to be only the touch of his lips, the haven of his arms. She couldn't think, couldn't breathe. It was as if she were poised on the edge of a precipice, in peril of plummeting endlessly. If he were with her, would she care?

Alex lifted his mouth from hers and held her close for just a moment. Dear God, what she did to him. Did she even realize? He had thought he'd been attracted to Caroline, but in comparison to the blaze that burned inside of him now she hadn't really meant anything to him. Slowly, languorously, his hand traced the curve of Samantha's cheek, buried itself in the thick reddish-gold glory of her hair. She was playing havoc with his senses, drawing him to her the way the shore pulled in the tide. He wanted to make love to her, so much so that it hurt.

"Samantha . . ." Her eyes, those wide innocent eyes, looked back at him. He'd always prided himself on being a gentleman, but he hardly had the strength to be one now. Being so close to her was delicious torture. His body told him to claim what he wanted, but his mind told him to stop. Samantha was too young, too untutored in the ways of love to know what was happening. He knew exactly where their kisses and embrace were leading. "I think it's stopped raining." His voice was a breathless whisper as he pushed her away.

"No, it hasn't, Alex. Listen." A sudden chill touched her and she longed once again for the warmth of him. Why had he stepped away? His sudden change of mood confused her. One moment he was whispering her name and holding her close, the next he acted as if she were poison ivy.

"It's let up a bit. I should be able to go back to town early in

the morning. I think we had better call it a day. I'm tired."
Without even looking at her, he sought the small partioned area
that had been her grandfather's sleeping alcove, leaving a frustrated and totally confounded Samantha behind.

32

The rain drummed down on the cabin, sending a persistent drip through the hole in the roof as Samantha tried her very best to get to sleep.

"Damn Cy Tyburn!" she grumbled, remembering all too clearly that time he had pushed his way inside the cabin, grabbed her, and made her loaded rifle go off. The bullet had gone right through the wood and sod above her bed. With all her other worries, Samantha had put off fixing it and now was paying the price. "Men!" Certainly they were a confusing and annoying lot. All except Gramps. "Even Alex." First he had kissed and caressed her so tenderly that the whole world had been spinning about her, then just as suddenly he had walked away. He hadn't even said good night.

Samantha curled up in a tight ball, trying to avoid the part of the mattress that was soaked through with rain. The spot was spreading, making it more difficult to find a dry place. She was cold, damp, and miserable for more reasons than one. She wanted Alex's arms around her, wanted him to keep her warm.

He was so very close to her, just on the other side of the partition. If only she had the nerve to go to him. What would he do if she did? Would he push her away again? Would he think her much too bold? Didn't he realize that she had lost her heart to him the very first moment they met? Perhaps he did realize and his coldness was his way of telling her the feeling was not returned.

Shivering against the chill and damp, Samantha pushed herself to the far corner of the bed. Soon there would be nowhere else to go. The rain was consuming the mattress. Her damned stubborn pride was the only thing keeping her from Alex's arms. Pride and fear. Fear of rejection. He had loved Caroline West, had come all the way across a continent to marry her, and now that dazzling but selfish woman had spurned him, had broken their engagement. How could she ever hope that he might ever feel such love for her?

Samantha stared into the darkness listening for any sound that Alex might make. Was he awake? If not, dare she wake him? Slowly she sat up and swung her legs over the side of the bed, trying to gather her courage. Why, she was nothing but a coward when all was said and done. As lily-livered as some damn-fool sissy. A Claybourne was supposed to be daring and brave, but crossing the short distance to where Alex lay seemed suddenly as harrowing as challenging an irate bear.

"Alex . . . !" Her voice was a hushed whisper, so faint that she wasn't surprised when he didn't answer. Hugging her arms around her body, she imagined it to be his embrace. She could see his strong body in her mind's eye. His lips. The startlingly blue eyes that always looked so pensive. The perfectly chiseled lips beneath his mustache. Lips that had been surprisingly soft. As she remembered the moment they had shared, her breath became heavier and an aching hunger for him surged within her. She had never felt desire until he kissed her, but now she recognized it for what it was. She had never been overly curious about where it all would lead but now that she'd had a sampling, she was wondrously inquisitive. There was only one way to find out. She could either stay huddled on her side of the partition, or go to him and tell him what was in her heart.

The wooden floor was cold to her bare feet as she traced a

path from her alcove to where Alex slept. Kneeling down by the bed, she whispered his name again. "Alex?"

"I'm not asleep, Samantha. Storms always keep me awake." His breath caught sharply in his throat as he looked up and saw her shadowed silhouette. "What is it?"

"I'm cold, Alex. So cold. There's a leak in the roof above my bed. I'm nigh onto freezing. Won't you please hold me in your arms again?" Before he had a chance to answer, she was beside him. The soft rounded curves of her breasts and stomach pressed against him as she pulled the blanket over her quaking form. Her head rested against his shoulder. Wrapping one arm around him, she cuddled up against him. "Now I'm warm. About as snug as I could be!"

Alex closed his eyes tightly and clenched his fists, taking a deep breath as he fought for control. He knew he would have to have the willpower of a saint to hold himself apart from her much longer. Dear God, she wasn't making it any easier for him. "I can get up and stoke the fire if you'd like," he breathed. He started to pull away, but her arms tightened around him, drawing him back down to the bed once again. "Samantha, do you know what you are doing?"

"Yes . . ." Something warm and deep flowered instinctively at the sound of his voice. Her fingers touched his arms and moved down to take his hand, entwining her fingers with his. "I'm not afraid."

Alex groaned, closing his arms about her as he pulled her into the curve of his hard body. Her hands reached out to touch him, to caress him, and the feel of those hands was his undoing. They swept all reason and caution from his mind. Alex captured her shoulders and bent his face to hers for a searing kiss, that reflected of his passion. Their bodies touched full-length and Samantha shuddered at the potency of the embrace. Through the thin flannel of her nightshirt she could feel every inch of his skin, every muscle. His breath seemed to be coming faster. She wondered if she was even breathing at all. Wordlessly she returned his kiss, trembling with pleasure as his tongue entered her mouth to probe the inner softness. She didn't even try to understand all that was happening to her but knew that Alex was the only man who could ever arouse such an urgent, glowing need within her.

"Sam . . . my beautiful Sam . . ." He gloried in the closeness of their bodies. He'd wanted to hold her, to kiss her, but he'd fought against his desire. Now he could only wonder at how right it felt. Samantha belonged in his arms.

Their lips touched and clung, enjoying the sweetness of newly discovered love. Lying together in the darkness, they moved their hands over each other, touching . . . exploring. To Samantha it seemed the most natural thing in all the world. Clasping her arms about his waist, she ardently embraced him, kneading his shoulders, his hard chest, pulling him even closer against her tingling breasts. She felt the shudder that went through his body and followed his lead, kissing him more deeply, then at last pulling away.

"Alex . . . I knew it would be like this. I knew the first time I saw you alongside the road. Being with you is like . . . like drinking a whole jug of moonshine or lying naked beneath the sun for a whole afternoon. . . ." The thought occurred to her that she wished with all her heart that she was completely naked beneath the gentle touch of his hands. "Do . . . do people make love with their clothes on?"

"No. Of a certainty, they do not." His fingers parted the neck of her nightshirt, unbuttoning it so that he could reach inside to feel the soft flesh of her breasts. He stroked and teased the peaks until she moaned low and whispered his name, yielding to those hands, relishing the incredible sensations. She was caught in a trance of mindless delight.

Alex was also ruled by his emotions. He wanted her so badly that all his resolutions to leave her chaste were quickly washed away. She was too tempting, too warm, too loving and responsive. He was a starving man, driven on by his hunger. She was the connoisseur's feast. Even so, he knew he had to be gentle. The thought that Samantha had never been with a man before filled him with a passionate tenderness. He would do everything he could to make what passed between them beautiful for her. She had said that she was *not* afraid. He would reaffirm that trust.

Stroking and caressing, Alex removed her flannel nightshirt, then moved away from her for just a moment as he slipped out of his shirt and underdrawers. Seeking her out in the darkness, he leaned over her, drawing her smooth naked body against his in a manner that wrenched a groan from his lips. Her skin was like velvet, caressing him like a thousand fingers.

"My sweet Samantha . . ." he whispered, pressing his face into the hollow of her neck. His mouth moved slowly downward from her throat to the skin of her bare shoulder.

Samantha tingled with an arousing awareness of her body. It was like discovering herself through Alex. Her body was intensely sensitive. The lightest touch of his hands or mouth sent a shudder of pure sensation rippling deep within her. As his mouth flamed a path over her body her stomach tightened. A hot ache of desire coiled within her and she reached up to tangle her fingers in the dark hair of his head. No matter what happened, she would have this moment to remember, she thought. This special moment with Alex. She would never be able to forget the passion of his mouth, the sweetness of his kisses, the all-consuming joy of being with him.

Like a fire, his lips burned over the soft mounds of her breasts, savoring the peaks with his mouth and tongue like the most cherished of treasures. "Your skin is soft," he whispered against her flesh, outlining the small circles until her nipples puckered into succulent buds. Samantha felt her heart move with love. It was as if in some way she was changing, blossoming as surely as flowers did when the sun touched them. Alex was her sun, warming her with his sweet ministrations.

Samantha wanted to tell him how she felt, but she couldn't speak. Instead she tried to show him, mimicking his caresses as she slid her hands over his body. His intake of breath, the way he gathered her deeper into his embrace, told her he enjoyed her tentative exploration.

Passion brought them to the edge of wild oblivion, yet even then Alex's concern was for her. "Do you want me to stop, Samantha?" he asked, his voice a husky whisper. "I will if that's what you want me to do. . . ."

"No! Oh, please, no!" Her words were a plea as she moved against him. Driven by emotions she no longer even wished to control, she wound her arms tightly against him and raised her mouth, hungry for his kiss. She felt alive and soaring. Her entire existence seemed to be focused on him and the experience of being with him.

Alex wanted to be gentle, yet it took all his self-control to keep his passion in check. His hands and mouth resumed their exploration until he was certain she was ready. His hands moved to encompass her small waist, then slid over the curve of her hips and the firm curve of her buttocks. His fingers moved down to her thighs, caressing their long, slender length. Samantha melted with every touch, sucking in her breath as she felt his fingers explore the center of her being. Her face flamed, but she did not pull away. Instead she opened up to him, knowing instinctively that Alex would never cause her pain.

"Relax, Samantha . . ." As if to give her warning of what to expect, he guided her hand to his manhood, allowing her to become accustomed to the feel of a man's passion. His hands spread her thighs, holding them wide for his entry, then slowly he guided himself into her softness. Their bodies met in that most intimate embrace.

Alex lay motionless until he felt her relax. Letting her grow accustomed to his invasion, he was infinitely gentle, taking absolute care as he pushed through the obstruction of her virginity. His kiss muffled her cry of surprise and he paused again, allowing her to learn the feel of him buried deep inside her. Like the currents of the river his body drew hers, joining them together.

Samantha was consumed by his warmth, his hardness. Tightening her legs around his waist, she arched up to him, wanting him to move within her. When he did, she was astounded by the pulsating explosion of her body, the pleasure she felt as they moved together. She had found a heaven she hadn't even imagined existed. How could she have ever dreamed it would be like this? It was as if she had been starving all of her life but had only just now discovered her appetite, as if in giving she had received the ultimate gift. She had never before realized how incomplete she was without him, but now she realized the shattering wonder of being whole. She was a child no longer, but a woman. A woman deeply in love.

Sensing her feelings, still breathless from the jolt of his own emotions, Alex held Samantha close in his arms, fondling her gently as they lay together. He couldn't get enough of her. Far from quenching his desire, what passed between them had made him all the more aware of how much he cared for her. From this moment on she was his, for all their tomorrows.

It was as if the sun had suddenly brightened, as if the winds had chased all the clouds of his nightmares away. It had been quite a while since Alex had known any peace, but now Samantha was like a balm to his soul. "Samantha." He whispered her name like a caress, still holding her close. With an answering sigh she snuggled up against the warmth of his chest. She wanted to continue to savor this moment of joy, this wondrous discovery of love, but as his fingers caressed her back, her eyes closed and she drifted off to sleep.

33

The rain stopped during the night. The day dawned bright and
cloudless. Golden sunlight washed the room and flickered on
Samantha's eyes, waking her. Yawning and stretching, she listened to the steady breathing of the man lying next to her. So it
had not been a dream after all. Alex *had* made love to her with
an exhilarating passion. Her heart began to race wildly as she
remembered each kiss, each caress, the breathtaking moment
when he had made her a woman.

Alex's arm lay heavy across her stomach, the heat of his body
warming hers. An awe-inspiring wave of peace washed over her
as she relaxed back into his embrace. If only life could always
be as perfect as it was this morning. Suddenly she had not a
care in the world. She wanted to sing out, to share her happiness with every living thing. If this was being "twitterpated,"
then she welcomed the heady feeling. She wanted to experience
more of this thing they called love.

Easing herself onto her elbow, she stared into Alex's sleeping
face. His cheekbones were high, the flesh across them a light

shade of bronze, his nose straight, his mouth finely chiseled. Beneath his nose was a tuft of hair that beckoned her touch. Tracing the lines of his mustache, she laughed softly as the bristles tickled her fingers. The word *handsome,* she decided, didn't do him justice.

"I love you, Alex," she whispered against his face, but he didn't waken and she contented herself with watching him sleep. Her gaze drifted down his body to linger on the rise and fall of his chest. A mat of hair covered the hard, smooth flesh there and Samantha remembered the feel of it against her naked breasts, a soft, tickling sensation that had left her breathless. She flushed, remembering every look he had given her, every time he had whispered her name with his husky cry of passion. Each kiss had seemed to tell her that now he belonged to her, that he truly cared.

A stray dark curl had fallen across Alex's wide brow and Samantha brushed it back out of his eyes with tender concern. Certainly he was handsome, but that was not all that drew her. The way he walked and held his head, his gentlemanly manners, his kindness to her, the intent way he had of listening when she spoke—all added to his charm. Closing her eyes, she put her head on his shoulder with a deep sigh.

Alex, on the other hand, was far from calm. Awake now and staring up at the ceiling, he tried to sort out his thoughts. He could not deny the poignant and soul-stirring passion that had been unleashed. Samantha was all a man could long for. Never had a woman touched his heart more and yet he was troubled, incensed with himself. His intentions had been honorable. To guide Samantha, to help her in her time of need, to be a shoulder to lean on. He had not meant for their kisses to lead to the ecstasy they had shared. He had not meant for them to become lovers. Not so soon. Not like this.

Gentleman. It was a word that had been drummed into his head since he was old enough to walk and talk. The Nicholson men had been expected to be polite and courteous, to show the mark of good breeding, to be respectful of the opposite sex. That was not to say that Alex had not succumbed to his hungers. He was a man with fierce appetites. It was just that he had learned early to seperate the ladies from those women who made it their business to ease a man's tensions. Despite his desire for Caroline he had held back from consummating their mutual passion. He had allowed her to put herself upon a lofty pedestal. He had never once given in to temptation. And Samantha deserved the same respect. Of all the women he had ever known, she was dearest to his heart. How then had he allowed his desire for her to get out of hand?

Gentleman! In the deep recesses of his mind he had fantasized about making love to her, drawn to her as a moth to a flame. She was beautiful. Young. Full of life. She had fascinated him right from the very first moment he had looked into her wide brown eyes and seen that look of haunting innocence. Behind her brashness and bravado, he had sensed her loneliness. An aching tenderness had filled his heart, a wish to protect her from the world's harsh pain.

Protect her! The words struck him full force. Had Cy Tyburn or any other man shared Samantha's bed last night, Alex would be as fierce as a lion, proclaiming the man to be the worst kind of cad. Samantha was vulnerable. The death of her grandfather had made her doubly so. Was it any wonder she had wanted to be held in his arms last night? She needed love and instead he had given her passion. He had taken advantage of her, there was no denying it. Samantha had lived her whole life on this mountain, beneath the shadow of her grandfather's protection. She was young and naive, little realizing the consequences of passionate indiscretion. Gossip. Scandal. Unwarranted condemnation. He, on the other hand, was older, wiser in both the ways of the world and matters of the heart. He was by all observations a sophisticated man. How then had he allowed himself to lose his head?

Samantha lay soft and warm against Alex, stirring in her sleep as he reached out to brush back a lock of her hair that had fallen into her eyes. A wave of tenderness washed over him, a determination that she would not be wounded by what had passed between them. There was only one answer, of course, and that was marriage. If the wedding night had come before the ceremony, then who was to know? Marriage. Somehow he would have to get used to the thought of being joined in wedded bliss to this spirited, courageous, stubborn, unspoiled beauty.

He doubted their life together would ever be dull. There was a great deal he wanted to teach her and so much that he could learn from her as well. A blending of East and West he thought, elegance and honesty.

Marriage. There was a smile on his face as he kissed her forehead and climbed out of bed. He hurried to get dressed, running over in his mind a list of all that needed to be done. A license, a preacher, a ring. Perhaps if they had the time he'd buy Samantha a wedding dress. Something white and lacy but without flowers. Somehow flowers seemed all wrong for her. A necklace of pearls, perhaps. He'd move her from this cabin to a hotel suite in town. Drudgery and hard work were no kind of life for his bride. Wan Lau and Patrick Trenoweth could run the mine.

Sitting on the edge of the bed, Alex stared down at her, realizing beyond a doubt that she had completely stolen his heart. He felt younger than he had in years. Samantha was like a breath of fresh air, like a walk in the moonlight. A rush of blood surged through his veins as he bent down to kiss her ear.

He watched her a long while, then set about the morning tasks.

Samantha stretched and dozed, then woke with a start. Had it all been a dream? She sat up, searching the room for Alex.

"Good morning." Dressed in his brown trousers and white shirt, the tails of which hung outside his pants, he looked very relaxed, standing over the cookstove. His hair was touseled and his grin was boyish. "Breakfast awaits you, a specialty of mine that I mastered in the army. An omelet."

"Scrambled eggs." Samantha laughed. She seemed to live on eggs.

"Eggs with a touch of wild onion and dandelion greens. *And* a few wild strawberries left over from last night. I was busy while you slumbered." His eyes ran over her with a hungry familiarity, and realizing her nakedness, Samantha found herself suddenly shy. Blushing, she wrapped a blanket around her slender form as she rose from the bed. Her hair was a mass of tangles, her face needed washing, she was achingly aware of her disarray. How foolish to feel that way after what had already passed between them, she thought, and yet she felt strangely shy.

Samantha hurried to dress, then washed her face and hands in the small china basin on the washstand. The water was warm. Alex had been busy. It gave her a special glow to know that he had made himself at home here. A wistful longing to share the cabin with him coiled within her. Was it really such an impossible dream? Running a brush through her hair, she stared out the window trying to gather up the courage to ask him. Would he want to stay?

"I think we had best take the wagon into town and get some supplies, Alex. Lots of supplies." She was a coward, couldn't quite find the words. "Though it *is* a challenge to live off the land. We don't really need to go anywhere. We could stay right here."

Coming up behind her, Alex put his hands around her waist, drawing her to him. He thought she meant that they should stay and make love again. "Mmm. I'd like nothing better, but there are a hundred things to be done," he said. "Last night changed so many things, Samantha." He felt suddenly bereft of words. How could he make her understand that although last night had been very special to him, he still felt a burden of guilt. He made a stab at it. "First and foremost, I want to apologize. I shouldn't have—"

"Apologize?" She was aghast. How could he say he was sorry for the most wondrous night of her life? The very word drove a painful wedge between them. "Apologize?"

"I'm older than you and wiser. I should have known the temptation would be too overpowering. You're beautiful and sweet and evidently I have little willpower. If I told you I hadn't dreamed of holding you in my arms, I would be lying, but last night was not the proper time." His blue eyes probed her brown ones. "But I will set the matter to rights."

"I wanted what happened between us, Alex." She was crushed at his words. "I wouldn't take away one kiss, one hug, one touch of your hand. I'm *not* a child. I knew what I wanted. I wanted *you*." Didn't he realize how completely she had lost her heart to him? Was this his way of letting her know her love would never be fully returned.

"And I wanted you. Very much." He could see by the look in her eyes that he had inadvertently hurt her feelings. "I've never met a woman quite like you, Samantha. You're very, very special to me." He shrugged his shoulders helplessly. He could talk business, handle himself quite well in every other situation, but saying the right words to Samantha now seemed to elude him completely.

"What I'm trying to say is that I want you to marry me."

"Marry you?" A chill touched her as she searched his face. She was almost afraid to speak. It was what she wanted more than anything else in all the world. To be married to Alex. To share his bed and his life. Even so, she felt tears burn her eyes. He wasn't asking her to marry him because he loved her. He was asking her because he felt guilty. He believed he had *taken* her virtue and must now right the wrong. But he had not taken anything she had not wanted to give. Couldn't he see that? Didn't he even realize how much he meant to her?

"We'll ride into town and get married this afternoon. It's not right for you to live all alone up in the mountains, Samantha. I'll make you a good husband. I'll take care of you and give you the love you deserve. My hotel room isn't big enough for two, but we can move into a larger suite until we find a house in town that you find suitable."

Samantha shook her head vigorously at the words he was saying. "No. I can't leave here. *This* is my home." She swallowed tearfully, letting her pride overrule her emotions. "I can't marry you, Alex."

"What?" He wasn't prepared for the possibility that she might say no.

Hastily she averted her eyes, knowing full well he would see the pain the words cost her. She didn't want him to feel he had to marry her. It was as simple as that. She would not trap him into a wedding as if he were some helpless animal being lured into a snare. She had her pride and the mine to think about. She just wasn't the type of woman who would be satisfied with a shotgun wedding. "I can't marry you, Alex."

"Samantha, you must!"

"No." He started to protest but she covered his lips with her fingers. "And I can't move into town. I promised my grandfather that I wouldn't give up the Siren Song, that I would stay right *here*. It's a promise I mean to keep."

Alex wanted to argue the matter, but in the end he had to concede to her wishes. She was young, with her whole life ahead of her, he reasoned. Perhaps too young to give up her freedom. She needed time. Marrying her was his greatest desire at the moment, but he'd waited this long to find the right woman. He could wait a little longer. Until then he would watch over her and protect her from afar.

"Stay at the cabin then if you must, then. I *do* understand how much the mine means to you." He kissed her lightly on the cheek, fighting the impulse to take her in his arms. He knew all too well what that would lead to.

"It's your mine now, too, Alex." Samantha leaned back against him, breathing in a deep sigh. If only Alex loved her, really loved her, she would have said yes to his proposal. The truth was she had thrown herself into his arms last night. She was the one who should feel guilty, and yet she didn't. Loving Alex had been glorious! If that made her a wanton, then so be it. "You won't be sorry . . ."

"Sorry that I became your partner? I'm not." Alex misread her meaning.

"Gramps told me that the Siren Song promised to be the highest-producing mine in the county and I believe him." She pushed the memory of last night out of her mind for the moment. "Patrick and Wan Lau and I intend to find that main vein just as soon as we can."

"And I'll be working right beside you." As she whirled around with a startled look of surprise, he laughed. "Did you think I would be content to sit on my *backside*? When I'm involved in anything, I give it all my effort, Samantha. I want to do more than just give you a grubstake." He relished the thought of being near her, of seeing her face when she found the gold.

"Then we had best get started." She answered his laugh with a smile of her own, wondering if she even dared to dream. Alex and she came from totally different worlds. They were as different as night and day, black and white, winter and summer, and yet she loved him. More than he would ever know. And perhaps if she loved him enough, someday he might come to love her too. Maybe then he would want to marry her for a far different reason than he did today. Even more than finding gold, that was what Samantha wanted.

Two

TO WORK AND
TO DREAM
The Siren Song Mine
and Central City
Autumn 1871

"Each morning sees some task begin,
Each evening sees it close;
Something attempted, something done,
Has earned a night's repose."

Henry Wadsworth Longfellow,
The Village Blacksmith

34

Samantha had said that a Colorado summer came late and left with tearful fury, but no matter how grudgingly it left, it had to make way for autumn. Alex stood outside the front door of the cabin gazing at the red, orange, and yellow leaves. The lush greens of summer had given way to the muted tones of fall. Though it was a cloudless day, there was a chill that hinted at cooler days to come. Even so, there was a languor in the air, a calm that was soothing.

That was not to say that the past several weeks had been easy, they had not. An awkward politeness had replaced the ease that Samantha and Alex had felt together before their night of lovemaking. They were on guard; they watched what they said, how they looked at each other. Though they talked of many things, there was no mention of that passionate rainy night. Yet with each glance it was obvious it had not been forgotten.

Though it was one of the most difficult things he had ever done, Alex was determined to keep his distance. Samantha was lovely, spirited, and drew his heart, but she was so young. He'd lived his life to the fullest, had known many women, but she was new to this matter of love. She undoubtedly saw him as her protector, her benefactor, her friend, the gallant man who had come to her rescue. Or perhaps she was in awe of him, little realizing that he was far from the perfect man she envisioned. No Sir Galahad but a man of flesh and blood with human frailties. Hadn't the war proved that beyond argument?

Time, he thought. Their relationship needed to work itself out. He would not take advantage of her infatuation. When the time was right, he would make love to her again. In the meantime he would content himself with her laughter and her smiles and would help her in every way possible to find that vein of gold.

Walking to the pump, Alex drew some water to quench his thirst, then stretched his aching muscles. He'd been working since dawn and had paused to take a break and a breath the fresh air. Mining was grueling work. Lifting heavy rocks, wielding the sledgehammer, pulling the ore cart, all had deepened his respect for Enoch Claybourne and for Samantha. She had courage, grit, and unwavering resolve that he could not help but admire. It had strengthened his own determination to see her quest succeed. If hoisting a sledge with a relentless fury and maneuvering a windlass would help make her dream come true, then he would concentrate his effort.

Samantha's dedication and determination were contagious. Her quest for gold was as fierce as her passion had been, he thought. Beneath it all was not greed but the thought of fulfilling her grandfather's dream, a dedication to his memory.

Alex felt he had rested long enough. Picking up a bucket, he filled it with water from the pump and headed back to the mine. The water in the bucket sloshed over and he paused, squinting his eyes against the sun, as a cloud of dust caught his eyes. Who could it be? The road was not used often. Someone had been doing a bit of mischief lately to sabotage Samantha's efforts. Just bothersome things, but annoying. One of these days the culprit would be caught red-handed, Samantha had said, and then they'd feel the sting of her buckshot on their backsides. Alex had no doubt but that she would do just that.

"Alex! Alex, old friend" came the call as the buggy rumbled up the road bringing Robert Cunningham's smiling face into view. "So this *is* where you've been hiding yourself. I thought you'd gone back to Boston to heal your broken heart."

Alex laughed. "Hardly that. I've been helping Samantha work her mine."

"Work? You said work?" Robert made a face. "That's something I avoid whenever possible. Seems there's always someone else who will do it for you if you know how to manage it." Jumping down from the carriage, he stood with his arms folded across his chest, appraising Alex, taking in the denim pants and flannel shirt. "Hmm, you're beginning to look just like a miner, breeches and all."

"I *am* a miner, Robert. At least I'm trying. It's damned hard work, to be sure, but I have to confess I've never been happier. Working down there with Jeremiah was aggravating. Up here is a world devoid of ambition, malice, pretentiousness, or greed. You should try it." Alex cocked one brow. "We have an extra shovel."

"Me?" Robert shook his head. "Not a chance. I get hives just thinking about it." Taking off his hat, he flicked his fingers through his thick auburn hair, brushing it free of the road's dust. "Think I need another haircut. Care to come back to town with me and spend some time at the barber's?" He clucked his tongue. "By the looks of that shadow on your face you most certainly could use a shave. Why, I daresay Caroline and J.W. would consider your appearance disgraceful."

"I daresay that you're right. I'm so glad to be away from them right now. Far away."

"Then you have no regrets?"

"Most definitely not. Caroline was *not* the woman for me. I should have realized that much sooner and acted accordingly. Samantha is far more enjoyable company." Just saying her name to Robert made him smile.

"Samantha, eh?" Robert looked toward the mine. "I should have known there was some reason for your sudden interest in mining." He laughed. "But I can't blame you. Samantha is very pretty."

"She's much more than that, she's . . ." Alex flushed under Robert's scrutinizing stare. "Well . . . I . . . I like her. I want to help her find her gold so that she can have everything she deserves in life. I'll fight anyone who tries to do her any harm, including Jeremiah West. You can tell him that for me if you want."

"Oh, no. If you want to let him know that, you can tell him yourself. J.W.'s riled enough as it is." Robert lowered his voice to a whisper as if fearful of being overheard. *Habit,* Alex thought. "He says he's going to get this mine if it's the last thing he ever does. Believe me, Alex, I'd be worried if I were you. Jeremiah is a very influential man in the territory."

"Perhaps that's true, but I'm not without my own connections, Robert. I haven't been idle all this time. I've been making various investments of my own. Making threats is one thing and will only get him so far." Alex clenched his jaw. "Samantha's no longer alone and no one's going to cheat her out of her mine while I'm around." Wishing to change the subject, he asked about the young man who had taken a shot at Jeremiah in the stables.

"He and his family moved out of town. Jeremiah was reasonably generous in paying for their establishment. Think he was afraid the fellow might try it again." At Alex's look of surprise he said, "Oh, yes, James Andrews told me what happened, Alex. And to think old J.W. has been all around town calling you a coward. If you ask me, it's very likely you saved his bacon for him, so to speak."

"Saved his bacon?" Alex threw back his head and laughed. "I thought Samantha had taught me just about every phrase, but that's a new one."

"Yeh, well, it's very possible you just might need someone to save *yours.*"

Alex sobered as he saw the look that came over Robert's face. "If you're worried about Cy Tyburn, Buck Cameron, or Slim Walker, don't be. I've handled them a few times and they don't frighten me. They're hardly more than mischievous boys. They don't pose much of a threat."

"Perhaps they don't, but I'm not sure the same can be said

for the new man in town. He makes Slim, Cy, and Buck look like amateurs." Robert twisted his wide-brimmed hat nervously in his hands. "Rumor has it he's a gunfighter who's already killed several men who got in his way."

"A gunfighter?"

"He seems to have taken a particular interest in you, Alex. He came into the barbershop that day you went after Samantha. Said he thought he knew you. I assumed it was a case of mistaken identity. Didn't credit you with knowing a man like that. But he's been asking all over town, asking about you by name."

"Who is he?" Alex didn't know any gunfighters. How could he when he'd lived nearly all his life in Boston?

"Says his name is Ben Cody. Do you know him?"

Cody. Ben Cody. The name did sound strangely familiar. Where had Alex heard that name? Closing his eyes, he tried to remember. The war. It had to be during those turbulent years. One of the soldiers in his unit whom he'd just barely known was called Cody. "Ben Cody." The image of hostile gray eyes hovered before him as the memory slowly came back. The resentment, the surliness of that soldier under his command. He was one of those always disobeying orders, drinking incessantly, making critical mistakes that could have cost other men their lives. Oh, yes, he remembered Ben Cody now. Alex had tried to be lenient, but it had done no good. The more he tried reason with the young soldier, the more his authority had been met with stubborn frowns. The soldier had even started a fight with Alex for no reason, a bout of bickering that had led to his incarceration in the camp detention cabin. They had gone into the battle of Chancellorsville without him, that brutal battle that had taken so many lives. It had been a bloodbath. A tragedy. A battle that young soldier was fortunate to have missed.

"Alex, do you know him?" Robert's question pulled Alex from the past.

"Yes. He was a soldier under my command in the war."

"The war? You've never mentioned it before." Robert sighed in relief. "An old war buddy? Thank goodness. I'd thought . . . I'd feared . . . that he was seeking you out with violence in mind.

"No need to worry. I never did him any great injury. He probably wants to talk about times I'd prefer to forget. He has no reason to harm me." With a shrug of his shoulders, Alex put the matter from his mind.

35

Robert disappeared down the road in a lingering cloud of dust. Taking out his pocket watch, Alex was disconcerted to see that it was already one o'clock. Their visit had lasted longer than he thought. Alex pushed open the creaky wooden door of the shaft house and stepped inside. It was suffocatingly dark, damp, and dismal. He paused to let his eyes adjust to the blackness, anxious to get back to work. It was taking them a lot longer to find the vein than they expected. Nevertheless, Samantha never gave any hint that she was prepared to give up. She worked every bit as hard as Wan Lau, Patrick, and Alex and never lamented her woes.

Lighting a lantern, Alex moved farther into the tunnel. A trickle of sandy dirt sifted down from one of the ceiling supports, reminding him of the danger. Samantha had warned him to be cautious. He couldn't help but wonder what his father would think if he saw him right now. Would he be proud or horrified? *Stunned* was the word, Alex thought. His father would be offended by the sight of his son dressed in denim, toiling away. He would never understand Alex's reasoning. Just like Jeremiah West, his first and foremost interest was money. Perhaps that was why Alex understood the banker so well.

Alex was careful in his steps, looking beyond the edge of his lantern light to the vast velvet darkness. It reminded him strangely of the future. No one could really see into the black void, nor could one know what fate had in store. He smiled as he thought about coming west to marry one woman and losing his heart to another. Life had many surprises, that much was certain. It was as unpredictable and exciting as Samantha.

A sudden draft from the tunnel blew out the flame of the lantern. Alex swore beneath his breath as he fumbled about in his pocket for a match. It was suddenly quiet. Eerily so. There was no sound of hammering, no sound at all. Breathing in the familiar odor of damp earth, wet wood, and mold, he put his senses on alert. The silence filled him with apprehension. What had happened? Hurriedly he relit the lamp and quickened his pace. The silence was shattered by a muffled shout as he collided with Samantha.

"Alex!" Her voice was a shriek in the semidarkness, echoing over and over again. Breathless, she grabbed for his hand. "Alex, I'm so glad you're back."

"Samantha, what's wrong?"

"Wrong?" She let out a gleeful roar at his solemn question. "Nothing is wrong, Alex. Hell, we've just done it! Found it! There's as much gold as in King Solomon's mines." Tugging his hand, she led him through the maze of the mine to a spot where Patrick and Wan Lau were working. The flickering light of the lanterns illuminated a shimmering layer of rock. "Gold, Alex." Her eyes were wide with excitement as she swept her arms in a wide circle.

"Gold." The walls of rock glistened. It was not at all as Alex had supposed it would be. He'd seen gold bricks, never raw gold. Nevertheless he was afraid to blink his eyes and find it had disappeared. After all this time it would be too great a disappointment.

"Gold and plenty of it." Striking at the copper-colored rock with her pick, Samantha loosened a large hunk the size of her fist and held it out to him. "Feel it. It's heavy."

"Richest mine I 'ave ever seen, and I 'ave worked a lot of mines." Patrick Trenoweth stepped forward with a jaunty air to explain how they had finally found the mother lode.

"Gramps was a bit wrong in his calculations. A bit off to the right. But it was there." Samantha held her head proudly. "There's gold *and* silver here, Alex." Her eyes were just as bright as the precious ore. "That's why there's a glitter of bluish-gray mixed with the coppery color. Gold is rarely found without a varying proportion of silver present. But this mixture seems to contain a larger amount of gold." She could barely contain her enthusiasm. Flinging her arms impulsively around his neck, she kissed him. Every fiber in Alex's body leapt in response.

"And so you've found your treasure," he said, beaming. He felt his heart swell with love. She had said she would find the gold, and she had. "I'm so happy for you, Samantha."

"Oh, Alex, I couldn't have done it without you." Her arms tightened about his neck. She was reluctant to let him go.

"Your grandfather knew what 'e was about, me beautay." Patrick Trenoweth grinned from ear to ear, as much from seeing Alex and Samantha standing so close together as from the morning's find. As Samantha caught his eye he winked.

"Gramps was right. It was here." She radiated excitement. "He said we would find the richest vein in the territory." A fleeting shadow of sadness crossed her face. "How I wish he'd lived to see this day and know just how rich a strike it is."

"Somehow I think he knows, Samantha." Capturing a lock of her hair, Alex pulled her closer and bent to kiss her forehead. "Where ever he is now, I can imagine him watching us and smiling."

"You think so, Alex?" That thought seemed to cheer her as she leaned into his embrace. "I hope so. I hope he is looking down from heaven this very minute and feels proud of me. I did it in part for him. I wanted to honor my promise. And now I have, with your help and Patrick's and Wan Lau's. Thank you. I couldn't have done it without all of you." The look of gratitude shone in her eyes, mixed with a soft glow of love. Her grandfather had warned her not to trust anyone, but he had been wrong. Alex was special.

Oh, Alex, she thought, *it feels so right when we are together.* Why hadn't he kissed her until today? Why had he held himself back from her all these weeks? It had haunted her, made her unhappy, fearing she might have done something wrong. She was dismally unsure of herself, calling herself ten kinds of fool for not marrying him when he'd asked. She should never have let her wounded pride get in the way. *If* he ever proposed again, she would say yes without a second thought.

Finding the gold had been as much for Alex as for her grandfather, if she were honest with herself. She didn't want Alex to see her as a poor, pathetic ragamuffin, an object of pity. She wanted his respect, wanted his love. Wanted to be good enough for him. Maybe now she would be. Nestling into his arms, she thought that even though she wanted his love, wanted him to feel as strongly about her as he had for Caroline West, at the moment she was content. For the time being just having him near was enough.

36

There was a festive mood at the cabin as Samantha, Alex, and their two companions celebrated the day's find. Wan Lau had strung colored paper from the beams in the roof, which seemed to dance in rhythm to the tuneful melodies Patrick plunked on his fiddle. The cabin rang with song and laughter. Samantha felt happy and carefree. Blissfully happy. Together they had found the gold that had teased and tormented her. Their success made her feel an overwhelming sense of pride. She'd proven old man West wrong. He'd thought he could goad her and provoke her into giving up, but she hadn't. With Alex's help she had stuck right by her guns, and in the long run it had paid off. Now she was rich. That thought made her giggle.

"And just what do ye plan to do wi' all that gold, me beautay?" Putting down the fiddle he was playing, Patrick reached for a bottle of whiskey at his side and put it to his mouth, letting the fiery liquid course down his throat.

"I don't know. Haven't really had time to think about it." She'd been so intent on the quest that she hadn't given much attention to figuring out what she would do if it succeeded. "I expect I'll use some of it to fix up the cabin." Alex had fixed the roof above Samantha's bed, but lots of other things needed to be done. Perhaps if she made it comfortable and cozy enough, Alex would consent to share it with her. Her eyes strayed to Alex and she blushed, afraid he could read her thoughts. "And . . . and maybe get me a few new dresses and some hair ribbons. I've been so busy, I suppose I've forgotten to look like a woman." Perhaps that was why Alex had avoided her. She had hardly looked feminine the past few weeks. The last time she'd worn a dress was the time he'd made love to her. Maybe he needed to be reminded of her femininity. Anyway, it was worth a try.

Searching for and finding three chipped earthenware cups, she poured a portion of whiskey into each of them for Wan Lau, Alex, and herself, then returned the bottle to Patrick. Together they toasted the Siren Song.

"I velly happy for you, missy. Velly happy." Wan Lau's usually pensive face was split ear to ear with a grin. "Now maybe Wan Lau can bring noble wife and honorable mother-in-law to this country. I save. I save."

"I'll help you!" Her head whirled, but not from the whiskey or the exuberance of finding the gold. It was the look she'd seen in Alex's eyes when she'd embraced him. He'd been friendly but so distant these past few weeks that she had despaired he would ever make love to her again. Now it seemed possible that those fierce fires could burn again. "Both you and Patrick deserve something special. A bonus! I'll use what we found today for that and of course I'll have to put some money back into running the mine. We've got a heap more digging to do. Why, we've only started."

The room was filled with merriment, but as the day wore on, Samantha was aware only of Alex. His voice was the only voice she heard, his face the only one that filled her eyes. She moved and talked and sang, but her thoughts had only one focus. The whiskey had made her feel warm and relaxed. Her head was spinning with the wild rhythm of her heart. When her eyes met Alex's, she smiled, sending a silent message. She wanted to be alone with him. She wanted to be held in his embrace. Leaving by the front door, she kept her fingers crossed hoping that he would follow. If he did, Patrick and Wan Lau would understand, would soon get over their pique at being deserted.

Samantha walked the pathway from the cabin to the mine, looking down at the ground. The wandering trail of footprints dotting the earth seemed to emphasize her relationship with Alex. His footprints and hers. There in the hard ground was the imprint of his boots and beside them the smaller indentation made by hers. Somehow it seemed it should always be so. Alex walking beside her.

"Samantha?" He had followed. Walking past the mine, Samantha headed for her favorite fishing spot, a place far from other eyes. "Samantha." Slowly Alex took her hand, warmed by the contact of her fingers with his. He was thoroughly charmed by her. Whoever said that East and West would never meet was very, very wrong he thought. Where the heart was involved, anything was possible. Undeniably she held his heart, though he doubted she really knew how much.

"Thought we might do a bit of fishing, Alex. Now that we've found the gold, we can relax, at least awhile." She squeezed his hand. "We'll catch some trout for supper tonight. You will stay, won't you?"

"Yes, I'll stay." How could he say no to her earnest invitation. For the time being he was resolved to watch over her and enjoy her company and let their relationship continue to grow. Friendship. First and foremost he wanted friendship between them. Samantha needed someone to care about her. To truly care. Alex did. She became more important to him with each passing day.

As the late afternoon sun shone down on their heads, Samantha and Alex sat cuddled together by the edge of a stream, dreaming and reflecting. "There are times when I wish we could stay just like this forever, Alex, without anything else to do but be together," she whispered.

"Mmm. Just you and me, Samantha." He put his arm around her shoulder, pulling her closer. "To me, this is paradise. The sky for our roof, the music of the flowing water . . ."

"You like being here with me? You don't miss the excitement of town?" Her voice trembled as she asked the question.

"I'm blissfully content." His lips caressed her forehead, then moved down her temple to kiss each closed eyelid in turn. He lifted her hair from the nape of her neck with stroking fingers, tracing a path to her ear. The touch was followed by warm, exploring lips that sent shivers up and down Samantha's spine. He'd thought he could blot from his mind the memory of her soft body beneath his hands, the hot sweetness of her mouth, the glory of her breasts, but he was wrong. He ached for her right now with a physical awareness that he could barely control. "Samantha . . ."

She waited in expectation, closing her eyes. Alex's lips and hands were igniting her as quickly as sparks to kindling. His husky voice breathed in her ear as his hands continued to do wondrous things to her senses. Suddenly a loud splashing sound disturbed their passionate reverie.

"Alex, the fish. I think you have a bite. Your pole is bending and bobbing." Grabbing the pole, Samantha thrust it into his hands. He pulled the fish into shore and Samantha put it in her hat for safekeeping. Then, with a smile, she wound her arms around Alex's neck. "Now, where were we? I think you were kissing me like this." Samantha moved closer, touching her lips to Alex's mouth, but he pulled away. "Alex, what's wrong?" The spell was broken.

"You're young, Samantha. I don't want to take advantage of you, though I like nothing better in this world than kissing you. You've seen where it leads. I should have known better than to come out here." Running his fingers through his hair, he sought to still the pounding of his heart.

"You don't like me in that way, is that it? Oh, Alex, I know I hardly ever wear a dress but I will . . . for you." Her eyes were bright with unshed tears. "I want you to like me, just a little."

"I do, Samantha. Very, very much. But I'm so much older than you are. Just a cynical old man at times. You're barely more than a girl." His touch was gentle on her cheek. "I'm eleven years older."

She stiffened. "I was eighteen two weeks ago! I'm not a child. Not by a long shot. My mother was much younger when she met my father, but she knew, just as I did. From the very first moment I saw you, I knew how I felt about you, Alex. And someday you'll feel like that about me too. I know you will. Until then I guess I'll just have to be patient."

"Samantha . . ." He started to explain to her the way he felt, but she silenced his words with a kiss. They lay side by side looking out at the churning water. "You are very special. You do know that, Samantha?" Alex said at last. His hand traced the curve of her cheek, buried itself in the thick hair at that nape of her neck. For a long moment he gazed at her before he slowly smiled. The look in his eyes made her feel beautiful and very content, told her that now everything would be all right. Nothing could be more perfect than the magic their being together created, she thought. There would be no more worries, no more unhappiness.

Samantha might have been less optimistic had she seen the buggy passing by the mine at that very moment. Alex would have recognized the black vehicle instantly. Flicking the reins in frustration, Jeremiah West chewed on the stem of his cigar as he guided the carriage down the long, winding road from the Tyburn's cabin and damned Samantha Claybourne to hell and back. She was the only stumbling block to his aspirations.

It stuck in his craw that Alex, whom he had once envisioned as his son-in-law, his partner, was helping the little hoyden.

Well, let them think themselves safe for a time. He'd give them a lull before the storm began. Perhaps they'd won for the moment, but he would have the last laugh. Of that he was certain.

37

It was a crisp autumn day. Ominous gray clouds raced across the sky. The gold and brown foliage around the cabin foretold winter. Rotting leaves covered the ground and crunched underfoot. There was a change in the air, Samantha thought, staring out the cabin window. In the weather, the sky, the leaves. There was a change taking place in her as well. She had told Alex that she was no longer a child and that was very true. Day by day she was slowly becoming more of a woman. Loving Alex had made it so.

Samantha looked at Alex now, watching as he hovered over the papers scattered on the kitchen table. He spent more and more time at the cabin of late. Finding gold had not simplified her life. Not by a long shot, she mused. Indeed, it had made it more complicated. Now there seemed to be a hundred things to keep track of. Now it went far beyond scrawling down a list of supplies in her grandfather's journal. Since the vein had been located, Alex had taken it upon himself to keep a careful account of money spent for supplies, tools, and timber to shore up the newly excavated tunnel. He kept a careful account of wages paid and bonuses given to the two miners working the Siren Song. She appreciated his efforts but they rankled her as well. Somehow it all made her feel as if she were no longer in control of the mine.

"I can write and I can cipher. Gramps taught me how, and also to read," she mumbled beneath her breath. Why, she could do sums in her head far more quickly than Alex, yet he always told her not to bother, that he would do it. Had it been any one but Alex, she would have been suspicious, would have questioned his intent, but one look at his engaging smile, his deep blue eyes, and she was lost. Thus she spoke not one word about her irritation and pushed all suspicion from her mind. Her grandfather had said many times that gold could turn the purest saint into a sinner, that a man would cheat his own mother where a nugget was concerned, but she knew Alex was different. She trusted him. Without Alex she might very well have lost the mine.

"What are you doing, Alex?" Wistfully, Samantha stared at the two fishing poles by the front door of the cabin. Usually at this time of day they went fishing. It was a way of rewarding themselves for a hard day's work. They would stretch alongside the bank, balancing their poles across a rock, and watch the sky. It was the most perfect moment of the day, a time she looked forward to.

"What am I doing? Some figuring, Samantha." Alex leaned back in his chair and stretched. Since Samantha had struck her rich vein of ore she needed him more than ever. As a favor to her he had spent hours keeping ledgers as well as carefully taking note of sound investments he could make in her name. He had even spent his nights at the hotel studying geology, learning more about gold and what the many forms of ore looked like so that he could be more useful to her. It gave him the satisfaction of feeling needed. When he thought about it, delved into his past, he realized that he had never really felt needed before. But Samantha relied on him and that gave him a glow of contentment. He found himself spending more and more time at the mine when he might have enjoyed the comfortable leisure of the town. He liked being here with her, enjoyed their moments together.

Now that he thought about it, Alex could see that he'd never known how to relax before, how to enjoy a bright sunny day. Even though he'd rebelled, Alex had absorbed more of his father's ambition than he'd realized; the need to achieve always overrode the enjoyment of life. Now he spent leisurely days walking in the mountains after days of hard work. Samantha showed him her favorite fishing holes and took him with her whenever she went deep into the woods to hunt. Alex was quite a marksman, Samantha remarked, for a man who didn't own a gun.

It was an uncomplicated way of life despite the toil and the ledgers. The kind of life that he had longed for. Samantha was an endless delight. He laughed with her, talked to her, telling her things he'd never told anyone else before. He shared her exuberance, her disappointments, and she in turn listened to his soulful outpourings with a tender patience that told him how much she cared.

Samantha was innocent, yes, yet in some ways she was also startlingly worldly and knowledgeable in what she knew of mining procedures and how to live off the land. She taught Alex all that she knew about mining, sharing her world with him just as he shared his expertise in business with her. It had proved a skillful blending, or so he thought. Together they would make Samantha Marie Claybourne into a very rich woman. Smiling to himself, he wondered just how Caroline and Jeremiah would treat her now that she had found gold. He doubted they'd turn up their noses at her now. He wanted to make certain that no one would ever snub her again. Dipping his pen into the inkwell, he sent it moving frantically across the page. Fortunes had been made and lost just as quickly, but he'd make certain that Samantha would never lose her fortune even if the vein of gold ran out tomorrow. Already she owned stock in quite a few businesses. With the same skill and concentration he used in investing his own capital, he insured Samantha's well-being.

Alex had been incensed when he'd learned of the incident at Professor Hill's smelter. He'd ridden into town and had it out with the foreman, who had mumbled an excuse. The money owed had been duly paid. To insure against such a thing happening again, Alex kept careful account of gold shipments to and from the smelter and always insisted on receipts for the ore delivered.

Birds chattered furiously outside the front door of the cabin, awaiting the feast of breadcrumbs Samantha strewed so generously at this time of year. Leaving Alex to his paperwork, she grabbed the bag of crumbs and stepped outside to feed them. Alex might be ignoring her but at least the birds were not. Swooping down, they chirped and scolded until the last crumb was gone. They reminded her strangely of the townspeople and how they had reacted to the rumors that she'd found gold. When she went to town, they didn't ignore her now but hovered about, squawking and trying to convince her to buy their wares. Why, she'd even been invited to several teas and luncheons, but being shy by nature, and feeling ill at ease with the townswomen, she had nervously declined.

"Oh, Gramps, I'm not certain at all that I like this business of having money," she whispered, looking up at the sky as if to see her grandfather's face. "I don't like people toadying to me just because of the gold. I'm still the same person I was before."

She'd seen how other newly rich people put on airs. Among the few concessions she'd made to her wealth were a new wagon, some hair ribbons, and a pink calico dress that Alex had admired in the dressmaker's window. The only other thing in her life that had changed was where she stored her gold. Because of Alex she had opened her first account at a bank that rivaled Jeremiah West's establishment. Though she had been leery at first, remembering Jeremiah's treachery and her grandfather's caution about bankers, Alex had convinced her that a coffee can or a mattress was anything but safe. But just to be on the safe side, she had hidden a bag of gold nuggets in a secret hole in the mine tunnel. Just in case. Banks had been known to fail. If such a thing happened, she would have a nest egg. Hadn't Gramps always cautioned her to be careful in such matters?

What would Gramps think if he could see me now? It was a question she had asked herself more than once of late. Would he understand her love for Alex? Would he approve the way she had given her heart, her trust? *Like stays with like,* he'd always said. *Only person you can trust is yourself.* The words haunted her. But she didn't have it in her to be like her grandfather. Living all alone was devastating. She needed Alex. Loved him. Wanted him. Being with Alex was right; she felt it in her heart. But as she walked back into the cabin she felt a strange twinge of apprehension as she watched him busily scribbling about on his ledgers. She was nearly jealous of his interest in the Siren Song. It was like having a rival.

"Alex! The sun is touching the mountains. If we are going to go fishing, we had best set about it before the sun goes down."

"Hmm? Oh, I'm sorry." Taking out his pocket watch, he gave a start of surprise. "We'll go right now. I'll finish up when we come back." Pushing the papers aside, he stood up. Grasping her shoulders, he bent forward to kiss her on the cheek. "I'm sorry if I've been ignoring you, but there is so much that needs to be done. Reaching in his pocket he pulled out a small velvet-covered box. "Before I forget, this is for you."

"For me?" Samantha's heart beat erratically. Hoping. Opening the lid, she gasped as she saw what was inside. It was a gold bracelet. "Oh, Alex! I've never had anything so fine. Thank you."

"There's an inscription on the underside, 'With love from Alex to Samantha,' and the date you discovered gold in the mine. It's a late birthday present. Happy birthday, Samantha." Enfolding her in his arms, he kissed her, a long and leisurely kiss, then broke away. "Put it on."

She did, her fingers trembling so badly that she was afraid she'd be all thumbs. Tears stung her eyes. No one had ever given her anything so lovely before. All her doubts about Alex, of what Gramps might have thought of their relationship, were swept away. "You already bought me a birthday gift." Having learned that her birthday was in the middle of August, Alex had insisted on a "late" celebration. Inviting Patrick and Wan Lau to a party in her honor at the cabin he had brought flowers—marigolds, geraniums, daisies, and sprigs of fern—the very first bouquet she had ever received. A box wrapped in colored paper had contained hair ribbons in a rainbow of colors. Since then she always wore one in her hair, even when working the mine.

"This gift is something special." It was a prelude to his asking her to marry him. He'd thought about doing just that these last few days, had in fact instructed the jeweler to begin crafting another piece of jewelry—a ring. Their relationship was growing every day and it seemed that all the right elements were there. Respect. Affection. Trust. A deep caring for each other. An all-consuming passion. Putting his hands around her waist, he kissed the soft hollow of her throat, his mind turning to amorous thoughts.

Sleep. That was a thing that often eluded him of late. Samantha had enfolded herself into his dreams with every look she passed his way. When he lay alone at night in his bed he knew exactly what it was that haunted him. His dreams were hot, torturous dreams in which she writhed under his touch. Awakening in the morning alone in his hotel room, he would remember how it had felt to hold her in his arms and would find himself still trembling with desire. Ah, yes, it was high time to claim her. His heart, mind, and body told him so.

He looked toward the bed and his mouth curved in a smile. Soon. Very, very soon he would remove the partition between those two beds, push them together to form one big bed for those nights when they stayed at the cabin. This time when he asked her to marry him, he would know the moment was right.

38

Jeremiah West sat a long time at his gleaming mahogany desk, staring out the window at the people who meandered by. All had smiles on their faces, and in his mind they were laughing at him. Laughing. Smirking. And why not? He'd been outrageously and thoroughly bested by a woman who was little more than a girl! He, Jeremiah West, who had boasted he could finagle an angel out of its halo, had been unable to devise a plan that would give him controlling interest in *that* little hellion's mine.

"I'm not beaten yet, not by a long shot. No one bests Jeremiah West." Oh, he was irritated, all right. First and foremost at Cy Tyburn, who had seemingly botched everything he'd been instructed to do. He was supposed to find a way to stop work on the Siren Song. By hook, crook, or any means available he was to have made it impossible for Samantha Claybourne to satisfy the first requirement of her claim, namely, that she work at least one day in three to make improvements in the mine. If the claim was not worked for a period of ten days, it could be declared vacant and reclaimed by someone else. He had planned it all very carefully, but somehow Cy Tyburn had failed. Just like an infuriatingly loud clock, the Siren Song kept ticking away, producing seemingly endless quantities of gold. Somehow he had to stop that clock.

Looking at the newspaper he held in his fist, Jeremiah West snorted in frustration. *The Register-Call* kept reporting on the Claybourne mine, calling it a "Cinderella story," detailing the "colorful" rags-to-riches tale of a "local" girl. It was exasperating. Infuriating. A painful reminder to him of what he might have had. A veritable treasure! And it had slipped right through his hands.

"That bungling fool!" Talking to himself all the while, he got up and paced the length of the rug. He'd hired *Tyburn* because he figured the Tyburns had as much reason to be resentful as he did. Birds of a feather, so to speak. It had seemed the perfect partnership, but more interested in his whiskey than in success Cy Tyburn had botched the simplest tasks. And yet he wasn't ready to censure the young man yet. He still had hopes of using him.

There had to be something he could do. Something. Anything. Could he convince the citizens of Central City that Stephen Tyburn really had been cheated out of his rightful share of the mine? Bribery was the answer, of course. Claims could be bought and sold at will, but to prevent fraud or coercion, each transaction had to be witnessed by at least two and sometimes five disinterested men. What if he could get those five men who witnessed Enoch's transaction to rescind their corroboration.

If enough money changed hands, a seemingly honest man could be persuaded to say that black was white and the sky a dark shade of crimson. A man would testify that a monkey was a chicken if he was paid enough hard, cold cash. It was a plan that deserved serious consideration.

"Ohhh . . ." His stomach burned and he clapped his hand over that agonized part of his body with a habitual gesture. At last he succumbed to the discomfort and stopped his nervous pacing long enough to walk to his desk. Inside was a box of baking soda and a spoon. Carefully he measured out just the right amount, his hands trembling so that he spilled a significant portion on the desk. "Damn!" he cried. Using the discarded newspaper to clean it up, he was transfixed by an article that had somehow previously eluded him.

"Property rights will soon be granted to miners who want to apply for a patent,'" it said. He read on, intrigued by the article and the possibilities it presented. Miners heretofore could lay claim only to mineral rights. The ore belonged to them but the government still owned the land. All that was about to change. The miner who wanted property rights in addition to mineral rights had to apply for a patent. Samantha Claybourne, in all reality, owned only the *gold* that came from the depths of the mine. Not her cabin, not her sheds, not the shaft house. What if he were able to buy the land right out from under her? How then would she go about digging?

Running to the door, he hailed a young, beardless teller with a growl. "You there, Watson, get Robert Cunningham in here on the double." It was about time for that two-bit lawyer earned his keep. "Lawyer," he snorted. They were as abundant as fleas on a dog in Central City. And why not? The only requirements were that the applicant be at least twenty-one years old, supply evidence of good moral character, and pass an examination before a judge, a few vague, simple questions, as it were. It was easy to gain admittance to the bar in the territories. Jeremiah had been Robert Cunningham's patron, his creator. He had made that brash young man what he was. Now it was time to cash in his chips. Samantha Claybourne would soon be eating out of Jeremiah's hand.

39

Wind whipped through the gulch, blowing Samantha's red-gold hair into her eyes as she walked up the boardwalk to Annie's Dressmaking Shop. The streets were a muddy quagmire and once or twice a passing carriage or wagon splattered mud on her pants. Luckily she was not wearing her dress, she thought, brushing herself off before she entered the store. Even so she was all smiles as she greeted the seamstress. A woman in love had cause to smile, she thought, catching a hasty glimpse of herself as she passed by the mirror.

"Are my dresses ready?" She felt familiar with the shop now, having suffered three fittings in as many weeks. She was determined to look prettier, more feminine, for Alex's sake.

"Mai Ling is putting the finishing trim on the green one right now. Weren't expecting you until later in the day." The woman behind the counter was apologetic. "I'll tell her to hurry, *Miss* Claybourne." Her manner toward Samantha had changed and Samantha could only suppose that the seamstress had read the article about her in *The Register-Call*.

"Oh, now, hold your shirt on. Don't want to put anyone out. I've got more than plenty of time to wait. Just leave her be." Spying a row of headless forms adorned with dresses, she gestured with her head. "I'll just amuse myself a bit by looking around."

One of the dresses was a wedding dress and Samantha reached out to touch its froth of satin, lace, and pearls. It was the prettiest thing she had ever seen. Long-sleeved, with a skirt made of yards and yards of flower-patterned lace, it seemed to shimmer in the early morning light. Like something a fairy princess might wear, she thought. For just a moment she envisioned herself wearing that dress, standing beside Alex in front of the preacher, hearing the preacher's voice proclaiming them man and wife. Reluctantly she tore herself away to examine the second dress, a blue velvet dinner gown with braid trim outlining a daringly low neckline.

"Why, I'd never be so bold as to wear something like this," she whispered. In shocked disapproval she looked at the tag proclaiming ownership, expecting to see Honey Wells's name there. Instead it read *Caroline West,* the name that stirred such unwelcome memories.

Turning her back on the mannequins, she strolled up and down the counter. Sitting on large blocks of sculptured wood was a variety of hats. Annie was a milliner as well as a dressmaker. Samantha stifled a laugh at some of the creations, wondering how any woman would have the nerve to walk the boardwalk wearing such a concoction on her head. Bobbing peacock feathers made one hat look as if it were going to take flight, another was covered with so many flowers that it looked like a garden. There were hats of every color and style: straw hats decked with ribbons, velvet hats decorated with lace and pearls, felt hats with ribbon ties, all perched side by side. Feeling bold, she picked up one of the plainest hats and put it on, turning her head from side to side to examine her image in the mirror. The feather tickled her nose, made her sneeze, and convinced her at once that it was not for her. Hats were a bother— except for her miner's hat. How it would look if she decorated it with feathers, flowers, and ribbons?

"Come along with me, Mary Anne. Annie should have my

dress done by now. *Robert* is taking me to the theater tonight. Jack Langrishe's group is presenting *Romeo and Juliet*." Caroline West swept through the door of the shop, letting it bang shut behind her. With her was a dark-haired woman from Caroline's circle, whom Samantha recognized. Suddenly anxious to avoid a confrontation, Samantha ducked behind one of the mannequins as the two women swept by.

"Robert? Is he a new beau?" The high-pitched voice sounded on the verge of a giggle.

"He's a lawyer who has an office in Daddy's building. Unlike my former fiancé, Robert is not a coward, nor does he argue with Daddy all the time about every little thing. Robert is completely manageable."

Peeking around the mannequin, Samantha could see the women examining a bolt of cloth as they talked. Why had she taken refuge behind the wedding dress, Samantha wondered? Was she afraid of coming face-to-face with Caroline and finding out that she wanted Alex back? Yes. She felt such a sense of relief to hear about Caroline's new escort that she nearly sighed aloud.

"Robert may be manageable but I'll never understand how you could let a man as handsome as your Boston gentleman get away. Why, I hear he's keeping company with that Claybourne hoyden. And he's as brazen as you please in his attentions."

"I didn't *let* Alex get away, as you put it, Mary Anne. Daddy made me realize that he just wasn't suitable to become a member of our family. I hated to break his heart the way I did, but it had to be done. Poor dear man, he was shattered. Why, even now, whenever I see him on the street, his eyes seem to be pleading with me to take him back. To give him my love again." She clutched at her chest. "But I didn't realize I'd driven him to such straits, made him so desperate. Keeping company with that little . . . well . . ."

It was all Samantha could do to hold her temper. She wanted nothing more than to hurl herself at these two jabbering cats and make them apologize. Instead she found herself burrowing deeper into the bustle of the wedding dress and straining her ears to hear the rest of the conversation.

"That little . . . hoyden . . . that little *draggletail* is very wealthy now, or so they say. Is it possible that your Alex is a fortune hunter? Such things have happened before. Why, just last year there was a woman who owned a mine and got swindled. A gambler sweet-talked her into a partnership, even proposed marriage. To make a long story short, he filed a claim, challenged her in court, and won the deed to her mine."

"Yes, I remember. I wouldn't put such a thing past Alex, let me tell you. Why else would he give a woman like *that* his time? Daddy told him again and again how much he wanted that silly mine. Now Alex has accomplished what Daddy couldn't, I suppose he'll find himself a very wealthy man. But he will break his ties to Samantha Claybourne at the very first opportunity, I daresay. You'll see."

"He will not! Alex wouldn't—" Samantha couldn't bear to hear anymore. How dare they say such things. Alex was not some scoundrel out to steal her mine. He was not! "Take it back!" Grabbing a shrieking Caroline by the bodice of her dress, Samantha stared her down. "Alex helped me. He gave me money when your father stole my gold dust. I won't let you say such things."

"Let go of me! You uncouth little . . ." Caroline's expression was a mixture of loathing and fear.

"Say you are sorry! Say it, before I get hoppin' mad and lose my temper!" Samantha tightened her hold. "I've had just about enough of you and your father, lady."

"Ohhhh!" Frantically Caroline pulled away, tearing her dress in the process. "Now see what you have done!" Seeking safety behind the counter, she raised her finger and shook it in Samantha's direction. "I'll tell my father. You'll regret what you've done today. Why he'll—"

"Put me in jail like he did Buck Cameron? I don't think so." Samantha's eyes flashed fire. "It's time old Jeremiah realized he's met his match. He has. You can tell him that. You can tell him something else as well. He'll never get his grubby hands on *my* mine. Alex will see to that. No matter what you think, Alex is on *my* side." Standing with her hands on her hips, one leg thrust forward, Samantha was scowling as Annie walked through the curtained entranceway to the back room. The anxious expression on the woman's face kept Samantha from saying all she wanted to say. Taking her package from Annie's outstretched arms, she left the shop in a huff, trying to wipe Caroline's callous, hateful words from her mind.

40

The noise of pounding hammers, the scraping of shovels, and the din of the workmen's conversation floated on the breeze to Alex's ears as he walked down Eureka Street. The excavation for Henry Teller's hotel was finished and the actual building begun. Robert Cunningham had told him that the cloudburst they'd had in July had accomplished in three hours what otherwise would have taken days. The structure was to be four stories high and it was whispered that Henry Teller planned to supply the hotel with water from its own springs. It was an ambitious venture in a city whose tallest building had never been more than three stories. Nevertheless, Alex wished the man well. Anyone who had business dealings with Jeremiah West needed all the luck he could get.

"Jeremiah West," he grumbled beneath his breath, remembering the happenings of late. There had been many attempts to interfere with work at the mine. Alex suspected it to be someone in the pay of Jeremiah West. There had been another roadblock; the ore cart had been upended; someone had rummaged through tools and scattered them about. Harmless deeds, but annoying. He was of a mind to confront West with his suspicions. The mischief had to stop. That was one of the reasons he was headed toward the West and Hatcher Bank this morning; a visit with Robert was the other. Robert, it appeared, now occupied Alex's old office. He found his friend there with the door ajar and his feet perched atop the desk. Suppressing a smile, Alex stepped inside.

"Alex! What a pleasant surprise." Robert grinned a bit sheepishly.

"You always did like that chair and desk," Alex responded dryly, raising one brow in a mocking manner. "It's a good thing I always made you feel at home." Closing the door behind him, he declined Robert's offer of a chair. "I won't be staying long."

Robert looked contrite. "Aw, now don't be angry with me, Alex. That tiny cubbyhole I rented upstairs was uncomfortable. When J.W. told me this office was available, I jumped at the chance to put up my shingle here. Can't blame me for wanting to live in plush surroundings." Opening the drawer of the desk, he grabbed a box of cigars and held it out to Alex. "Oh, that's right, you don't smoke. I forgot."

"I'm glad to see you coming up in the world, my friend. I hold no claim here. I can't talk long because I have a meeting with one of my investors. I'm going to build a boardinghouse for unfortunate individuals who are down on their luck. It was Samantha's idea." He smiled as he said her name and the look of happiness glowing in his eyes did not go unnoticed.

"Samantha, huh? You've been spending a great deal of time with her, Alex. Any wedding bells in your future?" He leaned forward on his elbow intently.

"If she will have me, yes. I love her very much," Alex admitted openly. There was no reason to keep it secret. "She said no once, but I'm going to ask again."

"You sly old dog!" Throwing back his head, Robert whooped with delight. "I knew it. I knew it. First time I saw the two of you together I was certain the sparks between you were too hot not to come to something." His voice lowered conspiratorially. "In case you haven't heard, I've been squiring Caroline about town. Believe me, you made the best of *that* bargain. If it weren't for this office and a few amenities, I'd follow your example and bid her good-bye. I thought I could cope with her vanity and her pride, but she's a bit more than even I can handle. Which only goes to prove that an elusive butterfly is often more alluring when it is out of reach."

"You're not in love with Caroline?"

Robert shook his head emphatically no. "I admired her, thinking her too far above me to even contemplate touching. When you broke your engagement I was certain I'd found my opportunity to acquire a place in paradise. I just didn't listen to my own advice."

"People seldom do. One day you'll meet someone who'll make you forget that any other woman ever existed. Like Samantha. That's my hope for you, Robert. To be as happy as I am now." Changing his mind, Alex pulled up a chair, settling himself comfortably as he leaned back. He enjoyed talking with Robert again. They fell into the pattern of easygoing conversation now as Robert gave a detailed account of what he had been doing the last two months, his women, his work. Most of his cases were simple ones—getting gamblers out of jail, filing new mining claims, settling disagreements between married couples. In turn Alex talked about his days at the mine, about Samantha and his hopes for the future.

"I hope that Jeremiah has come to realize that Samantha will never give up that mine."

"I don't think that he does, Alex. J.W. never gives up on anything once he's made up his mind. He's ruthless in his acquisition of power. He'll smash anyone to bits if they get in his way. Hell, he's done it time and time again. My advice to you is to keep your eyes open, always look over your shoulder, listen to every little whisper. J.W. resents Samantha with an intensity that is frightening. He wants to see her brought down from her lofty perch."

"I know that. Though I can't produce any evidence, I suspect him of foul play. I had intended to warn him on the subject. That's one of the reasons I came by today."

"Don't!" Choking on his cigar smoke, Robert gasped.

"Don't what?" Alex stared at Robert in surprise. His usually ruddy complexion had turned ashen.

"Don't confront J.W. And for God's sake don't get me involved." Looking over his shoulder cautiously, Robert lowered his voice. "I . . . I've got it made, Alex. For the first time in my life. I wouldn't want to rile the old man. I know you love Samantha but . . ."

The guilty look in Robert's eyes, the stammer, alerted Alex. Something was wrong. Bolting from his chair he was on Robert like a shot. "What's going on? What are you hiding? Tell me, Robert. I'm not a violent man, but by God I'll throttle the information out of you if I have to." As if making good on his words, he grabbed the young lawyer by the lapels of his newly tailored suit.

"Nothing . . ." Robert effected an innocent grin.

"Nothing? Don't lie to me my friend. I can read it all too plainly on your face." A nerve in Alex's jaw twitched as he looked the lawyer in the eye. "You and that scheming old man are hatching something. What? What?" His hand curled into a ball, wrinkling the other man's suit.

"I don't know. Though I wish I did. I'll keep my eyes and ears open just in case J.W. gets careless in his maneuvers." With a frantic twist of his torso, Robert tried to pull away from Alex's hold. "Let me go before you tear my suit."

"If you are instrumental in hurting Samantha in any way, I'll —" Realizing how close he was to losing control, Alex released him. "Please, Robert. Please. I've thought of you as my friend, considered you far above West's villainy."

Rising from his chair, Robert walked to the door and looked out, scanning the hallway carefully. Satisfied, he closed the door and turned to Alex. "All right. Samantha is a young woman with spunk. I admire that. And I admire you. I'd really hate to see her hurt by that vindictive old man." Robert related the conversation he'd had with the banker only an hour earlier. He told Alex about the newspaper article, of Jeremiah's plans to get property rights to the land. Samantha would own the gold, but Jeremiah West would own the road, the cabin, and the land the mine was on. "With all the merchants and most of the town officials beholden to him or, in his pay, he just might get away with it."

"The bastard! There must be a way."

"There is. Samantha's got to apply for a patent before J.W. does. There is every possibility that the tables can be turned before he even knows what's going on." Folding his arms across his chest, Robert was silent for a moment as he thought the matter out. "Looks like I can say good-bye to my fine cigars and my new office. I'll be lucky not to be practicing law out on the street if J.W. finds out I've warned you." He shrugged. "Easy come, easy go. Up one minute and down the next. But what the hell! I like you, Alex." A wide grin trembled on his lips. "I'd enjoy seeing J.W. beaten at his own game for a change."

"Then you'll help? I promise you, Robert, you won't be sorry. I'll hire you as *my* lawyer. I've got a few ideas about what this territory needs myself."

"Work with you, Alex?" Robert seemed elated at the idea. "Can I have an office like this? A lawyer needs to look successful if he's going to be taken seriously."

"Nothing but the best." Alex grinned.

"Well, then, let's get to work, *boss.*" Reaching in the desk again, he pulled out a wrinkled piece of paper and held it out for Alex's inspection. "This is what needs to be done under the new law conveying land from the United States government to a private individual. The steps are to survey, to post a notice of intent to patent, to post a sixty-day public notice in the local paper." He grinned. "Jeremiah thinks I'm doing this for him, but he's going to have a surprise in store."

Alex crumbled up the paper in irritation. "How in blazes did West think he could steal the property from under Samantha's nose? Surely there's some kind of justice even out here."

"Welll, I did foresee a few problems. I told him so. But J.W. thinks he can pay just about *anyone* to do just about *anything.* So far he's been right."

"Then I think it's about time he learned otherwise." The decision was made, the bargain sealed, and a plan set into action. With Robert's help Alex knew he would be successful in outfoxing the fox.

41

Ben Cody was restless. Bored. When he got bored, he got nervous. When he was nervous, his trigger finger itched to be used.
Gambling and drinking could keep a man amused for just so
long. He was tired of Central City. It was too big, too crowded
to be amusing. He had to watch himself. It seemed there were
always more than one pair of eyes on him whenever he walked
the street. So someone, he thought, had figured out his profession, it made them nervous and they were keeping him under
surveillance. Well, he wouldn't be here much longer. Once his
business with Alexander Nicholson was finished, he'd be moving on.

Alexander Nicholson. Just thinking the name made his stomach clench in a knot. He wanted to see the Major beg, just as he
had that fateful night. He hadn't bushwhacked him or shot him
in the back. He didn't want to spoil all his fun. He wanted
Alexander Nicholson to know exactly from where the bullet
that slammed into him was coming from. In the meantime he'd
kept his trigger finger quick by tangling with a man or two in a

dark alley, men of such little importance, they'd never be missed.

The Major was another matter entirely. Ben had been forced to use caution. Alexander Nicholson had aligned himself with the town's most influential citizen, a man whom it had seemed dangerous to cross. Now all that had changed. He'd heard the gossip bandied about. Alexander had come west to marry a rich man's daughter, but she had broken the engagement because she'd found out that the man she was about to marry was a coward. Refused to carry a gun.

Slamming his empty whiskey glass down on the bar, he chuckled at the thought. Coward. Major Alexander Nicholson, hero of Gettysburg, a coward! So the Major had lost his stomach for death. Strange that war could have such different effects on men. The Major had sworn off guns while he, Ben Cody, had learned to relish the power a long-barreled pistol conferred. Interesting. Amusing. Why, once he'd shot a man in the head just to see if the bullet would bounce to the right or the left of his bald pate. There were some who said that Cody was "Hell turned loose, Satan's executioner." Wherever he went, he was regarded with awe. If he was not a "hero," he was the next best thing to it.

Clearing his throat, Cody spit into the brass spittoon beside the bar. He'd have to be very careful lest his plan backfire. Unlike some others, the Major was no fool, nor was he slow with a gun. Ben remembered his markmanship all too well. Nicholson's intelligence and cunning made him a dangerous adversary. Unless he threw him off balance, Cody might very well end up as the victim himself. He would have to choose his time and act quickly.

He had no definite plan but supposed late afternoon or evening would be best. It was then that Central City became a noisy, busy town crowded with buggies and wagons, and people riding to their homes from the mines or stores. The stamp mills would still be going, drowning out any cries for help. Hell, if the piano player in the Silver Garter Saloon was playing his favorite song, he might even have accompaniment to his shooting.

Throwing money down on the bar, pulling his hat low on his face, Cody left the saloon. He strolled casually, pausing from time to time to scan the faces of passersby, hoping, always hoping, to come face-to-face with his quarry. Thus it was that he spotted Alex coming out of the bank. Stepping directly in Alex's path, he asked, "Say, mister, got a match?"

"I believe I do." Fumbling in his pocket, his mind still on his conversation with Robert, Alex didn't notice the man's face until he held forth the tiny wooden object. The look in those gray eyes chilled him.

"Much obliged." Taking time to light his cigarette, Cody slowly, insolently eyed Alex up and down. Seeing him up close brought back the past as if it had been only yesterday. High-and-mighty Major Nicholson. He hadn't changed a bit. Cody's voice was cold as he asked, "Haven't we met before? I seem to remember your face. I never did like it then and I don't believe I like it now. Ah, yes. The Major."

Ben Cody, Alex thought. He had changed, changed a great deal. The scar, the grim line in which he held his mouth, the cruel eyes—years of hard drinking and little sleep had ravaged the face and though Alex knew Ben Cody was a year younger than he was, Cody looked ten years older. The life he'd led was recorded on his face. The man inspired pity, not fear. The past six years could not have been easy ones for the man who now stood before him.

"I go by 'Alex' now, Ben. The war has been over a long time. I think we'd all like to forget it. I know I certainly would."

"Forget all that hoopla and excitement? Why I expect you were powerful sorry to see it end. What's it like to be a war hero, Major? To have it sung to the skies that you saved your men at . . . Antietam, was it? . . . or Gettysburg. I can't quite remember."

"It doesn't matter. I've put the war out of my mind." *And it would be well for you to do the same,* Alex thought, watching out of the corner of his eye as Cody fidgeted with the handle of his gun. A Colt Peacemaker, from the looks of it. His attempt to unsettle Alex by his actions and his stance was obvious.

"Put it out of your mind?" Ben Cody snapped his fingers. "Just like that! Well, I haven't and I won't." Taking two steps forward, he stood less than a foot away from Alex. "And I haven't forgotten just whose fault it was that I can't."

"The war was no one's fault, Ben. It was tragic. Senseless. Brutal. But for that we must all share blame. I don't think there is any disagreement that can't be solved peacefully if men just take the time to talk it out."

"Talk? Ha!" Drawing his long-barreled pistol from his holster, he held it in front of Alex's nose. "This is what men understand. This! It can make a giant as useless as Goliath, make a rich man as powerless as a pauper. It's the only thing anybody really understands." His lips curled in an evil smile. "Just remember that when you walk these streets at night. And be careful, Major, lest you have a little *accident.*" With mock courtesy, he tipped his hat. "But I can't stand here jawin' all day. Nor do I want to take up any more of your time."

"Ben . . ." Alex knew there was something in Cody's craw, something poisonous. Apparently it related to the time they had served together in the army, but what was it? That time spent in the brig? A small matter to cause such anger. "If there's something troubling you, let's have it out. Let me buy a whiskey at the Silver Garter and—"

"Just came from there, Major. Besides, just what would folks think if they saw you keeping company with me? Wouldn't want to shock 'em. Could spoil *my* reputation, you goin' without a gun and all." Turning his back on Alex, he made his way down the street, pausing only once before he was out of earshot. "Don't worry," he called back over his shoulder, fixing Alex with an icy glare. "We'll meet again."

42

The mirror glittered, bouncing bright rays of early morning sun into Samantha's eyes as she pensively studied her reflection. Would Alex be pleased? She hoped so. She wanted to look more *womanly* for him, wanted to make him proud when they walked the boardwalk in town today. She was *his* girl and she wanted him to revel in that fact, wanted him to be proud to have her on his arm. No one would call her "that Claybourne hoyden" today.

"Fuss and bother," she grumbled nonetheless. This business of being feminine seemed to take a great deal of time. Why, just the preliminaries had taken her an hour and she wasn't even dressed yet. She'd heated water on the stove and filled the old wooden tub and soaked and scrubbed in rose-scented foam until her skin glowed like a peach. She'd washed her hair in the concoction the woman at the general store had given her, then towel-dried it before the fire, and that had been only the beginning. Sitting in her frilly new drawers, chemise and petticoat, she toyed feverishly with her hair, using the wood and metal

curling iron to bring some semblance of order to her unruly
waves.

With a sigh, she put the last curl in its place and tied a mint
green ribbon around her head. The final result of her efforts
seemed suitable. The girl looking back at her from the mirror
agreed. The wispy bangs accentuated her large brown eyes, just
as the woman at the store had promised. The long burnished
curls, brushed back from her face and held in a slight cluster
over her shoulder, did indeed make her neck look long and
swanlike.

"Mmm." A stranger stared back at her, looking more like the
women who milled around the bolts of cloth in the general store
than Samantha Marie Claybourne. Twittering behind their
hands, they had gaped at her in amazement when she left the
store with a bottle of rose-water and lace-trimmed underwear.
Ducking into the livery stable Samantha had examined her
purchases and the dresses in awe. She'd conjured up three very
pretty dresses, all right. The dressmaker had done just what
she'd said. Couldn't have turned out any better if she'd sewn
them herself, if she'd been able to sew, that is.

Samantha remembered running her hands over each one.
She'd purchased a mint green muslin trimmed in white cotton
lace, a black-and-white checked skirt to be worn with a white
blouse with high-standing color and a periwinkle blue poplin.
The blue dress she had decided on. Alex had said that blue was
his favorite color. Putting on the black skirt and white blouse,
she had paraded her finery before the townswomen's startled
eyes.

"Found me some gold. Thought I'd dud out accordingly,"
she had informed the staring women, the very same women
who had once chastised Enoch Claybourne for the way he was
bringing up his granddaughter. "Might even buy me some perfume, if I have a hankering. The kind that comes all the way
from France." She'd done just that, wondering if she would
really have the nerve to wear it.

Staggering out of one store, her arms overloaded with boxes
and packages, she had even been the recipient of Slim Walker's
smiling appraisal. Reining in his mount, leaning forward over

the pommel of his saddle, he'd eyed her up and down. "That you, Sam?"

"Course it's me."

"Never seen you in a dress before. Looks right purty. Why, you even look like a *woman.* Thought you might be one, but I wasn't really sure." Climbing down from his horse he'd even been polite, helping her load the packages in her wagon. With a tip of his hat he'd taken his leave of her, promising he would stop by the cabin for a spell sometime. Despite Samantha's mumbled reply that she'd just as soon be visited by a polecat, he had tipped his hat and taken his leave of her with a wink. Though she could not admit it to herself, she'd been secretly pleased by his compliment. If Slim was appreciative of her new finery, Alex would be doubly impressed. More so today with her hair combed just right and the new green dress bedecking her freshly steamed and scented body.

Tugging and pulling first at the skirt, and then at the bodice, she laced herself up, adjusted the collar, smoothed the skirt with the palms of her hands, and appraised herself again. A lot of fuss and bother just to please a man! One concession she had not made, however. She would not trade in her boots for those dainty shoes she'd seen some fool women wear. She'd not have her grandfather look down from heaven and laugh. Flimsy little shoes with buckles or bows just weren't for her. Mountain living declared the need for something warm, thick, and strong on a person's feet. Besides, she was certain she could never maintain her balance on those scrawny, skinny heels. She'd most likely break her darned-fool neck! Alex would have to understand. A woman would do just so much.

Settling down in the settee, Samantha calmed herself by reading her grandfather's journal as she waited for Alex. He was late. That was unusual for a man who seemed to pace himself by his watch. Alex was always on time. She supposed there must be a reasonable explanation for his being late today.

"That Claybourne hoyden," she growled softly, remembering Caroline West and their confrontation at the dressmaker's shop. "Draggletail." She'd show her. She'd show them all. Every last person who had laughed at her. Imagine that woman insinuating that Alex was after her mine. Ha! They'd see. When she was

Mrs. Alexander Nicholson, they'd eat their words. Maybe that other woman had been swindled, but not Samantha. Never. They were wrong in thinking Alex was after her money. He didn't want her mine, he wanted her.

Samantha put down the journal, clasping it so tightly that she bent the cover. The conversation wasn't the only thing that troubled her. She had seen Alex going into Jeremiah West's bank. Knowing he had no money there, she had wondered what his errand could be, but once again she had put it from her mind. Still, he had seemed so desperately preoccupied these last few days. He was continually shuffling those foolish ledgers about and the papers he called stock certificates, or poring over pen-and-ink maps covered with oblong-shaped mining claims that overlapped each other in intricate designs.

Samantha shook her head. She should be grateful for his interest. Standing up, she paced the cabin, her eyes scanning the area with a trembling grin. Just as she was slowly changing to reflect Alex's influence, so was her home. Now there were curtains at the window, the interior had been painted, and two new upholstered chairs had been added to the sitting area. There was even a small desk for Alex. China plates and cups had taken the place of the earthenware crockery. Her tin cutlery had given way to knives, forks, and spoons fashioned from silver. Imagine, she thought. Eating with silver. True, she had vowed not to become "highfalutin'," but Alex was used to the finer things of life and she did so want to make him happy. Thinking about him now, worrying about him as the time stretched on, she walked to the door and opened it. Two men stood huddled together talking several yards away, as one of the men wrote something down on a piece of paper.

"You there, what are you doing on my land?" After all the mischief at the mine, it took very little to rouse her suspicions. Were these Jeremiah West's men?

"We're surveying, ma'am." The man who answered held a ball of string and was winding some of it around a stick.

"Surveying?" Anxiously she squinted against the sun to see just exactly what it was they *were* doing. Seeing them pound cornerstones in the ground, she knew they were being truthful and the truth frightened her more than if they had told a lie. "Surveying!" That could mean only one thing. *Claim jumping.*

In a flash she had her rifle in hand and was bounding out the door. Now that she'd found gold, every weasel and con man within a radius of a thousand miles would be after her mine. Well, no one would worm their way in here, no one. "You get on out of here. Hear me?" She ran a few steps, holding the rifle out before her. When she was in shooting distance, she halted and carefully took aim. "Get! I said get!"

"Whoa, woman. Don't shoot." The man with the string held up his hands.

"What are you doing here? This is my land." Samantha edged closer, keeping her eyes on the two men.

"Your land? No it isn't. Belongs to the territory. It's government land, at least now." A mocking smile played on the lips of the man who'd been writing.

"My grandfather staked a claim on the mine out yonder. Staked it out and recorded it, all proper and legal-like. So you just get back on your horses and ride on out of here before I get really riled and shoot."

"Aw, now, you wouldn't do that. Not a pretty little thing like you. Might hurt yourself. Woman hadn't ought to tote a gun." Calling her bluff, the man put his pen behind his ear and took a few steps forward. A carefully aimed bullet exploding at his feet stopped him in his tracks. "What the hell?"

"The next one will take off your toe, and don't think I don't mean it! I've been carrying a rifle since I was eight years old. Just because I'm wearing a dress doesn't mean I'm a piece of fluff. I worked for that gold and I aim to keep it."

"It isn't the gold we're interested in. We're just doing the job we've been hired to do." The man looked warily at her, thinking she just might carry out her threat and deciding he wouldn't chance it. "If you say so, you own the gold. Your grandfather most likely claimed the mineral rights but not the land. Honest, sister, it does belong to the federal government, at least for the time being. I'm just staking it out so the gentleman who hired us can file a claim. I don't ask questions, I just do what I'm paid to do."

"He's telling the truth. You don't have a quarrel with us."

The man with the string relentlessly rolled the twine back around the ball. He was even so bold as to whistle.

"Jeremiah West!" Samantha spat the name contemptuously. There wasn't anything too low for him to contemplate. "Well, you can tell him for me that I'll shoot anyone he sends up here. You tell Mr. West that I'd tangle with the devil himself to keep what belongs to me, even the federal government. I've lived in this cabin nearly all my life and he knows it. You tell Jeremiah West that he can go right straight to hell. That I'll *help* him get there if he sets one foot on this property again."

"Jeremiah West?" The man shook his head. "He wasn't the one who sent us, though I know very well who he is."

Samantha laughed scornfully. "Jeremiah didn't send you. You expect me to believe that? Might as well tell me that fish can fly! That villain is lower than a snake's belly and twice as repulsive. He sent you, all right. Don't know who on earth else would do such a thing."

"Alexander Nicholson did. That was his name. Dark-haired fellow that's a friend of the lawyer. They both gave me instructions Told me to hurry before anyone knew what they were about. Wanted to keep our doings secret, or so they said."

"Alexander Nicholson?" Samantha shook her head. "Not Alex. The very idea was preposterous. If she couldn't trust Alex, who in this world could she trust?

"I tell you he *did*!" Throwing the piece of paper on the ground, the taller of the men showed his frustration, then bent to pick it up again. "You can ask him if you want."

"Don't think that I won't, sooner than you think." Out of the corner of her eye Samantha spotted Alex's buggy. The way he sat so straight-backed in the seat made him unmistakable, even from a distance. "I'll ask him and when he says no . . ." She pointed the rifle at the taller man's midsection threateningly. Oh, she wouldn't shoot an unarmed man, of course, but he didn't know that. If she scared him enough, he wouldn't be back, no matter who ordered him. "Alex!" Still keeping the rifle aimed, she backed toward him as the buggy came to a halt. "Alex, I'm so glad to see you. We've got trouble here. These two have been surveying my land. Said you sent them. Don't they have a nerve."

"I did send them, Samantha. You *don't* own the land here, just the mineral rights. I wanted to file a claim so that—" He didn't have time to finish. In dazed fury she whirled on him.

"You sent them? *You* sent them! No. Don't tell me that. You wouldn't double-deal me that way. Say that you wouldn't, Alex." All the warnings her grandfather had whispered in her ears for so many years now came tumbling back full force. He'd warned her against trusting *anyone.* A man would cheat his own mother when it came to gold, he had said. *Isn't it possible that your Alex is a fortune hunter?* Words haunting her. "You *didn't* send them. There must be some mistake."

"He sent us, lady, just like we said, so he could file a claim. Now, let us go." Seeing she was distracted, both men slowly backed away, then took to their heels the moment they were out of rifle range. Samantha watched them mount their horses without trying to stop them. They'd said all she needed to hear.

"You were going to cheat me out of my mine." She shook her head, disbelieving even as she said the words. "You wanted to get my land. Wasn't a quarter share in the gold enough for you, Alex?"

"Let me explain. I wasn't after your mine, Samantha. Jeremiah West—"

"So you were in cahoots with him all the time only I didn't realize it. He couldn't get the mine fair and square so he sent you to sweet-talk me. Jeremiah West's soon to be son-in-law. Why couldn't I see?"

"That's not true and you know it." Alex was angry. To think she could make such an accusation after he had tried to help her. "Why would I have loaned you the money to keep this mine going if I wanted to steal it from you?" His voice grew louder as his frustration mounted. "Can you answer that one?"

"To earn my trust. To fandoozle me! Is that why you asked me to marry you, Alex? So you could have *complete* control of the mine?" The words exploded from her lips before she could think. "You bankers are all alike. Every lock, stock, and barrel of you . . . no scruples . . . I never meant anything at all to you."

"If you think that then you are a *fool*! If you can stand there and hurl such utterly stupid—" Taking a deep breath, Alex fought to control his emotions. How could she say such things? Doubt him?

"Stupid?" She raised her rifle, pointing it at him. "Well, you just follow those hired men of yours on down the mountain, Alex. If I see you up here again, any one of you, so help me I'll pepper your hides full of lead. I've said it once and I'll say it again. No one will get this mine away from me. Not even you!"

Alex clenched his fists, his cheeks were suffused with red. "Why you little termagant. Do you think you can solve all of life's problems by pointing a gun? Is that your answer? If so, then you have a lot to learn." Turning his back on her, he walked away but paused to shout over his shoulder, "I won't be back. When you've had some time to cool off and think reasonably, you can come to *me.*" Jumping into the buggy, he flicked the reins, startling the horses into a lively gallop.

Lowering the rifle wearily, sadly, Samantha watched as the buggy, horses, and rider became tiny specks in the distance. "Alex, come back. I'm sorry." She wanted to take back her words, wanted to follow him, but instead she merely stared at the road in numbed silence, at last allowing herself to succumb to her tears.

43

Alex's fury increased as he rode back into town. Women! What a confusing, irrational sex they were. "Add unappreciative," he mumbled to himself. He'd worried about Samantha from the very first moment he'd met her; he had intended to help her, to protect her, and what thanks did he get? Why, she'd practically called him a thief. In fact, she *had*! She had threatened him with a rifle! And all because had tried to guard her proprietorship of the Siren Song against Jeremiah West's invasion. It had proved a thankless task.

Samantha Claybourne was a stubborn, wild, undisciplined little hellion. What the townspeople whispered was true. Alex had seen another side to her now. She most certainly could be headstrong. He'd admired her independence, her strength, and her courage, but those qualities could be pushed to the limit. A man required a little softness now and then. And even more important was the issue of trust. That Samantha had been ready to think the worst of him with so little provocation stung him. He'd worked side by side with her in the mine for weeks on end, spent hours on her financial affairs. Yet when her temper was aroused, it was all forgotten. Suddenly, he had become her adversary.

"A little hellion," he swore, remembering the glint of anger in her eyes. And yet she had made a pretty picture standing there, all fire and sparks. The dress, her hair . . . Alex could feel his anger fading, knowing she'd worn that dress just for him. He remembered her kisses, her soft, clinging body and knew that he was lost. He simply could not do without her. She was in his heart, his soul, his very blood. He wanted to scold her, to shake her, to rebuke her for her lack of confidence in him, but he could not put her out of his mind. Never that. He wondered if he could ever stop wanting her.

He tried to understand Samantha, tried to imagine what her childhood had been like. Her grandfather had loved her, of a certainty he had, and yet he had kept her apart from other people. She had lived like a hermit. Even now Samantha was an entity unto herself, friendless and alone. It was that loneliness that had first drawn him to her and still touched him. Her grandfather had taught her not to trust, and with good reason. Perhaps her display of suspicion today was not so strange. Coming upon two men staking out her land, was it really any wonder she had jumped to the wrong conclusion? Surely, when she had time to think about it, she would come to her senses. Until then, Alex decided, he would continue in his efforts to secure her patented claim; he would do what he could to keep her safe from Jeremiah West's schemes.

The road was muddy and puddled from a recent rainstorm, and difficult to maneuver. The horses' heads bobbed up and down, their breathing labored as great billows of white vapor emerged from their nostrils. Slowing the animals down to a trot, he allowed them to cool off. He had been lost in his own thoughts, but now the world around him shifted back into focus. The sky was intensely blue, the mountains a blend of riotous autumnal colors. The chill proclaimed snow. Already there were patches of early snow on the faraway mountaintops. It was a wilderness paradise. Peaceful. Serene. Just as this unspoiled land was getting into his blood, so had she.

Alex thought about his feelings. He had initiated friendship, little realizing where it would lead. He could have backed away at any time but had allowed himself to become more and more involved until the inevitable had happened. She had won his heart with sweet innocence, then turned on him with utter distrust. Her behavior was outrageous. But even so he would be true to his word. He would wait until Samantha came to him. That was the way it had to be.

Central City loomed in Alex's path sooner than he thought it would and he kept the horses cautiously under control. The usual Saturday crowds wove their way along the boardwalks, mingling the sound of their chattering with the crunch of his buggy's wheels. Alex made his first stop at the surveyor's office, where he instructed the men who had staked out Samantha's land to draw up a detailed plan and field notes.

"You going to help her after she poked that gun in your ribs?" One of the two men looked at Alex as if he had lost his mind, but set about his assignment nonetheless.

The second step in securing the land was easy. Since Alex had paid for tools and labor the last weeks, he had records and could prove that at least five hundred dollars' worth of labor had been performed on the mine. He posted the notice of claim with intent to patent, paid the fee of five dollars per acre, and posted the sixty-day public notice in the local newspaper. To be on the safe side, he sent copies of each document to the land office in Denver, as well as a telegram instructing them that further information was forthcoming. The rest, he left to Robert.

Alex had other business to attend to in Central City. As he reached Lawrence Street he focused his attention on a wooden building across the street from the Hazard Powder Company. Now the building belonged to him. Alex had never intended to keep any of the money he made from his share of Samantha's mine. Secretly, he had put it all in a trust fund for her, and used his own funds to invest in the future—shipping, cargo, and transportation.

Alex knew his temperament was ill suited to banking. His brief employment at West and Hatcher's had proved that. He needed to do something that would actively engage his energies, that would be of real benefit to the booming town. He had decided upon a freight and cargo business. It was what he had done in the East, though his cargoes had traveled on waves, not wheels. He had invested his money in a stage line with the prospect of extending his routes to include the railroad lines. His cargo routes would join his father's shipping lines to create a circuit that transferred goods from East to West, from West to East, and even across the ocean to Europe. Already the need for supplies and mining equipment filled his ledgers.

SEA-LAND EXPRESS read the sign over the doorway. Alex had hired experienced teamsters to make the harrowing drive. There were two main routes into Central City and Black Hawk. One from the north via Dory and Golden Gate Road, the other from the south via Virginia Canyon Road, coming from Idaho Springs.

No longer a stranger to this hostile land, Alex had begun to understand its wants and its needs. He was a shrewd, observant man who saw that soon Colorado Territory would become the crossroads of the country. It already was to some degree, with California and the other newly acquired territories needing access to the east. Colorado Territory was growing rapidly, might even become a state, and when it did, his business would expand along with it to include the railroad. Oh, yes, he was here to stay, he thought, all the more so because of Samantha. Despite the angry scene at the cabin, he still cherished hope. He would busy himself with his own pressing affairs and wait patiently until she came to him.

44

The fire crackled and sparked, the cabin was filled with the acrid odor of burning cloth. Standing in her drawers and chemise, Samantha watched the last of the mint green dress disappear in the flames. Tearing the ribbon from her hair, she threw it into the stove, all the while chanting, "Damn him, damn him, damn him!" Tears came in an overwhelming flood, pouring from her eyes, rolling down her cheeks. Angrily she dashed them away. Alex Nicholson wasn't worth crying over. He wasn't worth her tears.

"Oh, yes, he *is*!" Her thoughts tormented her. One moment she raged at him, the next she found herself defending him. Restless and miserable, she was consumed by her conflicting emotions. Devil or saint, which was he? Over and over again she relived the morning's confrontation.

He had confessed to having sent the two men. He had said that he wanted to file a claim. That, then, was the end of the matter. He was worse than a cad. A man who would do such a thing was second cousin to a polecat! She had thought him so wonderful. Had thought he really liked her. Love made such awful damned fools out of women. Made them deaf, made them blind, and rattled their brains. Yes, she loved him. Fool that she was, she did. Even now she remembered the way he had caressed her and missed the touch of his hands. She, who had prided herself on being so self-reliant, so strong, was in reality nothing but a dumb, gullible, backwoods half-wit. She had fallen victim to his good looks, his charm. How he must have been laughing all the while.

Her grandfather had warned her. Right from the first he had been leery of her fondness for the Boston stranger, of all newcomers to the territory. He'd tried to tell her, but she hadn't listened. "Like stays with like," her grandfather had said. She was so unlike Alex. He was as sophisticated as she was naive. How could she have believed he would seek her out? How could she have been so silly as to think he would choose her over women who sauntered about in pretty dresses and perfume? It hadn't been her that attracted his interest, but the mine.

Watching the dying embers of the fire, Samantha sat cross-legged on the hard, wooden floor. A deep void chilled her heart, her mind was blank. Oh, Alex! His very name released a fresh flood of tears. She had been so happy these last months. He had made her feel loved and wanted, made her realize what being a woman really meant. His presence in the mine, working side by side, had brightened her world. Now endless days of loneliness were all she saw ahead. Riches, ha! All the gold in the world couldn't bring her what she really wanted: Alex.

Samantha didn't know how long she sat there still as stone, her mind in a chaotic jumble. She was like a coiled spring, tense, unhappy. She had thought love was kisses and happy endings. No one had prepared her for devastation. All her dreams and plans had been destroyed. Within the space of a few hours she had gone from utter contentment to darkest despair. Was there anything that could ease the ache in her heart?

It was over. Alex would never dare come to the mine again, not after her threats. She should be able to come to terms with that; it was for the best, after all. Instead, she could only grieve. She might never see Alex again. Surely he would not risk being shot. Would she really carry out her threat, even to save her mine? No. She could never under any circumstance harm Alex. No matter what she might have said. It had been a bluff, a bold taunt to save her injured pride. Yet, now that she thought about it, Alex had seemed equally irate.

"Let me explain," he had said. He had acted offended, insulted, as if he were the injured party. Samantha closed her eyes and tried to remember what he had said. "Why would I have loaned you the money to keep the mine if I wanted to steal it from you?"

Samantha's unhappy lethargy was shattered by sudden doubt. What if he was telling the truth? What if she had misunderstood? He *had* given her the money to keep the mine working. It was she who had approached him. And when she had offered him a third share, he had insisted on only a quarter. Was that the response of a greedy man? And when it came to sweet-talking, it was she who had climbed into his bed. Could she ever forget how hard he had worked or the look of joy on his face when he told her she had found the vein?

"Oh, Alex . . ." Samantha groaned, wishing she had stopped to listen to his explanation instead of going off half-cocked, as her grandfather might have said. She had been so busy screaming, she hadn't given him a chance to get a word in edgewise. She'd been judge and jury, condemning him within the blink of an eye. What if she'd wronged him? What if Alex had been telling the truth all the while? Could he ever forgive her? Could she ever forgive herself?

There was only one way to learn the truth: she would have to visit the district recorder. She ought to have reasoned that out before she raged and ranted. Bounding to her feet, she slipped into shirt, boots, and breeches hoping desperately that she was wrong. Going out to the shed, she saddled one of the wagon horses, slipped a bit between his teeth, and climbed up on his back. She rode down the mountain in a fury, scolding herself all the while. Her mind was a whirling pinwheel of fireworks, conjuring up her own bitter words, reliving the hateful scene again and again. When at last she found herself standing before the clerk, her voice shook as she made the inquiry.

"Ah, yes, that fancy-dressed fella," the young man recalled. "Polite as you please."

"So, he did file a claim?" Samantha clutched at the counter, afraid that her trembling knees would collapse under her. Did she still own the mine?

"He posted a claim of intent to patent. All nice and legal-like. Seems he was afraid of someone else beating him to it. Guess there's gonna be a lot of confusion what with the new law and all."

"New law?" Samantha felt as if she were strangling.

"You ain't heard? Miners can now gain rights to the land they're working, 'stead of just owning the ore. If you ask me, it all boils down to that railroad that's gonna be built. Has something to do with it, I'll reckon. Details were in the paper just a week ago and since then there's been more than just a few folks crowding in here asking questions. But that dark-haired fella beats all. Don't let no grass grow under his feet."

"Can I see a . . . a copy of the claim?" She was almost afraid to look.

"Don't see why not." Rummaging through his files, he located the right piece of paper. "There was another man asking after this same piece of property. Was mad as hell when he found out he'd been had. Offered me a bribe to tear it up, but I couldn't do that. Wouldn't have been honest. Besides, that fella in the fancy suit told me he was going to keep another copy on file in Denver. Seemed like a wily one, he did. Even had his lawyer with him and all." He held it out for her inspection. "Funny thing is, his name ain't even on the claim." He laughed in great gulping guffaws. "Unless his name is Samantha."

The name on the claim danced before Samantha's eyes, the room seemed to pitch and sway. The name all too clearly read *Samantha Marie Claybourne.*

45

Samantha stomped along the boardwalk, furiously angry with herself. She'd made a fine mess of things, she thought. It was going to be hard to eat crow, but that was what she was going to have to do. Alex had said she'd have to come to him and she had no other choice. She had learned a well-deserved lesson: A body had to trust someone sometime. From now on she'd be devilishly cautious in knowing her friends from her enemies. Alex had more than proved his friendship. She would find him. Somehow she'd make it up to him for raving at him and putting him in her rifle-sight.

Samantha pushed her way between a knot of miners, off work from their shift, and a straw-bonneted housewife. She let the crowd carry her along toward the hotel then hurried inside. The lobby was deserted and she supposed most people would now be in the dining room at supper. The desk clerk returned her stare with a grim set to his chin. When she asked for Mr. Nicholson, he turned up his nose and responded with a growled *no*, regarding her shirt, hat, and breeches with disdain. Waiting until he turned his back, Samantha scuttled past his wooden-grille cage and dashed up the stairs, but much to her dismay, there was no reply from his room. Though she searched the eateries, the stores, the bank, and even the saloons, she could find no trace of him. Disappointed, exhausted, she mounted her horse and rode back to the cabin. She would have to apologize to Alex another day. Tomorrow at the crack of dawn!

"Jeremiah West!" she swore beneath her breath. It was all his fault. If she weren't for him, her quarrel with Alex would never have happened. "Damn him!" It made her feel better to vent her anger on the banker, though at the back of her mind she knew she herself was to blame. With a deep sigh she slid from her horse.

Picking up a small rock, she hurled it down the mountainside, watching as it fell to earth. Picking up another rock, she threw it, farther this time, making a game of it, feeling her tension relieved by such playfulness. This time she sought to retrieve the rock, running down the sloping hill with a laugh. After all the days spent in the mine, it felt good to be out in the fresh air. Finding the rock was suddenly very important to her, foolish as it was.

"Omph . . ." Stumbling over an obstacle in her path, Samantha fell to the ground with a thud. Rising to her feet, brushing dirt from her breeches, she reached up to adjust her hat, thankful that her backside had cushioned the jolt and the only damage had been to her pride. Squinting against the fading sun, she started to retrace her steps when her foot encountered the obstacle again. Bending down to clear away the foliage, Samantha gasped in shock when she saw it was a man.

"Hellfire and damnation!" She dug frantically to fully unearth the bruised and bloody form. The fleeting mood of calm she had felt only a moment ago was gone, swept away by the sight before her. The man had been beaten, his eyes blackened, his nose broken. He was a pitiful sight, but his tortured groans proved he was alive. For that Samantha gave thanks. But who was he? Where had he come from? A man didn't just pop out of thin air. Nor were the lacerations and bruises the result of a fall. Clearly someone had meant to do him a great deal of harm.

How long had he been lying there? One hour? Two? Samantha calculated that he had landed on her mountain shortly before her return from Central City. Hovering over his unconscious form, she did her best to awaken him, alarmed by his ashen pallor. In desperation Samantha tugged and pulled, urging the man to rise to his feet, until at last her efforts rouse him succeeded and she saw him move his hand. Struggling under his bulky weight, she somehow managed to half carry, half drag him back to the cabin.

Stoking the embers of the fire, Samantha shook her head. "Whoever did this to you is a brute, mister." The firelight illuminated the pathetically swollen face of the man lying on Samantha's bed. His hair was red, as bright as any flame; his cheekbones large. More than that she could not tell. Below his broken nose, the lower half of his face was covered by a thick thatch of beard. It was a pleasant enough face, she decided, despite the damage that had been done to it. His plight and pain touched her and she hovered over him with soothing words, watching as he slept.

She had stripped away his blood-soaked shirt and breeches, leaving him in his long johns, and covered him with a blanket. She put cold cloths on his swollen eyes, salve on his cuts and bruises, tending his broken nose as best she could. That there seemed to be no life-threatening injuries gave her cause for relief. It was a long way into town and he didn't appear to be in any shape for a jarring ride. Better to leave him here. He had the look of a strong man. With proper care, he'd recover. If there were any complications, she'd fetch a doctor.

"You're all right here. No one will harm you. You're safe." She crooned the words over and over, glancing at the rifle she had loaded and ready. If the men who'd assaulted him came back, she was prepared. Her jaw clenched in determination, she sat down beside the bed, picked up her grandfather's journal, and skimmed the pages.

"Am I in heaven?" The voice was soft and husky. "Sure 'n' you must be an angel." The puffy eyelids fluttered open.

Samantha met the man eye to eye, brown eyes to green. "I'm no angel, mister. A whole bunch of folks in town will tell you that. But I am tending you."

"I'm glad this ain't heaven. Don't know if I be ready for that." Wincing with pain, he reached up to prod at his nose. "Broken. Me fine nose." He tried to get up, but Samantha held him back, explaining how she'd found him, coaxed him to his feet, and dragged him up the hill.

"Who did this to you? Who beat you and why?" she asked.

"Let's just be sayin' it was a disagreement between me and a few larger fellows. I fear they got the best of me, though I promise I did put up quite a fight." Suddenly realizing he was half naked beneath the blankets, he flushed. Searching through a large box in the far corner of the room, Samantha found a clean pair of breeches and a shirt for him.

"Thank you. I'm . . . I'm grateful." He raised his brows in question.

"My name is Samantha. Samantha Claybourne."

"Sean. Sean O'Brien. It's an Irishman I am, if you can't be tellin'." As Samantha turned her back he dressed himself in a hurry, letting out a groan here and there as he moved his bruised and aching limbs. Then he settled down to answer her questions, to tell the young woman who'd saved his life a bit about himself. He was a miner, originally from New York, who had gone to Virginia City to work on the Comstock. The dangerous conditions and pitiful wages had persuaded him to head west to the Colorado Territory and thus in November he'd arrived in Central City. "Instead of findin' a better life for meself I found another miser and men workin' fer a measly three dollars a day just to please his greed. 'Tis no decent wage."

Sean O'Brien had it in mind to inspire his fellow laborers to organize, to stand up together against the mine owners and demand better working conditions and higher wages. He had talked with the other miners, but all it had netted him was a kick in the ribs and a swollen, bleeding face.

"The miners did this to you?"

"No! Ah, no. I was kidnapped, abducted from town by a tall, grinnin' tawny-haired man and his two nasty companions. It's certain I am that they were hired to 'teach me a lesson.' They tied me up, threw me in a wagon, and drove me up this mountain. Late last night they set upon me and when they were done, threw me from the wagon like so much garbage. 'Tis hard to say what might have happened if you had not found me."

Samantha clenched and unclenched her hands, suspecting the answer to the question but asking it anyway. "Who is the owner of the mine? What is his name?"

"Jeremiah West. 'Twas the Little Duchess I was workin'. A mine not too far from here."

"Jeremiah West!" Samantha said the name with scorn. "Describe his henchmen to me." From the descriptions he gave her, it sounded like Cy, Slim, and Buck. Cy Tyburn and his gang working for Jeremiah West? She didn't like the sound of that at all. It was a grisly combination. Taking a chair once more beside the Irishman, she bid him to tell her the entire story.

It was a sad tale that enfolded. While most mine owners shut down mining operations on days when it was bitterly cold, West kept his open, driving his miners unmercifully. Going from the heat of the mine shafts and the sweat of their labors to the piercing cold outside, many of the miners had been stricken with pneumonia. One man had died from it. Instead of taking pity on the dead man's family, West, who owned the house they lived in, threw them out into the snow. Only the charity of the other miners had eased the widow's burden until she had managed at last to find work as a seamstress in Black Hawk.

"Jeremiah West is lower than a snake's belly!" Samantha shouted, shocked by what she heard. She knew the banker was ruthless in his dealings, but she'd never thought anyone could be guilty of such heartlessness.

But that was not the half of it. Sean O'Brien talked of falling rocks, of improperly shored-up tunnels and shafts. The mines were not timbered up as they should have been because Mr. West wanted to cut costs. The miners faced endless hours and perilous conditions. Only the hardiest and most skilled miners survived and stayed on the job.

"If a miner takes Sunday off to attend church with his family, it's out of his pocket. At but three dollars a day few can afford it. When we complained to Mr. West, he threatened to fire each and every one of us. Said the railroad was bringin' in wagonloads of Chinese to lay rails. Threatened to hire them instead at even lower wages."

"The unfeeling bastard! Seems to me that men who work so hard should at least be given one day off." Jeremiah West had condemned her grandfather for not sending her to church. How he'd looked down his nose at her grandfather, accusing him of not acting like a good Christian. What a hypocrite! West had done a great many people a great wrong.

"And there ain't nothin' we can do about it. He'll make good on his promise to fire them. I know that he will. And then whole families will go hungry. He has us just where he wants us." Sean O'Brien shook his head sadly. "And my big mouth has done nothin' but get me a good beatin'."

"No! You're wrong. There is something to be done." Samantha paced the floor in thought. "I've got me a mine. Bigger than the Little Duchess, nearly as big as the Black Ace. I know it can be a real producer. I think that mine might hold more gold than even I suspect." Folding her arms across her chest, she suddenly grinned. "Guess it's time to give ol' Jeremiah a run for his money. Tell you what. You have a job with me right now. I'll hire you on at five dollars a day. Seems to me a fair wage."

"It's a veritable fortune, it is. Five dollars! Nearly twice what he be payin'." Though it hurt him to do so, he smiled.

"And any of the others who want to come and work for me are welcome. Same terms. And I'll give them Sunday off to give thanks to the Lord, and they can tell Jeremiah West to go to the devil! They're all welcome at the Siren Song."

"I was right the first time, me girl."

"How's that?" Samantha cocked her head.

"You are an angel. A livin', breathin' real-life, wee blessed angel. You've not only saved me life but ya'll be saving all the others as well." He stuck out his hand, taking her fingers in a warm and friendly grip. "It's a deal. I'll bring you those who want to come. And you'll never regret the day you met Sean O'Brien. On that you have me word." Sitting down again, he sighed and closed his eyes. "An angel. A veritable angel. I think I love ye, Sammie dear."

"Blarney. Irish blarney, but nice to hear." Samantha watched as Sean O'Brien settled back into sleep, thinking seriously for the first time about what she had just done. Had she been rash? Foolhardy? Only time would tell.

46

The light from the lamp was burning low and Alex reached over to turn up the wick, at the same time straining to keep his eyes on the papers scattered before him. "We'll run six coaches, Robert. We'll stagger their schedules to include different days. Eventually we'll have three headed east and three west, then we'll branch out from there. I want all the coaches to be made by Studebaker. They're the best. I have six drivers and I want a man for each coach who'll ride shotgun. I'll leave it up to you to sign any necessary papers."

"Sure, Alex, sure. We've been over this before." Leaning back in his chair, a plush red velvet that he had picked out himself to go behind his new oak desk, Robert Cunningham stretched his arms over his head as he stifled a yawn. They'd been talking about Alex's stagecoaches for several hours now, working out all the details, and he was tired. "Only one word of caution: If you decide to ship gold, you'll need more than one man riding shotgun."

"I don't intend to ship any gold!" Alex's voice was sharper than he had intended.

"Not even Samantha's?"

"Not even hers." Alex was a bit surly at the mention of her name. He'd been so certain that Samantha would seek him out to make amends for their little quarrel that his temper was on the verge off erupting. Damn, what was wrong with her anyway? Why hadn't she come? He'd spent two sleepless nights worrying about her, wondering what she was doing, when she obviously hadn't even given him a thought.

"Woman trouble!"

"What?"

"Woman trouble. I recognize the signs. I can read you like a book, Alex. Samantha's done something to get your goat and it's eating you up inside. You've been trying to distract yourself with figures and details, but I know what's going on. I've been there eight—no nine—times before myself. Care to talk about it?"

"She had the audacity to accuse me of trying to steal her mine. Pointed a gun at me. By God, I think she just might have shot me if I hadn't ridden off in a hurry." He related the story to Robert, who promptly threw back his head and laughed. "What the hell are you laughing at? You wouldn't have thought it so funny if she'd pointed the gun at *you.*"

Robert managed the words between his giggles. "I'm sorry . . . it's just . . . just that I can imagine the scene! She's a lively one, all right. But I like her. I admire her spunk. Guess she gave you a surprise."

"Indeed. Up until now I'd thought . . . well, never mind. Forget it." Alex was restless. Anger and disappointment flowed in a fiery mixture through him. No amount of work, no attempt to take his mind off of the situation, seemed to help. He could not alleviate the tight knot in his belly. Fool that he was, he wanted to break his vow to wait until she came to him. But he *wouldn't*!

Robert stood up. "Come on." At Alex's questioning look he said, "I'm taking you out of here . . . to a place I always go to when I'm in a like state—a saloon."

Alex had little taste for hard liquor. He'd seen too many men drown in whiskey during the war to turn to it for comfort himself, but tonight he was ready to make an exception. Women, he thought sourly, could very well drive a reasonable, temperate man to drink.

"Well?"

"You're on."

"Fine. We'll drop off at my hotel and I'll lend you something to wear. If you go in there looking all dandified, there's liable to be a brawl. I hear there's been some trouble at the mines too."

Alex didn't argue. He knew instinctively that Robert was right. His sartorial style had gotten him into enough trouble already. Perhaps it was time for him to blend into his surroundings. He followed Robert across the street to his hotel, where he donned canvas breeches, a plaid shirt, and a leather vest, then together they strode down the boardwalk toward the "Concert Hall and Billiard Room." He thought with a half-smile how he had innocently mistaken the two-story white building for a theater when he first came to town. Perhaps it was a reflection of how much he'd still had to learn about the West. *And* about its women.

The smoke was thick as Alex pushed his way through the saloon's doors, a foglike haze stung his eyes as he looked around. It was a large, long room with a balcony running across the back. On the walls were paintings of cowboys, wagons, buffalo, horses, and the usual beer and whiskey advertisements. The clatter of bottles, discordant notes from the corner piano and the hum of men's voices mingled in a loud general din. Along the right side of the room was the bar with its dented brass foot rail; behind it, an array of varicolored bottles lined the wall. It was to the bar that Alex and Robert headed.

"Get something for you?" A dark-haired bartender officiated in front of the large, streaked mirror. Mopping up spilled liquor from the bar top with a yellowed white rag, he looked tired.

"Double shots of whiskey for me and my friend," Robert answered. Taking up his glass Robert held it high. "To the success of your new venture and to women. God bless them one and all. They can be the cause of a man's woes, but I for one couldn't do without them. They keep a man mighty warm on a cold winter night." Downing his drink in two gulps, Robert promptly asked for another. Alex did the same, letting the fiery liquid burn its way down his throat.

There were a number of miners in the crowded saloon. Some stood at the bar, others sat at the small round tables scattered throughout the room. Some played cards, while others amused themselves at billiards; all were drinking, a few were thoroughly drunk. A few games of keno and roulette were in progress as well as games of poker. Alex watched the losers pour grains of gold on the tables as one might sprinkle sugar on a pie. The recipient moved quickly to brush the gold into his own brown leather bag, pulling the strings of the pouch back into place.

"A few of the lucky ones," Robert whispered, nodding in that direction. "Lucky to have struck gold, that is. A miner who works another man's mine can't afford such frivolity."

"You spoke of trouble?"

"Well . . . J.W. has never been known for his generosity. I don't hold him blameless but I'm not certain he's really the villain in this. Seems three men have come into town from the West Coast, determined to stir the pot. Agitators. Using the miner's woes for their own gain. I've heard talk about one man, an Irishman who . . ." Robert was distracted by a big-bosomed brunette dressed in red silk and feathers who waved at him from across the room. She moved toward them, but Alex shook his head. The last thing he needed right now was another woman. With a shrug of her shoulders and a twitch of her hips, the saloon girl retreated.

Even now, standing at the bar, grumblings came to Alex's ear, angry talk he couldn't help but overhear.

"Know two men who were killed in cave-ins just last month."

"A fortune has been made out of the Black Ace and its all gone into Jeremiah West's pocket."

"The Irishman was right!"

Seeing that Alex was listening intently, the men lowered their voices. Then ambled across the room to join others, dancing with the gaudily clad saloon girls who swayed their hips, lifted up their skirts, and stamped their feet with apparent high spirits. Soon the room rocked with sound as the miners supplied the syncopation to the piano player's melodies, keeping time with their thick-soled boots.

"Say, I know you. Don't know if you remember me." Alex turned his head in the direction of the gravelly voice and found himself practically nose to nose with a grizzled old man with gray hair, leathery skin, and a handlebar mustache. "Tobias. Tobias Catwaller. I just signed on today as one of your drivers." The man held out his stubby, callused fingers for a firm handshake.

"Yes, I remember."

"Yeh. Yeh, and well you should. I promise to help you all I can, young feller. Been driving a stagecoach for nigh on to twenty years. Can drive that team blindfolded if need be. Know every inch of these hills." He smiled and Alex noted the wide-lipped, gap-toothed grin. "Can even do it with my hands tied behind my back."

"I won't ask you to do that. Just to keep your schedule." Alex stared at his empty glass, knowing he had to ask the question. Even here he couldn't get his mind off of Samantha. "Tobias, do you remember Enoch Claybourne and his granddaughter?"

"I do for a fact. Touchy as a grizzly bear in hibernation, old Enoch was. Didn't go much for folks snooping about. Worked his fingers to the bone, so I understand it. Especially after that partner of his nearly lost the mine in a game of cards."

"Partner?"

Tobias hooked his right foot on the brass rail, settling himself in for the story. "Stephen Tyburn. A no-good, lazy . . ." Tobias shook his head. "Never believed that story he was spreading 'round, about Enoch cheating him out of his share of the mine. Hogwash! He just wanted a little sympathy, but his lies ruined old Enoch's reputation. From then on he declared a little feud with the folks here abouts. He and that cute little mite of a granddaughter of his just about vanished, hardly ever left that mine site of his. Too bad, for him and for that young woman." He brushed his hat to the back of his balding head as a faraway look came into his eye. "Remember when I first brought her here. Frightened, lonely, and sad. Sat in the corner of the coach just huggin' her rag doll for all it was worth. Pathetic sight. Just lost her folks and was scared half crazy that she'd be sent to an orphanage. The old man wasn't sure he wanted her at first, but she sure did win his heart. A good woman, Sam. I'm real glad for her good fortune, I surely am. Maybe now these folks'll show her a little respect." The full lips puckered in a frown. "They haven't up to now. Why, I remember a couple of times seeing her scraping with boys nearly twice her size, fighting 'cause one of them called her grandfather a name. As a young'un she had more than her share of black eyes. But I never seen her back down, not once."

"No, I don't suppose she did." A strange warmth surged through Alex, melting his anger.

"And then the ladies stuck up their noses at her. Maybe people always mock what they don't understand. Anyways, everyone 'round got a lot to answer for. They treated Samantha Claybourne like a stray hound, but now she's showed 'em. Yessiree! She and that Irishman'll show them."

"Irishman? What Irishman?" Alex's back stiffened, remembering the miners' talk of such a man.

"Why, Sean something or other. Looked a sight when he came in last night, but he was smiling. Said he just might have found his pot o' gold. Guess he's going to be working at Samantha Claybourne's mine, him and some others." Alex's heart was pounding like a triphammer. An alarm went off in his brain, a warning of trouble. He had to warn Samantha. Putting down his glass, he murmured a few words of good-bye and headed for the door. "Where you going?" Tobias's voice was loud enough to make the others stare.

"Alex, don't go yet." Robert had succumbed to the temptation of one of the girls and was locked in her embrace, but he pulled away and moved toward Alex.

"Back to my hotel." He needed to get a good night's sleep if he was going to get up early in the morning. Ignoring Robert's protests, he hurried back to his hotel. Alex could hear the thud of his own boots, echoed by another sound as well. The heavy tread of boots, the jingle of spurs. He had the intense feeling of being followed, but whenever he turned around, he found himself alone on the deserted street. He was angry at himself for his apprehension. Seeing Ben Cody that day had jangled his nerves more than it should have. But not even Cody would shoot him down in cold blood.

The crisp explosion of a shot changed his mind. Alex threw himself to the ground. Another shot sounded as a bullet struck the boardwalk just inches from his head. As he rolled from the walkway to the ground below, a bullet struck his boot, making a permanent indentation. Another shot splattered mud in his face. Silence. Laughter. As suddenly as the shooting began, it was over. Alex heard the thunder of footsteps as the saloon doors were flung open and curious onlookers poured into the street.

"You shot, fella?" an old miner asked as Alex stood up.

"No. Whoever was shooting, was not trying to kill me. Or perhaps he was a terrible shot." He brushed the mud off his shirt and pants. He had a feeling he knew exactly who it was, but not why. It appeared that Ben Cody was much more dangerous than he had supposed. Perhaps there did come a time when it was too late for conversation.

Shaken but gaining courage with every step, Alex walked the distance to his hotel briskly. "Anyone been looking for me?" he asked the sleepy clerk.

"Not tonight." Alex had walked halfway up the stairs before the young man remembered. "But there was someone a couple of days ago. A young woman was inquiring as to your whereabouts."

"A young woman?"

The clerk wrinkled up his nose. "Not too well dressed, I must say. If it hadn't been for her long hair and for her . . . uh . . . well, I might have thought her to be a lad. She disappeared before I could get her name."

"Never mind, I know who it was." Alex walked up the stairs in a reflective mood, feeling oddly calm despite all the excitement. Was it the whiskey? No. It was the knowledge that Samantha had come to him after all. First thing tomorrow he'd ride up to the mine.

Dreams haunted Alex that night. Nightmares of blood and violence. Soldiers screaming out in agony, men falling around him. He'd had such dreams before, but now there was something different about them. Men moved around him but he simply stood there weaponless, a helpless observer to the carnage. He saw Samantha wearing a soldier's uniform, her red-gold hair billowing around her as she ran toward him, arms outstretched. Behind her, a sneer curling his lip, stood Ben Cody.

"Samantha . . ." Again and again Alex called out her name, trying to warn her. Though he tried to reach her, his feet were glued to the ground and all he could do was watch in horror as Ben Cody came closer and closer.

"Samantha . . . !" Alex was breathing hard and bathed in sweat when he awoke. His mouth felt dry, his hands clammy and cold. "My God." It had been a dream, only a dream, but somehow it had jolted him into awareness. All this time he had been running away from the past, being foolishly stubborn. He had appointed himself peacemaker, God's right-hand mediator, pacifist, moralist. Yes, he loathed violence. But Ben Cody's attack on him last night (and he had no doubt it was *that* gunman who had shot at him) had made him see things differently. A man could not force his own values on other men. There were those whose only way was brutality. Men like Ben Cody. A man had to hope for peace but be prepared for war.

In her way Caroline was right; Jeremiah, too. This was the West and not Boston. Thinking he could move about the streets without a gun was like trying to live in Kansas without a plow. Protect Samantha? How was he going to do that if he let himself be killed by some two-bit gunman with an ax to grind? Cy Tyburn, Slim Walker, Buck Cameron, could be managed by glib talk, but Cody was of a different ilk. He was a killer. Alex had read that in his eyes but had refused to listen to the inner voice that had warned him.

He sat up, swinging his feet to the floor. He had to face reality. He'd thought Samantha naive, but in some ways he was more so. To think he could shape this territory to his specifications had been a great mistake. He could only thank God that it had not gotten him killed yet. What if Cy Tyburn and his gang had been killers? Could he have talked his way out of trouble then? By God, no!

Hurrying to dress in the clothes Robert had lent him, he thought deeply about the matter. It was time he stopped punishing himself for the death of that young rebel soldier. The war was over, just as he'd told Cody. The future loomed ahead, a bright future with Samantha by his side. If his arrogant stubbornness didn't get him killed.

Strange, he thought, how the war had shaped their lives so differently. One had taken up the gun, the other had put his gun away. He'd heard that the war had left chaos in its wake, had spawned a species of lawless men, gunfighters who'd taken to the streets to vent their rage and bitterness. Most of them were Confederates, avenging wrongs done their families during the war. The West had given them a vast arena for their fury. They were loners taking out their vengeance on humanity for spoiled dreams.

Picking up his razor, Alex ran it quickly over his face, went to the door, and paused a moment before he went down the stairs. He knew exactly what he had to do. After last night only a very stubborn man or a ninny—a man out of touch with his sanity—would remain unarmed. Not that he was going to be foolhardy and strap on a gun. No. But his first stop would be at the gunsmith's. He would not chose Robert's knuckle-duster or Jeremiah West's derringer. Alex knew better than that. If he was going to carry a gun, it would be a six-shooter, such as he'd carried in the army. A six-shooter and a rifle. In the secluded woods near the mine he'd set about refreshing his skills.

As he entered the gunsmith's, Alex did not see the figure watching from an upstairs window in the saloon, nor could he possibly see the smile on Ben Cody's face. Opening the gunsmith's door, Alex was certain he'd made the right decision.

"That's right Major," Cody chuckled to himself. "That's exactly what I wanted you to do. It's a hanging offense to murder an unarmed man. Nor am I fool enough to meet you in a fair fight. What I have in mind is something altogether different. "Keep cool," he told himself. "All things come to those who wait."

48

The sun was a blinding bright orange orb, floating in the sky as Alex rode up the mountain road. The air was fresh as only mountain air can be early in the morning. He was happy. All the way up the mountain he'd thought of nothing but Samantha's smile, the dimples in her cheeks, the way her brown eyes glowed from within. Never had he felt this gut-wrenching need for a woman before, but it was there now.

Samantha's cabin was a welcome sight, a familiar haven. Climbing down off his horse, Alex hastened to the door, envisioning her embracing arms. She would be glad to see him, he thought. She'd whisper her apologies in his ear but wouldn't let her know he'd already put it out of his mind. He'd let her worry a bit, tease her, and then . . . Passionate fantasies teased him as he knocked on the door, but instead of Samantha's waiting arms he found a rifle pointed at his chest with deadly intent.

"What the hell? I'd thought you'd see reason by now!" A rekindled anger swept over Alex. "Well, if that's the way it's going to be . . ."

"Alex?" Samantha sighed in relief. "When I saw you ride up, I wasn't sure." She put down the rifle and tugged at his arm. "Come on in." Looking down at her boots, she avoided his gaze. "I . . . I came into town to see you. I was wrong, Alex. I should have known you wouldn't try to take the mine. I'm sorry." She stepped aside to let him pass through the door, then looked him in the eye. "And . . . and I thank you for what you did for me."

All the words of reproach he had planned died on his lips. She was so earnest. "It's all right." Smiling he added, "But the next time I come calling, please don't hold a gun on me."

"I had to be certain. There's been a bit of trouble."

Alex's eyes focused on the red-haired man lounging on the settee. He didn't need an introduction to recognize the man named Sean O'Brien. "Trouble? Would you care to explain, Samantha?" He eyed the man up and down, taking stock of his appearance.

"I found him lying facedown in the dirt on the mountainside a couple of days ago. You can still tell by his face that someone beat him up pretty badly. Cy Tyburn, I suppose. Sounded like him from Sean's description. I took care of him as best I could. He refuses to go and see a doctor. Men can be so stubborn!" She eyed Alex with regret. All she wanted was to fall into his arms, but Sean's presence put a damper on any thoughts of lovemaking. Instead she planted a hasty kiss on Alex's cheek.

"Cy Tyburn, you say?" He didn't like the thought of that ruffian being any closer to Samantha than his own cabin. "If you have any trouble with him . . ." His gaze was riveted to the red-haired stranger.

"Sean. Sean O'Brien, that's who I am. You're eyes be askin' the question of me." The Irishman stood up. His face was visible proof of the torment he had been through.

"He's a miner. One of Jeremiah's workers. Someone grabbed him in town, threw him into a wagon, and drove him up the mountain. They punched him in the stomach, ribs, and face, then left him in a ditch."

"Looks to me as if he'd want to see a doctor about that nose of his." Samantha's compresses had taken down a bit of the swelling in the eyes, but the nose looked extremely painful

"Ah, no. No! It isn't the first time I've had such a knock to me noggin'. I'll be all right. Sammie here has been an angel." Sean flashed her a grin, then held out his hand to Alex. "And just who might you be? Her husband? Her brother?"

"Alexander Nicholson. I'm a friend." Alex wondered at the man's prying. It seemed a bit more than just normal curiosity. There was something about the man that put him on his guard, yet he couldn't say just what it was. "I just started a new cargo business in town. Sea-land Express." Alex returned the proffered handshake.

"A cargo business, is it? Well, be careful. There'll be those who might not like to have you hornin' in on their business. I've found out, much to me disappointment, that not many folks in Central City are friendly."

"A cargo business, Alex?" Samantha was enthusiastic. It was one more reason to keep him in Colorado. Besides, one never knew when she might need a good, strong stagecoach to ship her ore to the mint. "That's real fine. . . ."

"But all the same take care. Look what happened to me." Sean O'Brien ran his fingers through his red beard. "What gets me goat is that I could have beat them one-on-one. Cowards that they were, they held me hands behind me back while each one took his turn." Walking to the stove, he picked up a mug and poured himself a cup of coffee. "But thanks to Sammie, I'll live to meet them another day. I'm thankful to her for more reasons than one."

"I've hired Sean to work the mine, Alex. Jeremiah West is paying his workers starvation wages, so I've told Sean that I'll hire any of the others who want to work for us."

"You've done *what*, Samantha?" So what Tobias had said was true. It hadn't taken much time for this Sean O'Brien to work his way into Samantha's trust. For all her suspicion and distrust, he had only to come to her like an injured lamb and her heart had gone out to him.

Samantha darted a glance at him. Something in Alex's manner told her he did not approve. "I've hired Sean to work *our* mine, Alex. I've told him that any of the others that are being similarly mistreated are welcome too."

Alex threw up his hands in exasperation. "You must have

lost your mind! You can't do it. You don't want to take on another man's quarrel, Sam."

"I had to." She folded her arms across her chest in defiance. Why didn't Alex understand?

"Jeremiah West is a powerful man, ruthless when it comes to business. I heard the grumblings in the saloon last night. There's going to be trouble."

"A man deserves a decent wage, I be thinkin'." Sean raised his brows. "Are you half owner in the mine?"

"I own a quarter, but I'm Samantha's financial advisor." Once again this red-haired man seemed to be overly interested in the matter.

Sean O'Brien clucked his tongue. "A *quarter*? Then it seems to me the decision is up to the lassie."

Alex turned his back in a huff. "Samantha, listen to reason. If you coax Jeremiah West's miners away, it will be a declaration of war. Don't you realize that? The complications that might arise are surely worth a thought."

She shook her head violently, sending her red-gold hair swirling in a soft, fragrant cloud about her face. "I don't care. He's taking advantage of the miners, forcing them to work long hours for little pay in mines that Sean says are unsafe. Jeremiah West needs his comeuppance." It stung her that he was taking West's side in the matter. She had thought he would greet her idea with enthusiasm.

"But you may be the one who's brought to heel instead." He'd come hurrying to her side only to find her under the influence of a total stranger. And who was this Sean O'Brien anyway? What did she know about him? "You're unschooled in such matters, Samantha." He stood looking at her with an unsettling stare, like a stern father protecting his child. His expression angered her. Putting her hands upon her hips, she met him eye to eye. Her silence was more potent than any words might have been.

"Now, now, now." Reaching out to take each one by the shoulder, Sean acted as mediator. "Don't be blamin' her, me boy. 'Twas I who told her me story. She's only tryin' to be of help. But if you ask me, everything has been goin' Jeremiah West's way for a long time now. Seems to be time for a bit of a change." He winked at Alex as if they shared some kind of secret. "And she's just the lassie to do it."

"Of that I have no doubt," Alex said dryly, "but I don't want Samantha in the middle of this. It's not her business. Samantha has a mine to run, but she can't hire every miner in the territory."

"Alex—" Samantha tried to interrupt, but Alex's upraised hand silenced her.

"I'm sorry for your situation. I know that there are men who try to take advantage of others, but there are ways to deal with them. The law, the courts." His protective instincts were on alert. Another time he might have been the first one to suggest going up against Jeremiah West. Now, however, he was staunch in his opinion to the contrary. He knew all too well that Jeremiah West could be a vicious adversary. He resented Samantha enough without adding fuel to the fire.

"The law? The law you say?" Sean O'Brien laughed. "The courts you say? It's well known that Mr. West can bribe a saint to testify against his own blessed mother. Conditions are getting worse all the time, me boy. And no one is willin' even to listen to our complaints, much less do somethin' about 'em. I tried to get the miners to stand on their own two feet, to band together, and all I got for me trouble was a busted noggin' and a one-way ride up the mountain. If not for the little lassie there I'd be meetin' Saint Peter at heaven's gates 'stead of talkin' to you. She's our only hope." With a sigh Sean O'Brien finished his impassioned plea.

Alex's eyes narrowed. To Samantha's surprise, he appeared unmoved. She had expected him to be just as outraged as she was to hear the story, but he merely stood there, shaking his head. But then Alex had never had to worry about money, had he? She understood the miners' plight. If not for their luck at the Siren Song, her grandfather's foresight in staking the claim, they might have suffered a like fate.

"Alex . . ." she whispered.

Alex directed his comments over her head, eyeing Sean up and down. "Samantha is not the answer. There has to be another way." He laid a strong hand lightly but meaningfully on her shoulder. His dark blue eyes held a poignant warning, cautioning her to be careful. Samantha didn't listen. Alex felt her stiffen beneath his touch.

"I have to be the answer, Alex. I've already committed myself. Claybournes never break their word. I've told Sean he has a job with me, that anyone who wants to come to work the Siren Song can. I meant every word I said."

Samantha's full lips tightened and she squared her shoulders. There came a time in a person's life when she had to do what she thought was right, despite what anyone else might think. Finding the bruised and bleeding man in the road had unnerved her, made her realize what could happen if a man like Jeremiah wasn't stopped. Nevertheless, she wasn't quite as calm and collected as she might appear. She had her own reservations. All the things Alex had said, she'd already told herself. Even so, she had made her decision.

"Then so be it. There is nothing more that I can say. I can only hope that you have not made a serious mistake." Alex's warning sounded ominous even to his own ears and he could only pray that he was wrong, for Samantha's sake. At the back of his mind hovered the image of Samantha lying bruised and broken at the foot of some hill, just as Sean O'Brien had been. The thought knotted his stomach and made his hands tremble. And yet what could he say? Samantha had the right to make her own decisions. It was her mine. The only thing he could do was to watch over her and be fully prepared to come to her aid if the need arose.

49

The events of the next few weeks enfolded like a giant chess game. Jeremiah West stormed and blustered. Some miners were threatened and bullied into staying despite poor conditions; others chose to accept Samantha's offer and came to work the Siren Song. When all was said and done, twelve names were written on the list and twelve men added their muscle and skill to Samantha's crew. Patrick Trenoweth was made foreman of the first shift and Sean O'Brien, foreman of the second.

Samantha boasted to Alex that it was as fine a gathering of men as she had ever seen. The miners were tall and lean, short and muscular—a melting pot that represented more than a few countries. Sean O'Brien brought two other Irishmen with him, another Cousin Jack—an experienced hard-rock miner or "gouger man" who'd come to the territory from Wales—and a smiling, jovial man from Italy. There was an Austrian, a miner from Serbia whom the others called a "bohunk," and, of course, Wan Lau. The others were at least second-generation Americans who had come to Central City from the states east of the

Mississippi. Sean O'Brien called it "the most interesting assortment of nationalities that had ever been assembled." But En-
glishman or Irishman, Austrian or Chinese, all were loyal to
Samantha, who had given them the chance to earn a decent
wage and live in dignity.

Samantha's decision, however, irrevocably changed her way
of life. No longer was the cabin her solitary retreat. Slowly but
surely other dwellings crept up the mountainside, and Samantha wondered in her heart what her grandfather thought as he
looked down from his place in heaven. He had been such a
solitary man, a veritable hermit. Some of his ideas and thoughts
had rubbed off on Samantha, making it difficult at first for her
to adjust to this "invasion." The once peaceful mountainside
was now a hodgepodge of hoists, engines, ore wagons, and
windlasses, the silence disturbed by the click, click of drills, the
screaming of the steam engines, the roaring boom of blasting
caps, and the clip-clop of the horses that pulled the ore wagons.

"Quite a change, isn't it, Samantha?" Alex asked one Sunday,
a warm Indian summer afternoon, as they sat on the creek bank
looking out at the water.

"I did what I had to do, Alex. I wanted to help the miners
and I have." Her tone was at first defensive, remembering that
it was Alex who had frowned upon hiring the miners. His manner seemed to infer that she might have some regrets, that he
had been right after all. Samantha stuck up her chin defiantly.
"And I would do it all again."

"I suppose it's not always possible to hold back the tide of
progress. I know there isn't a miner who doesn't cherish you in
his heart for giving him a fair chance." Sensing her pique, he
brushed his lips across her forehead. "You've taught me a lot,
Samantha."

"Such as . . . ?"

He put his arm around her, drawing her down beside him on
the mossy bank. "The colors of the rainbow, how many stars
there are in the sky, the songs the birds sing. The moments
we've shared have been precious. You've made me realize just
how beautiful the world really is. If it's selfish of me to want to
keep you all to myself, then I'm guilty."

She nuzzled her face against the warmth of his chest, all

sullenness banished by his words. Staring into his face she felt a
maelstrom of emotions and found herself lifting her head to
place a light kiss on his lips. She wanted to be with him always,
to share his laughter, feel his pain, protect him from harm. She
wanted to melt into him again, feel the intense pleasure of being
locked in his embrace and never let him go. Oh, if only he
would make love to her again.

"Being rich isn't everything it's cracked up to be, Alex," she
whispered. She felt a twinge of regret. The success of the mine
was demanding not only her time but Alex's as well. Lately,
they had so little time to be together. "The mine is taking up
more time than I ever thought it could. It's not just a matter of
digging anymore."

"One look at the faces of those miners, though, tells me that I
was the one in the wrong. Hiring them on has given a lot of
families hope. There comes a time when a person has to stand
up for what's right and you've done that, Samantha. And in
return you've made the Siren Song a bigger success than anyone
could have ever dreamed possible." It was the first time he'd
told her he was glad she'd taken the bold step that had put her
in competition with Jeremiah West.

"I wasn't really interested in making money when I offered
Sean a job. How was I to know . . . ?" Her generosity and
kindness had been rewarded tenfold. Now her mine was second
in size only to Jeremiah West's Black Ace mine and steadily
gaining. It promised to be the largest producing mine in the
Colorado Territory. An awesome accomplishment. In aiding
the miners, she had developed the mine into a thriving business
and made herself a very wealthy woman. "I didn't know that
it—"

"That's what makes it all the more special, Samantha. You
didn't know. You made your decision based on a wish to help
others and not on your own well-being. And now you've been
rewarded."

"Rewarded?" In some ways she was not so certain. Now the
Siren Song had become a huge enterprise, much too complicated for Samantha's liking. Without Alex she knew she
couldn't manage it. They both knew it. There were ledgers to
keep that were twice as detailed as before; equipment to let;

safety measures to monitor. The payroll now listed nineteen people. How could she help but remember the days she'd worked the small claim alone with her grandfather. How simple life had been. That Alex had his shipping business and his own books to keep further complicated matters. There were times when she wished she could turn back the clock to recapture those first moments of their being together again.

Alex raised up on his elbow to look at her. He sensed a wistfulness in her tone. "Yes, rewarded. You have succeeded where many have failed. You are a brave woman, Samantha. I hope you will always be happy. That's what I want for you. Contentment. Happiness."

"I'd be far more content if you were with me . . . if . . . if . . ." She couldn't find the words to tell him what was in her heart. Being together was important to her, but it was like looking at a glass of wine and wanting to taste it again. She wanted to drink the draft of his love to the full. Looking down at her hands, she curled then uncurled her fingers, slowly trying to gather the fortitude to speak her mind. All these weeks she'd been devastated by the way he held himself back from her, even in his kisses. "What I'm trying to say is that I . . . I want to be with you again . . . the . . . the way we were the night of the storm. It was the most perfect night of my life."

"Samantha . . ." His voice was a husky groan. "I've tried to keep things tranquil between us until I was certain that you—"

"That I what? That I knew my own mind? I know exactly how I feel, that what sparks between us is very right. I've told you before, Alex. I'm not a child. I—" She was taken by surprise as he wrapped his arms around her, joining his mouth to hers in a hard, deep kiss. His hands moved along her back sending spasms of tingling pleasure along her spine, then moved to touch her breasts. They lay quietly together and kissed for a long, long while. How long Samantha didn't know. All she knew was that it seemed like heaven to be with Alex like this. She wanted him, needed him, was only fully alive when he was at her side. To hell with propriety. If Alex was worried about her reputation, she'd soon convince him that it wasn't important to her. People had looked down on her for so long that she was used to it. What she did care about was being with him, loving him. Murmuring his name, she reached out to return his caresses.

"Samantha! Samantha!" The hoarse shout of her name broke the spell. "Samantha, follow me. 'Urry." Standing in the shadow of the trees, Patrick Trenoweth shouted frantically. For just a moment Samantha regretted having told him where she would be. His manner, however, clearly indicated that something was very wrong.

Jumping to their feet, rearranging their disheveled clothing as best they could, Samantha and Alex raced after the Cornishman. Samantha's heart beat wildly. Things had been so very peaceful. Had it been merely the lull before the storm?

"What is it, Patrick?" Alex asked the question for her.

"I always make me rounds on the hour and 'alf hour. It's a good thing I was on time." Patrick shook his head as he led them to the entrance of the main tunnel. "I walked along 'ere, pausing only briefly to look around. Something just didn't seem quite right. Then I smelled something burning. The smoke and stench filled me nostrils. I searched about and that's when I found this." Reaching down behind a clump of rocks, he brought forth several cylinders tied together, each one dangling a charred fuse. "Dynamite. The kind they use when they want a big explosion."

"Dynamite?" Alex had used it during the war. It had already replaced black powder and blasting caps in some of the mines. But it was not used at the Siren Song, and finding it now was clear proof of sabotage.

"I doused the fuses with water. We escaped 'aving a tragedy this time . . ." Patrick Trenoweth's cheek twitched in anger.

"But what about next time?" Chewing her bottom lip thoughtfully, Samantha avoided Alex's gaze. He'd warned her there might be a war, but she had ignored his admonition, so certain she could call West's bluff. Now the thought of what might have been made her tremble. She had thought to help these men, and instead had nearly sealed their doom. Was she really strong enough, adept enough, to best the churlish banker? She'd thought so. Now she was not so sure. A chess game. She could nearly hear the old man screaming *checkmate*. Well, he had not won yet.

"Guess it's up to me to make certain there isn't a next time." She knew immediately what she had to do. She'd confront her opponent on his own home ground, before half the town if need be. He was a smooth talker, but she'd make certain he didn't talk his way out of this one. Like it or not, he'd have a lot of explaining to do.

"Samantha, what's on your mind?" Alex didn't like the expression on her face. The set of her brows, the grim line of her mouth, signaled of trouble. "What are you going to do?"

"Tell that wily old coyote a thing or two. If he thinks he can send his henchmen to blow up my mine, he's got another thought comin'. It's about time someone told him what for." With a determined stride she headed for the entranceway.

"Samantha, no! Let the marshal handle this. Tell him your suspicions." He might as well have spared his words, he thought dryly. Samantha ignored his protestations without even a backward glance. Alex watched as she grabbed a rifle from the toolshed, mounted one of the horses bareback, and rode at a harrowing pace down the hill. Running from the entranceway, Alex grabbed his own horse and followed in pursuit. Now was no time for Samantha to be overly brave. Not with Ben Cody tracking him. It wasn't that he feared she was less than a match for Jeremiah, but that her daring might get her into far more serious trouble.

50

The pounding of his horse's hooves thundered in Alex's ears as he guided the animal at a frantic pace over the uneven road. It was a wild ride down the mountain trail as he followed after Samantha and he could not help but hold a grudging admiration for her horsemanship. Even without a saddle or bridle she maneuvered her mount flawlessly. He was at a loss to keep up with her. Nevertheless, he managed to keep her in sight, still hoping to overtake her and talk her out of her anger. She couldn't hurl accusations at Jeremiah West without proof. He had to make her see that. Her fiery words would only heat up the fire of controversy.

"Wait! Samantha, wait!" His words were lost in the wind. He was within a hundred feet of her when she slowed to take a bend in the road. Leaning low over his horse's neck, he called her name again. "Samantha!" This time she seemed to hear for she slowed her horse's gait down to a trot and allowed him to catch up with her.

"I'm not turning back, Alex! I'm not." Ordinarily she was

even-tempered, but the knowledge of what happened to Sean O'Brien coupled with Patrick's discovery of the dynamite had goaded her into indignant anger.

"All I ask is that you listen to reason." Alex grimaced, determined to talk some sense into her. "A man is innocent until proven guilty, Samantha. You can't just walk in and accuse someone of trying to blow you to kingdom come." She'd accused Alex unjustly and *he* had been innocent.

"I can and I will. I know he was responsible. If you can't see that, then you're blind." She had always striven to please Alex, but in this he was dead wrong. "He's an ornery skunk and I aim to reveal his stripes."

"You'll only fuel his hostility, Samantha. Wait, be patient, and if he is guilty, eventually he'll give himself away. When you have the proof you need, you can contact the marshal and make sure that he's justly punished. Don't bring yourself down to his level." His hand closed over her upper arm. "Come back with me, Samantha. You aren't really thinking clearly about what you are doing."

She shrugged off his hand with an angry grimace. Why was he taking Jeremiah West's side in this matter? "I'm thinking *very* clearly." It was all very simple to her. Jeremiah was the only one who had any reason to destroy her mine. "Jeremiah West put someone up to planting that dynamite. I know it and you know it. And I think it's about time the citizens of Central City knew just what kind of a weasel he is."

"And do you think they'll believe you? Will they take your word over his? It's not as simple a matter as you suppose. Ideally, right always overpowers wrong, but not where bribery and politics are concerned. "Think! Think this all out before you do something you may regret."

"I'm not a child, Alex. I can make my own decisions." Anger coiled in her stomach, intensified by pride and her unspoken realization that he *was* right. Half the town *would* side with Jeremiah West. Even so, she couldn't just sit by, hiding like a turtle in its shell, and put her miners in danger. "I can't let such a thing happen again, Alex. Next time Patrick might not find the lighted fuse and my miners will be using their picks and shovels in heaven."

"And that's your last word? You won't allow me to counsel you on the matter?" Samantha was just beginning to gain some respect in town. Would her rash action undo everything? "Think, Samantha, before you act." He did not even so much as flicker an eyelid to show his emotions, yet she sensed his ire.

"Maybe things are different out here than in your Boston, Alex. We can't always do things politely and proper-like. Hell, there's too many times when a man gets shot for no good reason at all, too many moments when a show of force is all a body understands. I've got to prove to Jeremiah West that he can't trifle with me. Got to stand up against him or all is lost. If I don't do that, then I might as well hand him the deed to the Siren Song on a silver platter." The place where he had touched her arm still tingled and she felt the urge to reach out to him. She didn't want to argue with him. Instead she wanted nothing more than to be back on the creek bank, lying in his arms. "I have to do what I think is right."

Neither spoke. Alex made no effort to touch her again, but as she urged her horse into a gallop she knew that he was following her. That thought was a comfort as she maneuvered her horse toward Central City.

Except for a few scattered buggies, the usually bustling streets were nearly deserted when Samantha and Alex arrived at last. The occupants of the vehicles were decked out in their Sunday best, the flowers and feathers on bright new bonnets swaying back and forth in the wind. It was the time of day when people were cloistered in an afternoon church service, eating their Sunday dinner at home, or blissfully exploring other pursuits. Jeremiah's beleagured miners were the unfortunate exception, toiling away with their picks and shovels as diligently on Sunday as on any other day. In hopes of finding Jeremiah, Samantha had visited both the Little Duchess and the Black Ace, only to be told that the illustrious owner had not been to the mines that day.

"He's getting ready for a dinner party," blurted one of the miners, emphasizing each word with a blow of his hammer. "Guess he didn't think fit to invite any of *us.*" A guffaw echoed the man's words.

Samantha might have asked more questions had she not been

spotted by the mine superintendent, a short, gap-toothed man who seemed always to be looking over his shoulder. "You've caused us trouble enough," he grumbled, pointing back at the road in defiance. "You ain't about to get any more of our miners." Samantha was on the verge of telling the man just exactly what she thought of that comment, but Alex's hand on her arm silenced her as they headed back out to the main road.

"A dinner party," Samantha whispered beneath her breath. She had thought to confront Jeremiah West privately, but now as the West's house came into view another idea came to mind. If she exposed his villainy before witnesses, he would have to curtail his schemes for a while, lest he come under severe scrutiny. Only a fool would blow up a mine when he'd been accused of plotting such an action in front of a crowd of onlookers.

"Samantha, I warn you once again." Alex didn't like the smile that trembled on her once frowning lips, and yet he sensed that argument would be of little use. Samantha had made up her mind. Even so, he could not help but admire her fortitude as he followed her through the double doors that led to the stately parlor. With her red-gold hair tumbling about her shoulders, her hands tightened around her rifle, she was an awesome sight. Such a stunning vision that the music stopped abruptly and all heads turned her way as she strode into the room like an avenging angel.

"Someone just tried to blow up the Siren Song," she thundered. Her chin thrust defiantly forward. One hand was on her hip, the other clutched her rifle. "Now who do you suppose would try to do a lowdown thing like that?"

There was a whisper in the crowd, then openmouthed, wide-eyed stares as the onlookers glanced first at Samantha then at Jeremiah West, who pushed his way through his guests with a growl of outrage.

"What is the meaning of this? How dare you barge in here uninvited?" His eyebrows met over the bridge of his nose as he peered through his spectacles at her. His scowl moved to Alex.

"Why, I'm just payin' a social call. I just want to ask you and these kind folks here what you'd think of a man who'd do everything in his power to get his hands on another person's property, even using dynamite." She pointed to a fat, balding man dressed in a black suit. "You, sir. What would you do if someone tried to steal your property from you?"

"Why, I'd see him hung! There are laws here pertaining to that sort of thing. Central City may be in the West, but we're civilized here," the man was quick to answer.

"Indeed we are. Yessiree, civilized. You hear that Mr. West?" Her eyes dueled with his and she was even so bold as to smile. "A body just doesn't tamper with things that don't belong to him."

"Nor does a young woman meddle in things that are none of her business." Jeremiah West seethed with anger as he hissed out his retort. This young woman standing before him had nearly ruined him. Half his miners had left to work her claim and if that wasn't bad enough, the other miners were threatening to strike because they'd heard that the Siren Song was paying better wages. "You stole my miners from me."

"I offered to pay hardworking men a decent wage. You were cheating them, Mr. West, just as you tried to swindle my grandfather out of his mine." Samantha drew in a deep, quivering breath, trying to calm her outrage. Alex had given her good advice when he'd told her not to hurl accusations. Still, it was difficult to hold her temper in check in the face of Jeremiah West's self-righteous stance. "But let's not let this get personal. Let bygones be bygones, I always say. The reason I came here tonight is to get answers to a few of my questions."

"Then state them, whatever they are, and get out of here. As you can see I am having a party. It's my daughter's birthday today and I will not have her upset."

As if taking her cue, Caroline West swept from the back of the room, dabbing at her face with a lace hanky. Looking up, her eyes focused on a point above Samantha's head, she gasped out, "Alex! Oh, Alex how could you?"

"How could he? Very easily. He just got on a horse and followed me here." Samantha couldn't help but notice the way the golden-haired beauty's eyes lingered on Alex's tall frame and she was only barely able to swallow her jealousy. Perhaps the flame that had burned in Caroline West's heart had not yet been extinguished. "But leave him out of this." Samantha returned the woman's look of venom with a heated stare of her own. "As I was saying, I have three questions. One, who else but you would profit by the destruction of my mine? Two, how much does it cost you to have your dirty work done for you? Three, now that you know I'm on to you and have warned all your friends here, are you gonna have the gall to try it again? If so, then you had better be forewarned, Mr. West, that I don't cotton much to yellow-bellied polecats. I'm a fighter. My gramps died in that mine. Hell, I was raised in that mine. Not you or anyone else is going to bully me into letting it go."

A stunned silence invaded the room as the elegantly clothed guests stared at Samantha Claybourne. Scorn was written on some faces, on others, disbelief, but a few expressions revealed they gave credence to her words. Samantha sensed it. Some of those gathered were eyeing Jeremiah West with suspicion.

"Get out! Get out of my house or I'll have you thrown out!" His nostrils quivered as he snarled the order. Jeremiah West turned nearly purple with rage. The nerve of the chit to come into his own house and make a spectacle of him this way. He watched as she turned on her heel and left the room with Alex following her. At that moment Jeremiah knew he would never rest until he had avenged the insult.

51

Bright rays of sunlight shone through the thick-paned glass windows, but the merriment of the midmorning sun did little to lighten the dour expressions on Jeremiah and Caroline West's faces as they partook of their breakfast. It was an unusually warm morning that promised another cloud-free autumn day, yet there was a sense of gloom in the dining room, an ominous silence that was disturbed only by the clink of glassware and the rattle of dishes.

"What ails 'e? 'Aven't touched a bite and me aslavin' away in the kitchen just to please yer appetite." Clucking her tongue in dismay, Mrs. Trenoweth cleared the table.

"What's wrong?" As Jeremiah threw down his rumpled newspaper, his face colored with anger. "That brazen little chit's appearance at my party last night is front-page news. But why should you care? Your goddamned ungrateful son has helped Enoch Claybourne's granddaughter screw me good. He did! If I wasn't such an upright citizen, I'd have him shot."

"Meaning no disrespect, 'e was only earning 'imself a living, sir." Balancing the stack of dishes she held in her hands, Mrs. Trenoweth stared her employer down. "You didn't 'ave any work for 'im. Man with a wife and children 'as got to earn 'is keep. Went to work at that mine to get money to feed 'is family."

"Now he's foreman of that mine despite all my attempts to lure him away. What kind of loyalty is that, for God's sake? *I* would make him supervisor of my enterprises except he's turned me down. Why, Cousin Jennie? Why? I've offered him twice what Samantha Claybourne is paying him." Pounding the table with his fist, he made the remaining dishes rattle as the table swayed precariously.

" 'E tells me 'e likes the young miss, that's why. All the men do. She treats 'em fair, she does. Gives 'im time off from 'is work when 'e needs it. When 'is eldest daughter was ill she advanced 'im three months salary so's 'e could take 'er to the 'ot springs to get 'ealed. Told 'im 'e didn't 'ave to pay back the money she'd given 'im. She gave 'im the land to build 'is cabin on, just to show 'er appreciation when they struck gold." Sighing, Mrs. Trenoweth smiled. "Patrick says 'er 'eart is as big as the 'ole territory. Says she always treats 'im fair."

"Fair? Rubbish! No one does anything for anyone unless there's a profit. She's no different from anyone else. You'll see. You'll see. Some day your son and all the others will come crawling back to beg me for their jobs but I'll laugh in their faces. Just you wait and see!" His voice was a roar. "They'll come running back, but I'll not have them. I won't." Rising to his feet, he confronted his cook nose to nose. "Ungrateful. All of you foreign bastards!"

"Daddy." Dabbing at her mouth with a napkin, Caroline pushed her chair aside as she hastened to his side. "Calm yourself lest you suffer apoplexy. Yelling won't do any good."

"Calm myself? After what happened last night? Bullshit! I don't hold with disloyalty. Imagine *her* marching into my own house!"

"But Daddy, it isn't Cousin Jennie's fault. Don't yell at her so." Tugging at his arm, whispering soothing words in his ear, she somehow managed to calm his ire. "Patrick Trenoweth isn't the one to blame, it's Alex." Looking Mrs. Trenoweth in the eye she motioned for the woman to leave. "Alex is the one who gave that Claybourne girl the money to keep that silly mine open. You should be mad at him. I know that *I* am. Keeping company with that uncouth little whore. Why, everyone in town knows just why he advanced her that money. Partner, my foot. She's nothing but an opportunistic little tramp who—"

"Hush up, Caroline. I don't want to listen to your peevish jealousy. I'm furious with him but only because he crossed me after all I did for him. Giving him a job in the bank when I hardly knew him from Adam. All because you'd set your sights on him. Well, we got more at stake here than just your pride." Plopping back down in the dining room chair, he leaned back and crossed his legs. "Jealousy isn't going to solve a damned thing."

"I'm not jealous. Who Alexander Nicholson keeps company with is no concern of mine, even if it is a disgrace. Obviously he isn't as well entrenched in society as you had imagined. Why I would dare say that—"

"Quiet, I said!" It was the first time he had ever raised his voice to her and he quickly amended his outburst by saying, in a softer tone of voice, "I need to think this matter through carefully." Reaching for the newspaper, he searched the black lettering as if therein lay the answer to his unrest. "I'm not beaten yet, not by a long shot." Oh, he was irritated all right. First and foremost at Cy Tyburn, who had botched a simple task, yet again. Even now an idea was dancing about in his brain. But no more dynamite. Not after her accusation. If the Siren Song blew, he'd be the first suspect. No, a more subtle approach was called for.

Wadding the newspaper up in his fist, Jeremiah West threw it to the floor, infuriated by the way *The Register-Call* had worded the story, insinuating that Samantha Claybourne's accusation deserved investigation, hinting at Jeremiah West's obsession with the mine. He'd have the editor's head! It was exasperating. Infuriating. The truth was, though he would not admit it to his daughter, that he *had* been bested. There seemed to be no way he could get his hands on that mine.

"If only you'd been woman enough to hold on to that damned Easterner, this would never have happened!" he rasped beneath his breath, turning his eyes in Caroline's direction. She was pacing up and down, obviously as agitated as he, but far from showing her any compassion, he barked out an order instead. "Sit down. You're fidgeting about is making me nervous."

"Ohhh!" Caroline's high-pitched wail shattered the air yet she obeyed, sitting across from him with her hands demurely in her lap. Her face was contorted as she sniffled. Tears welled up in her eyes as she said, "you're not the only one hurt by all of this, you know. I was jilted, like some plain-faced spinster the very same month I was to be wed. If not for my aplomb, I would have been shamefaced in this town, but I turned the tables on Alex. At least I have the satisfaction of knowing that everyone in Central City thought it was I who jilted *him.*"

Sniffing derisively, Jeremiah reached across the table to take her hand. "Listen to me and listen to me well, Caroline. I don't give a frog's ass who jilted who. All I know is that somehow, some way, you've got to get him back."

"No!" She pulled her hand away as if he'd burned her. "I don't want him. I don't need him. He isn't the only man in the world." She smiled coyly. "Robert Cunningham has been paying court to me with a ferocity that is extremely flattering."

"Hang Robert Cunningham. That no-account lawyer isn't worth a nickel. Besides, you aren't the only woman he's been seen with. Reminds me of a goddamn bee pollinating every flower in town."

"Daddy . . . please." In a flutter of embarrassment, she averted her eyes. She knew part of his anger was because Robert had abandoned him to work with Alex.

"Look at me girl." He willed Caroline to meet his gaze. "I said look at me! I've done many things for you. I've given you all the fancy carriages and dresses you ever wanted. You live as well as the queen of England herself. Now I'm asking you—no, *telling* you—to repay me by ensnaring that son of a bitch Bostonian."

Together Alexander Nicholson and Samantha Claybourne were unbeatable. She knew mining like the back of her hand; he knew finance and business. Jeremiah West had little doubt who had advised Samantha to invest in the new bank that was open-

ing in town. Ha, the woman who had once openly scorned
banks and bankers now practically owned one. What an unnerving joke. Next thing he knew, either she or Nicholson
would be running for territorial governor, for God's sake! It
might have been an amusing thought had he not been in such a
sour mood.

But on her own Samantha Claybourne would flounder, he
thought. She possessed no business sense at all. He could under-
mine her, ruin her, take over not only her mine but her bank,
her hotel, and her saloon as well. Piece by piece, he'd topple her
little empire until she was right back where she'd started. The
only flaw in his scheme was Alexander Nicholson, who insisted
on guarding the little chit as if she were made of solid gold.

"You have to win him back, Caroline!" His eyes assessed her.
She was perfectly beautiful. As soft and fragrant as a summer
rose. Certainly a worthy rival for that fiery hoyden. "I'm not
asking or begging, I'm ordering you to do it or be cut off without a dime."

"What?" Trembling from head to foot, Caroline stood up.

"You heard me!" He might be bluffing, but he could see by
the awestruck fright in her eyes, she didn't realize that. So
much the better. He'd been too lenient, spoiled her until she
was nearly worthless. Perhaps that was what had driven Alexander Nicholson away. But no more. "By hook or by crook, I
want you to drive a wedge between Samantha Claybourne and
her socialite beau."

"But how?" Caroline was aghast. Her pride was at stake. She
wouldn't go begging to any man. "*He* was the one who broke
off our engagement."

"I'll leave that up to you. Hell, you can tie him up for all I
care, lock him in a cage. Just keep him away from that vicious,
foulmouthed little upstart until I can get things under control."
Picking up a fork, he used it like a pen, frantically scratching on
the tablecloth as if it were a parchment.

Caroline eyed him in apprehension, fearing he was close to
losing his mind. "Daddy, what on earth are you doing? Have
you taken leave of your senses?" He was muttering beneath his
breath as if he were possessed.

"I'm doing a bit of figuring, Caroline. Trying to estimate just what the earnings must be from that mine. I could make good use of that money."

Now it was her turn to be condescending. "The Siren Song? Isn't that a bit hasty, Daddy? You don't own it. Perhaps you never will. It belongs to *Miss* Claybourne. Certainly she will never sell it to you. Steal it, then? Even you would not dare do that."

Her words stung him, the more so because it was the truth. And yet somehow he had to stop the little chit before she managed to get too much of a foothold. She was hurting him, more and more with each passing day. She had to be stopped. He had to think of a way to ruin not only Samantha Claybourne but Alexander Nicholson as well.

52

Alex read the account of Samantha's visit to Jeremiah West's residence over his morning coffee in the hotel dining room. Oh, it was amusing. It cast Samantha in the role of the heroine fighting to keep her mine against the machinations of an ambitious adversary, but it was one more red flag to be waved in front of a bull. He scanned the story again with trepidation. It would only fan the fires of the banker's animosity and somehow, some way, he would get back at her.

Alex's need to protect Samantha consumed him. She was getting in over her head, didn't understand the intricacies of business. There were other ways of striking back at someone besides dynamite. A sudden rise in the price of mining equipment was only one way. However, Alex was two steps ahead of the crafty man. He had already ordered tools from Denver, thereby circumventing Jeremiah's hold on the local merchants. For the moment he had the upper hand, but West's intentions bore watching.

There was another matter that concerned Alex as well. Sean

O'Brien. He was an agitator. Not content with his job as Samantha's foreman, he had apparently appointed himself spokesman for the miners from the Black Ace and Little Duchess. Using the dynamite incident as bait, he had lured all the miners to a rally last night. It had nearly turned into a riot. Carrying lighted torches as they descended from the hills, they had chanted their intent to earn a decent wage. The demonstration had taken the form of a parade through town with saloon keepers, the dance hall girls, and every ruffian in town taking part. Rocks had been thrown, broken bottles brandished. Only Alex's timely intervention had averted serious violence.

The door to the dining room was shoved open, slamming back hard as a man moved through the doorway. Looking up Alex saw the object of his thoughts, Sean O'Brien standing defiantly on the threshold. His clothes were muddy, his hair was touseled, his face showed visible signs of a fight. He swayed a little on his feet as he walked forward. One other thing that annoyed Alex was the man's penchant for drinking. He suspected that last night Sean O'Brien had been very drunk.

"You sent for me, your lordship!" The mocking bow and grin clearly stated the Irishman's resentment. Right from the very first he and Alex had been at odds, though the Irishman had carefully hidden his feelings.

"Yes, I did, O'Brien. I won't have you connected with another incident like the one that occurred last night. It reflects on Samantha and could involve her in trouble."

"Oh? And just what do you have to be sayin' about it? As I remember correctly it is Sammie who owns the mine and not you."

Alex clenched his jaw. "She does own the mine but believe me, O'Brien, if I see you instigating the kind of thing you did last night, I'll move heaven and earth to have you fired!" He took a sip of his coffee, but somehow it tasted bitter and he'd lost his thirst for it. "In case you've forgotten, I am Samantha's partner. I own a fourth share in the mine."

"And do you be ownin' Sammie as well? By the way you always be hoverin' over her, I'd say at least you think you do." Insolently he crossed his arms over his chest.

"Just what do you mean by *that?*" Alex eyed O'Brien warily.

He would have to be blind not to notice the way Sean had been ogling Samantha the past few weeks. Had he not known how steadfast Samantha was in her love for him, Alex might have been concerned. As it was, he was now very annoyed by the situation.

"I mean that you confuse me. As far as I can tell, you and Samantha aren't lovers yet you hang about her as if you claim ownership, tellin' her everything to do, treatin' her more like your daughter or sister—"

"It's none of your damned business." Alex bounded up from his chair.

"Ah, but it is. I've made it my business because you see I'm more than a little taken with her and I think you be causin' her more grief than happiness. I've seen the way she looks at you, like you're somehow just out of her reach. She's a woman not a girl, me fine lord. A woman to be taken into a man's bed not spanked and sent to her room without supper. . . ."

"I don't treat Samantha like a child. She's young. I'm merely protective of her. I don't want—"

"*She* wants to be loved, to be treated like a desirable woman. I can read it in her eyes each time you pass her by. She doesn't think she's quite good enough for your lordship but I think she's the kind of woman who would make a man swoon with delight." Picking up Alex's half-filled coffee cup, Sean O'Brien took a swig, then made a wry face. "You summon me to make an ultimatum which I won't be heedin', but I offer you this warning instead. I'm a patient man, a quiet man, but I know what I want when I see it, which is more than I can say for you. I think I can make Samantha happy if given half a chance."

"You won't be given any chance. Samantha belongs to me." Alex fought to keep control of his temper. He would never let Samantha be wooed by this hotheaded troublemaker.

"Oh, does she now? Well, we'll be seein' about that. I'll make you a little wager that I can seduce the lass before a week is out. Then we'll see who—" A well-aimed punch to the jaw silenced the Irishman. "Well, well, well. Perhaps you do care." Sean O'Brien held up his hands as if surrendering. "Just testing you, me boy. Just tryin' to get a perspective on the matter." He rubbed at his chin. "For a supposedly peaceful man, you pack quite a punch."

"I'd go to any lengths to see that Samantha is happy." Alex was so concerned with Sean O'Brien that he paid no notice to the man hiding behind the newspaper in the corner of the dining room. Ben Cody, however, had heard every word.

So the Major hasn't changed a bit, he thought with a smile. Still issuing orders. He wondered just who this "Samantha" was. Looking hurriedly through the newspaper story, he wondered if the two women were one in the same. Instinct told him they were. Hadn't he noticed Alex frequently riding out of town, headed toward the mines? He'd wondered what was so absorbing, had been irritated when Alex's absence in town had curtailed his plans for "fun." But perhaps the woman in Alex's life could make toying with him all the more entertaining. The next time he saw Alex heading up the mountain, he'd follow and be prepared for a little amusement.

53

It was an unseasonably warm day. The sky was clear without even a trace of a cloud. Only the slight breeze gave a reminder that it was autumn and not spring. Tying his horse to a post outside the mine, Alex searched for Samantha. All the way up the mountain road he'd cursed himself for a fool. Sean O'Brien was right. He had treated Samantha like a child. He'd been too blind to realize that his well-meaning celibacy had frustrated not only him but Samantha as well. Why had it taken the avowed desire of another man to open his eyes? He'd hoped to protect Samantha, but in his own foolish way he'd hurt her instead. Was it possible that she didn't realize how very much he cared? If so, he would soon inform her.

Alex found Samantha near the swimming hole, standing on the bank gazing out at the water. His eyes swept over her, trying to analyze just why this particular woman had come to mean so very much to him. Was it her smile, her courage? The trusting look in her eyes whenever their gaze locked and held? Love, he decided, was a combination of so many feelings. She amused him, entranced him, seduced him with her strange combination of innocence and guile. There were times when she was sweetness personified and all he could wish for was to hold her in his arms. There were also times when her stubbornness made him want to turn her over his knee.

But she is not a child! he thought. She was a woman whom he desired very much. Sean O'Brien's interest in her had awakened Alex to his own feelings, had sparked a surge of jealousy such as he had never felt before. A primitive emotion. A man seeking to assert a claim on his mate.

"Samantha!" At the sound of her name she turned and ran to him, throwing her arms uninhibitedly about his neck.

"Oh, Alex. I was afraid you were angry with me for what I did. But we haven't seen hide nor hair of Jeremiah West." The smile that trembled on her lips seemed to say that Alex had been wrong in his warning. "I'd say he'll stay as clear of me as if I had the measles." Shading her eyes with her hand, she looked in the direction of the mine, watching from afar as Patrick walked about. "Just to make sure my men are safe I've posted a look out. Today it's Patrick, tomorrow it'll be Fred Hennessy."

Alex remained silent. He was too busy relishing the sight of her standing so tall and proud. The breeze pushed her skirt against her legs, giving him a tempting view of her willowy thighs. She reminded him of the wind somehow. Soft and teasing at times, wild and unpredictable at others. Would he ever forget the sight of her sweeping into Jeremiah's parlor like a whirlwind? Though he had counseled her to turn back, worried at the storm she might provoke by her actions, he had nonetheless been secretly proud of her courage and resolve. Few men had been willing to come up against Jeremiah West, but Samantha had unswervingly stood her ground.

Taking his silence as condemnation, she stiffened. "I'm not a bit sorry that I stormed in there that way. I know that I was right. We won't have any more trouble, you'll see!"

"I hope you're right. Certainly it will keep the residents of Central City busy talking for a while. But that's not what I came to discuss. I came here to talk about us."

His expression was so sullen that Samantha knew a moment

of panic. Was he going to tell her how ill suited they were for each other? Had her bullheadedness angered him more than she realized? Her voice was a whisper as she asked, "What about us?"

"Are you happy, Samantha?" A long wisp of hair blew into her eyes and he gently brushed it away. "How do you feel about Sean O'Brien?"

"Sean?" She looked at him in puzzlement. How had Sean gotten into their conversation? "I like him. He's a friend. Why?"

"Something he said to me this morning . . . oh, never mind." He enfolded her in his arms, holding her close. "I'd never purposely cause you any pain."

"I know that, Alex." Samantha looked up at him, her eyes widening in question, her breath catching in her throat. There was a certain expression on his face that she hadn't seen there for a very long time. "Alex . . ." His name was smothered by a deep, leisurely kiss as his mouth claimed hers. Her mouth opened to him as she closed her eyes. His tongue was warm as it explored the wet, sweet cave of her mouth and she trembled against him. This was the kind of kiss she had been dreaming about, the kind that was a prelude to the wonders she had experienced that glorious rainy night. Samantha felt the heat and the strength of him with every inch of her body. She felt as if she were melting in his arms. The world whirled about her as she clung to him.

Alex drew a shaky breath as he lifted his mouth from hers. "I've been a pompous fool!" he whispered huskily into her hair. He clasped her tightly against his chest. Oh, how he wanted her! The touch of her mouth had ignited a fire in him that threatened to consume him. There was a curious roaring in his ears as he drew her farther into the clearing.

Samantha heard the quickened thud of his heart, felt a wave of delicious dizziness as she was swept up in his arms, carried to the edge of the pool, and lowered to the ground. The grass was dry, prickling, as it touched her skin, but she was beyond noticing. All she knew was that Alex was going to make love to her. After all these past weeks of hoping she was once again going to be his.

The small clearing lay still in the lazy afternoon sun, undisturbed by anything but a flock of birds that fluttered and took flight in the air. A small ground squirrel scampered about in search of food, scolding them for their intrusion. It was a tranquil setting. Mesmerizing. Protected by a clump of trees, it was a perfect lover's nest. It reminded Alex now strangely of Eden and he thought with a smile that he had found the perfect Eve. Samantha's secret pool, a sheltered paradise that she would share with him.

The ground was hard. Cold. But to Samantha's senses it was as soft as a feather bed. She arched toward him as he moved over her, caressing her. His fingers were at her throat, opening her buttons. His lips traced a fiery path down the curve of her neck to her just bared shoulder. His mouth was moist against her skin.

"You taste good," he breathed with a smile. Tugging at the ends of her sash, he cast it aside, then returned to his gentle ministrations. Brushing a soft kiss on her trembling lips, he gently explored the soft swell of flesh above her chemise. Soft moans of pleasure floated about them and Samantha suddenly realized they came from her own throat. Her hands clutched at his hair as she pressed against him.

Unmindful of the rocks and twigs, they lay side by side, delighting in the pleasure of kissing, of touching each other. Leaves tangled in her hair, but she shook them loose with a joyful toss of her head. Then her arms went around his neck. Answering his kisses with sweet, wild abandon, Samantha molded herself against him.

"What are you thinking, Alex?" Was he as blissfully happy as she was? She looked steadily at him, holding his gaze with her eyes. A quiver of physical awareness danced up and down her spine as he brushed his lips against her hair.

"You!" With a contented sigh he rolled over on his stomach, arms cradling his head as he closed his eyes. Propping herself up on her elbow, Samantha pulled a long, prickly weed and ran it teasingly up the back of his neck to his ear.

"And just what were you thinking about me?" He reached out to brush the offending weed away and encountered her hand. Just the touch of her caused a flutter deep in the pit of his stomach.

"What a lovely imp you are. How much lovelier you are without your clothes." Rolling over on his back, he opened one eye and reached for her hand. "I was wondering if I was going to remove them or if you were." Drawing her down again for another kiss, he whispered her name. Their lips touched and clung, parted and smiled against each other. They laughed joyously, intimately, as their fingers moved over each other, lingering and caressing. Then suddenly Samantha rose to her feet, tugging at her dress as she challenged him.

"I'll remove them. But you won't win my love quite so easily. You need some proper comeuppance for the weeks you've neglected me. I'll race you to the rock and back. Winner take all. Care to take my dare?" A small waterfall cascaded over the rocks, rippling the large pond with waves before journeying downstream in a trickling creek. With playful movements Samantha splashed into the water, ankle-deep, motioning him to come and join her.

Lifting her dress above her knees, she walked farther and farther into the water and as he pursued her she cupped her hands and sent a spray of water over him. Giving in to impulse, she pulled the dress over her head and stood in chemise and pantalettes. "Well, Alex. Are we going to race or aren't we?"

He answered by stripping off his shirt and tossing it to the ground. The rest of his clothing followed as he slowly and tantalizingly revealed the splendor of his naked body to her eyes. Hypnotized, Samantha was unable to take her eyes away from the magnificently masculine beauty of his body, the broad chest with its matting of hair, the wide shoulders, the flat stomach, the lean, taut flanks from which sprang the part of him that gave her such ecstasy. Her gaze lingered there as she wondered if all men were so marvelously fashioned. He reminded her of a sleek, powerful animal as he neared the water's edge. That he would choose her as his mate was her greatest hope. She loved him, desired him at this moment and always. In her heart she knew she always would, that she could never get enough of him. Answering his smile, she pulled her chemise over her head, dropped her pantalettes, and dashed farther into the water with Alex close behind.

The water came up to cover her breasts, her hair floated behind her like a cloud as the stream swirled around her. She was a graceful swimmer, taking the lead with strong, powerful strokes. She reminded him of a mermaid, some mythical water sprite. The sight of her so fascinated him that he soon fell behind, contenting himself with watching her, a burnished goddess skimming through the water. Time and time again his eyes were drawn to the slim curve of her waist, the long, lithe legs, the tempting curve of her breast. All the hungry promptings of his dreams rose up full force to conquer his very reason with desire. Pushing himself through the water with strong, bold strokes, he caught up with her, his hands closing around her shoulders, pulling her to him. The water buoyed them up as his arms captured her in an embrace.

Samantha felt the warmth of his breath on her neck. His strong, hard body sent a tide of tingling excitement through her. "Alex." His name was sweet and shivering as she whispered it against his mouth. Lifting her arms, she encircled his neck, wound her fingers in his damp dark hair. For an endless time they clung together, their wet bodies touching intimately as the water swirled around them. Time seemed to stand still as they looked into each other's eyes, listening to the sounds around them—the melody of the birds, the drone of bees, the soft whistle of the wind. His mouth closed over hers with fierce possession and he felt her shiver as the probing length of his manhood touched her thighs. Their bodies writhed together in a slow, sensuous dance as old as time itself.

Alex's hand moved over her body, past her stomach to the soft hair between her thighs, and she gasped at the shudder of ecstasy that rippled deep within her. All coherent thought seemed to have fled and there was only this moment, this man. She loved him. There was nothing as important as her inborn need to belong to him. As she gloried in the closeness of their bodies, it seemed to Samantha then that it was Alex to whom she would always belong. Her eyes were deep pools of darkest brown as she looked at him, and she felt her heart move with love.

"Samantha . . ." His hand traced the curve of her body, from neck to hip, crushing her to him, kissing her with a burning passion. He lifted her from the water and carried her to the shore. There he pulled her down beside him. "You little minx. You're a born seductress, my love." He was only human, not a saint. Most definitely unable to withhold himself from her deliberate enticement. Samantha was like a fever in his blood, as necessary to his survival as each indrawn breath. To hell with good intentions, he thought.

Alex explored her body as thoroughly and gently as if he'd never made love to her before, had never lain beside her on the mossy bank. Samantha trembled under his knowing touch, returning his caresses, running her hands over the smooth firmness of his chest. That he groaned with pleasure gave her confidence in her exploration. She grew bolder, sliding her hand across his taut stomach to touch his male hardness. It was proof of his desire and made her feel more confident, more sure of herself.

The moments that passed were a daydream of kissing and caressing, culminating in an unstoppable tidal wave of desire. Alex knew just how to touch her, how to tantalize her, and as she followed his lead she learned just how long to linger in her tentative probing as well.

Wrapped in each other's arms, they gave vent to the all-consuming desire that flamed between them. Samantha felt the ripples course through her blood, like the sparks of a radiating fire, consuming her as he probed gently between her legs. She writhed under his touch, arching up to meet him as he rose over her seeking the softness of her body. When he glided into her, it seemed to be the most natural thing in the world to be locked together. Something meant to be. Alex was her mate, her love. She cried out in passion as his manhood entered the moist softness of her flesh, holding him tightly as the world seemed to quake beneath them. Arching to him, she moved with him in joyous intimacy, enticing him to go with her to that world of sensuality and love they had traveled to before. The whole world became this man buried deep within her body. His kiss. The touch of his hands.

Samantha wanted to tell him how she felt, wanted to whisper

words of love in his ear, but her breath caught in her throat and she couldn't say a thing. Instead she fastened her arms around his back and clung to him as a wave of dizzying pleasure swept through them. What she felt was too beautiful for words. She closed her eyes wondering how she could have ever thought anything was important compared to this. She had no need of gold or riches when Alex was with her. To her he was the most important thing in the world. Even when it was quiet and her inner storm had passed, she kept her silence, afraid to break the spell. She'd wanted Alex to love her and he had.

When at last their pulses had slowed, as they lay together beneath the warm, embracing sun, Alex propped himself up on an elbow and looked at her. One hand was flung over her eyes, the other was pillowed under her head. Like a burnished silken cloak her hair was spread out around her shoulders. Reaching out, he touched her hair with a rhythmic movement of his hand, stroking, caressing.

"I've been more fool than gentleman, Samantha. Loving you was what I've wanted all this time. . . ."

"It's what I wanted too." She removed her hand from her eyes and raised a finger to his mustache to trace the contours of the prickly hair. "It can always be just like this between us, Alex. You can live at the cabin with me and never have to go back to that dreary hotel. It's here that you belong."

Alex shook his head. He wanted to get Samantha away from here, wanted her to live in luxurious surroundings. The cabin could be their retreat, but he had little desire to make it his home. "We can come up here on weekends. We'll take a suite of rooms in the hotel . . ."

"Live in town?" She wanted to be with him, but the thought of giving up the cabin made her shake her head. "No. I couldn't, Alex." They had talked about it once before. Though she wanted to be with him, fear held her back. Although the townspeople now minded their manners because of her prosperous mine, she still felt ill at ease around them. Perhaps she was just as much of a hermit as her grandfather had been, when all was said and done. "The mine . . ."

"Sean and Patrick can handle any important matters. Besides, I've neglected my shipping business far too long. Robert is always nagging me about my responsibilities . . ." Shrugging his shoulders, he confided in her, "No, it's much more than that." He told her the story of Ben Cody, not to frighten her but to warn her. "I don't want his obsession with me to cause you any harm. In town he wouldn't dare be too brave. Here he could be dangerous!"

"More than a mite so. Oh, Alex, it's all the more reason for you to stay with me *here*. The cabin could be your hideaway. And . . . and you know I'm a crack shot. If he even dared . . ."

Alex laughed. She was as intent on protecting him as he was on guarding her. It touched him. If only the essence of love could be captured, bottled, and distributed to each and every man, the world could be a marvelous place, he thought. He nuzzled her ear, whispering, "Put it out of your mind. We have other things to concern us." His hand was between their bodies, stroking her breasts, sliding down the velvety skin of her belly. "We need to make up for lost time." They lay touching each other, feeling again the wondrous rapture as they made love.

54

Streaks of lavender touched the sky as Alex rose to his feet and got dressed. The afternoon had passed all too quickly for the lovers. Slipping on her own garments, Samantha walked with him to where his horse was tethered.

"Alex, be careful!" Remembering all he had told her about the gunman, she was worried. She had noticed the rifle and long-barreled pistol he carried with him lately. Now she knew why he was suddenly armed.

"I'll be all right." He bent toward her for one last kiss. "I don't want you to worry. Just take a few precautions to ensure your safety."

"*My* safety? He didn't take a shot at *me.* Oh, Alex, if anything were to happen to you . . ."

For a moment he regretted having told her about Cody. "He's just trying to show his prowess. Bluffing. I don't believe he'll try to kill me, Samantha. If that was his intent, he would have done so that night. He's toying with me, like a cat with a mouse, in an attempt to make me atone for some imagined slight. I didn't tell you before because I knew it would worry you." He shook his head. "I shouldn't have said anything about it now. I haven't seen hide nor hair of him since. Perhaps he's left town."

"And perhaps he has not. . . ." Cy Tyburn was one thing, this Ben Cody another. "Stay with me, Alex. Don't go back to town. The cabin is small but it's big enough for us to share."

Her offer was tempting. With a fervent kiss he regarded her. "We'll talk about it tomorrow." He wanted to stay and would have but for a business meeting Robert had scheduled early in the morning. "Think about what I said, about coming to town."

Samantha nodded, choking back the words that would have marred an otherwise perfect day. Regretfully she watched him ride away, then trudged back toward the cabin. Pausing to sit on a rock, she ran her hands through her still damp hair, combing it with her fingers, tempted to saddle a horse and ride after him, to tell him she would follow him to the ends of the earth if he asked.

The sharp snap of a twig startled her and she spun around. "Alex?" So he, too, had felt the devastation of parting and had come back. She formed her mouth to say she had changed her mind, but the words never came. It was not Alex who rose up out of the bushes behind her but another man, one whose chilling gray eyes made her tremble. There was something about the man that gave warning despite his smile. "Who . . . who are you?" She could barely get the words past her lips.

"One of Alex's *friends.*" The twitch of his cheek sent the scar emblazoned there into a macabre dance.

"Alex's friends?" Samantha didn't recall hearing him mention any friends . . . Oh, my God! She thought, fighting against panic. This was the man Alex spoken of this very afternoon, the soldier-turned-gunfighter who had prompted Alex to carry a gun in his holster and a rifle strapped to his saddle. Seeing the cold, unrelenting expression on the man's face she understood what had prompted Alex to break his vow. He looked like a messenger of the very devil or, worse yet, Satan himself.

"I didn't frighten you, did I?" His manner said clearly that if he hadn't, he meant to do just that now.

"No . . . no." *Keep calm,* she told herself. *Don't show your fear.* Minutes passed slowly as he scorched her with his eyes, giving little doubt as to his thoughts. Apprehension squeezed Samantha so hard that she could barely breathe. If only she had her rifle. She stiffened as he stepped forward.

"I've wondered how to get to Alex. Now I know. You're his Achilles' heel. I saw it on his face when you were together."

He had been watching them make love! Of all the lowdown slimy snakes. She gasped as his hand whipped out to clutch cruelly at her arm. "Let me go! Please."

"Not until *I* want to."

"What do you want?" Her voice was so shaky, she could barely hear herself. His mocking laughter only added to her fears.

"Let's just say that you're going to help me right an old wrong. But first I want some of the same thing you just gave him." His fingers were brutal as he grabbed at her breast. "Another reason to incite Alex to a gunfight." He smelled of stale sweat, whiskey, and unwashed clothing, and she cringed as he drew near.

The very idea made her shudder. "You must be . . . be crazy to even suggest such a thing." That's right, show spunk, she thought. Above all she must *not* show fear. But dear God, now she knew how Alex must have felt that day he'd faced Cy Tyburn's gang. She'd been such a fool. It was so easy to be brave when you had a rifle.

He laughed deep in his throat, a mirthless sound. Holding her with one hand, he took his time lighting a cigarette. He struck the match on a tree, ignited a fire, and inhaled with pleasure. Blowing the smoke in her face, he said, "Crazy? Maybe. But I always have my fun. What are you goin' to do about it?" His tone was challenging. "Doesn't appear to me that you're in a position to do much." Suddenly, completely without warning, he slapped her. The blow knocked her sprawling. His hands were powerful, and she felt like she'd been hit with a club.

Samantha looked wildly about her. He was right. She was cornered. But up ahead were bushes and to the right a pathway that led to the cabin and safety. Slowly she crawled backward, pretending to cower, hoping to flee, but his grasp on her arm kept her prisoner.

"I'm going to slip between those hot little thighs of yours and then I'm going to send a message to Alex. When he plays the gallant rescuer, you can watch me shoot him."

"No!" She tried to reason with him. "If you kill him they'll hang you. Central City isn't like some of those flea-bitten towns out west. There's law and order and—" He slapped her again, harder this time.

"They won't hang me. Wouldn't dare. I've done pretty much just what I wanted all my life with no one to stop me." His eyes squinted as he looked at her. "Until I met that bossy Major. You'll never know how I sickened of dancing to his tune. It was because of him I was put in the brig, because of him I found myself in that stinking prison camp. I hated him more with each day that passed and swore that if I ever saw him again I'd get even. Now I will. I'll hurt him real good, through you." As he moved toward her she twisted desperately against him, kneeing him in the groin, somehow managing to wrest free. Frantically she raced up the path toward the cabin.

"You little bitch! I'm going to take real pleasure in choking the life out of you." Samantha could hear the trod of his booted feet as he came after her, the distance between them lessening with each step. She could hear the rasp of his breath as he clutched at her. Her heart was racing. Blood surged through her veins wildly. Her pulse beat at her throat.

The cabin door loomed like a blessed haven. Samantha tore through the door, but before she could shut and bolt it, Ben Cody was upon her, pressing her back against the door. Biting, kicking, and scratching, Samantha fended him off, but in the struggle he knocked over an oil lamp and sent it crashing. With a tinkling shatter it broke, spilling oil across the wooden floorboards.

"Well, now, maybe I'll just send up a signal so that the Major will come a bit sooner than I'd planned." With an evil grin he took out a match and set the oil ablaze. Flame sprayed in all directions. Samantha watched in horror as the fire spread rapidly, devouring all that she held so dear. The cabin was on fire, but this gray-eyed, scar-faced man wouldn't let her go. Instead he stared in fascination, blocking her way to the door.

55

Alex rode back to town at an increasingly slower pace as thoughts played about in his mind. First, he took his horse from a gallop to a canter, then to a trot, finally to a walk before stopping the animal altogether. He had it in mind to go back, to return to the cabin and tell Samantha that she'd won. If he could only have her on her terms, then he'd agree to live in the cabin. Wasn't there a part of him that had wanted to do just that all along? Yes, but he had been too stubborn to admit it. With a rueful smile he turned back, guiding the horse back into a gallop, thinking to himself that the winding road had grown so familiar that he could almost find his way blindfolded.

Feeling the rush of the wind against his face, Alex was startled by his horse's sudden erratic behavior. Nostrils flaring the stallion reared, nearly unseating Alex from his saddle. "What in the hell!" With mane and tail flying, hooves pawing the earth, the animal seemed crazed and only with the utmost skill was Alex able to get the horse back under control. "Damn you, Gypsy." He was cursing under his breath, supposing the cause of the bay's skittishness to be the scent of another animal, when the sight of smoke caught his eyes. Smoke. Fire. His eyes scanned the horizon. With a strangled cry he bent close to the churning muscles of his horse and guided the animal firmly up the road.

To his alarm he saw it was indeed Samantha's cabin. Flames leapt and blazed, threatening to engulf the entire building.

"Samantha!" A scream tore from his throat as he leapt from his horse, rushed toward the cabin, and pushed his way inside. "Samantha!" He saw her struggling with the man he recognized only too well. "Let her go, Cody. If you have a quarrel, it's with me, not her." Her dress torn, her hair in wild disarray, Samantha was a whirlwind of outrage and fury.

"Get out of here, Alex. He's going to kill you!" she screamed, her eyes wild with fear. "Alex!" He was going to die right before her eyes.

"You make a move toward that door," Cody hissed, "and I'll break both her arms." He would do it, Alex thought. Nothing was too low for a man like that.

"For God's sake, Cody, the cabin's going to go up like tinder." Already the fire had spread across the floor. "Let her go. You can do whatever you want with me." He'd been in such a hurry to save Samantha from the flames that he'd left his gun in the saddle holster. Now he regretted his carelessness.

"Let her go? Not a chance." Cody moved quickly, slapping Samantha across the face.

With a snarl, his blue eyes dark with rage, Alex lunged savagely for Cody, knocking his gun to the floor and freeing Samantha. Locked in frenzied struggle, Alex barked out his order. "Get out! Quick, before it's too late."

Samantha faltered. How could she rush to her safety while Alex was still in danger. Instead, like a wrathful fury she threw herself at the gunman's back, tugging and swearing. "Let go, you crazy fool! The cabin's going to burn down and us with it if you don't get out!" Her words seemed to pierce through the fog in his brain. Pushing free of Alex, he grabbed the gun before she could, then backed out the door, pulling Samantha along with him. All the while he kept the pistol pointed at Alex, using

Samantha as a shield to keep Alex away. His laugh was un-nerving as he stepped outside.

"Let her go!" Choking against the smoke, Alex staggered after the gunman and his unwilling captive. "Do what you want with me . . . but . . ."

"Well, ain't you a hero, Major. Noble. Trying to save a dam-sel from a roaring fire, even facing a man with a gun. Guess a man will do a hell of a lot for a piece of tail." His eyes gleamed with malice.

"Shut your filthy mouth." No one, but no one, would talk that way about Samantha—gun or no gun.

Piercing laughter answered. "Aren't you the brave one. Now we know how to rile him good. Just talk about his woman. You don't like that, Major? This ain't the *first* time I've followed you here."

"Samantha has no part in the bad blood between us." Alex tried to maintain a shred of calm, but it wasn't easy facing the barrel of a gun. "Where I come from a man leaves a lady's name out of a quarrel. You know that, Cody. It's me you're trying to goad. Let her go."

Ben Cody glared defiance. "You ain't no *Major* now to be giving me orders. No one here to put me in the brig now. Did you know that when the Rebs marched in I was taken to their prison? Libby Prison. I spent the rest of the war in that hell-hole."

So that was the reason for his hatred, Alex thought. "You weren't the only one, Cody. Several of my men were wounded and taken prisoner."

"But not you, Major." He loosened his hold on Samantha.

"No, I was lucky." Alex tried to talk reason. "But others were not. Many died in that battle you were kept from fighting. Listen to me, Ben. No one knows what's going to happen. No man can see his fate. You might very well have been one of the ones who died if you had been with us."

"Ha! Trying to soothe your conscience. Well, it won't work." He moved closer to Alex, turning his back on Samantha as if forgetting for a moment that she was there. "I hated you long before that. Hated all men like you who have everything they always wanted. Everything." He yanked at Samantha. "You!

Stop struggling if you want to save your fella." Fearing what might happen if she didn't do as he asked, Samantha complied. "I watched you at the pool, Major, and I have a hankerin' to poke her just like you did."

"No!" Samantha reached out to grab the gunman's wrist, pulling it forward to cancel his aim as she slammed her shoulder into his chest. The gun fired, but the bullet hit the ground. At that moment Alex struck out ruthlessly with his fist, catching Cody violently across the face. With a growl of anger Cody countered with his free fist, catching Alex on the chin.

"Alex, watch out. His gun."

Alerted by Samantha's timely warning, Alex tensed his body. Relying on the skills he had thought he'd forgotten, he kicked out violently, knocking the gun to the dirt.

The sound of flesh against flesh rent the air as each man landed blow after blow. They fell to the ground, rolling over and over as they struggled with deadly determination. Samantha was helpless to do anything but watch as each man suffered punishing blows. She'd never seen Alex like this. It was as if he had turned into a man she didn't know. *Coward,* Caroline had called him. How that haughty woman would eat her words if she could see him now.

The flames from the burning cabin danced higher, brighter, illuminating the faces of the two men. Alex had a cut over his eyes, Cody a lacerated lip. Their breathing came in ugly, rasping sounds. Still they did not stop.

Alex's head throbbed painfully, flecks of black danced before his eyes, yet he had no intention of quitting. He knew by Cody's grunts and winces that he was suffering.

Cody made a sudden move toward the gun. Alex threw himself down on the ground as both men scrambled for it. The pistol was between them. Then it was in Cody's hand. Slowly, coldly, the gunman clamped his fingers around the weapon and raised it to take aim.

"Oh, God. Alex!" A chill of fear danced up Samantha's spine.

Alex lunged out and slapped the gun away, driven by an insurmountable surge of fury that gave him strength to win out. Palming the gun, he turned and shot twice, hitting Cody once in the arm and once in the leg. In confusion, Ben Cody clutched at his wounds.

"Is this the only thing you understand, Cody? Guns? Bullets? Men like you are little better than brutes, brainless in your hate. You destroy and kill and maim. You would have shot me without blinking an eye and forced yourself on Samantha." He shook his head in disgust. "Shall I pull the trigger again? Shall I prove that I'm a man by taking your life?" With a mocking smile, he cocked the gun.

"No! No! Don't shoot me. Don't pull the trigger!" Cody groveled, down on his knees, his eyes round with fright as he pleaded for his life. "I'll leave town. I will. I'll never come near you again. I swear it."

With an unblinking stare Alex watched as the man before him seemed to take on another face. A young, beardless boy who'd never had a chance to plead for his life. A poor heroic youth whose only sin was to be in the wrong place at the wrong time, in having dreams of glory. Would Alex ever forget that face? Would he ever be able to atone for what he'd done?

"I won't kill you. You're not worth killing. But you can credit my clemency to a young Confederate soldier who was more of a man than you'll ever be." Still shaking with fury, Alex took long, deep breaths as he tried to regain his composure. His muscles were tense, his jaw set in a stern line as he watched Ben Cody struggle to stand. "Get a rope from my saddle, Sam. We'll take this brave gunfighter to the marshal." He looked at Ben Cody in disgust. "You and all your kind sicken me."

"Alex . . . ?" Samantha's voice was soft and breathless as she touched his shoulder. Tears filled her eyes as she watched him tie the gunman securely. The task complete, she threw herself in Alex's arms.

"You see, I'm not the saint I've led you to believe I am. I do have a temper. I try to keep it in check and I'm usually successful, but when he touched you . . . when he said—"

Putting her fingers to his lips, she silenced him. "You were a mighty fine sight, Alex. I was proud that you were fighting for me, to save our lives. No one's ever taken up for me before except Gramps. Guess that's why I've always been such a scrapper. It felt good to know that you care." She eyed the bound gunman warily, then turned her attention back to Alex, wiping the blood from his face. She leaned her head against his chest as she looked at the flaming cabin. The charred logs and the tumbled walls looked like the ruins of a gigantic outdoor campfire. Eventually, only the iron stove would remain, the chimney pipe standing upright like a lonely sentinel. Dark gray smoke swirled in the air like an ominous thundercloud, embers glowed orange where the fire had already blazed itself out. She fought against the agonized wail that threatened to tear from her mouth. The cabin was gone. All her precious memories and recollections. Soon it would be nothing more than a smoldering ruin.

"I'm sorry, Samantha."

"He overturned a lamp in our scuffle. Then he lit the match that started the fire." Her breath escaped in a long, shuddering sigh.

"I wanted you to be with me in town, but not like this. I know how precious your memories of your grandfather are, how much you valued all the things he left behind. If it will make you happy, I'll build you another cabin."

She shook her head. "No, thank you, Alex. It just wouldn't be the same." She entwined her arms in his with a weary sigh. "Gramps said that sometimes a person had to call a spade a spade. The past will always be a fine memory, but I have to carry on with my life. I'm not really needed up here. Not like I used to be. Sean and Patrick can keep things under control. There's no need for me to be hovering around. I realize that now." Stroking his face, she smiled. "I guess fate just has a strange way of telling a person when it's time to stop being a child and come to terms with the new twists and turns life has taken. Gramps was a hermit of sorts and I suppose just got used to it. But now I think I'm ready to tackle the whole damned town if need be."

They loaded Ben Cody into Samantha's wagon and hitched up the horses. Glancing back one more time, Samantha wiped the tears from her eyes.

"There's a suite of rooms in the hotel across from mine. I've been saving them for you. It won't be anything at all like living up here, but I think you'll find it comfortable until we can make more permanent arrangements. Like getting married."

"You want to marry me?" Her eyes, still wet with tears, glowed with sudden joy. She had been so afraid he would never ask her again.

"Will you be my wife?"

"Yes. Oh, yes!" It seemed she had a lot to learn and now was just as good a time as any. She'd hold her head up, she'd go into Central City and smile. She was going to be Alex's wife. Perhaps when all was said and done, fate had a mighty potent way of taking a hand.

Three

A DUEL OF
HEARTS
Winter 1871–Spring 1872

"She's beautiful and therefore to be woo'd:
She is a woman, therefore to be won."

William Shakespeare,
Henry VI, Part I, V, 3

56

Snow. An ocean of white greeted Samantha's eyes as she looked out the hotel window. Winter had arrived earlier than usual, driving the snow before it with a relentless fury. Samantha watched the icicles that hung suspended from the eaves, lengthening into frozen spears. It was a beautiful world. Being with Alex made it more so, and yet there were still times when she had to pinch herself to make certain she was not dreaming. So much had changed since she'd met Alex that spring day. And now she was going to become his wife!

Oh, Gramps, she thought, *if only you were still here to share this happiness with me.* Winter at the cabin seemed a lifetime away, but she still remembered how her grandfather had carefully stocked up on supplies and prepared to hibernate in the cabin like a bear with its cub. Each time the door opened the wind had driven fine granules of white snow across the room. There were days when the snow had made it impossible to go farther than the backhouse. Waking up late in the mornings, she had remained in bed as long as she could, huddling beneath her blankets. Then the mad dash across the room to stand on the cold, splintery floor until she could pull on her clothes. A continuous routine. First the fire was kindled, then the ice had to be broken in the large bucket that was filled at the pump every day. There was bacon to slice and fry, coffee to brew. Now everything was done for her. At the snap of her fingers anything she asked for was brought to her door by servants anxious to please.

"Yes, Miss Claybourne. No, Miss Claybourne. Anything you say, Miss Claybourne." Wealth had raised Samantha in nearly everyone's esteem. There were days she looked in the mirror and expected to see someone else staring back at her, instead of the very same face. She really hadn't changed. Only their perception of her had altered, making her more acceptable in their eyes. Money was power, a balm to make people forget another's faults, or so it seemed.

Samantha watched as Alex trudged through the snow below her window, making a trail of footprints on the boardwalk. Catching his eye, she waved, then hurried to the mirror to smooth her hair. Gone forever were her denim pants and flannel shirt, replaced by calico and poplin dresses in various hues. The one she wore today was a bright shade of yellow. She listened for the sound of Alex's footsteps in the hall as she straightened her collar, then hurried to open the door. Alex stood there grinning, his arms full of packages.

"Everything you ordered, Samantha. I think you must have bought out the stores, my love. And I'd be willing to wager that not a one of these is for yourself." Alex never ceased to marvel at Samantha's generosity. She seemed to feel that sharing her good fortune with others was the most natural thing in the world. He wondered if there was a selfish bone in her body.

"Let me see . . ." Taking some of the parcels from his arms, she pulled at the twine around the large box. "The dress for Myrna, Patrick's oldest daughter. Pink calico. There's a dance at the church tomorrow night and she's becoming a young woman." Her voice lowered to a hush as she spoke in confidence. "She's in love with the baker's son. I want her to look pretty." Plucking at her own dandelion-colored poplin skirt, she smiled. "First dress I ever wore for you, *my beau,* was that blue-and-white polka-dot cotton with the tiny white buttons. I thought I looked pretty foolish."

"I thought you looked grand." Shrugging out of his jacket, Alex flung it on a chair then brought his face close to hers for a brief gentle kiss. "You were astonishing. Both Robert and I were completely entranced." He could still recall his first glimpse of Samantha even as she stood before him. Now she had dresses in every color of the rainbow and looked lovely in every one. But Alex suspected it was all done just for him. Samantha would always be more comfortable in breeches and shirt. Despite her bonnets, skirts, and curls she was still that bewitching, unconventional young woman he had once mistaken for a boy. Riches had not changed her and that pleased him.

"Who would ever have guessed that someday I'd have all of this. . . ." With a sigh she made a grand sweep of her hand, indicating her plush surroundings. "Sometimes I think I'm going to wake up and discover its all been a dream." She scanned the large, elaborately furnished room. A thick Persian rug covered the polished wooden floor; dark blue velvet chairs and a matching settee flanked by walnut lowboys and side tables formed an intimate setting before a handsome fireplace. On each table sat an elaborate lamp with a wick that turned up or down depending on how much flame was needed to light the room.

"It's real, Samantha. Not only this suite of rooms, but the hotel as well. "The 'Enoch Claybourne Hotel.' How does that sound to you?"

"Sounds just fine. My tribute to Gramps. I hope it makes him feel proud." Every time she looked at the gold letters spelling out her grandfather's name, she got goose bumps. It was her memorial to the man who had given her such love and molded her young life. Enoch Claybourne had often claimed that when all was said and done, the only thing a man really left behind was his good name. It was the thing he had most valued and had instilled in Samantha, a determination to guard and revere the Claybourne name. Now that name hung proudly in carved and gilded letters above the entranceway of the fine two-storied building.

"Actually, you are his greatest memorial." Alex smiled, putting the rest of the parcels down on the settee. He kept a similar suite of rooms across the hall in an attempt to maintain the strictest propriety, though he spent most of his time in Samantha's suite. His shaving cup and razor on the bedroom nightstand and his suit hanging in the closet attested to that fact.

"I wonder what Gramps would say if he could see all of this." Samantha returned to the window and ran her fingers down the velvet draperies. There was even a double door that opened onto a small balcony. Mahogany . . . velvet . . . Persian rugs. Elegant, Alex called it. Downright gaudy is what Gramps would have said. Now it was home to Samantha.

"Your grandfather would be amazed." Alex pulled one of the purchases from its nest of brown paper. "The fiddle you wanted for Patrick. It came all the way from New York." Taking the instrument from its case, he held it out for her inspection.

"His old one had a cracked neck. Lord, but won't he be pleased?" She poked in a sack and brought out a bright red confection made of paper. "And the Chinese lantern for Wan Lau."

"Came all the way from San Francisco, or so the storekeeper said." There were seven more packages in all, each for one of the mine workers or a member of his family. Samantha was quick to reward loyalty and scrupulously honest in her dealings with her workers. She was kind to their families, understanding of their problems and sympathetic to their needs. When she had heard that Honey Wells was about to lose her saloon, she had rewarded the woman's kindness to her by giving her the needed money.

Was it any wonder, Alex thought, that they all loved her? Nearly as much as he did. He wanted to wake up every morning and find her beside him, wanted to see her swell with his child, wanted to grow old with her. There was no other woman who could ever make such thorough claim to his heart.

"Has anyone ever told you that you're an angel?" Alex drew her into his arms, his kiss one of hungry passion. There was not another woman on earth as intoxicating as Samantha. She was a rare treasure, a child-woman who enchanted him more with each passing day. Even the sunlight seemed to add to the spell of the moment. Shining through the thick glass panes, it cast a soft, golden glow over the entwined lovers, illuminating faces that radiated contentment.

Samantha felt herself bursting with happiness. Life just couldn't get any better than this. As long as she was with Alex, she knew she'd be happy. Responding to his kiss, she ran her fingers along the beloved planes of his face. She craved his touch, was drawn to him like a moth to a candle flame. In his arms was where she always wanted to be, and she reached up to fold her arms about his neck, ardently embracing him, wanting—

A loud knock at the door interrupted their sensual reverie. "Let's ignore it," Alex whispered playfully into her ear. His hand reached for and found the softness of her breast as he gently pushed her toward the settee in a fluid motion that never disrupted their embrace. The sofa was soft beneath them as they lay side by side. Alex's muscled strength strained against her as he unbuttoned her bodice. The touch of his warm, seeking fingers on her naked breast was a welcome sensation and she moaned low in her throat with pleasure.

"Mr. Nicholson? Mr. Nicholson, are you in there? Miss Claybourne?" Another loud knock shattered the spell. With agonizing effort Samantha brought herself back to reality. Rising from the settee, hastily rearranging herself, she answered the door to find the tall, skinny sandy-haired hotel clerk gazing back at her. His face was suffused with a blush as he said, "I . . . I didn't want to bother you but . . . but there is someone downstairs looking for Alexander Nicholson. Said it's important. When . . . when he wasn't in his room I . . . I knew . . . uh . . . thought he might be with you." His eyes darted into the room beyond her. "And I see that he *is* here."

"Yes, we were discussing business," Alex said icily, adjusting his cravat. It irritated him that this callow youth should interrupt them and unnerved him lest his wagging tongue create gossip. Alex didn't want Samantha's reputation compromised. With a look of regret he followed the young man down the hall, forgetting his jacket in his haste. Thinking the visitor to be a business associate and remembering Alex's admonition of how

important it was for him always to look dignified, Samantha
picked up the gray jacket and followed.

Making her way down the long carpeted stairs, Samantha
started to call after Alex, but the words died on her lips. It was
not a man who waited below but a woman, an impeccably
dressed vision in pale blue. Caroline West. Dear God, what did
she want with Alex? Taking a step back into the shadows, Samantha watched with apprehension.

"Oh, Alex, darling, I just had to see you." Caroline's voice
was high-pitched and melodious as she greeted him. "I've been
such a fool. Life without you is just too tedious to mention. I
miss your kisses, your smile, the way we used to stay up together to watch the sunrise." Samantha watched in fascinated
gravity as the golden-haired woman took a step forward, winding her arms around Alex's neck. A frigid blast as cold as a
winter wind enclosed Samantha's heart as she heard the woman
say, "I love you, Alex. I want you back again. . . ."

Samantha wanted to race down the stairs, to tear Caroline's
arms from around Alex's neck, but instead she turned her back
in agonized silence. It was too painful a reminder that Alex had
come all the way to Colorado to marry *her.* Turning, she fled up
the stairs too late to see Alex pull free of Caroline's clinging
arms.

"Caroline, please, I don't want to create a spectacle. People
are watching us." He was suspicious of her sudden show of
affection, especially after her sharp, twittering tongue had tried
to unman him. She had babbled the lie all over town: She had
broken off her engagement because he was a coward. Why was
she suddenly here now spewing sweetness and smiles?

"Let them watch. I don't really care, Alex. All I know is that
we made a most grievous error in staying apart for so long."
Grasping his arm with a familiarity that was nothing short of
bold, she tried to renew their embrace, but Alex held her at
arm's length. "Alex . . . !"

"There's been no error, Caroline. You are not the woman for
me nor am I the man for you. What we had was infatuation, an
illusion that disintegrated when we came to know each other
better."

"No!" His rejection stung her. Only the remembrance of her

father's harsh demands kept her from unleashing her full fury upon him. Instead she feigned tears. "Alex, how could you hurt me so? How could you even intimate that what we had is over?"

"Because it is. It was passion that we shared, not love, Caroline. I know that now and so will you when you meet the right man." He said the words as gently as he could, not meaning to cause her pain. "I've met someone else, someone I have grown to love very much."

"Samantha Claybourne!" She spat out the name, her determination to remain calm shattered by the thought of the miner's granddaughter laying claim to Alex. It was just too humiliating to think that he could possibly prefer that little hoyden to her.

"Yes, Samantha Claybourne. My fondness for her has developed into love. She's like a walk in the forest, refreshing and unspoiled, caring. . . ."

"She's a rude, crude, uncouth little hellion is what she is! How could you, Alex? How could you do this to me? The whole town knows that she's your mistress. They know the reason you lent her that money for her mine. But to—" Alex's hand silenced any further ranting as he cupped it over her mouth.

"I won't hear another word. Samantha is going to be my wife. That is all I need to say on the matter. I certainly do not need to explain myself to you, Caroline! Nor will I allow you to make her the subject of your poisonous gossip. Say what you want to about me but don't malign Samantha." There was a roaring in Alex's ears as he fought to hold his temper in check. He looked, to Caroline's eyes, like a scowling, ominous stranger. There was not even a spark of affection in those blue eyes staring back at her. At that moment she knew beyond certainty that she had lost him.

"Your . . . your wife?" she stammered. Her father would be furious when he learned that she had failed. He would berate her, show his anger, and perhaps even make good on his promise to withhold the spending money he had, up to now, so freely allowed her. She would have to beg for every new hat and it was all the fault of Alex. Alex and that nasty little tomboy who had so stealthfully ensnared him.

"My wife. I intend to make my life with Samantha."

"Marry her for her money, you mean." At last her anger bubbled forth in a spew of incautious words. "So that's why you've taken up with her, why you speak of weddings and love. Do you think I don't know? She's one of the wealthiest women this side of the Mississippi and now you think she's good enough for you. Well, she won't be rich for long. Not when my father—" In horror at what she had nearly revealed Caroline put her gloved hand to her mouth.

"What are you telling me, Caroline?" Alex clutched her shoulders and forced her to look at him. "What is your father up to now?" Shaking her none too gently, he tried to appease his curiosity. "Tell me! Tell me!"

"Nothing. Nothing. I was just angry, that's all." With a frantic burst of strength Caroline broke away, intent upon putting as much distance between herself and Alexander Nicholson as possible. There was another way to accomplish her goal, she thought sourly as she glanced over her shoulder at Alex from the front door. If she could not snare the gander, she would turn her attentions to the golden goose. She would drive a wedge between Alex and Miss Claybourne, all right, just as her father had ordered. She would go to Samantha Claybourne when Alex was not hovering about; they would have a heart-to-heart conversation. A bit of girl talk. The thought made her smile as she left the hotel.

57

Samantha watched the door in agonized apprehension, waiting for Alex's return. She wouldn't give him up to that spoiled, cow-eyed, pale-faced blonde; she just couldn't. Not after all they'd been through together. Alex belonged to her, not Caroline West. That snobbish female had given up all rights to Alex when she'd broken their engagement just because Alex wouldn't tote a gun. She didn't love him, couldn't have any real affection for him if she'd turned him loose. Why, then, was she here now, trying to snare him again? Did she think that he was partner in the Siren Song, now that the mine had struck a rich vein of gold, that he was merely another rich prize to be claimed? Or had she other motives? It didn't matter. Samantha only knew that she'd never give Alex up without a fight.

"Caroline West!" The very sound of the name incensed her. Damn the woman. Damn her father. They had been nothing but a pain in the backside for a long, long while. Picking up a silver teapot, Samantha hurled it at the door, regretting the action as the door opened and Alex stepped inside.

"Samantha?" He eyed her curiously, then bent down to pick up the artfully crafted object. "Is something wrong?"

"No. No." She couldn't tell him what she'd seen, what she'd overheard. A man had a right to his privacy. She didn't want him to know she'd been spying on him. Besides, she feared to bring up the subject, was apprehensive about what he might say. "I was polishing it and it just flew right out of my hands."

Her expression was so earnest, so serious, that Alex's eyes brimmed with suppressed laughter. He suspected that she was annoyed at the hotel clerk who'd interrupted their lovemaking but too embarrassed to admit it.

"Then I urge you to be more careful," he said with a grin. Enfolding her in his arms, he kicked the door shut with his foot. "Now, where were we before we were disturbed?"

His mouth captured hers in a long, languorous kiss that took Samantha's breath away. For a moment she forgot her fears about Caroline and gave herself up to the fierce sweetness. Her lips opened under his, her entire body tingled with the exciting sensations that were now so very familiar to her. Alex always kindled a fire within her just by being near her, touching her. It was such exquisite torture, such poignant pleasure, that she sighed.

Alex looked down at Samantha's closed eyes and felt a wave of protective tenderness. He'd meant to tell her about Caroline's visit, but now he thought better of it. There was no need to upset her with something that was unimportant. Caroline West was his past and Samantha Marie Claybourne was his future. His arms held her against his heart as his kiss deepened. Perhaps seeing Caroline, realizing how close he'd come to marrying the wrong woman, made Samantha all the more precious to him.

Samantha's arms crept around Alex's strong neck, drawing him closer. She'd make him forget Caroline West, drive all thoughts of that pampered ninny out of his head. Her heart moved with love. Deep inside her was the fierce need to belong to him. She was a woman, Alex had made her so with his gentle teachings. She was *his* woman, she could never belong to another man. There was nothing as important at this moment as this chance to give herself wholly to him.

Always before, Samantha had been the recipient of caresses and kisses, but now it was she who aroused Alex's desire, running her hands over his body. His sharp intake of breath, the way that he groaned out her name, emboldened her. Slowly she reached up, unbuttoned his vest and pulled it off. His linen shirt followed, baring the masculine strength of his chest to her view.

"I just never tire of looking at you, Alex. Don't reckon I ever will." Her palms slid sensuously over his tight flesh, stroking the hair of his chest with fascinated familiarity, slowly exploring every inch of him. "You're pleasing to the eyes. Very pleasing."

"So are you." The soft material of her poplin bodice tightened across her breasts, teasing his eyes. Deftly unlacing the ribbons, he pulled the bodice down around her shoulders, exposing the soft swell of her bosom to his touch. His long fingers gently stroked and caressed the peaks, then compulsively his hand closed over the soft flesh. He urgently sought out her mouth in a hungry fusion.

Samantha's hands moved with sensuous fascination as they slid down his back to his hips. Her hands tugged at the waistband of his trousers as their bodies caressed. Slowly, purposefully, she undressed him in a manner meant to fire his passion. *Caroline West be damned!* she thought. She'd blot that woman out of his heart and mind.

"If this is your reaction, I hope to God we're interrupted again and again." His voice was husky as he teased her. He stripped away her skirts and petticoats until all their garments lay at their feet. Caressing the small of her back, his hands slid downward, cradling the curve of her bottom in his palms. Pulling her up on her toes, he pressed her against him as his kiss grew fiercer. Their bodies writhed together in a slow, delicate dance. His arms tightened around her waist as he pulled her so close that she was certain she could feel every hair of his chest against her swollen breasts. Between their bodies she felt the provocative, insistent pressure of his maleness and experienced a jolt of devastating desire. The warmth and power of his warm, taut body straining so hungrily against hers set her aflame.

"Alex . . ." Her tongue slid past his teeth to explore his

mouth as she kissed him hungrily, passionately. She trembled as his hand moved over her body from shoulder to thigh, stopping to caress the flat plain of her stomach.

"Shall we move to the bedroom?" Without waiting for her answer he picked her up in his arms, carried her to the bed, then gently laid her down. Smoothing back the hair from her face, he lay down beside her. Alex reveled in the sheer delight of the texture and pressure of her body against his skin. She was as soft as velvet, he thought, her desire a vibrant match for his own. "Your skin is so smooth," he whispered, burying his face between the soft mounds of her breasts. With his lips he outlined the circles of her nipples. He could feel the pounding of her heart, beating as furiously as his own. Trailing his lips along her soft flesh, he sought out that place where her heart beat and reverently kissed her there.

Samantha shivered again. Her fingers clutched at his shoulders, moved to the dark hair of his head, seeking to press him even closer to her bosom. She heard him take a deep, shaky breath, felt a quiver in the hard muscles of his arms as he embraced her.

At last he lifted his head, looking down at her tenderly as he breathed, "My feisty Samantha . . . so beautiful . . ." Their lips met again with an explosion of passion. He pulled her onto him, mingling his legs and arms with hers. He lifted his head and his mouth claimed hers with fierce possession. Then she was opening up to him, relaxing as she gave herself up to the flood of heat that pulsed between them.

Blue eyes locked with brown as they both hung suspended in time, moving together in the ultimate passion, climbing together, soaring then gliding slowly back to earth. Muted sunlight washed the room, warming her as she watched the rise and fall of Alex's chest. She loved him so very much. If you loved someone with all your heart and soul, how could they help but love you back? Love was an all-encompassing need to give.

She closed her eyes, wondering how she could have ever thought anything else was important. Even finding gold was as nothing compared with the treasure she held in her heart. Samantha's only thought was of her contentment. Surely Alex could not give a second thought to Caroline West after the bliss they had just shared. Nestled in Alex's arms, she thought how foolish she had been to be so afraid.

58

Pushing open the door to the balcony, Samantha leaned out and took a deep breath of the sun-warmed air. The sun shone on the newly fallen snow, flickering, shining. *Sparkles* and *sunshine*—those two words best explained the way she felt today after spending such blissful moments in Alex's arms. She felt carefree and startlingly happy, and why shouldn't she? She had everything any woman could ever want. Most importantly, she loved Alex. If she wasn't exactly certain of the depth of his feelings for her, she wouldn't worry. She felt enough love for both of them and that was a start.

The thick Persian rug felt soft and soothing to her bare feet as she walked about the room in a dreamy haze. Running her fingers through her coppery hair, she recaptured every precious moment of lovemaking in her thoughts as she closed her eyes. She had been foolish to fear Alex's encounter with Caroline West. Could he help it if the woman came brazenly to the hotel to see him? Surely if Alex felt any stirring of emotions for his ex-fiancée he would have revealed it to her last night. And yet he had been extremely restless, agitated in his sleep, fretful over something. What?

"I won't even think about it," she vowed, gathering the folds of her morning robe and pulling them snugly against her body. Gramps had always warned that people often "borrowed trouble," but she wouldn't allow herself any trouble today. Not when the day promised so much.

Alex's gray jacket still lay on the settee, another reminder of the passionate night they had spent together, and Samantha walked across the carpet to pick it up. Holding the jacket against her chest, she had just conjured up Alex's handsome visage when she was startled out of her reverie by the sound of insistent knocking. Thinking it to be the hotel clerk, she opened the door, staring in frozen disbelief to find Caroline West standing before her, the last person on earth she wanted to see.

"What do you want?" Samantha's look of surprise melted to a frown as her eyes squinted in displeasure.

"My, my, my. What a greeting." Caroline's heavy-lidded eyes appraised Samantha with undisguised disdain, taking in the flannel nightgown beneath the robe, the touseled hair. "Aren't you going to invite me in? I thought surely *you* would have acquired *some* manners."

Every muscle of Samantha's body stiffened at the reproach. With as much dignity as she could muster, she gestured for the cold, proud beauty to enter. She was achingly conscious of each passing second as she waited for Caroline West to pull off first one glove and then the other before deigning to take a seat on the settee. The woman's head turned from side to side as she examined the room with exacting scrutiny.

"So this is Alex's little love nest," she said at last in a mocking tone that left no doubt as to her meaning.

"Alex spends some time here with me. Yes." Samantha proudly stood her ground. She would not let some prissy snob in velvet and lace intimidate her.

"Quite a lot of time, or so I've heard the gossips say." Caroline regarded her through narrowed eyes, an amused expression on her perfectly profiled face. "Why, the whole town's talking."

"Let them. I don't give a damn!" Samantha was perilously close to losing her temper. Stalking to the door, she opened it wide. "Say what you have to say. Don't beat about the bush. If you have something in your craw, spit it out and then get out of here."

"All right. I'll come to the point." The thin lips curved up in a satisfied smile, reminding Samantha of a cat she had seen once who had cornered a mouse. "I made a mistake in giving Alex up. I was foolish to even compare him to the other men. I erroneously weighed him against other men who stride about armed and prepared for a challenge and found him wanting. But the measure of a man is in his manners, not in being a bully. To come to the point, I want him back."

"No!" Samantha tried to hide her fear. "I won't let you have him." Clenching her fists she shook her head furiously. "You had him tied but you untethered him."

Throwing her head back, Caroline West gave in to gales of laughter, finally managing to catch her breath long enough to say, "Oh, my dear, you really are too much."

To be laughed at in this way ignited Samantha's temper. With a purposeful stride she closed the distance between them and stood menacingly close to the other woman. "Stop braying like a lamebrained jackass before I pull out every hair on your tightly curled head. I won't be laughed at. Not by you. Not by anybody." Something in her manner warned Caroline not to trifle, for she stopped giggling just as quickly as she had begun. "That's better. Now, hightail it out of here before I do and say things I might regret."

"I won't laugh anymore. In truth, I suppose it's not a laughing matter. Alex has certainly gotten himself into a mess *this* time." Her voice held more than just a hint of sarcasm as she said, "I suppose you *love* him. Of course you do. Alex can be very charming. And he's handsome."

"Alex is unlike any man I've ever met before. Yes, I love him. And he's no coward. I saw that firsthand. But you've said your piece. Now you can go." She wondered if it would scandalize the hotel if she threw this woman bodily out in the snow.

"I won't go until I make you realize. Sharing a bed with you does not mean that Alex loves you. A dalliance, that's all it will ever be. An amusement. I can well believe that Alex has *never* met anyone quite like you before." Her tone of voice marked her comment as an insult. "But men never marry their . . . well . . . their bedmates. A man wants a woman of his own class. And you're hardly that."

"Alex *is* going to marry me!" Caroline's insufferable poise, her condescending way, her arrogance, made it difficult for Samantha to keep her own balance. She wanted to fly at the woman, scratch out her eyes, shake her until her teeth rattled, force her to take back her words. She was so riled, she could barely think. Feeling as if she were drowning, suffocating, she somehow managed to say, "I've got money. The mine has given me all I could ever hope to need. I'd wager I've got nearly as much as you. Hell, maybe even more."

"Money perhaps. But you lack breeding. Your way of dress, your words, your manners, the way you glower and come so close to shouting at me, all mark you for what you are. Totally unacceptable to live in Alex's world, unsuitable to be his wife no matter how much gold you might have been able to acquire from your little mine." She shook her head almost pityingly. "Despite our . . . our little differences, I hate to see you hurt. Alex came to Central City to marry *me*. Foolishly, I pushed him away. He was lonely, dejected. And I would suppose he felt at least a measure of fondness for you. Pity for you when your grandfather died. But now that I'm willing to take him back, he is only too anxious to come to my arms. Only his guilt at having compromised you keeps him away. That and his silly proposal."

"No . . . !" Samantha was shattered. What this woman said was true! Alex had come to Central City to marry this golden vision. He would have done so had Caroline not been put off by his refusal to fight. Now this woman was reasserting her rights, and though Samantha loved him with all her heart, she had the sinking feeling that she was no match for Caroline. Hadn't she thought from the very first that Caroline West was the perfect match for Alex? They both shared a world of elegant dress, speech, and manners. A world where Samantha would never belong.

"Can you imagine what his parents would think of you? What his friends would think of you in Boston?" Seeing Samantha's hesitation, she hurried on. "You would hardly fit into the strict social circles of that proper town. Why . . . Alex would be ruined." Lifting a hand to her hair, Caroline patted each strand into place. "Alex can't stay here forever, you know."

Samantha stared at Caroline numbly, self-doubt and sadness clutching at her heart. People spoke of falling in love, of the whirling, spinning ecstasy of it. Now she felt only the pain as she fell to the earth with a thud. Hadn't she always been realistic? Gramps had taught her to keep her feet on the ground and yet she couldn't let go of her dream. "I don't care about Alex's parents. Only him. I love Alex. Much more than you ever could."

"And you think that's all there is to it? Love? You silly, foolish child." Slowly, gracefully, she rose to her feet, brushing at the skirt of her impeccably styled periwinkle blue velvet dress. "He doesn't want you. He's merely too honorable a man to push you away for fear of breaking your heart. But someday, when he returns to his senses, he'll realize the terrible mistake he's made." She shrugged her shoulders disparagingly. "Oh, perhaps here, despite the rumors and twitterings, you'll manage to keep him in tow, but someday, when he longs to return home to Boston, he'll find you an embarrassment. He'll resent you and any affection he feels will turn to hatred. I can't make it any plainer than to say you are as mismatched as a pebble and a jewel."

"I won't give him up. No matter what you say, I'll make him love me. I will." Samantha was aware of Caroline's stare and turned her head away so that the haughty woman wouldn't see the tears that misted her eyes. "I love Alex and I won't give him up to anyone. I won't!"

"We'll see." The voice was soft and low, but it was as if the woman shouted. "I give you fair warning, I will do everything in my power to get Alex back. Think on that. All's fair in love and war." Again Caroline's voice tinkled with laughter. "I suppose you can classify our little 'talk' as a skirmish." With a rustle as soft as the wind she was gone in a swirl of perfume, leaving Samantha alone in a room that had suddenly become cold and dark.

Samantha didn't really know how long she sat staring out the window. Nor did she really care. She felt numb. Devastated. Helpless for the first time in a long while. Alex was the light in her world and suddenly the storm clouds threatened to extinguish her happiness. The question was, what to do about it? How could she compete against the beautiful, calculating Caroline? How could she hope to rival such a woman? Caroline West was all the things she was not. Poised. Ladylike. As icily beautiful as a distant star. She was the woman Alex had loved, perhaps still did.

And yet I love him so, she thought trying to assuage the ache in her heart. She sat still as a stone, facing the possibility that she would lose Alex. Her throat was dry. Her eyes ached from crying. With agonizing clarity she knew the worst was yet to come, and that knowledge unnerved her. She felt hot; she felt cold. She wanted to run away, to flee the pain of facing Alex and asking him if he still loved Caroline. What would she do if he said yes? How could she live without him?

Caroline's terrible words swirled about in her head: *Your way of dress, your words, your manners . . . unacceptable to live in Alex's world. You would hardly fit in . . . someday . . . he'll realize the mistake he's made . . . he'll find you an embarrassment.* The memory made Samantha's face burn. For a moment, she felt shame, then suddenly that shame and sadness turned to anger. How dare that woman say such things! She didn't know beans in a bag! Why was she sitting here feeling sorry for herself, bemoaning the fact that she had lost Alex before it had even happened? What kind of fighting spirit was that? She'd fought Jeremiah to keep the mine, hadn't she? Wasn't Alex even *more* important to her? War, Caroline had called it. Indeed it *had* come to that. She would fight for Alex with every breath, with every nerve, with every fiber of her being. She was not some harebrained coward who'd run off with her tail between her legs. Anything worth having was worth fighting for. Hadn't she learned that by now? She'd never run from a fight before and she wasn't about to start running now.

If Alex wants a lady, someone with hands as soft as a baby's behind, someone acceptable to his friends and family in Boston, *she* could become that woman, she thought with stubborn resolve. Nothing was impossible. She would fight fire with fire. She would prove she could be just as good a lady as that whining, spoiled, disdainful Caroline West. She would out-lady that lady if that was what it took to win Alex's heart.

Quickly she moved about the room This was no time to sit about moping. There was a great deal to do. Gramps had always said that you couldn't make a silk purse out of a sow's ear, but he was wrong. She would prove it to herself, to Caroline West, and to Alex.

Stripping off her robe, pulling the flannel nightgown over her head, Samantha shivered. It was an awesome thought, to change herself completely, and yet she would do it. She had to if she meant to keep Alex. Lacing up her dress, pulling on her boots and coat, she took a last deep breath and stepped through the doorway.

59

Samantha trudged along the boardwalk in a dither. It was all well and good to decide to become a lady, but just where was she going to find a teacher? She wasn't acquainted with any of Central City's highfalutin upper crust, she thought with a sigh. And even if she did know them, she would have been loath to trust them. What she did must be kept secret, at least for a while. No one, especially Caroline, must know what she was about.

"Drat and damnation!" Now that she was determined to do this thing, it seemed an impossibility. Because of Gramps's aversion to people prying about, Samantha had very few friends. Alex, of course. Patrick, his wife and family. Wan Lau. Several of the other miners. But not one of them could be of any help to her in this venture.

In disappointment she walked up and down the street, reading the letters sprawled across each storefront, each sign hanging from a door. Walking all the way up Main Street, she chided herself, certain that if she kept walking, she'd soon find herself in Nevadaville. Still, it did her good to keep moving, to concentrate on the buildings instead of her thoughts. She passed by the Central City Bakery, the Roworth and Lake Grocery Store, remembering the day Alex had helped her load supplies, A. Jacobs' Clothing Store, coming at last to a wood-fronted building with a large lettered sign that proclaimed THE MONTANA.

A theater, Samantha thought, standing up on her tiptoes to read the program attached to the door. She'd never been inside a theater before. Her grandfather had called them "scandalous," certain that those who made their living parading about on a stage must be up to no good. No matter how she had cajoled him, he had refused to take her into town to see a performance. But now she was here.

The Taming of the Shrew, she read, wondering just what kind of an animal *that* was. Her grandfather had told her that sometimes animals were trained to do tricks and prance about before a gathering of people; she supposed such was the case. Listed below those bold letters was a list of names. Edward Singleton. Fannie Gardner. In darker letters it read, "Jack Langrishe presents Teresa Templeton." The program proclaimed her to be the most renowned actress in the West and an accomplished drama coach. Samantha read on to discover that the actress held sessions on the "intricacies of pronunciation." How to talk and how to walk. Instantly, she knew what she was going to do: hire this woman to teach her.

Pushing open the door she entered the darkened building, stumbling over chairs as she worked her way toward the only source of light, a lantern that glowed on the high wooden stage. After the bright sun it was difficult to adjust her eyes to the dim lighting, but when she did she could see that two people, a man and a woman, were standing on that platform.

" 'Good morrow, Kate, for that's your name, I hear,' " called out the man.

"Oh, no, my name's Samantha." Her voice came out in a hoarse croak as she moved closer.

" 'Well have you heard, but something hard of hearing,' " the woman answered. " 'They call me Katharine that do talk of me.' "

Katharine, that was a name Samantha had never heard before. She thought to ask this Katharine just where she might be able to find Miss Teresa Templeton, but before she could ask the question the man started talking again.

" 'You lie, in faith; for you are call'd plain Kate, and bonny Kate, and sometimes Kate the curst; but, Kate, the prettiest Kate in Christendom; Kate of Kate-Hall, my super-dainty Kate . . .' " He stopped talking as his eyes settled on Samantha. "We are closed, miss," he barked out in obvious irritation. "There is no matinee today. Come back at seven o'clock."

"I want to see Miss Teresa Templeton. I must see her." Samantha was not to be denied. "Please tell me where I can find her."

"We're in the middle of a rehearsal. Can't you see that?" Bending over the stage, he glared down at her, his face illuminated by the lone footlight.

"Leave her alone, Edward. We know these lines backward and forward. Let's call it a day." Slowly, gracefully, the woman walked forward. "I'm Teresa Templeton, my dear. What can I do for you?"

"I want you to coach me. To teach me how to talk and walk just like the advertisement outside says. I want you to show me how to be a lady. I don't care none about being an actress. I want to learn how to always say the right things, act proper in all situations, and know how to be mannerly. I'll pay you anything you ask if you can accomplish that." Determination glowed in Samantha's eyes as bright as the footlights.

"She doesn't have time. That advertisement is meant to bring in *actresses*. Jack Langrishe is starting up another acting troupe. Teresa isn't running some finishing school."

"Be quiet, Edward! Leave the girl alone." Cautiously walking down the steps of the stage ladder, Teresa Templeton took Samantha by the hand. "Come along with me to my dressing room, young lady, and we will talk about it. Despite what my colleague tells you, I think I might be able to find some time to do as you request." Pulling Samantha along, she led her to an area at the back of the stage and lit a lamp. "It's not very fancy. I'm used to much larger dressing rooms, but it serves well enough."

It was more cubbyhole than room, Samantha noted, with a

curtain that pulled across the entrance instead of a door. A large overturned crate was littered with tiny boxes, tubes and bottles. Above the crate, nailed to the wall was a round mirror. There was a backless chair which Teresa Templeton pulled out for Samantha to sit on and a rope that was strung from wall to wall. From that rope hung a variety of colorful dresses that looked as if they had come from ages past. Samantha couldn't resist reaching out to touch them.

"My costumes. My character in the play is very well dressed, at least after she wins her husband's favor and they stop bickering." Teresa Templeton laughed, a melodious sound. Picking up a powder puff, she dabbed at her nose. "The hem of one is rather scorched, I fear. It brushed against one of the footlights a few nights ago and caught fire. Needless to say there was a lot of excitement *that* night."

Samantha gasped as she saw the red gown with its blackened skirt. "You must have been very frightened." The memory of the fire in the cabin was still very vivid in her mind. "I'm scared of fire, leastwise when it gets out of control." She turned her attention to the actress, appraising her. Teresa Templeton appeared to be in her early thirties until one got a closer look. A careful scrutiny revealed the tiny lines at her eyes that crinkled up when she laughed, the darkened smudges beneath her eyes that told of late hours and little sleep. Her hair was a honey-colored blond touched with wisps of gray at the forehead. Tightly curled, it framed a remarkably pretty face that for the moment was devoid of all the paint and makeup Samantha had heard actresses always wore. Gramps had decried such cosmetics whenever he spoke of the evils of the theater. The woman's figure was somewhat plump, but she was still a ravishing sight in her pale pink dress. Samantha was intrigued yet she couldn't say why; perhaps it was the proud way the woman held her head.

"This is my very first time in Central City but I'm coming to like it," Teresa Templeton was saying. Her gray eyes were soft as she met Samantha's stare. "But that's not what we came to talk about. Tell me about this determination of yours to study diction with me. You seem just fine the way you are."

"I'm not! I don't know any pretty words and I lose my temper when I ought not to. Even though I wear pretty dresses I look as fashionable as a goose in a henhouse. And I don't know the right things to say." Samantha took the woman's hand imploringly, her eyes pleading. "Oh, please. You gotta help me. I love him but I'm gonna lose him for certain to *her*. Alex is a gentleman. He comes from Boston where everything is fine and proper. I want him to feel proud of me. I want to be a lady, his lady." The story tumbled out in a flurry of stammering words. She found herself telling this woman about the first time she'd met Alex, of her disappointment upon learning that he'd come to the territory to get married. She told of her grandfather's death and her resolve to keep the mine, of Alex's kindness to her and his generous loan of the money she needed to keep and work the mine. Each time she mentioned him, her eyes brightened and she couldn't help but smile. "And then his fiancée broke the engagement because she thought Alex was a coward. But he's *not*! He just wanted to keep a vow he made during the war about not carrying a gun." She recounted the fact that they had become lovers, averting her eyes as she spoke. "We were happy, so very happy, until *she* decided she wanted him back." Samantha's voice shook with anger as she recounted Caroline West's visit, the insulting words she had spoken. "I've got to be honest with you, I wanted to run away at first, but then I knew I had to fight for him. A woman has to do anything she can to hold her man. That's when I decided I had to learn to be a lady. So that I can go to Boston with Alex and he'll hold his head up high. I want him to feel proud of me. I want to be part of his world." She shrugged her shoulders. "Hell, I never wanted to be before. I was happy just being me, but I guess sometimes that's just not enough."

"So you want to be just like this woman who scorned you. Are you certain? You seem to me to be perfect just the way you are. Clothing and manners don't always make a woman a lady. It sounds to me as if this haughty rival of yours is the one who lacks breeding." For a moment a look of sadness clouded her eyes. "If this young man loves you, he will accept you just the way you are. And if he does not, then he isn't worth your tears. Believe me, I know. I once loved a man as much as you care for your Alex, but he left me for a woman who had a great deal more money than I could ever possess. It broke my heart at the time, but now I realize that sometimes fate is kinder than we know."

"I can't take the chance on losing Alex. I think he cares for me a great deal. At least I've got to try and win his love. A Claybourne never gives up. Please . . ."

Teresa Templeton slowly shook her head. "All right. If you want to give that proper miss a taste of her own medicine, I'll do as you ask." Taking Samantha by the shoulders, she turned her around and around. "First and foremost we must get you some *stylish* dresses, shoes, and hats. Tastefully elegant. By the time I am through with you, every man on the street will turn and stare. Your beauty will make your rude rival look like a mouse by comparison." She trilled out her laughter. "I think this is going to be very enjoyable. Like having my own fashion doll. But the lessons will be tedious and boring," she warned. "I'll drive you unmercifully, make you walk with a book on your head, repeat the same phrases until you are hoarse."

"I don't care. I'll do anything that you ask."

"Then let's get started. Right now. Right this very minute." Grabbing her hat, tying it under the chin, she laughed again. "I know just the right dressmaker. She's skilled and she's prompt. Within the next week she should be able to finish at least one new outfit."

Samantha watched Teresa Templeton leave the dressing room, hesitating just a moment before she followed. The old Samantha would soon be gone and a new Samantha would take her place, she vowed. And Caroline West be damned.

60

It was long after dusk when Samantha returned to the hotel. She was exhausted but joyously happy as she thought of the task ahead of her. As Miss Templeton had said, it was "a long road to success," but she had taken the first step. At least when the week was out, she would be dressed for the part. That thought had been her only comfort as she'd been forced to stand stark still before the dressmaker. Measured and remeasured a hundred times, poked and prodded with pins, asked over and over which laces and ribbons she liked, which colors she preferred for her gowns, she had become so impatient that she had told the flustered woman she really didn't give a damn, only to be severely reprimanded by Teresa Templeton.

"If you are going to be a lady, Samantha, you must hold your temper in check," she had said. "Profanity is taboo. If you must give vent to your frustration, say something a bit less colorful. 'Fiddlesticks,' for example. At least until you become more demure."

"Fiddlesticks?"

"Fiddlesticks."

Samantha had tucked that word into a corner of her brain, bringing it forth again and again as the day progressed. The dressmaker's was not the only place they had visited. Teresa Templeton seemed to be having the time of her life taking Samantha to visit the shoemaker, the jeweler, and a woman who owned a millinery shop. Before the day was even half over she had purchased or put in orders for six hats, ten dresses, seven pairs of shoes, and a score of delicate lacy unmentionables that were to be worn beneath her gowns—drawers, petticoats, camisoles, and chemises. She had even agreed to wear two instruments of torture—a corset and a bustle. All because of her desire to please Alex and outdo Caroline West. This was *war* she reminded herself, and she had to win the battle. Alex would be so proud of her when her transformation was complete. With that thought in mind she had bid the actress good-bye with a promise to meet her at the theater at eight o'clock sharp. Tomorrow morning her lessons would begin again.

Alex was waiting for her when she came to the head of the stairs, pacing back and forth in front of her door. As he caught sight of her he hurried forward, a worried look on his brow. "Samantha, you were supposed to meet me at the proposed site of the boardinghouse at two o'clock. Where were you?"

"Damn!" She choked the word back as soon as it was out. "Fiddlesticks, Alex. I guess I forgot." Her confrontation with Caroline West had so upset her that she'd let the appointment slip her mind.

"You forgot?" How unlike Samantha it was to forget anything, Alex thought. She had a remarkable memory. "I was afraid that something might have happened to you." She looked so contrite that he didn't push the matter. Instead he gathered her into his arms and brushed his lips against her ear. "I missed you. You seem to be a habit with me," he whispered. "As important as going to sleep at night and waking up in the morning."

"Am I, Alex?" His words pleased her and she smiled. "I hope I'm a habit you never want to break." She wanted to tell him about Caroline's visit, but she held her tongue. She would not play on his sympathies. Would not keep him tied to her by promises. She wanted Alex's happiness above everything else. If that meant setting him free, then she would. It was his decision as to which woman he would choose, not Samantha's. She wanted him to make the choice out of love and not from a feeling of obligation. But in the meantime she'd give Caroline West a hell of a fight, she thought with a smile.

61

Alex stood before the bedroom window staring down at the steeply sloped, snow-packed road below, watching as the town came to life. Even at the crack of dawn there were people milling about, merchants and miners anxious to start their day. It reminded him of a disturbed anthill, everyone going in different directions. But nearly each one of those poor souls was in danger. Jeremiah West was like an octopus, spreading his tentacles slowly and surely over the town, reaching all the way to Black Hawk and Mountain City. He was ruthless, obsessed with money and domination. Only he and Samantha stood in the man's way. That Samantha was a target for another of his devious schemes, Alex had no doubt. Caroline had warned him: something perverse was brewing. Alex wasn't certain just what it was, but he was resolved to find out.

Turning away from the window, Alex gazed at Samantha still asleep in the bed. Her strawberry blond hair spread across the pillows like rich strands soft silk framing the heart-shaped face that had grown so dear to him. Her long, thick lashes shaded

her cheeks. Dear God, he loved her so. More than anything in
the world he wanted to protect her, to shield her from turmoil
and trouble.

If only we could retreat back to the mountains, he thought.
They had been so happy there. In that tiny, sparsely furnished
cabin, Alex had been content for the first time in his life. For
those all too few precious weeks, they had been able to shut out
the world. Now it was threatening to close in around them at
any moment. Far from bringing them happiness, Samantha's
newly acquired wealth had complicated their lives. It made her
a vulnerable target for unscrupulous men, endangered her na-
iveté, gave them less time to spend together. Where would it all
lead?

"Ah, Sam. Sam." Unable to resist the temptation, he bent
down with aching tenderness to touch a strand of her hair. She
was the woman he wanted to share his life and love with.
Hadn't she crept into his heart right from that very first day?
"Oh, Samantha don't *ever* change." She was his haven in a
storm of disillusionment. Her innocence and unselfishness were
proof of how people were meant to be: not cold and grasping,
using others for their own gains; but warm, open, and caring.
Samantha was never one for practiced wiles, for fluttering eyelashes, empty chatter or meaningless words. She was a rarity. A
treasure of the heart, his heart, as beautiful and real as the
mountains that had sheltered her all these years.

A slight smile curved Alex's lips as he thought of their first
meeting. She had been all bristle and fire when she'd confronted
Caroline, announcing that she had "saved his hide," but she
had been vulnerable as well. Perhaps it was that which had first
drawn him. She had seemed like a blossom in search of the
sunshine, reaching out to him with her unassuming affection.
He had intended to offer friendship and comfort, but somewhere along the way his fondness for her had turned to love.
Holding her in his arms, making love to her, had bound him to
her. She had given herself to him so openly, so completely, that
now the thought of ever parting from her was unthinkable.

I should have married her long ago, he reproached himself.
Why hadn't he? Was he a fool? His relationship with Caroline
had left him, as Samantha might have said, "gunshy." He had

been afraid that the magic he felt with Samantha would fade
away, just as it had with Caroline. He had been apprehensive.
Wary. What he had not let pierce his stubborn brain was that
Samantha would never disappoint him, never change. She
would always be passionate, honest, unaffected, and unspoiled,
a fey creature with an infectious zeal for living. He wanted her.
He would never love another woman the way he loved Samantha. When the jeweler finished the ring, when she became his
wife, he would make up for his stupidity in not plighting his
troth earlier.

As if Samantha sensed his thoughts, her lips formed a smile
in her sleep. Moaning softly, she turned over on her side, moving closer to Alex. He remembered the way she had clung to
him last night as they made love, almost desperately, as if she
had feared he might vanish. She had murmured something
about wanting to please him and had snuggled her slim body
into the hollow of his. She had been totally uninhibited, fiery,
igniting in Alex a blaze of mindless delight. Then she had slept
cuddled up against him, her arms wrapped about him, her
breasts pressed tightly to his chest. A wave of protectiveness
had swept over him then as it did now.

For several moments he sat on the edge of the bed, watching
as her eyelids fluttered open. When her copper-colored eyes met
his, he smiled. "Good morning." He pressed his lips against her
forehead in a light kiss and stroked the hair back from her face.

"Good morning." Stretching like a cat, she stifled a yawn,
then met his smile. "You're up awfully early aren't you, Alex?
Usually you stay cuddled up with me for a while, before you go
back to your own room."

"Believe me, you are very tempting." Suddenly he wanted to
sweep her up in his arms and carry her away, far from all the
dangers that threatened. Jeremiah and Caroline West could fly
to the moon for all he cared. Moving closer to her he found his
gaze wandering over her lingeringly, like a caress. "I have a
wonderful idea, Samantha. We haven't been up to the mountains in such a long time. Let's slip away this morning. Just the
two of us. We could hitch up the sled, bundle ourselves up in fur
rugs." He winked. "We could chop a hole in the ice and dangle
our poles although I venture a guess that we wouldn't even care

if we caught any fish. We might even go for a walk like we used to do, then search out a secluded cave, build a nice fire and make love."

Samantha hugged her arms around her body. It was such a delicious idea. She missed being up in the mountains, the freedom she had always had there. Most of all she missed those special moments she and Alex had shared. "It sounds like a fine idea, Alex. We can—" She stopped in midsentence as she remembered. Teresa Templeton. She had promised to meet her this morning. "I can't!"

Alex raised his eyebrows in surprise. "You can't?"

The truth trembled on her tongue. It was so strange to have a secret, but she had no choice. "I'm going to . . . I have some business to attend to, some things that must get done." She looked at him regretfully. "But it sounds like a mighty fine idea. We'll do it some other time."

"Yes, some other time." He was curious but didn't pry. "Well, at least we can have a leisurely breakfast together."

"What time is it?"

Alex took out his gold pocket watch. "Seven thirty-five."

"Oh, no!" Bounding from the bed, she was all thumbs as she hurried with her toilette, brushing her hair in hurried strokes, washing her face and hands. Tying her hair back with a ribbon, she concentrated on getting dressed, murmuring "fiddlesticks" as she fumbled with her fastenings. Hurrying forward, Alex tried to help.

"I've never seen you in such a state. Surely there's no need for such haste." Always before it had been he who kept a strict eye on his watch, he who had such an aversion to being late. Samantha always believed that what needed to get done would take care of itself.

"I'm late. I . . . I have to meet someone at eight o'clock." She avoided his eyes. "It's a surprise. You'll see." Giving him a hasty kiss on the lips, she flew out the door and raced down the stairs. Alex watched as she left the hotel, then, picking up his razor, he shaved the nightly stubble. He'd stop by his office building and talk with Robert. Perhaps he'd had better luck in finding out what was going on than Alex had.

Picking up his jacket and straightening his cravat, Alex

traced the path Samantha had made, out the door and down the stairs. Walking the boardwalk in the crisp morning air, he reached the office just as it opened its doors. Pushing his way through the crowd of merchants waiting to transact the day's business, he found Robert at his desk munching cheerfully on a biscuit.

"Alex!" Robert exclaimed, holding forth a wicker basket. "Have a biscuit. Elizabeth made them."

"Elizabeth?" Alex succumbed to the tantalizing aroma and took one, sinking into the seat of a leather-padded chair as he bit into it.

"The beauty you saw me with several weeks ago. The little dark-haired bird with the large bosom. She may not be able to carry a tune, but she certainly can cook. It is only one of her . . . uh . . . assets." He wiped his mouth with the back of his hand and rolled his hazel eyes suggestively. "Ah, women. I love them all. Blondes, brunettes, redheads. Tall and short, plump and lithe." He shook his head as he wiped the desk clean of crumbs. "Sometimes I wish I were a sultan, so I could have them all. . . ."

"You're incorrigible!" Alex doubted that Robert would ever settle down. "Is it any wonder I keep you far away from Samantha?"

Robert grinned sheepishly. "I'd never—"

"I know." Alex stopped his banter and his expression sobered. "Have you had any success? Have you been able to discover what is going on with our illustrious Mr. West?"

"Only that he has been in a particularly cheerful mood lately. It's unnerving. Something is going on, but what it is, I still can't tell. He's hardly spent two minutes at the bank. He's been cavorting all over town." Robert tugged at his sleeves and Alex could see that his jacket was too short, ill fitted to his tall, gangling frame. "And he's been withdrawing a great deal of money."

"When I worked here he seemed far more inclined to put money *in* the bank than to take it out. He seemed pleased to have other people invest in *his* projects, however." Alex clenched his jaw, deep in thought. He'd kept careful contact with Patrick Trenoweth, certain that Jeremiah West had something sinister in mind. Sabotage? If that was the case, the sheriff and his deputy had been forewarned. Jeremiah would be the first and foremost suspect. Alex doubted that sabotage was still on the banker's mind. But what was he planning? What had Caroline meant by her careless remark?

"Oh, and I forgot. Two days ago, just after our first talk I saw J.W. with Cy Tyburn."

"Cy Tyburn?" That sneering ruffian was hardly the kind of man Jeremiah West would keep company with, unless . . .

"Saw the two of them get into a wagon together. They headed up the middle road."

"The one that leads to the Siren Song?"

"The Siren Song and the Tyburn cabin. Could have been just a social call, but I don't think so, Alex. Alex?" Robert gasped as he was hauled unceremoniously out of his chair. "What are you doing? Where are we going."

"I want you to come with me. I think it's time I paid our mutual friend Caroline West a visit. I don't want to tempt fate." Somehow, some way, he would find out what her father was planning, even if he had to choke the answer out of her. That was Alex's intention as he dragged Robert out the door.

62

Samantha pursued the matter of becoming a lady with the same intensity she had displayed in working the Siren Song. She was an eager learner and Teresa Templeton a strict teacher.

"First you must learn to walk gracefully so that when you enter a room all eyes will be turned your way. You must look like a swan. Watch." Shoulders held back, waist bent slightly forward, the actress glided across the stage. "Now you."

Samantha had a bounce to her walk. Swinging her arms back and forth, she crossed the stage with a spirited stride. "Like that?"

Teresa Templeton smiled as she shook her head. "We'll have to use the book. Keep your shoulders back and your arms at your side. Your posture must compensate for a bustle. We in theater call it the "Grecian bend." Imagine yourself as the letter S. The top of the *S* commencing at the forehead with the last curve of the *S* passing over the bosom and through the bustle you will be wearing." Once more she demonstrated, then putting a leather-bound copy of Shakespeare's sonnets on Samantha's head, watched as she took her turn across the planked wooden platform.

An *S,* Samantha thought, trying very hard to envision herself in the shape of that nineteenth letter as she walked slowly forward. It was impossible. She couldn't concentrate on her forehead, her arms, her bosom, and her backside and still keep the book from falling! She felt clumsy. Foolish. She was ready to abandon the whole idea until she thought of Alex. What a woman wouldn't do for the love of a man! She wondered if he had ever been privy to such a show of foolishness and decided that he had. His dignified walk was one of the very first things she had noticed about him.

Again and again Samantha walked across the stage, a full twenty-five times, she counted. At last she was able to cross the full length twice without toppling the book from her head. Puffing out her chest with pride, she basked in the warmth of Teresa Templeton's praise.

"One thing I will say for you, Samantha. You never give up!" the actress said with an amused smile. "And as you can see, nothing is impossible if you continue to practice it." It was time, the actress declared, for a rest before they began on the next phase of the lesson. Leading Samantha backstage to a small stove nestled in a corner, she filled a kettle with water from a large water barrel and placed it on the burner. "I thought we would have a spot of tea. It's a habit I acquired on one of my European tours."

"You were in Europe?" Samantha was notably impressed.

Running a hand through her honey-blond curls, Teresa Templeton sighed. "It was one of the highlights of my career. Perhaps if I hadn't been running away from my unhappiness, I might have enjoyed it." As she looked at Samantha her gray eyes were sad. "As it was, I had been deserted by a man who told me over and over again that he loved me. A man who left me with child. My husband!"

"And he just up and deserted you?" Samantha was indignant. "Why that mangy polecat." Watching as the older woman measured out three spoonfuls of tea from a brightly painted canister into a strainer, she pleaded to hear the story. "Sometimes it does a whole heap of good to pour it out, and I'm a mighty good listener. And . . . and I really am interested." Settling down on an old wooden chair, holding a chipped china tea cup, she listened to the sordid story.

"I was eighteen years old when I met him. He seemed to be everything a woman could want. Tall and smiling with light brown hair that always seemed to fall into his eyes. He was very romantic, writing poems and bringing me flowers. It seemed that I had found the man of my dreams." Her voice was low and husky as she told the tale of meeting the newcomer at her father's store. "It was his first week in New York. He had come from Omaha. Needless to say I felt sympathy for him, being in an unfamiliar city. Though he was five years older than I, nevertheless I took him under my wing. I introduced him to influential people my father knew, hoping it might help him in his chosen career. He was a bank messenger, but he had aspirations of one day owning his own bank."

"A banker!" Thinking of Jeremiah West, Samantha scowled.

"To make a long story brief, we got married. The first six months of our life together were ideal. I couldn't have been happier. Then my father's influence secured him a position as assistant teller with a raise of ten dollars a week." She paused as she took a sip of her tea. "Perhaps it was the pressure of becoming a father that frightened him. I suppose it's possible the thought of such responsibility was what prompted him to leave. Whatever it was, I awoke one morning and found his note. He'd left New York and he'd left me as well. It was devastating. Right from the first, he had played me for a fool so that my father would help him attain his aspirations."

"He left you? Wasn't there something . . . ?"

"There was nothing to be done. And most tragic of all, the shock upset my father so violently that he suffered a heart attack. Rightly or wrongly, my mother blamed me. We quarreled. In desperation I joined an acting troupe who took me in."

"And your baby?" Samantha squeezed the cup so tightly that it nearly cracked.

"I . . . I lost my child." Gathering up the cups, she seemed close to tears but quickly regained her composure. "My name was Clara then. Clara Barlowe. But that young woman has long since died to be replaced by Teresa Templeton. I've had, I suppose, a very good life. Fame and a reasonable amount of fortune." She forced a smile. "Women who played western theaters, actresses, had a head start on the road to success because any measure of beauty attracted a crowd, talent or no. Now I am proud of my craft. My only love is the audience that applauds me each night."

"How sad." Samantha wondered what she would do if Alex just up and left her. The thought was overwhelmingly gloomy. "I'm sorry. I don't know if I could survive such a thing."

"You would survive. Like me, there is core of strength within you, Samantha. I recognized that the moment you walked through that door. Yet you are vulnerable and loving too. I want you to win your young man, to have the happiness that eluded me. That's why I agreed to help you. It wasn't for the money." Teresa Templeton drew herself up tall. "Now. You did not come here to chat with me all day, nor to hear the tragic story of my life. There's more to being a lady than walking across the floor. You must learn how to talk, how to sit, the right way to hold a teacup. The right moment to smile. A lady always lets a gentleman open doors for her." Opening the stage door, she demonstrated.

"Why? I can do it myself." It sounded foolish to Samantha. "Hell, by the time you wait for them to get to it, a body could be out the door and on her way." Realizing she had used a swearword, she blushed.

"Because that's the way it's done. Men are strange creatures, Samantha. They like to consider themselves our superiors. They like to think us weak and themselves strong. A lady always plays on this philosophy. And learns to manipulate a gentleman's supposed protection."

"That's the damnedest thing I ever heard. Why, I could never—"

"Then there is no use going on." As if dismissing her, Teresa Templeton turned her back and started to walk down the stairs to her dressing room.

"Wait!" She'd come this far; she might as well see just what this business of being a lady really did entail. Alex. She must remember Alex. Someday when they were married and he swept her back to his home in Boston, she'd remember all this foolishness and be much the better for it. She would be able to hold her head up with the best of them. "I'll . . . I'll do anything you say."

Thus began a tedious morning of saying "How do you do" a hundred times or more with marbles in her mouth. She learned which words to say and which were forbidden. Learned it was always *isn't* and never *ain't*. Banished the familiar word *tarnation*. Was told quite pointedly *never* to refer to men as "gents." Even the way she sat down was scrutinized. A lady always lifted her bustle and crinolines before sitting down. The next time they drank their tea, Samantha followed the actress's example of holding her little finger out.

"Men abhor a woman talking about important matters. A lady talks of the weather, her coiffure, or her new hat." It sounded to Samantha as if being a lady suddenly turned a woman into a brainless jackass! Even so, she kept her thoughts to herself. If being a lady would please Alex, she would give it her best try. Certainly it was true that Caroline West never seemed to talk about anything of merit and Alex had been smitten with her right from the very first!

At last Samantha was given a respite from her grueling exercises as the noon whistle pierced the air. Teresa Templeton had a matinee to prepare for. With a smile and an outpouring of glowing praise for Samantha's accomplishments, she dismissed her. Squinting at the bright sunlight as she stepped outside, Samantha retraced her steps back to the hotel.

It was warm for a winter's day. Halfway between the hotel and the theater was a small café. Crossing the roadway with her newly learned gait, Samantha entered and let her eyes adjust to the light. She gasped as an all too familiar profile caught her eye. Alex! And across from him sat the golden-haired enchantress Samantha recognized only too well. Caroline West! Alex was with Caroline, listening to her twittering babble as if she were the most entertaining woman in the world. He was leaning forward, closer, as if fearful of missing a word, so intent that he didn't even notice as Samantha looked on.

How could he! How could he make love to her, whisper words in her ear, and then march right off to enjoy another woman's company? Had Caroline won after all. Samantha covered her mouth to hold back the sob that threatened to give her presence away. She would win Alex back, show him that Caroline wasn't the only woman in the world. The fight wasn't over yet. Turning her back, she fled to the hotel, her determination doubled. Still, when Alex knocked at the door that night, she sent him away for the very first time ever.

63

Alex lay awake staring up at the ceiling, trying to sort out his thoughts. He was in a foul mood, frustrated for more reasons than one. Everything seemed to be going wrong and he didn't quite know what to do. First and foremost was his relationship with Samantha. In the last few weeks he had noticed a subtle change taking place, one he didn't like at all. It was as if the woman he thought he knew so very well was being transformed right before his eyes. She was quieter, more subdued. Always before she had voiced her opinions sharply; now she agreed with almost everything he said. When they were together, her thoughts were clearly elsewhere. When they *were* together, that is. She had been preoccupied lately, spending hours and hours at her mysterious appointments. Had Alex not known the kind of woman she was, he might have suspected she had another lover.

It was impossible to sleep. The empty place beside him emphasized his loneliness. He wanted to go to her, to make the short trek across the hall and knock on her door, but something held him back. Perhaps they needed some time away from each other. Samantha was young and vibrant and he feared he was being overly critical of her. She was like a young bird trying her wings. He could not begrudge her. After all the grueling work in the mine, she deserved to be frivolous now and again. If a new hat, a new dress, made her happy, then certainly she should have it. And yet there were times when she reminded him eerily of Caroline, primping before the mirror, agonizing over just which dress to wear. What had happened to the sweet, outspoken girl who had so enchanted him? Had her newly acquired wealth changed her? If so, he was deeply disappointed.

Rising from the bed, he walked across the room barefoot and lit the lamp. Running his hand through his hair, he thought the matter out. The incident with Caroline, the deterioration of their relationship, was making him skittish. Picking up the velvet box that lay on the nightstand, he opened it and looked at the two shining rubies that shone like fire in the lamplight. Two hearts touching, that was what the ring signified. He had intended to give it to Samantha tonight, but at the last minute had hesitated and left it behind. As long as he had any doubts, he would not give it to her. To him, marriage was forever. He had to be absolutely sure that she was the woman to share his life, to walk beside him. And yet at this moment, aching for her as he did, he knew beyond a doubt that he loved her.

"Oh, God!" Closing the lid on the box with a snap, he shook his head. If only things could go back to the way they used to be. He wanted the old Samantha back, the laughing, carefree wood nymph whose laughter and smiles brightened his days, not the young woman who was becoming an imitation of Caroline West, concerned only with her appearance.

He cringed at the memory of his encounter with his ex-fiancée. Therein was another frustration. Robert, coward that he was, had abandoned him and Alex had suffered her company without acquiring a crumb of information. She had been secretive, and more than a bit smug, confident that he would one day come running back to her. Despite all his denials, Caroline had taken leave of him with an irritating smile and the taunt "We shall see!"

Blowing out the lamp, Alex reflected on his life in the still of the night. As the eldest son of a prominent man he had been forced to take on responsibility early. His life had been an established routine until the war had shattered his hopes and taught him a lesson: Money had no importance if a man had no peace of mind. He had moved about in a listless dream until he met Caroline. She had promised so much—a whole new beginning, a new future in a life west of the Mississippi. Instead, Caroline had shown him just how wrong a man blinded by beauty could be. Then he had met Samantha and been touched by her innocent charm. He had discovered true love where he least expected to find it. Yet now she, too, seemed to be changing right before his eyes.

I'm getting old and cynical, he thought. Samantha was not at all like Caroline. They were complete opposites. He was creating his own disquiet and all because Samantha was taking joy at last in testing her feminine wiles. In truth, she did look stunningly beautiful in her stylish new dresses. Alex couldn't help but notice how the men ogled and the women stared with envy. She *was* the most eligible young woman in all of Colorado. Why shouldn't she delight in her newfound desirability? He should feel proud and not critical, he scolded himself, putting the troubled thoughts from his mind.

Later, in the early morning, he sat drinking a cup of coffee in the hotel dining room, relaxing as he scanned the Sealand ledgers. He seemed to have the Midas touch of late. All his investments had been profitable, including Samantha's stocks and bonds. The financial future he'd wanted for her was secure.

"Mind if I sit down, Alex?" Without waiting for an answer, Robert pulled out a chair and plopped himself down on it with a triumphant sigh. "I finally found out just what old J.W. is up to," he confided, motioning to a passing waiter to bring him a cup of coffee. "You won't have to rely on prying the information out of Caroline."

"That's a relief." Alex nodded to the waiter to refill his cup. "Which reminds me. Just where did you hurry off to Tuesday? A fine friend you turned out to be."

"I'm sorry, Alex." Robert looked contrite. "But I know you'll forgive me when you hear what I've learned. It was Caroline's prattle about the railroad that set me thinking. I spent all afternoon yesterday doing some investigating. I wouldn't be a bit surprised if J.W. hasn't bitten off more than he can chew this time."

"What do you mean?" The dining room was beginning to fill with patrons so he lowered his voice.

"Seems J.W. got it into his head to buy up all the available land surrounding Samantha's mine. All of it! Cy Tyburn has been bullying those who won't sell, strong-arming them and using scare tactics if they didn't cooperate." He lit a cigar, puffing smoke into the air. "He was nearly a hundred percent successful, except for Patrick Trenoweth, that little Chinaman, and Sean."

"Good God! I should have bought that land myself. Now Jeremiah's got Samantha right where he wants her." Alex slammed his fist down on the table, sending a spray of coffee sloshing over the rim of the cups. "If only I'd known."

"It's worthless land. J.W. paid three times what it is worth, and all because he had hopes of selling it to the railroad." Robert rocked back and forth in his chair seemingly unconcerned by the possibility.

"He will sell it. You don't have to tell me all the details for me to know what is in his mind. He'll let the railroad push Samantha off her land. I've seen the way they work. Samantha might be able to stand up to Jeremiah, but she won't be able to hold out against the Denver Pacific." Alex stood up so suddenly that he sent his chair toppling. He made his way up the stairs to Samantha's room with Robert following close behind. He knocked at the door impatiently. Whatever needed to be done, he would do it if he had to face the devil himself.

"Alex? What is it?" Samantha looked tired but was already dressed to go out. Another "mysterious" meeting? Alex thought glumly. Well this was far more important.

"Robert just informed me that your nemesis, Jeremiah, has bought up all the land surrounding the Siren Song."

"What? Why that dam—" She covered her mouth self-consciously. "I mean . . . how . . . how dare he. The nerve of the man." She fought her instinct to rush for a rifle. Though she wanted to go storming after the banker, she held back, remembering all that Teresa Templeton had taught her. Above all she must not lose her temper and go blundering about. A lady would never do such a thing. But how would a *lady* react to the situation at hand? Samantha wasn't certain, but she seemed to remember the actress saying, "men are strange creatures . . . they like to think us weak while they see themselves as strong. A lady always plays on this philosophy to manipulate a gentleman's supposed protection."

"Get your coat, Samantha. We'll go and have this out with Jeremiah West once and for all." Alex thought bitterly that Samantha had been right all along. There was little to gain in polite conversation at this point. He remembered the day she'd stormed into Jeremiah West's house to berate him in front of his guests. "Got to stand up against him or all is lost," she had said. "Too many moments when a show of force is all a body understands." This was one of those moments.

"I can't go, Alex. Not now." She'd promised Teresa Templeton that she would be prompt this morning. There was going to be a grand ball to initiate the opening of the hotel and Samantha had made plans to attend. It would be her chance to make Alex proud of her, to witness all that she had learned. The actress had gone to great lengths to find a dancing master for Samantha, to teach her how to waltz. How could she be so unappreciative as to just now show up?

"You can't go?" Her answer stunned him. He had expected her to react to the news with brimstone and fire.

"I . . . I have to go out. I . . . I have an appointment." She fluttered her eyelashes in the way she had been taught. "You go, *darling*. I'm certain that you can handle the matter. You always know just what to do, Alex." Tying her bonnet beneath her chin, she gave him her most radiant smile, proud of herself for showing the proper restraint. She was sure that Caroline West herself could not have displayed such poise. Brushing past Alex as she walked through the door, she stroked his cheek affectionately. "I'll be back in a little while and then you can tell me all about it."

"Was that really Samantha?" Robert was as astonished as Alex by her reaction. "Are you at the right door?" He chuckled softly. "Whew. Women! They never cease to surprise!"

Alex watched Samantha glide down the stairs, a troubled

frown on his face. "I don't know what's happening to her, Robert. A disturbing change has come over her these past days. Sometimes I blink my eyes and expect to see Caroline looking back at me."

"Oh?" Robert shrugged his shoulders. "I rather like the change. I wouldn't mind her calling *me* "darling." Besides, I've been trying to tell you that there is no need to be upset. The railroad won't buy the land that J.W. confiscated. J.W. is stuck with acres and acres of rocky ground. Even his friendship with Henry Teller didn't do him any good."

"They don't want the land?"

"Seems it's proving more difficult to lay track up the canyon past Black Hawk than they thought. Gonna need a trestle to cross Black Hawk's commercial district. Costly. Anyway, they turned J.W. down flat. So much for his aspirations. . . . Of course, I suspect he'll try to sell the land back to its original owners, but something tells me that old J.W. just might have made a serious error in judgment this time."

64

Tap, tap, tap. Jeremiah West drummed his fingers on the desktop in angry thought. He'd taken a gamble and he'd lost most miserably. Picking up a pen, he tried to venture a guess as to the exact figures. Enough money to make him decide that he would have to be very frugal from now on. There would be no more extravagance for the Wests and that included Caroline.

"Damn! Damn! Damn!" He'd hoped that he could kill two birds with one stone on his latest venture. He had placed his money on the hope that Alexander Nicholson's cargo business would be ruined by the coming of the railroad and that Samantha Claybourne's property would be gobbled up in the railroad's quest for land. He'd heard of it happening before. Instead he held the deed to property that was utterly worthless. And it was *her* fault he faced financial ruin. Her stubborn insolence would lead him to madness.

The bare, skeletal trees stood dark against the window, like menacing strangers. Jeremiah West felt a flash of fear. From the corner of his eye he thought for a moment he saw someone peering through the window at him, waving his arms in anger. He was on edge . . . jumpy . . . nervous. Because of his monetary straits and declining profits, he had cut back his mine workers wages once again, requiring more hours for less pay. The action had stirred resentment among the miners and there had been disgruntled threats on his life. There had been mumblings about a strike, grumblings of violence. He'd had dreams in which he'd been chased by rioting throngs of miners. To insure his safety he'd hired Cy Tyburn on as his personal bodyguard. The bumbling oaf had to earn his keep in some way, he reasoned.

"I'll show them. They'll think twice before they tangle with me," he said aloud, trying to calm his jittery nerves. It was Sean O'Brien who really unnerved him. That rabble-rouser had been meeting with the miners, urging them on to a strike. In his loud booming voice he had publicly denounced the owner of the Little Duchess and the Black Ace mines. He had cajoled and he had shouted, stirring up an already angry crowd. "Huh. Samantha Claybourne's foreman. No doubt she put him up to it." Oh, he would give anything he had to put that haughty little chit in her place.

The door to his study opened with a resounding bang. Jeremiah jumped in alarm, reaching in the desk drawer for his gun. His voice was shaky as he asked, "Who's there?"

"It's only me, Daddy." With hatboxes piled all the way to her chin, Caroline entered the room. "I wanted you to help me decide if I should keep all four. I don't think I like the straw bonnet at all."

"Take them all back!"

"What?"

"I said take them *all* back to that silly little shop where you got them. We can't afford them. Your extravagance is going to ruin me." He bounded from his chair threateningly.

"You can't mean that." Ignoring his words, Caroline proceeded to take the hats out of their boxes one by one to model them. "I like this one with the flowers. Makes me think of spring. Don't you, Daddy?"

Jeremiah's angry growl was her answer. Blustering about in irritation, he proceeded to stuff each hat back in its proper box.

"There will be no more frivolities in this household. Do you hear me? No bonnets, gloves, or dresses. I will not allow you to lead me to the paupers' den, daughter or no."

"But I must have a new dress. We've been invited to the grand opening of the Teller House. Everyone of any prominence will be there. You can't expect me to wear a dress that everyone has seen before." She was aghast, her mouth open, her eyes wide.

"I do!" Folding his arms across his chest, he paced the room. "I told you what would happen if you couldn't be of use to me. Well . . . I don't see Alexander Nicholson pounding at the door. This morning's paper hints at a wedding between your Boston beau and that sniveling little hoyden. That tells me quite clearly that you failed."

"I don't believe Alex will marry her. He just couldn't." Caroline's voice was shrill with bewildered frustration. "Besides, you're just taking out your anger on me when it should be pointed at yourself. I didn't buy that worthless mountain land, you did. I didn't invest in the wrong stocks and bonds." She stifled a sob. "You have impoverished us, not me. It would seem that instead of berating me for not having Alex eating out of my hand, you should take a good look at yourself." She sniffed derisively. "If you're so intent on keeping Alex from marrying Samantha Claybourne, maybe you should marry her yourself. If you ask me, it's the only way you'll recoup your losses *and* get your hands on her filthy mine." Turning her back, she flounced out the door, leaving the hats behind.

"Marry Samantha Claybourne!" Jeremiah stifled an oath at such a preposterous idea. Samantha Claybourne couldn't stand the sight of him and he certainly had no affection for her. Yet the more he thought about it, the more the idea appealed to him. Samantha Claybourne was a very rich woman.

Pacing the floor, chewing an unlit cigar until it was nearly in shreds, he argued the matter with himself. He was a desperate man. He'd lost money at an alarming rate the last few weeks. The Teller House had cost much more than had first been proposed and he had invested funds he could ill afford. The railroad to Central City had been postponed. Even his choice of stocks and bonds had been disastrous.

"Marry Samantha Claybourne." He knew it was too late to court her, though in his day he might have been more than a worthy rival for Alexander Nicholson. No, Samantha Claybourne would laugh in his face if he even dared to offer the proposition. Even so, he knew that if he could force her to marry him, everything she owned would belong to him. It was a potent temptation.

Abduction! It was the only way. Samantha Claybourne had been invited to the grand opening, had accepted the invitation. What better time would there be to spirit her off? Surely Cy, Buck, and Slim could handle the details. Once they were married, he would find a way to make her a manageable wife. If she proved to be a nuisance, well . . . He'd handle that matter when he came to it.

"Ah, yes, a wedding." Throwing back his head, Jeremiah West laughed for the first time in weeks.

65

Samantha clenched and unclenched her hands nervously. Looking out the small window of the theater, at the calm and cloudless sky, she felt the grip of fear. Just as surely as winter had given way to spring, she, too, had transformed herself and yet she felt uneasy. It was like straddling a fence and not being comfortable on either side anymore. She was no longer the old Samantha, but just who was she?

She had been dubbed the "belle of Central City," dressing in fancy gowns, exchanging her horse and wagon for a fancy carriage. She wore diamonds, lace, and perfume. Men who used to think of her as just "Sam" now treated her with deference. She had even received flowers and candy from those who thought they might steal her away from Alex. It was cause for celebration. Why, then, did she feel so empty? So lonely?

"Alex," she whispered. She was the most eligible woman in all of Colorado, with more men than she could count at her feet, and yet the one man she wanted above all was slipping away from her. Day by day she sensed it in his kisses, his touch, and the way he spoke her name. She had hoped to lure him away from Caroline, but Samantha could only suppose that, though he would not admit it, his heart was still in the haughty blonde's keeping. Not that he had been unfaithful; she knew it was not in Alex's nature to do such a thing. But even so she knew she would not be happy until *she* held claim to his heart.

"Oh, Teresa, I just don't know what to do. I thought it would be so easy. I thought I could compete, that Alex would be so proud of me." Turning from the window, Samantha walked slowly back to the stage. "Instead we hardly even see each other anymore. I wonder if he's even noticed that I have changed. He's never mentioned it to me, never once told me he was glad. He just keeps staring at me as if I'd suddenly sprouted a wart on my nose or something."

"Did you ever happen to think that maybe he liked you just the way you were? He asked you to marry him long before you made your decision to become a lady." Teresa Templeton studied the earnestly beautiful face. Her heart went out to the girl, but she sensed that Samantha had been wrong in her aspirations. As she had told Samantha once before: If Alex didn't accept her just the way she was, then he would never really love her.

"He asked me to marry him because he felt sorry for me. I've thought it over in my mind. Alex looks upon me as a child, someone who's alone in the world and needs his protection. In a way he's right. I do need him. If not for Alex, I wouldn't have all that I have now. He counseled me, guided me. I'm appreciative and yet I want him to look upon me as a beautiful *woman,* the way he set his sights on Caroline West. I want to prove to him that I can be just as stunningly pretty as she, and just as refined." She let her breath out in a long-drawn-out sigh. Her head ached unbearably from all the discipline she had practiced today. Tomorrow was the grand opening of the Teller House and she had been going over and over the appropriate manner to initiate a greeting. "How do you do? It's a lovely evening isn't it? I'm so pleased to make your acquaintance. Allow me to present my fiancé, Alexander Nicholson. It is a pleasant evening but with just a hint of a chill. Yes, I would gladly accept your kind invitation. It is with honor that I say yes to this dance."

"But Samantha." Teresa Templeton was dubious about the situation. "If your Alex was so taken by this Miss West, why then isn't he with her? Haven't you thought about that? You're the one whose company he seeks."

Samantha toyed with the sleeve of her dress. "That's just the way Alex is. He's a gentleman. He'd never jilt me for that woman even if he did love her. He has too keen a sense of honor."

"And perhaps he loves *you*. That's what I hope for you, Samantha. I want you to be happy, to live a fairy tale that never ends. I want you to have the happiness I might have had if my Jeremy hadn't left me." Teresa Templeton shook her head, trying to dispel the thoughts whirling in her brain. She hadn't thought of Jeremiah Westbrook in years, not until that first meeting with this interesting red-haired child, yet now it all came back to her so vividly, she could almost see his face before her eyes. She had loved him once, as stirringly as Samantha loved her Alex. Pray to God, Samantha would not suffer a similar heartache.

The stage was a flimsy construction of wood and metal braces, with ropes, curtains, sandbags, and pulleys hanging overhead. A catwalk had been constructed across the ceiling so that a young boy could change the meager scenery—canvas backdrops and painted trees. Scanning the drearily lit building now, Teresa Templeton thought sadly how it reflected her life. Unreal. Imaginary. She wanted Samantha to find happiness in the real world. Surely anyone who had worked so very hard to win the love of a man deserved to be rewarded. That was her hope as the lessons proceeded.

Gaslights flickered at the foot of the stage, mumbling voices outside the door reminded the actress of the time. It had escaped her today. Now it was nearly time for the matinee. Samantha's last lesson. Now she must make her own way in the social world.

"Good luck tomorrow night, Samantha dear. I know you can do it!" Her eyes misted with tears. This young woman had so quickly captured a place in her heart. She had almost begun to think of her as a replacement for the child she had lost so long ago.

"I'll try." Samantha bit her lip. It was unladylike to carry on, yet she felt like hugging the actress who had become her only female friend. With the exception of Honey Wells, Teresa Templeton was the only woman who had ever shown her kindness. "I'll prove to you that all your time hasn't been wasted." It rankled her that the actress had been snubbed when invitations had been mailed out. Surely Teresa Templeton was more of a lady than most of the women who walked about town with their noses in the air. She was suddenly struck with an inspiration, one that made her tell a white lie. "My invitation said that I could bring an extra guest. Why don't you come with me? Please, Teresa. You can be my good-luck charm. You can keep your eye on me and tell me how I'm doing."

"Oh, no, I couldn't!" Teresa Templeton's confidence faltered momentarily. She was an actress, hardly socially acceptable to the elite group of the city. Samantha was so naive, she didn't know that strict propriety forbade her from mingling. And yet there was such a pleading look in those large brown eyes that she was tempted to flout propriety just this once. She wanted to see Samantha make her debut, if only from the shadows. With that thought in mind she laughed softly and graciously accepted Samantha's offer.

66

Wrapped in a cloud of fatalism, Samantha settled back in her corner of the carriage as it rolled down Eureka Street. She fidgeted nervously, trying to remain calm, but in truth she wondered why on earth she'd ever decided to go to this affair. She had been the one who insisted they go, not Alex, and now she regretted it, wishing she could send word that she was indisposed. She had twisted her ankle, was abed with the ague, had suddenly taken the vapors. Surely the Sacred Thirty-six alarmed her more than a horde of raging bees. She wondered if her legs would support her when she got out of the carriage.

"Do . . . do you like my gown, Alex?" She was even tongue-tied around Alex tonight and could barely form the question. She so wanted his approval, wanted to hear him say that he thought her beautiful.

"It's stunning. Yes, of course, I like it." Alex shook his head in irritation. How many times must he tell her that he approved of her gown? Phrasing the question in various ways, she had asked him at least fifteen times within the hour. It had begun to annoy him. He had no interest in this ridiculous gathering, but Samantha had insisted that they go. She had talked of nothing else for days. She reminded him of every woman he had ever known, concerned only with outshining every other woman she met.

"And . . . and my hair?" She had instructed her maid to arrange it in an elaborate coiffure of curls heaped atop her head, with bangs and side ringlets that framed her face. The hair at the top and sides of her head was frizzed.

"Yes, yes, I think your hair looks just grand." He leaned back and gazed sullenly out the window as the carriage came to a stop in front of the hotel.

"You look stunning, Samantha." Teresa Templeton squeezed her hand reassuringly. Alex Nicholson's aloofness surprised her. Something was wrong here. Very wrong. She had the apprehensive feeling that his affection for Samantha was cooling, that all her primping, far from pleasing him, only aggravated him. If only Samantha had listened.

"I spent the whole day in a bubble bath just so I would look all right. Perfuming. Curling. Preening. Whew!" She glanced at Alex, but he scarcely seemed to hear her. He was quiet now, but she was certain that once she made her grand entrance, once he realized she made Caroline West look like a plain-faced schoolmarm, he'd perk up.

The carriage door was opened by a little man decked out in a dark blue suit. Samantha drew in a deep breath as she stepped through the door. She felt self-conscious. These were the very same people who had snubbed her for years, who had considered her far beneath them. She didn't want to be laughed at. Could she remember all that she had been taught? As she looked over her shoulder at Alex she knew he would never even guess the courage it took to get out and walk up the boardwalk.

Eureka Street was thronged with a gala crowd. The brilliant lights, the swimming sea of faces, the heady trill of music coming from the hotel, combined to intoxicate her. It was as if she were watching her own entrance into the hotel from afar, as if someone else and not Samantha Claybourne were walking through those double doors. Gripping the fan that hung from her wrist, she was determined to make Alex proud if it was the last thing she did.

There was a mirror in the entranceway and Samantha took one last look at herself. She was wearing a gown in the latest style, the close-fitting aqua blue silk outlining her figure. The skirt was flared beneath the bustle, decorated with pleating and bows of a darker hue. The high stiff collar forced her to keep her neck straight, her chin up. Cut to a *V* in front, the bodice emphasized her bosom, though she did feel slightly scandalous to be exhibiting such a daring neckline. At her ears were diamond earrings, safely attached to her newly pierced ears. Around her throat was a diamond necklace. In her hair were ostrich feathers—dark blue, white, and a blue that matched her dress. It was the shoes, however, that annoyed her. High-heeled with pointed toes, they squeezed her feet unmercifully. If not for Alex . . .

She would outshine Caroline West. She would. She would! Adjusting her long white gloves, giving a final pat to her hair, Samantha glided across the floor with an air of importance. Didn't she own the largest gold-producing mine in the territory? Wasn't she wealthy? Hadn't she learned etiquette? Drawing another deep breath, she waited for the butler to announce her, then walked in step with Alex through the archway.

The room was swarming with guests dressed in their utmost finery, all intent on showing off their newfound wealth. It was a stunning array of elegant dresses and finely tailored suits in a luxurious room where voices buzzed and blended in excited chatter. But the voices stilled to an awesome quiet as Samantha made her entrance. Like a flock of birds startled by a cat, Samantha thought. Nevertheless the oohs and ahs and staring eyes dispelled any last doubts she might have had about her appearance. She *had* dazzled them, but that was only the beginning.

Under the glow of public admiration Samantha blossomed. Alex studied her intently, apprehensive yet proud at the same time. She had shown these twittering peacocks, he had to give her that. Were it not for the fact that he feared losing her to this fawning, ridiculous crowd, he might have been more pleased. He didn't begrudge her triumph. Oh, no, never that. She had become quite a lady and he didn't object, but somewhere along the way he seemed to have lost his "real" Samantha. She wasn't *his* Samantha anymore.

The crowd closed around Samantha and Alex, but she was carefully poised. Extending her gloved hand, her cheeks were flushed, her eyes bright with pleasure as she acknowledged the introductions. "How do you do, Mr. Teller. I am most impressed with this magnificent hotel." Even Jeremiah West greeted her cordially, taking her hand and placing it to his lips. Without any indication of her true feelings for the man, she murmured politely, "Good evening, Mr. West." It was Caroline's expression that pleased Samantha the most, however. Dressed in a blue gown that paled by comparison with Samantha's own, she stared openly, her complexion taking on a slight tinge of green. Remembering Caroline's warning that she would never fit into Alex's world, it was exhilarating to know she'd made her eat her words.

Samantha looked behind her, intending to whisper her thank-yous to Teresa Templeton, but the actress had disappeared. Though she scanned the walnut-and-damask-decorated room, she couldn't find the actress anywhere. With a sudden twinge of regret she wondered if Teresa Templeton had even followed her inside. She'd been so concerned with her own entrance that she hadn't been paying attention.

"My friend . . . she's not here," she confided to Alex. He was looking at her with an expression she could not quite describe. "I must find her. Why, if not for her . . ."

"I saw her slip out the front door. I believe she knew immediately that those clucking hens were chattering about her. I believe she wanted to save you any embarrassment." He thought to himself sadly that the Samantha he knew would have taken the actress by the arm and defiantly paraded her under these snobs' noses.

"Oh, no." Samantha took one last look behind her before she was pushed none too gently into the dining room. Sitting at Alex's side, she suffered through the long-winded speeches, toasts, and backpatting as the occasion got under way. Though she was virtually starving, Samantha tried to hold her ravenous appetite in check, declining a second helping. Throughout dinner she was elegant, amusing, and demure. Though Caroline insisted on flirting with Alex and nearly made her lose her temper, she never once gave her annoyance away. The time had come for Alex to make his choice. There wasn't anything more she could do. If he didn't realize by now just how much she loved him, he never would.

"Why, to say it is grand is an understatement," Caroline trilled. "The furniture alone cost twenty thousand dollars. The parlors are perfect marvels of elegance. And there are ninety guest rooms."

Samantha found the Teller House cold and dank despite its Brussels carpets, crystal chandeliers, and many rooms. She was far more comfortable at her own hotel. She listened to conversation and comments circulating around the table and tried to look interested. The truth was, she was bored. Only the memory of Teresa Templeton's stern denouncement of yawns saved her from giving in to that gesture. Yawning, like scratching, was a thing ladies did *not* do in public.

At last, when Samantha was certain she couldn't bear to hear one more word about the Teller House, the assemblage moved form the dining room to the grand ballroom. She tapped her toe as the musicians began. "The music is lovely, isn't it?" she whispered from behind her fan, longing for Alex to take her by the hand and lead her to the floor. "I . . . I believe it is a waltz." She waited expectantly.

"I thought I'd sit this one out with you, Samantha." His toes were tapping as vibrantly as her own, but, assuming she didn't know how to dance, he was making the sacrifice. When she was suddenly whirled onto the floor by a rotund, mustached man who looked much like a walrus, he was taken completely by surprise. Shocked, he watched Samantha glide gracefully across the floor. Why, she'd told him she'd never even been to a square dance, and yet here she was twirling about the floor as if she'd been born to dance.

"Why, Alex, what happened to your 'Cinderella'?" Grabbing his arm, Caroline West positioned herself in his arms. "It seems only right that we dance. You belonged to me before *she* came along." Alex had no choice. She had already maneuvered her way onto the dance floor. He couldn't avoid her without being rude.

Samantha viewed the sight of Alex dancing with Caroline sadly, feeling more than a twinge of jealousy. Even so, she was not without her own admirers. In a whirl of satin she was swept about the room as she struggled to maintain her smile. She had been so mockingly pleased with herself, but now she wondered if she had lost the "war" after all. Would Caroline West always be a wall between them? It appeared so. It was a sad truth she had refused to accept. She had held such hope, thought she could compete. Now she was not so certain. Could she live with the fear that one day Alex would go running back to the woman he had come so many miles to claim?

"Why so glum? You've taken this party by storm. You surely are the most beautiful woman here." Robert Cunningham took her by the arm, leading her into another waltz.

"Alex."

"Alex?"

Samantha expelled a long-drawn-out sigh. "I'm beginning to think it's time I faced reality." She looked toward Alex and the clinging Caroline and wanted to cry. "Alex is everything that I am not. I tried so hard but . . ." Why was she confiding in this man she barely knew? She couldn't say, but somehow his easy, friendly manner drew her out. "I'll always be afraid of losing Alex, of not being worthy of his love. Maybe it just was never meant to be."

"Losing Alex?" He looked at her quizzically. "Whatever do you mean?" Seeing the direction her eyes took, he shook his head, laughing softly. "To Caroline? Caroline?"

"She wants him back." Samantha buried her face in the warmth of his shoulder, fighting her tears. "She came to the hotel to talk with me about the matter. She told me she was sorry that she had given Alex up and warned me that she intended to have him back. She told me that there would be a war between us and that . . . that . . . Oh, Robert!"

Robert paused in midstride, shaking his head in violent denial. "She didn't give Alex up, Samantha. It was Alex who broke the engagement."

"What?" Samantha was afraid to believe his words. He was

just trying to soothe her. "But the gossip was all over town. Everyone said that she had decided not to marry Alex because he was a . . . And . . . and she told me the same thing when she came to inform me of her intent to reclaim Alex."

"She was saving face, Samantha. It was the story she spread all over town to keep people from guessing the truth."

"A story?"

"A story."

"She told me I would never be suitable to live in Alex's world and . . ."

Robert took Samantha by the hand and led her to the courtyard, a glassed-in area decorated with potted palms and a trellis of vines. "We've got to have a serious talk about this, Samantha. I don't know what Caroline told you, but it was Alex who broke the engagement. Caroline is a trial sometimes, a daddy's girl. Alex found her too vain, shallow, and selfish to make a proper wife and he was man enough to admit he'd made a mistake. Caroline twittered that little tale about Alex's cowardice in an attempt to save face. He, being a gentleman, let the matter rest."

"Alex is no coward!" she emphasized with the tip of her fan.

"I know. He saved Jeremiah West's life, though I doubt he heard one word of gratitude. Alex is my friend, a man I admire a great deal." He kissed her lightly on the cheek. "I'm glad he fell in love with *you*. I think you make a perfect pair."

"Fell in love with me?" She felt dizzy but knew it wasn't from the wine she'd had at dinner. Alex loved her and not Caroline West! Her heart soared with joy. Tumbling from her lips came all her doubts, her hopes and dreams for a life with Alex. She told Robert about Caroline's visit, about her determination to make herself into a lady so that she could win his love, be good enough for him.

"Alex loves you just the way you are, Sam. He's told me so a million times or more. There's never been any threat from Caroline West. Not now, not ever." He grinned. "Now, show a little of that spunk Alex is always telling me about. Go and get your man. I have no doubt but that he will be most grateful to you for saving him from that little cuckoo's company."

"Alex loves *me*!" She increased the tempo of her fan, only to drop it. Robert stopped to pick it up, handing it to her with a wink. He started back toward the ballroom and motioned for her to follow, but Samantha shook her head. A shout of jubilation was welling up in her throat, but her eyes were red and she needed to regain her composure. "You go on, Robert. I'll be out in a minute. And . . . and thank you. You've proven to be my friend as well as Alex's tonight. I won't forget that."

Alex had broken the engagement. She still couldn't believe it, yet she knew that Robert wouldn't lie. All this time she had been so apprehensive and there had been no need. Such a fool, such a silly fool. She should never have doubted Alex, not even for a moment. She whirled about in her own private dance, feeling happy and blissfully carefree. All these months she'd put herself through needless heartache, borrowing trouble. Oh, what a story she had to tell Alex. He would laugh with her when he related the trials and tribulations she had suffered to become a lady. The one thing that had been gained from this, however, was her newfound poise. She wouldn't be afraid to meet his family now. Hell, she wasn't afraid to meet the queen of England! She could be a lady now whenever she wished. Wrapping her arms around her body, she closed her eyes and giggled with joy. A noise, the sound of someone bumping into a chair, alerted her to someone else's presence in the room. Samantha whirled around, intent on identifying the person who had intruded on her solitude, but before she could glimpse a face, she was gripped from behind. Strong arms encircled her waist, a large hand clamped over her mouth, stifling her screams.

67

Alex was trapped in the arms of a double-chinned matron who squeezed him tightly against her large bosom as the music pulsated around them. Turning his head as far over his shoulder as he could manage, he looked in the direction Samantha and Robert had taken. So much for friendship. Robert had headed toward the courtyard. To show Samantha the newly blooming flowers? A wave of jealousy washed over him.

". . . and Henry Teller has extended an invitation to President Grant himself to visit our blossoming city," the woman was saying. In a monotone voice the matron recited the virtues and advantages of the mining town that was being proclaimed the "Queen of the West."

Alex's eyes were riveted on the door, watching as Robert returned alone. Where in the devil was Samantha? At first he was relieved that she was not with Robert, then curious, and finally, worried. She was out of her element here, as innocent as a spring lamb among voracious wolves. There was not been a man in the place who had not looked at her with a covetous eye. Even Jeremiah West had openly stared.

". . . there really isn't a decent theater in Central City. I told Henry that I would be more than willing to offer my support if he was serious about his intent to build one in the future. After the success of this hotel I would not be at all surprised . . ." Her cold blue eyes appraised him. "I don't believe you have heard a word I have said . . ." She followed his line of vision toward the door.

The music had stopped. Alex extricated himself as politely as he could and strode across the floor toward Robert. "Where's Samantha?"

"She's coming, Alex. She wanted to dry her eyes before—" Robert yelped in surprise as Alex grabbed his arm and held him in place.

"If you did anything to upset her . . ."

"Me? She was crying over *you*." Robert pushed Alex's arm away. "She thought you were in love with Caroline, old boy. Of course Caroline had something to do with that. It seems she paid Samantha a little visit a while back." Robert related his conversation with Samantha. "Women can be ruthless when it comes to their egos, especially our dear Caroline. Seems she not only announced her intent to win you back but took great pains to tell Samantha how ill suited she was to associate with you. Said you would be ruined if you ever took her back to Boston."

"What!"

"Caroline told Samantha she would be an embarrassment to you. That's why Samantha changed. She did it for *you*, Alex."

"The clothes, the jewelry, the difference in her walk and the way she phrases her words . . . all for me?" He was deeply touched. He considered the flush of guilt that came over her lately whenever she swore. He had even come upon her walking across the living room with a book on top of her head. Samantha was not caught up in being rich. She had taken herself unmercifully to task because she wanted to be good enough for him. Good enough? Why, she was the most priceless treasure in the world! And yet had he ever told her that? Had he ever really told her how very much he loved her? To his mortification he realized that he had not. He had been raised in a very reserved family, had learned to keep his emotions to himself. Though he did indeed love her, perhaps he had never told her just how much.

"That woman . . . Teresa Templeton . . . who is she?" Alex had a suspicion that she had played a part in Samantha's transformation. Determined to ask the woman herself, he finally found her standing quietly in the corner, a punch glass in her hand. Anxious for Samantha's future, she told Alex how Samantha had come to her determined to make herself into a lady, resolved to fight for his love.

"And like a damned fool I acted sullen, resentful. She wanted me to give her my admiration and instead I . . ." Alex remembered the brief glimpse of fear he'd seen in Samantha's eyes when they entered the hotel and realized just how much courage it had taken for her to put herself on display. By God, she'd been splendid!

"Even Jeremiah West took a second look," Robert was saying. "Course now, he did much the same thing himself. Coming west, changing his name from Jeremy Westbrook to Jeremiah West. He wasn't always the haughty banker. Just an ordinary man from Omaha, Nebraska. Came a long way up from being a bank messenger to owning a veritable empire."

"What did you say?" Teresa Templeton had turned visibly pale. "No. It couldn't be. After all these years . . . I . . . I . . ." She put her hand to her throat as she shook her head, trying to calm herself. The musicians paused briefly as they prepared to play yet another waltz, and it was in that moment that Teresa thought she heard a muffled scream.

"Samantha!" Alex had heard it, too, and without another thought he ran in the direction of the sound.

68

Samantha struggled in the grasp of her captor, trying her best to scream. From out of the shadows Buck Cameron and Slim Walker emerged to taunt her with their grins. She knew at once who held her. Cy Tyburn! Enraged, kicking and thrashing about, she fought to regain her freedom.

"Struggle all you want, Sammie. You'll not get free of me. We got a little score to settle and now's as good a time as any." He dragged her struggling to the back of the hotel and out the door. "You've been one sore pain in the ass, Sammie, but I reckon your *intended* can tame you." Taking his hand from her mouth, Cy Tyburn laughed uproariously.

"My intended? Just what in hell are you talking about, Cy Tyburn?" In her anger she forgot all the careful coaching. "Just take your hands off of me. I'll make you cry uncle if you don't."

"Oh ee! Ain't the lady feisty, huh, Buck? Old Jeremiah's gonna have his hands full. Think he must be plumb loco, wanting to marry her."

"What? Marry Jeremiah?" The thought was too preposterous. Instead of fear it inspired Samantha's giggles. "You've lost your mind, Cy," she gasped between gulps of laughter. "Why . . . why I'd just as soon marry *you!*" She jabbed him in the ribs. "Now let me go." He loosened his hold, brushing the tips of her breasts as he did so. "Cy Tyburn, watch yourself! I'm short on temper tonight."

"I'll let go of you if you promise to be a good little gal."

"I'll act like a lady, if you act like a gentleman and stop grinning like a buffoon." She wanted to scream, to let out a yelp that would bring the whole hotel running, but she held back. She didn't want to embarrass herself or Alex. Besides, Cy Tyburn didn't scare her. She'd always been able to hold her own with him. "Now, tell me what's going on. If this is your idea of a joke, I don't think it's very funny."

"It's no joke, my dear." Jeremiah West stepped from the shadows into the moonlight. "I'm going to do you the honor of marrying you. You, my dear Miss Claybourne, are going to be my wife."

"Why, I wouldn't marry you if you were the last man on earth! Has everyone suddenly gone crazy? I love Alex. I'm going to marry *him.*" Samantha looked nervously about her. Buck, Cy, and Slim were closing in, forming a tight circle around her. She shouted for help, infuriated by their manner.

"Keep her quiet, Cy." Jeremiah looked over his shoulder anxiously. "She'll make me look like a fool."

"You are a fool if you think you can get away with this! I'll die before I'll say I do."

"Don't tempt me." Jeremiah's eyes glittered maliciously. "My carriage is in front. Do you think you can subdue her long enough to get her there? Quietly?" In answer Cy, Buck, and Slim grabbed Samantha. Taking his neckerchief off, Slim used it as a gag while Cy clutched at Samantha's arms and Buck held her frantically kicking legs. It was like some ghastly nightmare. Samantha winced in pain as she was pushed and pulled through the bushes. Then somehow, miraculously, Samantha managed to break free. Taking to her heels she fled toward the door, screaming at the top of her lungs, making it as far as the glass-encased courtyard before she was again subdued.

"She's more than likely startled half the territory by now.

That scream of hers . . . !" With a vicious tug at her arm, Cy Tyburn watched as she winced in pain. "Come on, Sammie. I don't want to hurt you none. Leastwise not *too* much."

"Don't you cause her any pain. I won't have none of that." At least Slim Walker was not against her, Samantha thought. Her eyes pleaded with him to help her. "There wasn't anything said about hurting Samantha. If there had been, I wouldn't 've agreed to be party to it."

"Shut up, Slim! It's about time Samantha got her due." Buck Cameron's voice was a growl. "Been lookin' forward to this for a long, long time. Ever since she took it upon herself to rescue that dude. That shot she aimed at me could have ruined my shootin' hand."

"Take her to my pa's cabin. Got a preacher waiting there." For just a moment Cy Tyburn looked at her a bit regretfully. "Too bad, Sammie. I kinda had you pegged for myself. Thought you'd come to your senses eventually and see that Eastern fella wasn't for you." He whispered in her ear. "But if you ever get tired of that *old* husband of yours, I'm sure I could be persuaded to lend my services. Just remember that."

In indignation Samantha managed to twist the heel of her shoe ruthlessly into Cy Tyburn's foot. In pain he cried out, loosening his hold just enough for her to break free once again. This time she pushed her way inside the Teller House, hiding in the shadows. The muffled thunder of footsteps announced the pursuit of Cy Tyburn and his gang. She could hear Jeremiah West's enraged command to find her.

Suddenly the room was filled with light.

"What's going on here?" Alex's voice! A lamp was lit and the light illuminated her face. "Samantha! What in blazes!"

"They were trying to abduct me, Alex! Those damn polecats were going to take me away." Her voice was a croak.

"Well, they won't be doing that now." With measured strides Alex walked forward, shielding Samantha as he stepped between her and Cy Tyburn.

"Keep out of this or I'll batter your face so hard even your own mother won't recognize you. Do you hear that, dude?" With a grunt he hurled himself at Alex, swinging. Alex stepped aside with the graceful motion of a dancer. Cy Tyburn stumbled off balance but came up swinging again.

"Alex, be careful!" Skillfully, Alex blocked a blow to his jaw and replied with a punch to Tyburn's nose, that well-chiseled flesh of which he seemed so vain. Groping at his face to ascertain that nothing was broken, Tyburn wiped the blood away and came at Alex yet again as Buck and Slim watched in agitated silence.

Cy Tyburn connected with Alex's jaw then hit him in the head. Engulfed by a wave of dizziness, Alex staggered back, shaking his head to clear it.

"Gonna give you more than that, dude." Lowering his head, he charged, but Alex sidestepped him again, managing to aim a blow that grazed Tyburn's jaw. He connected again with the other hand, hitting his adversary in the neck.

Like a boxer, Alex used his fists, coming at his opponent with a left and right and then repeating the pattern. In less than a minute he had taken the fight out of the blond rowdy. "Had enough? I'm willing to quit if you are." Wiping the blood and perspiration from his face, Alex hovered over the bruised ruffian. A murmuring crowd had gathered in the doorway to view the combat.

With a look of venomous hatred, Cy Tyburn stood up, but he nodded. Buck and Slim held their ground, obviously reluctant to meet the same fate. "Should have helped me take him," Cy Tyburn grumbled at them under his breath. "Fine friends you are." He glowered at Slim Walker. "You should have shot him!"

Slim Walker shook his head. "I wouldn't shoot an unarmed man, not even for you," he said. "Seems to me its about time we showed the dude a little respect. Anyone who can beat the tar out of you has more guts than we gave him credit for."

Samantha ran to Alex's arms as a twittering crowd gathered behind them. Everyone assembled could see Alex was no coward. She felt proud. Like a knight for his lady, he had fought for her. She'd never loved him more than she did at that moment.

"Jeremiah West must have lost his mind, Alex. He told me he was going to force me to marry him. What a rotten, sneaky way to try and get my mine!" Shakily, she pointed her finger at him.

Throwing up his hands in feigned innocence, West rolled his

eyes. "A misunderstanding. It was Cy Tyburn who was trying
to do the young woman harm. I merely came upon the scene to
offer my help."

"That's not true!" Samantha was indignant, though she did
manage to maintain some semblance of poise for the benefit of
the onlookers. "He was going to spirit me away——"

"It wouldn't have done him any good." Stepping into the
room, Teresa Templeton edged closer to Jeremiah West. "Dear
God, it *is* you! I'd know that profile anywhere. Jeremy. Jeremy
Westbrook." She'd thought it to be an illusion, her imagination,
but now there was no doubt. He was the man she once had wed.
Despite the changes time had wrought, she recognized him.
"This man is *my* husband. He deserted me like the scoundrel he
is, but since we never divorced we still are legally wed."

Samantha watched as Jeremiah's West's face turned as pale
as a ghost's. "Clara . . . !"

"It's Teresa now. Teresa Templeton. I buried my past just as
easily as you buried your memories of me." All the angry, re-
proachful speeches she had filed away in her brain deserted her
now. Instead she centered her attention on Samantha. "But you
will never harm this lovely young woman again. I'll make certain of that, Jeremy. If you ever come anywhere near her again
I'll . . . I'll . . ."

The room was buzzing as the assembled guests whispered the
news. One white-haired grande dame with a monocle attached
to a long, thin stick, held the banker, and the woman who
claimed to be his spouse, firmly in her sights. "An *actress,*"
Samantha heard her gasp. "Jeremiah West was married to this
woman? Then he was a bigamist! What about his marriage to
Caroline's mother?"

It was certain to be the scandal of the year, but far from
feeling triumphant, Samantha felt sorry for Teresa Templeton.
So Jeremiah West had been a scoundrel even in his younger
days, she thought. Samantha wondered what the legal ramifica-
tions of this astounding revelation would be. Teresa was still his
legal wife.

"I don't envy her," Samantha whispered into Alex's ear.
"But I sure as hell am glad you came along just when you did. I

can't imagine being Jeremiah's West's wife." Throwing back her head, she laughed.

"I would have had to make of you a widow, my love. I would never let any man lay claim to you except me. I love you, Samantha." Drawing her into the shadows, he kissed her. "Robert told me the whole story." He shook his head. "Ah, Sam. Sam. When I think that you changed so drastically just for me, I don't know whether to be angry or glad. To know you love me so much sends my heart on a wondrous flight, and yet I know I should—"

"I wanted to make myself into a lady, to be a part of your world, Alex. Caroline West was right. The old Samantha Claybourne would have been the outrage of Boston. You would have been embarrassed to take me back home with you. . . ."

"No, never. I love you just the way you are, Samantha! For a moment I thought I'd lost you. I haven't, have I?" He wound his arms around her waist. "If I thought I had, I'd get on the next stage and leave town. The thought had crossed my mind."

"Leave town?" She was indignant. "You just try that, Alex. Why I'll get my rifle, follow that stage, and drag you back by the hair of your head if need be! Why, I'd—" The burning touch of his lips silenced her. Oh, she loved him so, but she had learned a very important lesson tonight. She had tried to be just like Caroline West and had very nearly lost Alex. She guessed people were a whole lot better off being themselves. She hadn't tried to change Alex, had she? No. She'd loved him just the way he was.

"You have my heart, Samantha. Now and forever." Taking a tiny black velvet box from his pocket, he opened the lid. Inside was the most magnificent ring Samantha had ever seen, two fiery red stones encircled with diamonds. "I had the jeweler make this up especially for you."

"Rubies."

"They represent hearts. Your heart and mine, Samantha. The diamonds represent the thread of love binding us together. A never-ending circle." Taking her hand, he slipped it on her finger. "There will never be anyone else for me, Samantha. Only you. Always you." He tilted his head so he could look down into her eyes and saw that she was smiling. Resting his chin against her cheek, he asked the reason for the mischievous look in her eyes.

"I was just thinking," Samantha whispered. "Cy Tyburn mentioned that there was a preacher waiting up at his father's cabin. If you wouldn't mind riding all that way, perhaps there could still be a wedding. . . ."

GLOSSARY OF MINING TERMS

Assay– test of an ore to determine its value

Claim– parcel of land in a gold field, staked out and recorded by title; piece of land a person is legally entitled to mine

Fool's gold– iron pyrite, a mineral composed of silicon and oxygen that is often mistaken for real gold

Hard-rock mining– underground mining; quartz or lode mining, in which ore is usually removed by blasting

Lode– fissure in rock formation containing gold-bearing ore. Principal vein called the "mother lode"

Placer mining– recovery of gold from deposits in sand, dirt, or clay (often in an active or ancient streambed) by panning

Quartz– crystalline mineral, often transparent, in which gold and silver veins are most commonly found

Retort– vessel or chamber in which substances are distilled or decomposed by heat

Shaft– perpendicular (or sometimes inclined) hole sunk from the surface to work a mine

Stope– steplike excavation underground for the removal of ore, which is formed as the ore is mined in successive layers

Tunnel– subterranean horizontal passageway, such as in a mine

Windlass– horizontal barrel supported on vertical posts, turned by a crank so that the hoisting rope is wound around the barrel

Winze– passageway, usually connecting two tunnels at different levels

Reckless abandon. Intrigue. And spirited love. A magnificent array of tempestuous, passionate historical romances to capture your heart.